NO ESCAPING LOVE
by
Sharon Kendrick

GW

For Ken and Robina,
with love.

CHAPTER ONE

SHE might just—*just*—make it.

Shauna flung her suitcase and holdall into the empty compartment, clambered in and slammed the door shut just as the train began to move away.

She'd made it with seconds to spare, but, glancing at her watch with a grimace, Shauna realised that, although this might be the express train from Dover to London, it would need to sprout wings and fly if it were going to get her to her interview on time.

She looked out of the window and cursed the stormy skies which had made her ferry crossing so turbulent, before pulling the now crumpled advert out of her holdall. Oh, please—if anyone up there is looking down on me—let me get this job, she thought, as she read it for the umpteenth time.

WANTED

Assistant to businessman in Central London.
Hours erratic. Salary excellent. Accommodation
available. Initiative and enthusiasm a plus—
along with conventional office skills. Languages
essential, including *fluent* Portuguese.
Apply in writing to Box No.4204

She had applied, and had received a type-written reply, requesting that she attend for interview at

Ryder Enterprises at sixteen-hundred hours today.
The letter had been signed 'Max Ryder' in a firm
and rather flamboyant signature.

Some luck, she thought ruefully. It sounded a
peach of a job—and she was going to be late.

Exactly three hours later Shauna arrived at Ryder
Enterprises, feeling as if she'd been run over by a
steamroller. Two years of working in the relatively
laid-back atmosphere of Portugal had left her ill-
equipped to cope with the frantic bustle of the
London Underground.

Struggling with her baggage, she pushed open the
heavy glass door and sank into an opulently deep-
pile cream carpet. A waft of cloying perfume hit her
like a solid wall and her heart sank as she saw the
other women in the room. She was in the wrong
place! She must be. There was no way that she had
anything in common with the other occupants of the
room. She stood out like a sore thumb.

The three females sitting around a glass table the
size of an ice-rink who had been laconically chatting
with each other all froze in unison as they looked
her up and down. Their assessment lasted less than
five seconds before they gave a group demonstration
of superior dismissal, then renewed their conversation, ignoring her completely.

Shauna stood stock-still, frozen with indecision,
momentarily debating whether or not she should simply turn right round and leave, when she heard a
polite cough, and stared across the room into a pair
of smiling eyes. The smiling person wore spectacles,

had a slick, dark bob and was seated behind a desk. She was speaking now, and it took a couple of seconds for Shauna to realise that she was addressing her.

'I'm Mrs Neilson,' she said. 'And you must be...?'

'Shauna,' she said clearly. 'Shauna Wilde. I'm so sorry,' she walked forward and put her case down by the desk, 'but I'm late.'

Mrs Neilson looked down at a list of names before her. 'Yes, you are,' she agreed. 'And by over an hour, too.' She looked up, her eyes apologetic. 'I'm very sorry, but I'm afraid that Mr Ryder won't tolerate unpunctuality.'

'Oh, but he must!' said Shauna hastily. 'Please?' She smiled at the receptionist, a pleading look in her eye. She had a lot riding on getting this job. 'I've come straight from the Continent—all the way from Portugal. I was making brilliant time but then my ferry was delayed. Can't I just wait until he's interviewed the others? He might see me then.'

'He *might*,' said Mrs Neilson doubtfully, then gave a small smile. 'You can try. Take a seat—but I can't promise anything.'

'Thanks.' Shauna walked over to a chair, dropped her belongings defiantly on the ground beside her and sat down. The eyes all turned in her direction. Well, she decided—this is a game that more than one can play, and she began to stare back.

The more she saw, the more uneasy she became. The three women looked so much *older* than her, and confident. And assured. Very assured. Apart from one elegant creature with short hair—and that must have been cut by someone with a degree in technical drawing, judging by the precision and angles of the style—they had the kind of untamed lion's mane of hair which every woman knew took at least an hour in front of the mirror to achieve. Tousled, yet perfect—while Shauna's was scraped back like a schoolgirl's.

Shauna's hair was undoubtedly her best feature, but black curls which tumbled waistwards were hardly practical for everyday wear. Maybe she should have had it cut to a more manageable length, but she had long since given up going to a hairdresser's for just that purpose. Every hairdresser she'd ever met had managed to talk her out of it.

Shauna looked at the women again. Oh, *why* hadn't she bothered to put some make-up on? Because you slept on the boat and it would have smudged, spoke the voice of reason—and a tiny loo on the train was hardly the place to accurately apply your mascara!

As she waited she considered furtively scrabbling around in her holdall and going off to try and camouflage her shiny face, when a final despairing look at the group convinced her that she would stand no chance against them. They were band-box neat and perfectly co-ordinated. As sleek as well-groomed pedigree cats with their up-market clothes, and Shauna felt like a moggy who'd been left out in the rain all night.

Had things in England really changed that much? she wondered. Was this kind of high-powered dressing really *de rigueur* for a job as a businessman's assistant? Nervously, Shauna tugged at the cuff of her suit.

A door behind the woman at the desk opened, and a blonde sashayed her way out of the room without a word.

Mrs Neilson looked up. 'Would Miss Stevens like to go in next?'

The woman with the short hair headed for the inner sanctum, and Shauna dived into the bottom of her holdall, seriously worried now. Was the job all she had supposed it to be? Had she missed something? Been more naïve than usual? Did these women really look like your run-of-the-mill PAs? Suppose the advertisement was a cover for something else—what had she thought about it sounding too good to be true?

She located the letter nestling against a railway timetable and the remains of an apple-core and read it again. Twice.

No. If there was some subtle message in it then she, Shauna, was too dense to fathom it out. And let's face it, she thought, if you go in there and some guy offers you a job in his massage parlour, then you smile politely and head for the door.

Shauna's fingers, when they replaced the advert, were trembling. She had read about places like this in the Sunday papers. Her imagination began to run away with her. What if they wouldn't let her out? What if a strong hand were to snap itself over her wrist with steely strength...? Don't be so ridiculous, reprimanded an inner voice. Everyone else is getting out, aren't they?

The last woman—a luscious-looking strawberry blonde—went in and the phone on Mrs Neilson's desk bleeped. She picked it up and listened.

'Yes, Mr Ryder—she *is* the last, but Miss Wilde has turned up.' There was a pause. 'Yes, I know she's late, but apparently she's travelled a long way to get here…'

Shauna could hear an angry-sounding voice at the other end of the phone.

'I realise that,' interjected Mrs Neilson. Another pause, while she listened to the voice. 'In my opinion—yes.' She replaced the receiver and looked at Shauna. 'He says he'll see you after the last applicant.' She stood up. 'I must go—I've got a hungry husband at home, champing at the bit,' she grinned. 'Mr Ryder will escort you down to the entrance when the interview's over.' Her voice dropped to a whisper. 'Good luck.'

'Thanks.' Shauna watched her retreat out of the glass door and began to twist at the black corkscrew curl by her ear, a habit which she'd had since childhood, and one which invariably made her look about sixteen, instead of twenty-three.

She must be crazy! She'd be alone in this building with this man Max Ryder—someone she didn't know from Adam! Get out now, the voice urged her. Out of this office, into the lift—press for ground floor, and you're away. She picked up her holdall, and her heart sank to see the strawberry blonde striding out, her eyes glittering, her face a mask of fury.

'Bastard,' she muttered, scarcely audibly, and tottered out of the room on high heels like stilts.

Shauna, now seriously alarmed, sprang to her feet and began walking after her, when a deep voice stopped her in her tracks.

'Going somewhere, Miss Wilde?'

Her heart in her mouth, she turned round reluctantly. 'I don't think I'm suited for the job,' she blurted out, and then her mouth stayed open. She had been conjuring up an image of a small, squat man, with olive skin—possibly with a patch over one eye—and stubby, fat fingers covered with a tasteless display of ostentatious gold rings, but the deep-voiced Mr Ryder couldn't have been more different.

Initially, because he was wearing a suit, she decided that he looked respectable, but closer inspection convinced her that respectable was not the right description at all. Respectable men weren't *that* good-looking!

Every cliché in the book could have been used about this man. Intense. World-weary. Brooding. She'd often read about eyes being like chips of ice and had wondered what that meant. Now she knew. The narrow green eyes which were studying her so closely were as cold as glass. His skin was lightly tanned and his mouth was set in an uncompromising line. She tried to imagine him laughing, and failed.

He was tall. I mean—*I'm* tall, she thought. But this man made her feel like some tiny little thing, which was an entirely new experience for Shauna. He had dark, dark hair with just a bit of a wave in it—a wayward lock curled darkly on the collar of a shirt which even she could tell was silk. The tie was silk too—a pale grey affair which toned perfectly with the darker grey of his suit, a suit which fitted superbly, falling in folds from the broad shoulders, folds which hinted at hard muscle and sinew...

'I beg your pardon?' he was saying.

Shauna's grey eyes were like terrified saucers. 'I don't think I'm suited for the job,' she repeated. 'I'm sorry if I've wasted your time.' And proceeded to stare open-mouthed at him again, like a terrified young kitten who had just chanced upon a jungle cat.

'Do please stop gaping at me like an idiot,' he said impatiently. 'And how on earth do you know you're not suited for the job, when you don't know what the job entails? Unless you do know what the job entails, in which case you must be clairvoyant.'

Recognising the heavy sarcasm, she shut her mouth hastily and gave him what she thought was a sweet smile. Humour him, she thought.

He began to look worried. 'You're not about to be ill, are you, Miss Wilde?'

She shook her head. So much for charm! 'I feel fine,' she lied.

'Good,' he said curtly. 'Then, as you've been so good as to give me your time, and I—' here he broke off to glance at a discreet pale gold watch on a tanned wrist '—have set aside mine—then perhaps we could conduct the interview on more formal lines?'

She gulped. 'Sure.' She hooked the holdall over one slim shoulder and picked up her suitcase.

He gestured with his arm. 'After you?' he suggested.

Knowing at once how poor Androcles must have felt as he walked into the lion's den, Shauna stepped unwillingly into the inner sanctum and her eyes lit up.

'Oh, but—it's beautiful!' she exclaimed, as she slowly took in her surroundings.

There was a huge window which took up almost a complete wall, filling the room with a bright, clear light. London lay mapped out before them like a painting. Then other details of the office began to register—the black ash table, a tiny oak bonsai tree and a sheaf of neat papers its only adornment. And the thickness of the pale coffee-coloured carpet in this room made the deep pile of the one in the outer office seem positively threadbare. She'd never seen such an obvious display of wealth, and her earlier misgivings returned to assail her.

'The view I mean,' she finished tamely. 'The view is beautiful.'

The green eyes narrowed. 'I like it,' he said gruffly. He indicated a chair with a wave of his hand, obviously expecting her to sit down, but she remained standing.

'Just a minute,' she blurted out. 'I want you to know that I would never consider doing anything— illegal.'

Dark brows shot up. 'Illegal?' His voice was incredulous. 'Would you care to elucidate?'

She felt on slightly shaky ground, but it was too late to back off now. Assert yourself, some inner

voice urged her. Don't let yourself be intimidated by
your surroundings. 'I'm afraid that I'm just not interested in escort work,' she managed. 'Or—massage.'

'Massage?' he enquired faintly. '*Massage*? Pray
tell me, Miss Wilde—has the front of my building
changed dramatically within the last few hours? Am
I the victim of a practical joke? Is there now some
lurid neon flashing ''Girls! Girls! Girls!'' outside?'

'No, of course not.'

'Then why on earth should you think that I'd be
running some kind of cheap racket like that?' The
green eyes glinted ominously.

'Because—because of the other applicants,' she
burst out. 'They just didn't look like the type of
women who'd be applying for secretarial jobs.'

'Perhaps you could be a little more specific—what
exactly was wrong with them?'

She squirmed a little under his scrutiny. 'They
looked far too glamorous for that kind of work.'

His mouth turned down at the corners. 'Not glamorous, Miss Wilde. I don't consider glamour to be
the over-application of perfume, coupled with a
wholly inappropriate use of make-up. Tacky is the
adjective which springs to mind. Whereas you...'

She didn't know what description he might have
considered suitable for her, because he broke off in
mid-sentence to study her even more closely than he
had done before.

She was glad that the Mediterranean sun had
tanned her skin—at least it camouflaged the slight
rise in colour which his perusal brought to her

cheeks. She knew that she looked clean, and fairly neat, but that was about all that could be said. The black ringlety curls which fell almost to her waist had been pulled back into a french plait, the neatest way of wearing it, but already another corkscrew-like strand had escaped and kept streaking across her face in a dizzy spiral. Her face was completely free of make-up. The legacy of her background had given her naturally long black lashes which fringed the unusual grey eyes.

She wore a navy linen suit, plain and simple. Perhaps not the *best* colour choice for her, but eminently the most practical. Unfortunately she had had it for several years, so the skirt was the wrong length—it brushed to just below her knee instead of this season's style which was several inches above. Her navy leather shoes were completely flat—when you were as tall as she was you *didn't* wear heels!

She met his eyes mutinously, her chin lifting fractionally, peeved at such a leisurely appraisal.

His next words, however, were completely unexpected. '*Gostaria de se sentar, agora?*'

'*Obrigada,*' she said automatically, pulling out a chair from one side of the desk and sitting down, her legs tucked neatly together.

His eyebrows shot up somewhere into the dark hair, as he walked round to the other side of the desk and sat facing her. 'I don't believe it!' he exclaimed. 'You actually speak Portuguese?'

'Of course I do—the advert specified it.'

'It may have specified it, Miss Wilde—but I've been interviewing for three days now, and you're only the second person who has understood and responded to the simplest statement in that language.'

Shauna's eyes widened. 'You mean none of the others today…?'

The tone of his voice bordered on contemptuousness. 'There's one thing, and one thing only, that the assorted bunch I saw today had in common, and that was their avid interest in that ridiculous article—as opposed to the job I'm offering.'

'What article?' asked Shauna in bewilderment. 'I'm not with you.'

The green eyes viewed her with suspicion. 'Then you must be the only woman in the country who hasn't read it.'

'But I haven't *been* in the country,' she pointed out.

He mentioned the name of a well-known women's magazine. 'They decided to do a piece on the fifty most eligible men in Britain,' he growled. 'And since then, it has caused nearly every female coming into contact with me to display even more of the ripe-plum syndrome than usual.'

Shauna had had enough. True, she hadn't exactly warmed to any of her fellow interviewees, but his words were a slur on women in general. She began to rise from her seat. 'What a disgustingly arrogant thing to say—'

'Oh, do sit down, Miss Wilde—you're not in the running for an Oscar, you know. You object to the truth, do you—however unpalatable?'

'I object to your colossal ego,' she said primly. This rejoinder actually brought a wry half-smile to his lips, the first since the 'interview' had commenced, and Shauna was taken aback—his whole face had softened for a moment. The thawing of the glacial green eyes was a definite improvement, she decided.

'My ego may be colossal,' he stated. 'But facts are facts. I'm rich and I'm powerful, and I've known enough women to recognise a blatant invitation when I see it,' he told her arrogantly.

I'll bet you have, she thought fiercely. This man was so big-headed that she was surprised he could walk through the door! 'Well, you needn't fear any "blatant invitation" from me,' she said crossly.

He leaned right back in his chair, his head resting in the palm of his hands, with the careless grace of some jungle feline just before it pounced. 'In that case, Miss Wilde—you could be just what I'm looking for.'

She sat upright in the soft leather chair, meeting the bright green gaze with a candid stare of her own. 'Just what *are* you looking for, Mr Ryder? Your advertisement didn't make it very clear, I must say.'

The green eyes had narrowed to alarming slits. 'Oh, must you? And how would *you* have worded it?'

'I would have thought it was fairly obvious—if you wanted only fluent Portuguese speakers, then the advert should have been written in Portuguese.'

There was a pause. The look he gave her was very measured. She half thought that she saw the merest hint of humour twitch at the corner of his mouth, but then decided that it must have been a trick of the light.

'You are, of course, absolutely right, Miss Wilde. If only the young woman from the specialist staffing agency who came here to take ''details'' of what I required had been credited with your common sense.'

She ignored his sardonic tone. 'Didn't you tell her what you wanted?'

'Of course I told her!' he barked back. 'But she wasn't listening. She spent the whole time wittering on about ''what a beautiful house you have, Mr Ryder'' and ''your photograph didn't do you justice at *all*, Mr Ryder'',' he mimicked.

Shauna gave an almost imperceptible click of disapproval. How *could* she have done? she wondered. Women like that gave women in business a bad name. Quite apart from the fact that you wouldn't need a degree in psychology to recognise that a man like Max Ryder would be completely turned off by such an obvious approach. A man like him would have women in their hundreds, if not *thousands* running after him.

He was still looking at her. 'Am I to understand that you don't approve of women using sex appeal at work?'

Her grey eyes were cold. 'Certainly not. I hope you complained to the agency?'

He shrugged broad shoulders. 'I just shan't use them again. Let's hope I don't have to.' He stared at her consideringly. 'You seem very interested in this staffing agency, Miss Wilde—perhaps you have an affinity for that kind of work?'

'But I'm being interviewed for *this* job, Mr Ryder,' she answered sweetly. She knew that ploy of old. People in power wanted nothing less than one hundred per cent commitment—give them any indication that some other job might suit you more, and you'd be out on your ear. And besides, this job offered her a roof over her head. 'Would you like to tell me a little about it?'

A spark of humour glimmered in the green eyes. 'How about "Tyrant requires PA. Hours long, pay lousy"?' He began to chuckle quietly.

'And is that the truth?' Shauna asked.

A tanned hand moved forward to tap a pencil on the surface of the black ash desk. 'No, I lied about the pay—that's good! The tyrant bit you'd have to make up your own mind about—but I don't suffer fools gladly. I've been called some rather unflattering names in my time,' he said softly. He leaned over to push the bonsai tree a fraction to the right, and then, as if satisfied, settled back in his chair again.

'I buy and sell,' he explained. 'And I deal mainly in property. Since the market has flattened out in this country I've diversified a little, and I'm doing several deals in Europe. At the moment I'm in the process of buying a plot of land in the Algarve which I intend turning into a golf and holiday complex. The project is estimated to take two years minimum, hence the need for an assistant who can speak Portuguese.'

'But you speak it yourself!' she protested.

He shook his head. 'Enough to get by—and I'm very good at ordering in restaurants—but the subtle nuances of the language all go over my head, and I need to understand what is being said. I certainly can't get to grips with legal jargon. Which reminds me—just how good *is* your Portuguese?'

She needed no second bidding. This bit was easy. She wanted to make it clear to him that she, at least, was *not* here on false pretences. That unlike the others she was—as she had stated in her application— perfectly fluent in Portuguese. She spoke rapidly, deliberately making her speech both formal and colloquial—impossible for anyone but the seasoned linguist to understand. When she had finished, she saw that another wry smile had appeared. 'How much did you understand?' she queried.

'Very little,' he admitted. 'You speak very quickly, and your pronunciation is superb.'

She inclined her head, relishing what she accurately assessed was a rare compliment. 'Thank you.'

The eyes were curious. 'How come?'

'How come what?'

'That you're so fluent?'

She hesitated just a little. 'Well,' she said lightly. 'I *have* just spent two years working as a PA in Portugal.'

He waved his hand in the air dismissively. 'I know that. But you must have been pretty good before that? You wouldn't speak it as well as that after just two years.'

He was probing, and she resented it. She didn't want to have to give him a potted history of her life, see pity cloud those enigmatic eyes. She indicated the papers which lay on the desk before him. 'As you'll see from my résumé—I studied languages.' Her grey eyes instinctively flashed a warning.

There was an answering flash in the dark emerald depths. 'To which the same argument applies.'

He was not, she decided, the kind of man to be put off. He was the kind of man who would take a prize for getting blood from a stone. She made up her mind to give him the barest facts possible. 'My mother—was Portuguese,' she stated baldly.

'And your father?'

'Irish.' A flat statement, which dared him to pursue the subject further.

'Unusual combination,' he remarked.

'So I've been told.' She cleared her throat. 'So what you need primarily, Mr Ryder—is an interpreter?'

If he'd noticed that she'd neatly steered the subject away from her parents, he didn't show it. 'Mainly,' he replied. 'But as well as shorthand and typing, I need someone to be my right-hand man, so to speak.' He smiled briefly. 'Or woman, I should say. Someone who will know exactly what I know, and will therefore know how to deal with any urgent business should I not be available. I employ a great many staff not only in this country, but all over the world. Every time some trifling little problem arises, I don't personally want to have to deal with it.' The green eyes held her directly in their full, magnificent gaze.

'I need cables sent,' he continued. 'Documents translated, airline tickets booked, business associates met at the airport. I may need you to travel abroad with me.'

'That sounds like very long hours,' she observed.

'Absolutely. But in return you will be paid handsomely. You'll have first-class accommodation in London, if you want it, and extremely generous holidays. So what do you think?'

'And how much is the salary?'

The sum he mentioned almost made her fall out of her chair.

'Will you be needing accommodation?' He looked at her quizzically.

'Yes, I will,' she nodded. 'Could you tell me what that consists of?'

There was a moment's hesitation. 'There's a large penthouse flat at the top of this building—part of that will be yours.'

It took her precisely ten seconds to mull it over. He would have to be the worst tyrant ever created to justify her turning a deal like this down. Yes, he seemed a big-head of the worst order, and he himself had admitted that he'd been called some 'unflattering names' in his time. She could think of a few herself! She stared into those unusual green eyes. Surely he couldn't be *that* bad?

And the job—the job was everything she wanted. A secure base, with money to save until she decided what she really wanted to do with her life. But then again, he hadn't offered it to her, had he? No doubt it would be the old, old story of 'I've several other people to see'.

'It sounds very—adequate,' she said cautiously.

This last remark inspired a throaty laugh. 'Adequate? What a ghastly word! Miss Wilde, if you're going to work for me you must promise me faithfully that you will never use the word "adequate" ever again.'

She let the flippancy go. 'You mean—you're—you're offering…?'

His face was quite serious again. He gestured to the sheaf of papers on his desk. 'I've seen your references, which are excellent—though you, Miss Wilde, would probably have said "adequate". You satisfy all my other criteria—your Portuguese is fluent, you seem bright enough—oh, and you don't fall into the man-eating tigress mould.'

Meaning, thought Shauna acidly, that I'm a plain Jane.

'And one other thing,' his voice was lower now. 'You need this job, don't you?'

Yes, she needed the job, but she wasn't desperate. She knew that nothing was a bigger turn-off than desperation. 'There are other jobs,' she said coolly.

He smiled. 'The job's yours if you want it.'

She had actually been reaching for her holdall, when she stared at him, not believing her ears. 'Pardon?'

'The job's yours,' he repeated. 'If you want it.'

She still didn't believe it. 'Just like that?' she asked cautiously.

'Just like that.'

She pretended to hesitate, but she got the impression that he wasn't fooled for a minute.

'In that case,' she said, resisting the temptation to leap up into the air, 'I'd be happy to accept.'

'Good.'

'When would you like me to start?'

He frowned. 'Is tomorrow too soon?'

She wanted to make amends for her earlier flights of fancy. 'Tomorrow's fine.'

A piercing look came into his eyes. 'Today, you were late,' he accused.

'There was a...' she began, but he held his hand up.

'I'm not interested. I'm prepared to overlook it once—it won't happen again.'

'No,' she said quietly—she wouldn't dare!

He closed his eyes briefly for a moment, and yawned. She noticed how intensely weary he looked, and wondered whether that was work, or play. When he opened them again, he found Shauna staring at him intently.

He blinked. 'What is it?'

'Your last assistant,' she ventured. 'Why did she leave?'

He stiffened, and the green eyes became cold again. Shrugging his shoulders, he said, 'For—personal reasons.'

Repressing hysterical thoughts, she forced her voice to sound casual. 'Oh? And what were they?'

He paused for a second. 'I'm afraid it was the old story—she fell in love with her boss. That by itself isn't a sackable offence, but I'm afraid she let it affect her work.'

There was no mistaking the warning in his voice. Don't make the same mistake, it seemed to say.

Resisting an urge to comment on the girl's mental state at the time, for surely she must have been loopy to fall for such an insufferably arrogant man, Shauna gave a prim smile. 'Well, don't worry, Mr Ryder—I can assure you that I will not fall into the same trap.'

'Good,' he said abruptly. 'I'm very glad to hear it.'

But Shauna thought he didn't sound one little bit convinced.

CHAPTER TWO

MAX RYDER'S next words were, however, brisk and businesslike. 'I assume that you've clothes and stuff to collect?' He looked down at Shauna's rather battered suitcase. 'Or do I take it that's the sum total of your worldly goods?' he asked sarcastically.

'No, you do not!' she retorted indignantly, pushing away a dark curl which was tickling the corner of her mouth. 'Don't forget—I *have* just come off the boat. As a matter of fact—I've got two more suitcases.'

'So where have you left them?'

'They've been in store at some friends' flat.'

The green eyes beneath the dark brows were looking at her questioningly. 'Local?'

'Yes,' she nodded. 'In London.'

He gave a heavy sigh. 'Are you being deliberately obtuse, Miss Wilde?' He glanced at the pale gold watch. 'I'm expecting a call from Paris at eight—I can give you a lift to collect your belongings, then when we get back I'll show you over the flat.'

She shook her head, so that two more curls wiggled out. For some reason, she was reluctant to be driven there by this man. He was her boss, and—she had to admit—dangerously attractive. She didn't want contact with him spilling over into her private life. 'That's very kind of you, but I can manage on my own, honestly.'

'Oh, for God's sake!' he exclaimed impatiently. 'I'm not trying to unlock the secrets of your soul—I'm simply offering you a lift. Why struggle on the Tube when you can do it in comfort? And if you're worried about some boyfriend—ex or otherwise—rushing out to hit me on the jaw, then don't. Like the proverbial wise man—I'll hear, see nor speak evil!'

The very idea was laughable. She simply couldn't imagine anyone having the temerity to hit *this* man on the jaw! Quite apart from anything else it looked as though it were fashioned from granite.

'I happened to share with two lawyers, not cavemen,' she retorted. 'And they live in Hampstead.'

To her surprise, the questioning ceased. 'Hampstead's miles away,' he said briefly. 'It would take you all night to get there. Come on—we'll take the car.'

She followed him in silence out of the office and into the lift. At the ground floor he introduced her to Charlie, the commissionaire. Then he ushered her through heavy revolving glass doors and outside, where the light was fading rapidly from the sky. The typically October temperature had plummeted rapidly now that the sun had disappeared and Shauna shivered involuntarily, her linen jacket seeming totally inadequate. She hadn't thought he'd been looking, but he noticed immediately.

'I hope there's a thicker coat among your things?' he commented.

'Yes, I've got an overcoat.' She didn't like to say that all her things would probably look to him as if they'd come out of the Ark! Two years was a long time in fashion, and department stores had only recently begun to realise that not all women were of medium height and build. Shauna, being tall and very slim, had always found it notoriously difficult to find clothes to fit her.

Their steps led them to the back of the building, where he unlocked a cunningly concealed car-port to reveal the low, sleek lines of a Mercedes. He was a good driver—confident, but not over-confident. He drove the powerful machine well within the limits of the city's speed restrictions. She thought it rather a waste to have such a powerful car if he lived in town. They headed north.

'So tell me,' he said, 'how on earth you managed to survive two years working in a foreign country on your own.'

'What's that supposed to mean?' she declared indignantly.

He shrugged, the glimmer of a smile playing on his lips. 'If you thought I was running a massage parlour and escort agency, then your imagination must have been working overtime when you were abroad.'

She flushed. Her daydreaming had got her into trouble on more than one occasion. 'I'm surprised you gave me the job.'

A brown hand expertly and swiftly changed down into second gear as a taxi shot out of a side-street and into their path. 'I had a strong gut feeling about you, and I tend to rely on my instincts—where business is concerned, at any rate,' he finished.

She began to wonder how he might respond where his emotions were concerned. If indeed he had any! She remembered his conceited remark about women displaying the 'ripe-plum syndrome'—meaning, presumably, that they all fell eagerly into his arms, she thought acidly. But he'd been nothing but disparaging about her fellow job applicants, so he obviously wasn't desperate for scalps to notch up. She sneaked a surreptitious side-glance at him in the darkness of the car. How old would he be? Early thirties? Involved? Someone as eligible as Max Ryder would be bound to be involved. Except that she couldn't recall seeing any photographs in that vast office of his. Come to think of it, it had been one of the most impersonal rooms that she had ever been in. Stark and dramatic. Even the bonsai tree on the plain black desk had given nothing away. Stunning, but impersonal. A bit like him, really.

'So you managed to spend two years on the Continent without getting yourself into any scrapes?' he probed.

The way he said it made her feel about ten years old. 'I'd been used to working in Portugal,' she defended. 'After two years I knew the job inside out and back to front. I got back to England and suddenly I felt like a stranger in my own country. When I walked into your building I felt totally out of place— it was so outside my experience that I imagined the worst possible scenario.' She tucked one of the errant curls behind her ear and looked at him slightly nervously. 'Do you understand what I mean?'

Unexpectedly he said, 'I believe I do.'

The curl sprang back. 'Can we forget it, and put it down to travel fatigue? By the way—it's left here.'

The car swung up the tree-lined road. The trees were beginning to lose their leaves now. It seemed such a long time since she had lived here—a lifetime ago, really. Nick and Harry had been great flat-mates to have—kind and protective, just like the brothers she'd never had.

'Nice area,' he commented.

'Yes, it is. Could you pull up here? It's the second house, behind the van.'

The powerful car pulled smoothly to a halt. He turned to face her in the semi-darkness. 'I'll wait here,' he said. 'Let me know if you need a hand with anything.'

'Thanks.' She climbed out of the low car, walked to the front door and pressed the bell.

She had to wait several minutes, and was contemplating leaving a note, when the door was opened and a tall, tousled-haired young man stood stock-still, and then a grin split his face in two.

'Shauna!' he said in surprise, and then, 'Shauna!' again in a tone of delight. 'You dark horse, you! Why didn't you say?'

'Because I didn't know until recently,' she laughed. 'And you know the advert you sent me? I got the job!'

'You got the job!' he echoed in delight, and before

she could stop him he had caught her up in his arms and whirled her round and round.

'Put me down, Harry,' she giggled. 'You'll give yourself a hernia!' But as he carefully lowered her back on to the step she saw over his shoulder that Max Ryder was no longer sitting in his car, but lounging against the bonnet—his expression in the darkness unreadable, but, even in that outwardly re- laxed stance, there was no mistaking the coiled ten- sion in the long limbs. Obviously, he must have seen Harry embrace her, and she wondered why she should mind that he had.

Harry looked at her closely. 'You look fabulous, Shauna,' he said quietly. 'But pensive. Come in. Have a drink?'

She shook her head regretfully, eyeing the famil- iarly shabby hall with affection. 'I can't. I've got someone waiting. He's offered me a job and accom- modation. I'm here to collect my stuff.'

'So? Invite him in, too.'

Shauna took in the overflowing books, the half- empty wine bottle, last Sunday's—and the Sunday's before that!—newspapers littering the floor. She could just imagine the minimalist, bonsai-loving Max Ryder fitting in here!

'I don't think so, Harry,' she smiled at him fondly. 'He hasn't even shown me the flat, yet—and he's expecting a phone call from Paris. But I'll come round another night—you can cook me one of your famous Bolognese sauces, and we'll catch up on all the gossip.'

Harry frowned. 'If only we hadn't let your old room out.'

'I would hardly have expected you to hold on to it for two years!' exclaimed Shauna. 'That would be stretching friendship a little too far!'

'No, I suppose not.'

'It was good of you to keep my stuff for me.' She looked at her watch. 'Listen, I'd better not keep—'

'No, of course not. I'll get your stuff.' He retreated into the larger bedroom. 'Nick will be sorry to have missed you,' he called out. 'Did you know he's in love?'

'He wrote and told me! What's she like?'

He reappeared, carrying two large suitcases. 'Great—when she's not sitting gazing at him like a lovesick puppy!'

'You next, then,' teased Shauna.

'Is that an offer?' he smiled.

They heard a loud toot from outside before she had a chance to reply. Shauna knew immediately who it would be.

'That'll be my new boss,' she explained. 'I'd better go.'

Harry pushed the curtain open a crack. 'Flash car,' he observed. 'What's he like?'

Shauna peeped out—he was *still* standing there. 'The kind of man your mother told you never to go out with—well, *most* mothers,' amended Shauna.

'Lucky devil,' said Harry gloomily. 'I have the opposite trouble—instant parental approval—very boring!'

There was a momentary pause. 'Thanks for my free holiday,' he smiled. 'I had a great time.'

He'd travelled out to Portugal in the summer, and her boss had put him up for the fortnight.

She grinned her agreement. 'Me too. And thanks again for finding me the ad.'

They stood for a moment, hands clasped like the old friends they were—their brief and youthful romance long forgotten. 'I'll carry your cases to the car for you,' he said.

A dark figure loomed up out of the shadows. 'There's no need for that,' contradicted a deep voice, and Shauna started to see Max Ryder standing there, automatically moving away to break the contact, wondering what had caused the faint upward curl of his lip.

She performed the necessary introductions, but she thought that her new boss was decidedly lukewarm in his greeting, and Harry was uncharacteristically taciturn. In fact, for some reason neither man seemed to like the other very much.

Amid promises to call soon, Shauna and Max roared off down the street. There was silence for a moment. Then he spoke.

'I thought I asked you not to be long,' he said tetchily as he put his foot down on the accelerator. 'I hope I'm not going to miss my call.'

'Sorry,' she said automatically.

Max gave her a sideways glance. 'After such a fond reunion, I'm surprised your lover doesn't want you to stay with him.'

So he *had* seen them embrace. 'He is not my

lover,' she said, in an angry voice. Not any more, she thought. An attempt at young love years ago which had fizzled out almost as soon as it had started. Not that she was going to explain that to *him*. He was her boss, and he had absolutely no right whatsoever to comment on her private life. 'And even if he were, it's none of your business.' Which didn't come out at all the way she had intended it to.

She saw his hands tighten on the steering-wheel, as if he was not used to being spoken to in such a way, and she might have tried to amend her snapped response, but a glance at the cold, hard profile told her that she would be wise to say nothing, so she stared out into the night as Hyde Park swept by them.

He didn't speak again until they had arrived back in Mayfair. He was not, Shauna decided, the type of man to engage in meaningless pleasantries.

'I'll show you the apartment now.' He frowned as he glanced again at the pale gold wristwatch. 'You must be hungry.'

So he was back to being civil. 'Starving,' she admitted.

This time, the lift went right past the third floor where he'd interviewed her, and the doors opened straight into an enormous sitting-room. The carpet was white, and littered with Persian rugs. The walls were also white, with several large modern canvases which fitted in perfectly with the simple leather furniture.

Shauna suppressed a gasp. Surely he couldn't mean that *this* was her flat? Compared to the dark cubby-hole she'd had in Lisbon, this place was like a palace.

'The kitchen's through here,' he was saying. 'There's a bathroom off that passage over there, but of course your room has its own, *en suite*. This is your room here.' He pushed open a door to reveal a sumptuously appointed bedroom, decorated in palest eau-de-Nil. 'You'll find that—apart from work— we'll hardly see one another.'

Shauna's mouth fell open. 'We? What do you mean ''we''?'

He sounded impatient. 'The flat has three bed- rooms, and a great deal of living space. We'll hardly be on top of one another.'

Suddenly the tall, dark figure of Max Ryder ap- peared very slightly menacing, and involuntarily she took a step back. 'But I didn't know I was going to be sharing with *you*!'

'Oh, for God's sake! We are living in the twentieth century, you know!' he retorted. 'Men and women *do* share flats these days—as you've obviously done yourself before. Or perhaps you consider yourself such a little sexpot that you think I won't be able to keep my hands off you?'

'No, I don't!' she parried, a blush creeping into her cheeks as her mind became alight with vivid im- ages that his words had conjured up.

'Well, that's something,' he said, with a kind of grim satisfaction. 'Because, believe me, the last type of woman to attract me is some tall, skinny kid who doesn't look old enough to be out of gym-slips!'

Shauna glared at him. It was one thing to decide

that the man before her was the last person she'd ever fall for—it was quite another to discover that he felt exactly the same way—and his disparaging remarks made her bristle with indignation. Share a flat with *him*? Why, she'd rather share with a gang of escaped convicts!

'And what about—privacy?' she asked primly.

He gave a hollow laugh. 'Privacy? Will you stop acting like the original vestal virgin? Slightly redundant anyway, since we've just collected your stuff from your ex-lover.'

He managed to make a young love-affair sound so *sordid*, she thought, her grey eyes sending out sparks of indignation.

'You'll have all the privacy you could possibly want,' he continued. 'For a start, I'm away in the country most weekends. Secondly, your room is on the opposite side of a very large flat, and it has its own bathroom. So does mine. So the chances of your coming across me in the raw are pretty remote.' His eyes narrowed. 'The good news for both of us is that I'll shortly be having the flat divided into two completely separate apartments. It would have been done already if *I* had been here to sort the damned builders out. Unfortunately, I've been out of the country.'

That explained the tan, thought Shauna.

His eyes were mocking as they surveyed her. 'Now, are those arrangements secure enough for your Victorian sensibilities, or would you like me to throw in a chastity belt while I'm at it?' He gave an unexpected grin as he saw her colour heighten yet again.

'You know, you really are going to have to do something about that blushing, if you're going to work for me. And you a woman of the world!'

His teasing immediately defused the atmosphere. 'I am *not* a woman of the world, if that means what I think it means.'

He was staring at her curiously. 'Tell me, you didn't lie about your age in your letter, did you?'

'Oh, for goodness' sake!' she flung back at him. 'Of course I didn't lie! Do you always think the worst of people, or are you just used to people lying to you?'

'All the time,' he mused. 'Particularly women, and particularly about their age. Except that they usually lop a few years off, whereas in your case...'

There was something distinctly unsettling about the way those green eyes bored into her, she thought, but, refusing to rise to this, she stared steadily at him. 'Will you be needing me this evening?' she asked pointedly. 'Because I'd like to unpack and—'

He shook his head. 'You're free until tomorrow morning at ten sharp. Oh, and there's one more thing—house rules.'

'I am very tidy,' she interrupted. 'And I do not leave dirty dishes in the sink.'

'There's a dishwasher, actually—and the maid comes in twice a week. No, I've only one rule and that's no overnight guests. I don't care who you go to bed with—just don't do it here. I don't intend to have my sleep disturbed.'

She went white beneath her tan and glared at him. He was obviously going out of his way to shock her, but he was going to be disappointed—she had absolutely no intention of rising to his challenge, *or* of offering him any information on the current state of her love-life. The question was whether she could put up with working for a man who could be quite so contentious. She continued to stare at him as she contemplated the only alternative, which would be to walk out of here right now.

She couldn't. It was a brilliant job—she'd never find another like it. And if the only fly in the ointment was the conceited Max Ryder—well, surely she could put up with that? And at least he had made it perfectly clear that he wouldn't dream of making a pass at her, so in that sense, at least, she was quite safe with him.

The green eyes had been observing her with the faintest touch of amusement. 'Changed your mind, have you?'

She pretended to look perplexed. 'Changed my mind? About what?'

'Staying.'

Her wide mouth closed in a determined line. Roll on the day when the builders arrived! 'Certainly not, Mr Ryder. I look on it as a challenge.'

The glimmer of a smile. 'Call me Max. And there's plenty of food in the kitchen. Help yourself.'

'Thank you very much,' she answered politely, but, as she closed her bedroom door behind her, she reflected that her voracious appetite of earlier had mysteriously disappeared.

CHAPTER THREE

SHAUNA unpacked her cases and her holdall and hung everything up in the vast mirrored wardrobe, deciding wryly that she would really have to invest in some new clothes. What she had was OK, but there was so little of it. In Portugal she'd lived mostly in lightweight clothes which were totally inappropriate for the approaching English winter. At least the stuff she'd picked up at the flat was warmer, but, even so, it now looked terribly dated.

The bathroom looked like something out of an ideal home advertisement—all mirrors and lights and expensive-looking glass-topped bottles. She took a long, luxurious bath, which was heaven after all the travelling, and finished off in the shower, untying the rampant black curls and smothering them with shampoo, then conditioner. It took her almost half an hour to dry them, and by that time she was exhausted and barely had the energy to brush her teeth and climb into the king-sized bed. It had been a long day.

She had thought that she wasn't hungry, but her stomach obviously thought differently since she woke up in the night feeling distinctly empty. She sat up in bed, rubbing her eyes with the back of her fist, her heart sinking when she saw that her watch read only four a.m.—hardly the proper time to eat. Her stomach rumbled loudly in protest. Perhaps if she was *very* quiet, she could go and raid Max's lar-der—he'd told her to help herself, after all.

She climbed out of bed and pulled on her robe. Barefooted, she quietly opened the bedroom door and listened for a moment. She could hear nothing other than the faint ticking of a clock somewhere in the distance. Max Ryder's bedroom door was closed, thank goodness. Silently she padded over the thick pile of the carpet, the soft woollen strands tickling her toes. She reached the kitchen and gently opened the door.

Whatever else he might or might not have done, Max Ryder certainly ate well. The fridge was full of salads, cold meats, cheeses, fruit, and an expensive-looking box of Belgian chocolates. Further hunting produced a bread-bin, and she cut herself two enor-mous slices of brown bread, buttered them, and lay-ered salad and ham between them.

She had just found a full carton of orange juice and was about to open it when she heard a sound behind her and whirled round to find Max Ryder standing at the door, wearing nothing but a pair of faded denims—and only half-zipped, she noted in horror before averting her gaze from them so hastily that the carton of juice slipped from her fingers.

At precisely the same moment, they both lunged for the juice, Shauna's outstretched hand making her lose her balance, her bare feet slipping wildly on the shiny tiles. She would have fallen awkwardly had his arm not reached out automatically and, as she top-pled, he caught her.

Winded, she sagged against him, momentarily too

dazed to be aware of anything other than his strength as he held her, of the tingling warmth of his hand as it casually spanned her back, and then, as her senses returned, she realised to her horror that she was clasped close to him, that her breasts were jutting firmly against the warm skin of his bare chest—their shape clearly defined through the wool of her robe. A strange wave of dizziness assailed her and colour washed her cheeks as she saw that the way she was leaning against him had caused a bare breast to slip free of the confines of her robe, so that almost the whole of the milky-pale globe—untouched by the hot summer sun—was visible.

She heard him swear beneath his breath and she hastily pulled away, breathing rapidly, unable to meet his eyes for embarrassment as she pulled the gown tightly around herself, as if it were armour-plating. The thick maroon dressing-gown had been chosen with no concessions to fashion, warmth and hard-wearingness being its main function, but all of a sudden she might have been clothed in some feminine little wisp of satin, she felt so exposed under his gaze.

'What the hell are you playing at?' he grated, in a loud, harsh voice, and she noticed a small muscle working on his left cheek. He pushed her out of the way almost roughly, slammed the orange juice down on the work surface, and stood facing her.

'Is this your idea of entertainment?' he demanded. 'Hurling things around the kitchen at this God-forsaken hour? Not to mention yourself!'

'That was an accident—I slipped on the floor. You frightened me,' she protested.

'Frightened you? You're bloody lucky I didn't rugby tackle you to the ground,' he snapped. 'I heard noises, and I thought it was an intruder.'

The remark about the rugby tackle was a little too close for comfort. 'Oh, for goodness' sake! Does this mean that every time I walk around the apartment you're going to start throwing yourself at me like the caped crusader?'

The green eyes were cold. 'As I recall,' he said icily, 'it was you who threw yourself at me.'

'And I told you it was an accident! I am now sharing this flat with you, in case you'd forgotten, and that means that from time to time I will be making some little noise or movement,' she said, sweetly sarcastic.

'It sounded like Nelly the Elephant stomping around,' he retorted. 'And do you always make a habit of eating sandwiches at four in the morning?'

Boss he might be—custodian he was not! 'I eat when I'm hungry—like now! So if you wouldn't mind letting me get on with it...'

'I'm going,' he snapped moodily. 'Just try and make less noise on your return trip, will you? And put the light out.'

As he stomped out of the kitchen, she had to resist a very strong urge indeed to stick her tongue out at him. She waited until she heard his door close quietly, before perching on a stool and shakily pouring herself some juice.

He had implied that he was a tyrant. *Tyrant*? That

was the understatement of the century! She could
have provided a far more colourful description! He
was the foulest-tempered, meanest man she'd ever
encountered. She bit into the sandwich viciously. He
also had one of the best bodies she'd ever seen—and
she'd seen hundreds, bronzed and posing on beaches
all over Portugal. There hadn't been a trace of sur-
plus flesh on that frame, even when he bent down.
He had also been perfectly at ease with his semi-
clothed state, completely unselfconscious, which was
more than could be said about her.

She bit into the sandwich again, wishing that she
could dispel the sinking wave of disconcertion that
washed over her as she recalled the way that her
breasts had pressed against him. The way in which
her robe had fallen open... She pressed her knuckles
to the sides of her head, the sandwich forgotten.
What if he'd thought it deliberate? His ego was so
immense, his opinion of women so low, that he probably hadn't put it past her to wake him up in the
middle of the night, and then to drape herself pro-
vocatively all over him, like some amateurish *femme
fatale*.

A small groan escaped her. Please don't let him
think that, she prayed. After all, hadn't one of his
criteria for employing her been that she didn't 'fall
into the man-eating tigress mould'?

She finished off the rest of the sandwich and
stacked her plate and glass in the dishwasher. As she
tiptoed back to bed, she resolved that, unless there
was a fire, Max Ryder would never again see her in

any form other than fully dressed—that way there could be no misinterpreting her motives!

Although there wasn't much of the night left, Shauna opted for sleep, and, much to her surprise, it came. When she opened her eyes it was nine-fifteen and bright sunshine was streaming in through a crack in the silk curtains.

Ten o'clock sharp, he had said, so she had to hurry, although, as she towelled herself dry after a brief shower, she decided that it wouldn't come as any great shock to her to learn that he had reconsidered his job offer after the orange juice incident.

She dressed in a simple black tunic, but she relieved its starkness with a scarlet ribbon at the nape of her neck which loosely tied back the thick black curls.

Feeling ready to face the world—or, more importantly, him—she opened her bedroom door, hoping against hope to find the sitting-room empty, but she was out of luck, for he sat there at the table by the window, as large as life, with a coffee-pot steaming in front of him.

He looked up as she entered, and she braced herself for a barrage of abuse, or a cold dismissal, but there was neither—he barely glanced up from his newspaper, except to say, 'The coffee's fresh,' gesturing to the pot before him.

She hesitated for a moment, and eventually he looked up at her, his expression as inscrutable as if it had been carved in marble.

'About last night,' she began.

'Forget it,' came the curt rejoinder.

What was it that made her persist, when his tone expressly forbade it? 'But I...'

'I said *forget* it!' The green eyes looked as dark as jade.

'I didn't want you to think—' she began stubbornly. What? That she'd been out to seduce him?

'Listen to me,' he interrupted exasperatedly. 'I thought nothing. Do you understand? *Nothing.* You may have thought it appropriate to act like some damsel in distress—personally I thought your reaction was way over the top.' A cynical smile twisted his lips. 'Cowering in the corner, defending your supposed honour. Believe me, what I saw was less than I'd have seen on any beach anywhere in the world, and certainly nothing to get excited about. So can we please drop it?' He picked up his newspaper summarily. 'Now eat up your toast like a good girl,' he finished sarcastically.

She forced her hand to remain steady as she reached out for the coffee-pot, scarcely crediting what she'd heard, too stung by his cutting put-down to be able to think of a suitable retort. Nothing to get excited about! What a nerve! Of all the high-handed, arrogant swines, she thought as she determinedly ate her way through one slice of toast and began a second—she was not going to let him see how angry his hurtful comments had made her, by being off her food!

No wonder he was paying her such a high salary— danger money, that was what it was! And now here she was, ensconced in the home of this unbelievably rude man. The future certainly did not look very promising.

She pulled one of the newspapers on the table towards her, but couldn't really take much in. She thought what a strange picture they must make, sitting drinking early morning coffee together, when they were virtual strangers. But didn't that happen all the time with flat-sharing? They said you never really learnt what someone was like until you lived with them. What surprised her was that Max Ryder wasn't already living with a woman—in the *full* meaning of the term.

She realised that she knew absolutely nothing about him, other than the obvious...that he was tall, dark and handsome and—according to him, at least!—had a lethal effect on women. When she looked up from the paper, whose words were a mystery to her, her grey eyes all dreamy and miles away, she found him surveying her curiously.

'A woman who doesn't chatter in the morning— now that *is* something I could get used to.'

And here, no doubt, he would be rewarded with gushing thanks, she thought drily. 'Didn't you say you wanted to start work when we'd finished our coffee?' she asked coolly.

Her raised his eyebrows by just a millimetre. 'Why, certainly,' he murmured. 'If we could just convene to the office, I'll give you a list.'

He picked up a green silk tie which he had thrown over the back of the chair. It was almost the exact colour of his eyes and Shauna found herself wondering if he'd chosen it with precisely that in mind!

She followed him out. It felt odd to be travelling down from the flat to the offices just two floors below. A bit like going from a hotel bedroom down to the dining-room, she decided, then bent her head quickly to study an imaginary spot on her black patent shoes. Bedroom! Now, what on earth had made her think of hotel bedrooms? Thank heavens that Max Ryder couldn't read her mind!

Mrs Neilson, the receptionist, was already in place. 'Morning, Max,' she smiled.

'Hi, Rosie. You met yesterday, but may I formally introduce Shauna Wilde, who got the job?'

Rosie Neilson extended a perfectly manicured hand. 'Nice to see you again, Shauna. I knew you'd walk the job, the moment I saw you.'

'How d'you do?' said Shauna politely, slightly alarmed at this. I hope I'm nothing like the last assistant, she thought. The one he had to get rid of!

'We'll be in my office all morning,' said Max. 'Can you hold all non-urgent calls for the first hour?'

'Will do. I'll rescue you with coffee later.'

Shauna and Max went into his office, and, from that moment on, he kept her busy—and how! For the first hour she scribbled furiously in a small notebook while he explained the framework of his day. 'Although, of course—no two days are ever the same,' he said.

He gave her the phone numbers of clients and colleagues, of hotels he liked to stay in, and restaurants he favoured. As far as she could make out, he had so many fingers in so many pies that he could have done with a couple of extra sets of hands!

After the first hour was up, the phone on his desk began to ring. The first call was from Paris, and he dealt with that himself, speaking in a very passable French accent. Then he set to—dictating a whole heap of letters, and asking her to write one to his Portuguese lawyer.

'These are the main points I want to make—just make it formal, but flowery—you know the kind of thing they like?'

She nodded. 'I do.'

He went out for early lunch—he didn't say who with, she assumed it was business—leaving her to fend for herself in his absence. Surprisingly enough, she coped, even when Mrs Neilson went off at lunchtime.

She typed the letters he'd dictated and he came back just before five and pronounced himself satisfied. She supposed it would have been too much to ask that he actually beam his gratitude; instead she had to make do with a brisk 'Thanks' before he informed her that he was going out for the evening and gave her a spare set of keys to the flat. She mystified and infuriated herself by wondering just who he was out with.

Within a few days she had settled into some sort of routine. She worked hard—he certainly expected it!—perhaps harder than ever before in her life. He was exacting, demanding and critical to the extreme if she fell short of his own standards of excellence. And yet she found the challenge of working for such a hard taskmaster strangely satisfying. She became determined that he should not find her deficient in any of the skills he expected her to have.

Once, she caught him listening to her conducting a conversation entirely in Portuguese, the expression on his face a cross between amusement and irritation. She suspected it peeved him that she was fluent, whereas he was not!

In the flat she saw him less than she would have imagined—he was right, it *was* very big. He went out some evenings, never saying where, never inviting her to go with him, but then, why should he?

Once or twice, she'd answered the phone to a woman with a distinctively low voice called Marta. She was bursting with curiosity to know who she was, but he always took the calls in his bedroom.

Shauna tended to disappear to her room after supper to read, or, if he wasn't around, she'd watch TV or a video. Once, she had dinner with Harry and Nick, and Nick's girlfriend, Heather—but Shauna knew immediately that it wouldn't become a regular thing. Nick was too much in love, and Harry was studying for his Bar exams. Sadly, she recognised that they had all inevitably grown apart since they'd been at university together.

A fortnight went by with Shauna scarcely seeing Max at home, and she made up her mind to try to break the ice a little. After all, they *were* flatmates, and, just because they were also boss and employee, that shouldn't in theory preclude some sort of friendship.

One day—just before he set off for lunch—she

casually asked him whether he'd be eating out that evening.

He grimaced. 'God, no—I've had a surfeit of restaurant food this week.'

Perfect! She would cook one of her wholewheat spaghetti dishes as she'd sometimes done with Harry and Nick, and get to know a little of the person behind the enigmatic façade of her employer. Except that it didn't quite turn out like that...

Max emerged from his room at around eight to find the table set for two and Shauna busy stir-frying vegetables, her face pink and shiny from the heat.

His brow creased suspiciously. 'Having company?' he asked, his tone leaving her in no doubt what he thought of *that* idea.

She smiled. 'Not exactly—that is—I hoped that you might like to join me?'

'*Whaat*?' he queried.

Her smile faded a little. 'I was just rustling up some supper for myself, and, as you weren't going out tonight, I thought...' Her voice died away as she saw his face. If she'd suggested dining on old socks he couldn't have looked more aghast.

He looked at the frying-pan, which contained the snow-peas, baby corn and zucchini, and gave a barely suppressed shudder, before turning the direction of his gaze back to Shauna, the green eyes looking distinctly unfriendly.

'Let's get a couple of things straight, shall we?' he said, in a deliberately neutral voice. 'The way to my heart is not through my stomach—got that?'

She frowned non-comprehendingly. 'I don't—'

'Neither am I,' he continued relentlessly, 'going to be impressed if you start baking cakes your granny taught you to. Similarly, flowers filling the apartment, or the smell of fresh coffee wafting through the air, are less likely to fill me with admiration at your home-making skills, than with boredom.'

The fullness of her mouth became distorted into a straight line as she bit her bottom lip in anger. 'I don't know what you're talking about,' she snapped.

He leaned forward as if to emphasise his point, so close that she could see the dramatic contrast between the bright green of his eyes and the stark jet of their centres. 'Then let me tell you. I am talking about your little "womanly wiles",' he sniped sarcastically. 'Why is it that whenever I'm around women they suddenly show an irresistible desire not only to cook and sew, or to endlessly straighten already straight pictures, but also to coo with delight whenever they spot a baby or a fluffy kitten?' he mused sarcastically. 'Perhaps you could throw some interesting new light on the subject?'

The primary rule of deference to one's superior flew straight out of the window and there was a momentary flash of rage in her grey eyes before she quelled it. No need to let him see how much his conceited rejection had hurt her. She managed a scornful laugh.

'Over-reacting *just* a little, aren't you, Max?' she enquired mockingly. 'I've hardly been out at dawn picking mushrooms to prepare a lavish banquet. It was a simple supper that I thought you might like to share—if I'd known it was going to cause *quite* so much fuss, then I wouldn't have bothered. I shan't again.'

'Good,' he said curtly. 'I am sick of women deciding that I am to be the lucky recipient of their search for a permanent partner. I am *not* looking for love. Understand? And now I'm going out.'

Speechless with indignation, she watched as he walked to the door, the electric light gleaming on the dark, tangled waves of his hair, watching his every stride, every damned muscular move of him, and it wasn't until he had slammed the front door that she allowed herself the luxury of a very loud and very graphic expletive.

A fortnight later, Max was dictating another letter for her to type and standing in front of the enormous plate-glass window which dominated the office, when the phone on the desk began to ring and Shauna reached out to pick it up.

'Mr Ryder's office,' she announced briskly.

'Is Mr Ryder there?' asked an efficient-sounding female voice.

'Who's calling, please?'

'This is Queen Mary's School.'

Max was looking at her enquiringly.

'It's Queen Mary's School,' she said, pressing the mute button on the phone.

He took the receiver at once, looking slightly puzzled as he did so. 'Hello?'

She couldn't help noticing that his expression changed from puzzlement to something fast approaching anger, or that his barked monosyllabic questions had become increasingly terse.

He gave a curt goodbye and replaced the receiver noisily as he got to his feet. 'I have to go out now, Shauna. I may be some time.'

She was dying to know what connection he had with Queen Mary's School but she didn't dare ask. She'd never seen him look quite so angry before.

He was away for hours and didn't reappear. Shauna typed the letters he'd dictated, and then a special messenger delivered some legal documents which were entirely in Portuguese, and she began to translate them, enjoying the challenge of making sense of the formal and rather stuffy terms used.

At six, there was no sign of him, and at six-thirty she decided to call it a day. She took the documents up with her to the flat and had just placed them neatly on the dining-room table when she heard the front door slam and looked up to see Max.

She was torn between waiting to gauge his mood before she spoke and a very natural desire to demonstrate that she'd shown initiative in translating a complicated piece of Portuguese. Prudence lost.

'Hello,' she said. 'I worked until six-thirty. I've left the letters on your desk—oh, and these arrived...' She stopped in mid-sentence, suddenly aware that the bright green eyes were hard with anger.

'What is it?' she cried. 'What's happened?' But he didn't answer, just continued to stand there, staring at her.

'Max...' Even now, his name still sounded unfamiliar on her lips. 'What is it?'

There was a long silence. 'It's my daughter.' The

deep voice was harsh. 'She's just been expelled from school.'

His daughter! Just imagining him as a father required a major adjustment in thinking, and she felt an unmistakable lurch in the pit of her stomach. If there was a daughter, then somewhere there must be a wife...or an ex-wife...

He carried on speaking as if she weren't there. 'Damn and *damn*!' he exploded.

She took a deep breath to steady her voice. 'What's happened?'

He stared at her. 'My daughter has what's euphemistically termed an "attitude problem". Her boarding-school have not taken kindly to the fact that she's been found smoking. Again.'

'And won't they reconsider?'

He shook his head. 'Nope. That's what the phone call was about this morning. That's where I've been all day. This was the "last chance", as they say.'

A daughter! She just couldn't imagine it. 'How old is she?'

'Thirteen,' he said automatically, and then must have seen her raised eyebrows. 'You don't think I look old enough to have a thirteen-year-old?' he queried. 'I was a child bride,' he finished sarcastically.

She wondered what had caused the bitterness in his voice. 'It's just that—well—I haven't noticed any photographs,' she faltered.

He turned abruptly and walked across the room to his bedroom and returned moments later carrying a large, silver-framed photo. He handed it to her. 'This is my daughter,' he said.

Shauna stared at the face of the young girl and realised that her mother must be very beautiful indeed, for, although the child owed her slanting green eyes to her father, Shauna saw that the sculpted delicacy of her features had not come from him. She found something strangely appealing in the way the child stared defiantly at the camera, as though daring it to make her smile.

'She's very beautiful,' she said.

'Yes,' he replied shortly.

For some reason which she didn't quite understand, she was reluctant to ask the next question. 'And—what about her mother? What does she say?'

There was a long pause. 'She doesn't have a mother.' He walked towards the drinks cabinet. 'Do you want a drink?'

'No.'

He tipped some whisky into a glass and drank half of it off in a mouthful. 'She's dead,' he stated baldly, glancing up, the green eyes narrowed. 'It's all right. You can spare me the platitudes. It all happened a long time ago.'

She was mature enough to realise that he wasn't lashing out at her, but his curtness hurt, nevertheless. She shifted in her seat a little, surprised at his frankness, surprised that he should confide in her at all.

'So what do you plan to do?'

He set the glass down on the cabinet, and began to loosen his tie. 'They're sending her home tomorrow. I'll have to find another school for her. It's going to mean some disruptions. There isn't room for her to come here, and anyway—it isn't suitable. I have a house just outside Oxford, in the country. There's no way round it—we'll have to transfer the business down there, until I can get her into a new school.'

She noticed that he hadn't asked if she minded being uprooted, had just assumed that she would tag along, like a pet poodle, and perhaps he read something in her expression, for a frown appeared between the dark brows.

'Is that OK with you?' he asked grudgingly.

As a considerate question to his secretary, it barely registered on a scale of one to ten, but Shauna had a soft heart, besides which, objections from her were the *last* thing he needed right now. 'No problem at all,' she said. 'Go anywhere, that's me. I'm footloose and fancy-free, with absolutely no ties.'

He looked surprised for a moment, then nodded. 'Good. We'll leave first thing.' He hesitated for a moment. 'I feel I should warn you—she won't make things easy for you. She can be—very difficult.'

Like father, like daughter, thought Shauna, but she smiled at him. 'That's OK,' she said.

CHAPTER FOUR

'ARE you one of Daddy's mistresses?'

Shauna almost choked on the apple she'd been chewing. 'I beg your pardon?'

The green eyes met hers mutinously. 'I said, are you one of Daddy's mistresses?'

Shauna was determined not to look shocked which, she was sure, was the whole point of the exercise. 'I'm your father's new assistant. My name's Shauna Wilde.'

'Assistant!' The young voice was scornful. 'That's a new one! I suppose you'll spend all your time trying to get him into—'

'Bianca!' Max came into the room before she could finish the sentence, although it was perfectly clear to Shauna what she had been about to say.

'That's enough!' he warned his daughter. 'If you can't behave properly, you'll be sent to your room—and I mean it.'

'Yes, Daddy.' The child suddenly flashed her father a brilliant smile which illuminated her whole face.

Yet she was more than a child, thought Shauna. She was that volatile mix of child-woman, poised on the brink of adolescence. The photograph had not done her justice, she decided. It had not been able to accurately convey the almost porcelain-like translu-

cence of her skin. She had tiny, neat wrists and limbs
and looked sleek and well cared for. Only her trou-
bled eyes betrayed her turmoil of adolescent emotions.

Shauna and Max had driven up from London that
morning, and, after he had dropped her at the house,
he had driven to the school to collect his daughter.

Shauna had been astounded to see Max's house—
'Seekings'—a double-fronted Queen Anne building
set in elegant and mature grounds. Now she could
understand why the London flat was so bare, and so
characterless. The flat was not a home—*this* was
home.

It was full of beautiful old furniture, floors scattered with jewel-bright rugs, and impressive oil-
paintings hanging on deep crimson walls.

Shortly after Shauna's arrival, a plump, old-
fashioned woman appeared on the doorstep. 'I'm Mrs
Roberts, the housekeeper,' she told Shauna. 'Normally I only work the weekends Mr Ryder's here,
and when Miss Bianca's on holiday, but Mr Ryder
rang me last night and said what had happened,' she
explained, as she showed Shauna her bedroom.
'Sounded desperate, he did, poor dear. I know he'd
like me here more often than I am, to keep my eye
on her, and so on—but I've a husband to look after.'
The smile on her tired face faded a little. 'Invalided
from work now, he is.' Her voice dropped. 'She's a
right handful is Miss Bianca. Had her own way for
far too long, she has, and twists that father of hers
round her little finger. A right handful.'

And Shauna, on coming face to face with the slight

blonde creature, her elfin features doing nothing to disguise the rather worldly calculating expression in her eyes, would have tended to agree with Mrs Roberts. But she had been there herself. Once, she had been a lonely, confused schoolgirl, a little like this.

'I'll get the rest of the bags in,' said Max.

Shauna and Bianca watched in silence as he headed back towards the main hall.

Bianca's eyes flashed with pleasure. 'So are you sleeping with him, or not?' she demanded.

Shauna bit back the instinct to snap back. She was being tested, and she knew it. 'No, I am not,' she said firmly. 'And who on earth taught you to say things like that?'

'Oh, at school,' said the young girl airily. 'Everyone knows about sex at school.'

'Then it sounds as though you're better out of that particular school, doesn't it?'

'Except that me being here puts a spoke in the wheels, doesn't it? It means that I'll be forever playing gooseberry.'

'No, you won't,' said Shauna gently. 'I'm here to type and phone and translate, that's all—until your father sorts out a new school for you.'

The expression was truculent. 'Oh, yeah?'

Just at that moment Max came back into the room, and the conversation was brought abruptly to a halt.

'Mrs Roberts is just about to serve lunch,' he said. 'Do you want to freshen up, Bianca?'

'Sure. I know when I'm not wanted.' She strode out of the room, her hips swinging in a curiously adult way which only served to make her seem younger and more defenceless.

Max turned to Shauna. She thought how much older and wearier he'd become in the last twenty-four hours. There were lines around the bright eyes, lines which she foolishly found herself wanting to massage away with her fingertips.

'I'm trying very hard not to rise to those kind of remarks,' he said. 'I hope you'll understand that underneath that hard exterior there's the little girl I once knew trying to get out.'

She suddenly found herself wanting to reassure him. To tell him that she had no intention of sitting in judgement on his daughter. 'You don't have to explain anything to me, you know,' she said softly. 'I'm just here to do your work for you.'

He looked at her for a long moment, those strange, green eyes seeming as though they had the power to read her thoughts. The colour rose in her cheeks as for the briefest second she thought how near he was, how close his lips looked, and then she stepped back self-consciously. 'Did I hear you say something about lunch?'

'Yes,' he replied, still looking at her. 'Come through to the dining-room.'

The dining-room looked like something out of a film set. Three places had been set at the far end of the table, which sat in an alcove overlooking the gardens. There were fresh flowers on the gleaming wood, and crystal glasses and damask linen napkins. It was a long time since Shauna had experienced such correct formality, and she felt ridiculously underdressed in a simple skirt and soft grey sweater which matched her eyes. Max, she thought, would have fitted in anywhere—the fine quality of his clothes spoke volumes—and Bianca hadn't simply freshened up, she had changed out of her school uniform into a violet and green sweat-shirt, with the shortest matching skirt that Shauna had ever seen. All of a sudden she felt like a poor relation.

'Isn't that a little short?' commented Max.

Bianca's voice was triumphant. 'You should tell that to some of your girlfriends, Dad. I thought you *liked* women who showed their legs.'

'That's enough!' he growled.

Shauna refused wine and poured herself a glass of mineral water, making a huge effort not to smile. *Touché*, she thought with amusement.

'Can *I* have some wine, Dad?'

'No, you certainly can't—will you please just eat your soup?'

After lunch, Bianca was taken into the study with her father, much to her disgust, presumably for a long and serious talk, thought Shauna, whose own afternoon was spent telephoning various contacts to alert them of the temporary change of address. The lines to Portugal were being unpredictable, and she spent a tedious half-hour waiting to be connected to Max's lawyer in Lagos.

While she listened to the interminable crackle of the international lines, she found herself thinking about Max's antipathy towards women. Well, that didn't tie in with all Bianca's comments about his 'mistresses' as she called them. But here again, a lot of men professed not to like women much—but that didn't stop them going out with them! Shauna banged a stamp firmly on to an airmail envelope with her fist. The subject of Max Ryder's conquests was taboo, to her at least. She wasn't going to make the mistake of her predecessor.

Dinner, though technically perfect, was a near disaster. The salmon mousse, the chicken Véronique and the *tarte aux pommes* might as well have been sawdust because Bianca alternately sulked and sniped at every available opportunity.

Shauna could see Max restraining himself from biting back an angry retort, and it seemed fairly obvious to her that they should have some time on their own.

She stood up. 'I'll skip coffee, if you don't mind. I'm going to turn in.'

Max's face darkened. 'Please don't feel you have to go because Bianca has decided to forgo good manners.'

Bianca scowled, and Shauna knew a wave of empathy. They were so alike, these two—both sitting there with angry faces—one so fair, and the other so dark, but both with those amazing green eyes. 'It's nothing to do with Bianca,' she smiled. 'It's more to do with being half-dead on my feet!'

Max rose, his face becoming a series of strange, shifting shadows as he moved out of the soft blaze of candlelight. A half-smile caught at the corners of his lips.

'Thanks for all your help,' he said, and Shauna felt as though he'd thrown her a bouquet.

'No trouble,' she answered. 'Goodnight, Bianca.'

'Goodnight,' came the sullen reply.

In the privacy of her bedroom, she untied the thick, dark curls and began to brush them in long, rhythmical strokes. She stared at her reflection in the mirror, the large grey eyes serious. Inadvertently, Bianca's presence had sparked off memories of her own childhood...

She was startled out of her reverie by a soft tap on the door of her bedroom, and she crossed the room to open it. A tall figure stood on the threshold.

'Max!' she said in surprise.

He seemed oddly hesitant. 'I wasn't sure whether or not you'd be asleep. I wanted to talk to you.'

She gave silent thanks that she hadn't changed into the silky nightdress which lay neatly folded on her pillow. She opened the door wider, in an automatically friendly gesture. 'Of course. Come in.'

There was an infinitesimal pause before he stepped into the room.

Hard to imagine a greater contrast than between the man and the room. The frippery of the predominantly feminine bedroom served only to emphasise his masculinity—the tall and muscular frame making everything seem fragile and insubstantial. She wondered fleetingly how many other women had made that gesture of inviting him into their bedrooms, and hoped that he would not misconstrue the meaning of hers.

He gestured to the window-seat. 'Do sit down. And don't look so afraid—I'm not going to bite you,' he growled.

'No.' It was hard to describe just what she *had* been feeling—but she certainly wouldn't have classified it as fear! She perched on the edge of the window-seat.

He remained standing and she had to strain her neck upwards in order to look at him. 'I didn't want to talk downstairs, where we could be overheard,' he began.

'By Bianca?'

'Yes.'

She gazed at him curiously, at his narrowed eyes, the taut lines around his mouth.

He began to move restlessly around the room, and it was several moments before he spoke, still in that fierce, growling voice. 'I know that she can be awkward,' he said abruptly. 'But it hasn't been easy for her.'

'I'm sure,' she agreed quietly.

He shot her a suspicious look, and moved to stare out at the dark night, his back to her, his stance unyielding. When he eventually turned round, the green eyes were flinty. 'I suppose that, like all women—you'd love to hear the gory details?'

She didn't rise to that one, taking instead the opportunity to dare to ask the question which had been foremost in her mind since yesterday. 'Has—has her mother been dead for a long time?'

His voice was flat. 'She died when Bianca was a baby. In a car crash.'

'Things must have been very hard for you both,' she said carefully.

He shot her a quick look, but, seeing nothing other

than calm attention in her grey eyes, sat down at last on the seat next to her, the long legs outstretched, his profile all hard lines. 'Yes, it was,' he said grudgingly. 'Very hard. Everyone assumed that I wouldn't want to keep the baby. My wife's family tried very hard to get me to give her to them. But I knew for certain that I wanted Bianca. She was the one good—' He hesitated. 'I wanted to keep her,' he said finally. The look he gave her did not invite questions. She got the distinct feeling that this was not something he often spoke of.

'The business was still in its very early stages,' he continued. 'But as I had started it up—and was working from this house—a nanny seemed the ideal solution. Not so,' he said wryly. 'It became a series of nannies. Bianca was a difficult baby, not surprisingly—who cried constantly. I clashed with the older ones who thought I was too soft with her. And some of the younger ones,' his voice sounded bitter, 'seemed less interested in caring for a small child than in bemoaning the lack of social life here in the village.

'I thought that things would improve when Bianca started school, and we could dispense with having these transient nannies. There would only be a few hours after school until I finished work when she would need someone to look after her—and Mrs Roberts agreed to do that.'

He moved the powerful shoulders in a small shrug. 'The trouble was that it didn't quite turn out like that—the business grew, and I was having to work later and later. Inevitably, my deals meant that I had to stay over in London and, occasionally, abroad. Mrs Roberts had family commitments of her own, and was unable to provide the kind of erratic care which Bianca needed—and neither was it fair to expect her to.

'The decision to send her away to school wasn't taken lightly—but I couldn't see an alternative. Bianca, perhaps understandably, saw the move as one of rejection.' His face darkened. 'And since then she has acquired quite a talent for getting herself thrown out of schools.'

'What kind of schools were they?'

He gave a humourless kind of laugh. 'Oh, I've tried them all, believe me. Progressive ones. Strict ones. Segregated. You name it, and I've tried them. Tomorrow I try again.' He shifted his position a little. 'It's late,' he said suddenly. He got to his feet, and, in an instinctive movement, held both his hands out to help her up off the window-seat. 'You look tired.' His voice sounded almost harsh. 'Get to bed.'

Breathlessly, she realised how close they stood, so close that she didn't dare look at him for fear that he might read the dizzying sensation of pleasure in her eyes, and she could have let him go on gripping her hands like that all night, if it weren't for the fact that any toe-curling feelings of pleasure were strictly one-sided.

As he bade goodnight to her, it occurred to her that he hadn't been a bit put out by having a long conversation with her in the privacy of her bedroom. A lot of men might have found it difficult to concentrate on what they were saying, given the implications of that.

But Max hadn't had the slightest difficulty concentrating, and why not?

Because he didn't see her as a woman, did he? She was just Shauna, his secretary. And a skinny kid, as he'd once said.

Oh, hell, she thought.

CHAPTER FIVE

SHAUNA slept deeply and a vivid dream came to
haunt her. Through a warm mist a figure was trying
to find her, but, each time she reached out, the figure
retreated. She woke up with an empty feeling of disappointment, and, as she dressed in a simple black
skirt, teamed with a crisp white blouse, she reflected
that she had spent almost all her life alone.

What must it be like, she wondered, to wake up
with someone beside you every day—to laugh with,
to kiss, to make love with…? To do that with a man
like Max Ryder? mocked a voice in her head, but
she hushed it, defiantly dragging a brush through the
wayward black curls.

Max and Bianca were already at breakfast, and
they looked up as she walked into the sunny dining-
room. Bianca's eyes widened as they saw her.

'Good grief!' she exclaimed. 'You look exactly
like a waitress!'

Shauna flushed. Her outfit was serviceable and
neat—but it *was* over three years old. She opened
her mouth to defend herself, but Max had already
butted in.

'Don't be so rude, Bianca.' The narrow green eyes
swept up and down over her figure, as if he were
seeing her for the first time. 'I'll give you an advance

on your salary, and you can buy yourself some clothes.'

'That isn't necessary,' Shauna told him stiffly, beginning to feel like a scarecrow.

'I'm insisting,' he said firmly, and took a piece of toast from the rack.

'I could come and help you,' said Bianca gleefully.

Shauna smiled at this, as she sat down and helped herself to bacon and tomatoes. She could imagine what Bianca would try to make her buy! 'We'll see,' she said non-committally. Perhaps if they went on a shopping trip together, it might encourage her to be a little less hostile.

'Dad, what am I doing today?'

'The reading you've been set,' he growled, 'will keep you fully occupied, I imagine.'

'Dad—*please* could we have today off? Could we go riding? Oh, please, Dad!'

Max frowned. 'What you fail to have grasped, young lady, is that your presence here is not due to your old school granting you an unexpected holiday. You are here because you've been expelled. And if you think that I'm going to reward you for that by taking you riding, then you've got another think coming. Besides, I have to ring round all the schools.'

Shauna watched the girl's face. She had noticed the sullen, rather jaded expression disappear when she had asked her father to take her riding. All at once, she had seen the little girl behind the façade, breathless with excitement and anticipation. She took a deep breath.

'I could ring round the schools for you.'

Bianca shot her a grateful look, while Max directed a glare.

'This has nothing to do with you,' he scowled.

'Of course, the *last* thing I want to do is interfere,' she said meekly. 'I just thought that the fresh air might do you both good.'

There was silence for a few long seconds, then, unexpectedly, Max threw his head back and began to laugh. It was a totally uninhibited movement, and, as she stared at the firm column of his neck, the mushroom which she had been chewing suddenly lost all its flavour.

He lowered his head, and the green eyes met hers. 'You sounded just like my old matron,' he said gravely.

Great! she thought. If she wasn't being the skinny kid, she was being compared to some old battleaxe!

'I suppose,' he sighed, 'that, as I'm outnumbered, I shall have to gratefully concede.'

'Oh, Dad! Thanks!' A whirling, small blonde figure hurled herself at him, hugging her arms tightly around his neck.

Shauna felt a lump rise in her throat, and she stood up quickly, grabbing at two plates and stacking them on top of each other. 'I'll just clear these away, and then get started.'

'You don't have to do that,' said Max gently. 'Leave them for Mrs Roberts.'

'No, I'd rather help. Honestly.' She hurried from the room, not wanting them to see her own vulnerability at witnessing the unrestrained show of affection between daughter and father. Evidently, beneath the skirmishes of their relationship ran a deep vein of genuine love and regard—something which had been sadly missing from her own childhood.

She took the plates through into the kitchen where the big, old-fashioned stove gave out such a comforting warmth. Mrs Roberts, her hands full of suds, came towards her smiling, wiping the calloused red hands on to the floral apron.

'You shouldn't have done that!' she exclaimed. 'That's what I'm here for.'

'You shouldn't have to wait on me,' answered Shauna. 'I could grow to like it! Now, where's your dishwasher?'

'She won't let me buy her one,' said a deep, amused voice behind her.

The beautiful bone-china plates almost hit the stone-flagged floor, as Shauna turned round to face Max. He wore no tie, and a button of his shirt had come undone, giving Shauna a glimpse of the smooth brown skin of his chest, and she was reminded of that first night at the flat when he'd confronted her, the chest then completely bare, wearing nothing but those faded, half-zipped denims.

The memory completely drove all coherent thoughts out of her head. 'Pardon?' she said stupidly, thinking what a pity it was that he didn't smile like that more often.

'She refuses to have one near the place—a dishwasher.'

'And rightly so,' affirmed Mrs Roberts. 'Machines

to do this, and machines to do that. Pretty soon, people will have forgotten how to use their hands.'

'As you can see—we're living in the Dark Ages here,' said Max, his head on one side, observing her. 'Thanks for offering to ring round the schools.'

Shauna put the plates on the draining board. 'Pleasure,' she replied. 'It won't take long to ask them to send us their prospectuses.'

'Good.' There was a pause as they walked out of the kitchen together, towards the study. 'You know, I get the distinct impression that I was out-manoeuvred by you at breakfast.'

She feigned surprise. 'Who—me?' she enquired innocently.

He laughed again. He had been doing rather more of that than usual this morning, she noted. 'We'll be back in time for lunch.' He hesitated, his eyes skimming the black skirt which hung just below her knees. 'Your salary's on the desk in my study. Use it.'

Quite why this should have flustered her so much, she didn't know. She wished that the skirt had been shapelier. 'I'll do that,' she said hastily.

His expression was thoughtful. 'I'd better go and change.'

She walked slowly into the study, thinking that working for him was perhaps not going to be as easy as she had anticipated. Not if he was going to be so—so *charming*. Was this how it had started with the last girl? she wondered. Had he begun to trust her, to confide in her? Had he let his guard slip? Only to find that the loyalty of an employee had suddenly turned into unwelcomed and unasked-for love? As long as she was careful not to make the same mistake. He was not looking for love. Hadn't he told her that himself?

She worked all morning, busying herself with phoning round schools, having to break off now and then to speak on Max's behalf to lawyers in Porto Mâo who were dealing with the purchase of the golfing complex.

Mrs Roberts brought her tray of coffee at eleven—steaming, fresh and strong—accompanied by a small plate of florentine biscuits.

Shauna leaned back in the chair, and smiled. 'Thanks, Mrs Roberts. You're spoiling me.'

'You make sure you eat them,' said the housekeeper. 'You're all skin and bone.'

If anyone else said that, she'd scream! And anyway, she wasn't *that* thin. Her waist and hips may have been slender, but her bust more than made up for that. It was the bane of her life.

At twelve-thirty she left the study to wash her hands before lunch when she met Max and Bianca in the hall. It had obviously been a successful outing, because they both looked relaxed and happy, and Bianca was bubbling over with good humour. She spied Shauna.

'Oh, Shauna!' she enthused. 'It was *fantastic*! Really great! Dad, have I time for a shower before lunch?'

'Definitely,' he replied, pretending to wrinkle up his nose.

Bianca bounded away, taking the stairs two at a

time, and Shauna was left alone with Max. He had obviously ridden his mount very hard, for the thick, dark hair lay in tangled wet waves plastered to his head. His forehead was beaded with sweat, and the light shirt he wore beneath his riding jacket clung to his torso.

There was something so raw—almost primitive— something so ridiculously and overwhelmingly *masculine* about him, that she started trembling, and couldn't stop.

'You're not cold, are you?' he enquired assessingly.

His response killed her reaction instantly. Perhaps the 'skinny kid' should take to wearing thermal vests, she thought ruefully. 'No, I'm not. But you will be— if you don't get out of those clothes.'

Now what had she said? She flushed scarlet. 'I didn't mean—' she stuttered. 'That wasn't a proposition.'

His gaze was very steady, his face serious, but there was a hint of laughter flashing in the green eyes, a trace of humour uplifting a corner of the firm mouth. 'Really?' he said softly. 'You *do* disappoint me, Shauna.' And then he left, leaving his secretary dry-mouthed and weak and *angry*, too. What the hell was he playing at? He'd warned her off, and yet now he was teasing her, flirting with her, playing with her emotions as a cat would a mouse. And he wasn't stupid. He must know perfectly well how lethal his own particular brand of charm was, exercised deliberately like that.

As her pulses slowed to normal again, a fleeting

fear crossed her mind. Please God, she prayed. Don't let me fall in love with Max. Don't let me become another victim of that cold and unfeeling heart.

At dinner that evening, Bianca did not come down.

'She's tired after her ride,' explained Max. 'She had soup and toast in the kitchen with Mrs Roberts, and is at present listening to some awful row on the radio, and drinking a mug of cocoa. All of a sudden she's beginning to look like a young girl again, and not a pastiche of older women she's seen in fashion magazines.'

Shauna felt unaccountably nervous as her earlier fears came back to haunt her, sitting alone with him at the gleaming table, the candles casting strange shadows around the room, as Mrs Roberts brought in dish after delectable dish. She drank more wine than she had intended, or than she was used to, and as its warmth flooded through her veins it washed away every tension.

They chatted in desultory fashion, and had just finished the cold lemon soufflé when he leaned back in his chair, eyeing her speculatively.

'No ties, hmm?'

She blinked. 'I beg your pardon?'

'You. You told me you had no ties. I'm interested to know why.'

She tried, without success, to shrug her shoulders nonchalantly. 'It isn't much of a story.'

He frowned. 'I can't believe you don't have any-one.'

'Well, I don't.' Her voice shook slightly in spite of her bravado. 'My parents were divorced when I was nine. My father went away, and we never saw him again. It broke my mother completely. I looked so like him, you see—and she couldn't bear to have me around.' She twisted the stem of the wine glass between long, slim fingers. 'So she sent me away to boarding-school.'

'As I did with Bianca, you mean?' His voice was harsh.

Her grey eyes surveyed him calmly. 'No, Max. Nothing like that. Circumstances forced you to send her away. My mother didn't want for anything materially—she could easily have kept me at home. She *just didn't want me*,' she emphasised, and, pushing her chair back, she walked over to the spitting glory of the log fire, crouching down to warm her hands in front of it, so that he couldn't see her face.

'Go on,' he said.

She found herself wanting to tell him. She gazed into the flickering flames. 'I was a lonely child, even at school. Always daydreaming. I think I used to retreat from the reality of my life by living in a fantasy world. My mother's visits to me were—infrequent, to say the least. It was a bit of an embarrassment, at school, how little she cared.' She forced herself to sound bright, not to betray any of the pain which had dominated her school-days.

She turned to face him again. 'I had no idea what I wanted to do, really, but, as I'd been brought up speaking Portuguese, Spanish and French, languages seemed the obvious choice. Then my mother remarried.' She paused as she saw the question in his eyes.

'Oh,' she shrugged. 'He was no evil stepfather figure. Harmless and innocuous enough, but we had nothing in common. I was in my first year at university, when the news came that the plane carrying my mother and stepfather back from their holiday had crashed. It's funny—even if you've had a bad relationship with your mother, it can still hurt like hell when she dies.'

'I'm sure,' he agreed quietly.

'When the will was read, it transpired that they had indulged themselves royally and had built up a mass of debts. The house had to be sold to pay them.' He was looking as though he wanted to hear more, she thought. 'Consequently, I was fairly broke at college. I worked at night, weekends—you know the kind of thing.'

'Must have been hard?'

She flashed him a smile. 'Not really. I was lucky to be there. And when I finished—I took off to see a bit of the world.' She wished he'd stop looking at her like that. Didn't he realise that that crooked half-smile, the unexpectedly tender softening of his eyes, made her want to curl her fingers possessively around those strong hands? To feel him as close to her as he'd been last night?

'So what made you come back?'

She shrugged, the thick swaths of black curls surrounding her oval face like a dark cloud. 'You can't keep drifting forever. Sooner or later you have to settle down. And it might as well be now.'

'Oh, Shauna,' he said suddenly, softly.

She rounded on him furiously. 'Don't say it like that! Just don't! I don't want your pity!' The sudden movement caused a rippling movement of the silky blouse across the swell of her breasts and she saw his gaze drawn to it.

Something in the room had changed. A sensation as tangible as electricity crackled in the air. He tore his gaze away from her breasts, and their eyes met, and locked.

Her tongue darted out to lick her lips—fear, or something very like fear, had dried them, had set her heart racing, her pulses hammering. She heard his sharp intake of breath.

'I don't want your pity,' she repeated weakly.

'It isn't anything remotely like pity that I'm feeling right now.' He stood up in an abrupt movement which caused his chair to scrape roughly against the polished floor. It sounded deafening. She thought that he was about to walk out, but she was wrong, for he walked towards her, slowly and deliberately, until he stood looking down at her, his eyes burning, a message in them she couldn't read, or perhaps she could—for she moved forward at the same time as he pulled her tightly into his arms, his hands spread possessively across her back, her face buried in the warm masculine scent of his shoulder. She didn't know whether he intended to pacify or to stir her, but she found herself pressing or being pressed against the hard length of his body, her body moulded into his as if glued there. She looked up and their eyes met for the briefest of moments and then he bent his head and swiftly, almost brutally, began to kiss her.

His mouth tasted sweet, and of wine—soft, hard,

tantalising, demanding, and her lips opened welcomingly beneath its pressure. He pulled her even closer, and she became breathtakingly aware of the muscular strength of him—every sinew and every fibre. She thought that she felt his hands flutter towards the heavy and achingly sweet straining of her breasts, but it might just have been the frantic beat of her heart.

In a deliciously heady haze she instinctively moved her hands from his shoulders to thread her fingers into the glorious blackness of his hair, when he pulled himself away from her as brutally as he had begun. His breathing was ragged and his eyes looked black in the candle-light, and haunted.

'Dear God!' he exclaimed. 'Dear God in heaven! What the hell am I thinking of?' and he thrust her away from him.

Her senses screamed their mutiny and, her heart still racing, she stared at him, thoroughly confused by his reaction. 'What—what is it?' she stumbled. 'What's wrong?'

He met her gaze, his face a tight, angry mask. 'That should never have happened.' He muttered something indistinct under his breath and strode to the door, leaving her still reeling as she listened to him mounting the stairs with an angry step, while she found herself incapable of any movement, other than a weak collapse into the armchair behind her.

CHAPTER SIX

SHAUNA stumbled up to her bedroom when she was certain that Max was no longer around. Automatically, she stripped off her clothes and pulled a white gauzy nightgown over her head.

She stared back at her reflection in the mirror, at the glittering eyes and flaming cheeks. She lifted cool fingers to wonderingly touch her lips, now dark and swollen from the pressure of that heady kiss.

Was it simply because it had been—so long? When had she last been kissed? A year ago, maybe— with Ramón, the Portuguese doctor she'd dated briefly. But it hadn't been like *that*. Nothing like that.

Max's kiss had set her on fire. She had responded to him with a stunning eagerness and lack of inhibition, and then he had ruined everything by his horrified reaction to finding her in his arms.

Oh, hell, she thought as she climbed into bed. What on earth was she going to say to him tomorrow? Worse still, what was he going to say to *her*?

Sleep, not surprisingly, eluded her until the first light of day had begun to creep around the curtains and consequently she awoke feeling headachy and grumpy.

She should have stopped him, she definitely should have stopped him. But he was just as much to blame. He had been the one who had made the first move. It had been he who had crossed the room and grabbed her in that almost brutal way. True, she hadn't exactly put up a fight—but he had been the instigator, not she.

Her bravado disappeared as she slowly descended the elegant, curving staircase. Let's face it, she thought, if Max Ryder had decided that she was just another eager little secretary with the hots for him, then she would be out of the door and sent packing as fast as you could whistle.

She heard footsteps.

'So there you are!' said an accusing voice, and a neat blonde head peeped out from behind the study door. 'I've been waiting for you for ages!'

The greeting was so friendly, so unexpected, and so unlike the stormy reception she had been anticipating, that she started, having to hold on to the heavy oak banister for support. 'Oh, it's you, Bianca! You startled me.'

Bianca ignored this. 'You look terrible.'

'Thanks,' said Shauna wryly.

'No, I mean—you've got big black shadows underneath your eyes. You and Dad haven't had a row, have you?'

Shauna's heart sank. 'Why do you say that?'

'Well, you look like death, and Dad went storming out of the house, first thing, looking furious.'

And she knew what had caused that fury. 'Did he say where?'

Bianca looked at her out of the corner of her eyes. 'Only that he'd be back tonight.'

'Tonight?' Why hadn't he said something? Was he so embarrassed by last night that he couldn't bring himself to talk to her?

'So you'll have to look after me, won't you?' Bianca's voice was wheedling.

Shauna shook her head. 'I can't,' she said flatly. 'I have to work.'

'But it's Saturday!' said Bianca triumphantly. 'Nobody works on Saturday, do they? And besides—we're going shopping.'

Shauna put her head to one side, so that a dark plait fell forward over her shoulder. 'We are not.' With that determined set of her mouth, Bianca looked uncannily like her father, she thought.

'Oh, but we must! Dad's given you an advance and you've got to get some new clothes—'

'I am not in the mood for shopping.' In all honesty she felt like crawling back to bed and hiding under the sheets for the rest of the day.

Bianca's smile was winning. 'Don't say you can't drive?'

This, coming from a thirteen-year-old! 'Of course I can drive!'

'Well, then. The car's in the garage—I can direct you into town. And besides,' the green eyes, so like her father's, were suddenly watchful, 'what else are you going to do with me all day, if you don't take me shopping?'

Shauna hesitated. Put like that, a shopping trip seemed like the better option. Blast Max, she thought. He might have been angry with her, or with himself, but that was really no excuse to disappear—

leaving her in the role of baby-sitter to a child she hardly knew, and who had a reputation for being capricious. Still, a shopping trip might at least take her mind off recent developments.

She nodded her head. 'Oh, very well—you win! I take it I've got time to drink some coffee first?'

'Sure,' grinned Bianca. 'I'll go and get changed.'

Shauna had never driven a Range Rover before, and she eased it up the drive with care, reflecting on how strangely enjoyable it felt to have this excited teenager beside her, keeping up a cheerful running commentary as they drove towards the nearest town.

'That's where I rode my first mare. And that's where the Cheriton cows escaped and blocked the road for *hours*.' She pointed to a large, grey-stoned house. 'And that's where Rupert used to live. His mother still does.'

Shauna changed gear. 'Who's Rupert?' she asked casually.

'He was Daddy's friend. And Mummy's. My godfather. Oh, look—it's one of the Denver twins on his bicycle—I think he's gorgeous. Can you slow down, please?'

'No, I can't!' Shauna laughed, deciding that her boss's daughter was more like thirteen going on thirty!

They parked in the multi-storey car park, and Shauna was suitably impressed by the new, brightly lit precinct, with all its shops under one roof. Any reservations she had begun to have about such an impromptu shopping session quickly disappeared, simply because Bianca didn't give her a chance to change her mind! She steered her with great resolution in through the glass doors of a shop she would never normally have gone in, and, within minutes, had pulled out a selection of garments.

'You should *never* wear drab colours,' Bianca announced. 'With your hair and colouring you should have bright clothes.'

Shauna found it slightly shaming that a thirteen-year-old should be so knowledgeable about what suited her, and the lethargic sales assistant, who didn't seem particularly interested in any kind of selling, looked up to heaven on more than one occasion.

'How do you know so much about clothes anyway?' grumbled Shauna, as she pulled a cherry-red cashmere dress down over her hips.

'Daddy says I inherited it,' announced the child proudly. 'Because Mummy was a model—before she had me, anyway.'

Shauna was totally unprepared for the unreasonable flash of resentment that this piece of information produced. A model? She stared in the mirror. 'I can't wear this,' she said suddenly. 'It's far too short.'

'You've *got* to have it,' said Bianca decidedly. 'You've got legs all the way up to your armpits. In fact,' she screwed up her eyes a little, 'you don't look bad at all.'

'Thanks a bunch!'

'Don't mention it!'

But her mood lifted again as she bought leggings, two sweaters, the cherry wool dress, and a black cotton jersey dress which she wasn't at all sure about, but which Bianca convinced her that she *had* to have.

After lunch, more shopping and then a film, it was dark by the time they walked back to the car and drove home companionably.

'Are you really not interested in my father?' asked Bianca suddenly.

Third gear was reached with a horrible grating sound. 'Why on earth do you ask that?'

Bianca shrugged. 'Well, you said you weren't the other day—'

'And I meant it,' interposed Shauna hastily. 'He's my boss, Bianca. End of story.'

Bianca moved one moccasin-covered foot up on to the dashboard. 'Pity,' she sighed. 'He never meets anyone like you normally.'

'I'm not sure I like the sound of that!' Shauna laughed. 'What kind of people does he usually meet, then?'

'Oh, you know—rich ones. Beautiful ones,' she said gloomily.

'Well, that's the biggest backhanded compliment I've ever heard!'

'I didn't mean it to be. The women he meets— well, they always smile at me with their mouths, but never with their eyes. They see me as an obstacle, you know.'

Shauna's heart went out to the girl, suddenly looking so young and unsure. 'I'm sure you're imagining it,' she said gently. 'I bet they like you really.'

The young voice affected uninterest. 'They don't. They just pretend to when Dad's around. But I don't care.' There was a pause. 'Shauna—can I tell you something?'

'Blast!' The headlights picked out the startled gaze of a rabbit, and Shauna swerved just enough to miss it without risking an accident. By the time they had recovered, she remembered that she had halted the girl in mid-flow.

'Sorry, Bianca—what were you saying?'

The girl shook her head. 'It doesn't matter now. We're almost home.'

Shauna thought that Bianca seemed increasingly tense as the big car crunched up the gravelled drive. She could see the study light on, and Max's car parked at the front of the house. I'll collect the bags later, she thought, as she jumped down from the driver's seat. Bianca was still strangely silent, and, as Shauna put her front key in the lock, the heavy door was yanked open from the other side, and she had to struggle not to topple inside.

Max was standing there, his face a study in anger, the eyes narrowed to slithers of icy jade, his hands resting on the lean hips, his legs apart.

'Where the *hell* have you been?' he demanded, and Shauna shrank back from the fury in his voice.

'I—' began Bianca.

'I am speaking to Shauna,' he said coldly. 'I assume that she was the one driving the car. You'd better go to your room, Bianca, until I send for you.'

With what sounded like a strangled sob, Bianca tore up the stairs.

She could hear his breathing, coming fast and heavy. She steeled herself not to remember how similar it had sounded last night, after they'd kissed, but faint colour had washed into her cheeks before she could block the thought out completely. What on earth had made him so angry?

'You'd better come into the study,' he ordered, and she followed him automatically, too stung and confused to formulate a coherent question.

In the study he turned to face her. The only light in the room came from a lamp on his desk, and the intensity of its glare was concentrated in a small area, leaving the rest of the room gloomy and shadowed. In this light, the blackness of his hair and the dark shadows on his face made him look almost demonic. She stared back at him.

'Where the hell have you been today?'

It was a struggle not to sound defensive, and yet, she thought, she hadn't done anything wrong. 'I went shopping,' she said. 'With Bianca. You told me I could use the car any time. We had lunch, saw a film, and came home, that's all.'

'That's all?' He sounded incredulous. 'You don't think it matters that you disappear with my daughter for most of the day? That I arrived back this morning to find you both gone, and sat around all day not knowing where you were, worried sick? And you say "that's all"?'

Her confusion cleared immediately, and the import of his words became crystal-clear. Bianca, for whatever reason best known to herself, had lied to her. Had tricked her into taking the car into town and disappearing for the day. But it was up to Bianca to admit that to her father. She wasn't going to tell tales, not when he was in *this* kind of mood.

'I'm sorry if you've been worried,' she began, but his words cut across her.

'What right did you have to countermand my orders?' he interrupted. 'Perhaps you thought that whetting my appetite with your attempts at lovemaking last night would give you some position of authority?'

She gasped aloud at his words, but he carried on as if he hadn't heard her.

'Or maybe you play a cleverer game than that.' His smile was the most ruthless she had ever seen. 'If you think that befriending my daughter is the route to my heart, then don't bother. As a ploy it's been used before.'

It took a few seconds for what he was saying to her to sink in, and the disbelief became hurt, and then anger. Her voice was shaking, and the words bubbled out hotly like boiling toffee.

'How *dare* you?' she demanded. 'Just how do you dare? I can't even believe that you'd think it! Suggesting that I was nice to your daughter because in some way I thought it could get to you. Of all the arrogant, unforgivable things to say!' She glared at him furiously. 'I don't know what has made you quite so cynical about women—but haven't you considered that your warped view of humanity is actually *damaging* to the child? Don't you think that she's picking up on all your distorted values? Is that what you want? Tell me, Max Ryder—do you want a child who trusts no one? Just like you?'

His face had gone white and he opened his mouth as if to speak, but she was there before him.

'Well, don't worry. I won't be here to see it. I don't want to work for a man like you. I won't live like this, and I'm giving you notice. I shall be leaving in the morning.' And, saying this, she turned and ran.

She almost scrambled up the flight of stairs to her room, and, as she leant weakly against the door, she realised that she was shaking like a leaf. Legs which felt as though they had been carved from wood took her over to the bed, with its frilled and flounced canopy, and slowly she sat down.

So that, she thought, was that. The best opportunity she'd had to make something of herself was now a thing of the past, but all the perks in the world could not compensate for the monstrous things he had accused her of. A huge salary was one thing, but she could not and would not tolerate living in such a climate of mistrust and hostility.

She must have been mad not to even consider that Bianca had not been telling the truth. She had walked into that little trap as willingly as the fly to the spider. Why should the girl suddenly have undergone such a remarkable change in attitude? She, Shauna, had been ridiculously naïve.

But she had taken Bianca at her word—and was that such a terrible thing? Because hers was a trusting nature, in spite of all the knocks she'd had. In spite of her parents, and her being orphaned at a relatively young age, her soul had remained intact. Unlike *his*.

Her face burned with anger and shame as she recalled the look on his face as he'd spoken of her 'attempts' at lovemaking. *Attempts*? What was he implying? That they'd been deficient in some way? She allowed herself a grim smile. He was a liar. She had enjoyed it, and *so had he*.

She was wearily thinking about packing her things together when there was a tap at the door. She made no answer. It would either be him or his daughter, and she had no inclination to see either of them.

The knocking resumed.

'Go away!' she called.

The voice was deep and curiously resigned. 'No. We need to talk.'

The smouldering resentment which she still felt was temptation enough for her to fling open the door and meet his gaze with one of belligerent stubbornness.

'What for? Haven't you said enough already?'

'Please,' he said, quite gently.

One word, but a word which she guessed he'd used very little in his life. A word which, when spoken in that soft tone he'd adopted, pushed all the fight out of her.

'What do you want?' she asked, in a small, defensive voice.

He stood just inside the room. 'I've just been speaking to Bianca,' he said, still very quietly. 'She told me the truth—that she'd conned you into believing I'd gone out for the whole day and left you to look after her. Why the hell didn't you tell me what she'd said?'

'Because you didn't ask.'

'But you let me believe that—'

She held her head very high, her eyes on a level with the chiselled lips. 'No,' she contradicted. 'You believed what you wanted to believe. You'd already made your mind up, hadn't you? And what would you have had me do? Tell you that your daughter had been lying? Expose her to the kind of fury which you vented on me? Is that what I should have done? No way, Max. I'm big enough to stand up to bullies, but she isn't.'

A muscle began working furiously in his cheek; his face beneath the tan had gone almost grey. She'd gone too far.

'I'm sorry,' she said. 'I shouldn't have said that.'

He stared at her. 'Why not? It's the truth, after all.'

There was a pause as Shauna struggled to find the right words. 'I've an idea, if you'd like to hear it,' she said tentatively.

Dark eyebrows disappeared, his mouth a tight line. 'The magic solution?'

She ignored the sardonic note in his voice. 'I think that Bianca getting herself expelled and deliberately fooling me into playing hookey with her—knowing just how much it would annoy you—is all a form of attention-seeking behaviour. I'm just trying to imagine how she must see it. She doesn't get to see you very often, so she's deliberately naughty—and that gets her your undivided attention. It's not good attention—but it's still attention.'

He gave an impatient wave of the hand. 'So what are you saying I should do? That I should move the company down here permanently and send her to the local day school? That's as unworkable now as it was five years ago.'

She looked at him steadily. 'Can I make a suggestion?'

His mouth twisted wryly. 'Suggest away. Solve my problems for me, Shauna. Wave your magic wand.'

Her idea had all the brilliance of simplicity. 'What about weekly boarding?'

He frowned. 'What?'

The words came spilling out in her eagerness. 'I mean—you may have already given it some thought, but it strikes me as an ideal compromise. Find a school as close to here as possible that takes weekly boarders. Bianca will board mid-week, while you're in London—and come here every weekend. It'll give you more time together.'

His expression was one of mocking surprise. 'The first woman who has ever suggested I spend *more* time with my daughter, rather than less,' he said sardonically.

She didn't offer a comment on this, but the tight line of her mouth registered her disapproval.

'You don't think she'd find that disruptive?' he asked. 'Neither fish nor fowl, not fitting into one place or the other?'

'I think it's just what she needs,' Shauna said quietly. 'At my school, we all thought that the weekly boarders had the best of both worlds.'

There was a long pause. She saw a light flare in the green eyes, and momentarily the harsh, tense lines on his face disappeared. 'I'll look into it tomorrow.' He stood up slowly and looked at her. 'You will stay?' he asked.

She stood looking at him, knowing that she would stay. The perfect job, she thought wryly—there was no such thing. Certainly not *this* job, anyway—and Max Ryder was the reason why. He was the antithesis of the perfect boss. He could be difficult, moody and autocratic, she knew that.

Yet as she stared at the hard, enigmatic face, she discovered that it was easy to ignore the voice in her head which was clamouring to be heard. The voice which was asking her if she was being entirely truthful about her motives for staying. She pushed aside the nagging question of how much her growing feelings for Max were affecting her decision. Sometimes feelings should be left well alone, not analysed out of existence.

She gave a small nod. 'Yes, Max. I'll stay.'

CHAPTER SEVEN

IT WAS a bright, clear morning and Shauna breezed downstairs in a light-hearted mood which matched her outfit. The jade-green angora sweater which she wore over her jeans echoed the swinging hoops at her ears, and the jet-coloured curls were caught up at either side of her head by combs of exactly the same shade of green.

As she walked into the breakfast-room, Max lifted his head, looked at her very hard, and frowned slightly.

'I've got a smut on my nose?' she hazarded.

He shook his head. 'You look—nice,' he commented. 'That's all.'

The compliment was hardly lavish, but it made her feel ridiculously pleased, so she took refuge in teasing. 'Nice?' she giggled. '*Nice*? And this coming from a man who once berated me for using the word ''adequate''!'

There was a glint in the green eyes. 'OK, then— you look better—than you used to.'

Now why should that half-baked compliment fill her with a silent, frustrated rage? Surely it wouldn't have hurt him to have hunted around his not inconsiderable vocabulary for something more flattering than 'better'. Unless, of course, that was all he thought she *did* look.

All she knew herself was that she looked radically different from the girl she had been when she first arrived. Oh, the difference a slick of lip gloss made! And, taken in hand by the undoubtedly talented Bianca, she had discovered that dressing up could be quite fun. The drab clothes had been bundled up and donated to the local thrift shop, and Shauna had decided that she would never look back!

It was hard to believe that the shenanigans of a fortnight earlier had ever occurred, such was the air of ordered calm which had descended on the household.

After Max had left her that night, a tearful Bianca had come to her room.

'Please don't leave,' she had sobbed. 'I'm so sorry I lied to you.'

Shauna had heard her out, and had then gently pointed out that her behaviour was going to hurt no one more than herself in the end, and would drive a wedge between her and her father.

At last, a place as a weekly boarder was found, and Bianca professed herself delighted with the scheme. The best news as far as Bianca was concerned was that the new school didn't want her to start until after Christmas, as it was felt it would be too disruptive to begin mid-term.

'She's going to go to her grandparents in Scotland on Boxing Day until term starts,' Max had told her. 'So we're incarcerated here until then.'

Which, as far as Shauna was concerned, was like winning the pools. She loved the work and she loved the countryside. She would have liked to have thought that her relationship with Max had altered since all the disruptions, but no such luck. The most it seemed she could hope for was the kind of grudging respect he had demonstrated when she helped him pull off a remarkable deal ahead of a rival, but, other than that, he gave little of himself away. Polite, yet curiously distant—he remained the most unfathomable man she had ever met.

They worked together in the mornings, and in the afternoons he usually left her with more than enough letters to occupy her, while he went riding with Bianca.

She grew used to living with him, but her reactions to him were unpredictable.

Once, she had walked into the kitchen to be confronted by his back view as he leaned over the table, reading a newspaper. Thankfully, he didn't notice her for a second or two, and she stood rooted to the spot, dry-mouthed, riveted by the sight of faded denim clinging to and moulding the narrow lines of his hips.

Did he always have such an effect on women? she wondered. Such a *physical* effect? She'd never experienced anything like it before, and it had started to trouble her. The memories of him, and her unique reaction to them, had begun to haunt her at night when she lay alone in between the exquisitely laundered lawn sheets. Sleep had become an elusive creature which she pursued hopelessly as she tried to blot out the stormy yet nebulous dreams which left her feverish and confused when she awoke with a start from them.

Quite apart from anything else, they were together

so *much*. From breakfast until bedtime. And still it wasn't enough for her. She found herself resenting it when he drove to the nearby town without her. In bed at night she listened for his footsteps when he mounted the staircase to his bedroom, her heart foolishly racing as she heard them pause—or was she just imagining them pausing?—then its beats subsiding into agonised disappointment as they passed by to his own room. It was playing havoc with her nerves.

Perhaps it would be better when they returned to London, she reasoned. She could catch up with her old college friends, and gradually forge a new life for herself, so that she only saw Max at work.

So why was she dreading that moment so much?

She had already observed with wry amusement that Max's full-time occupation of Seekings seemed to have spread around the county, since invitations for him began to flood in. Her only comfort came from the fact that he didn't seem overjoyed by his popularity.

At breakfast one morning he eyed the pile of cards at his place with disgust. 'Damn these society matrons!' he snapped, as he began to slit the envelopes open. 'I refuse to endure being introduced to their giggling daughters.' His expression altered slightly. 'Oh—here's one for you, Bianca.' He scanned the letter before handing it over to his daughter.

Bianca read it eagerly. 'Oh, Dad, it's from Sally Bartlett—we used to have riding lessons together. Remember? She's invited me to go over for the day to see her new pony—oh, can I, Dad?'

Max smiled. 'I'll ring her mother later.' He caught her expression. 'I said *later*. I'm not promising anything.'

Bianca was dropped off at Sally's the following morning, and when Max returned he walked into the study to find Shauna typing.

'Get your coat,' he instructed. 'We're going out.'

'Out?' Her grey eyes lit up.

'Bianca isn't here—it's an ideal opportunity to drive to Bristol to talk to my accountant. I rang to confirm last night.'

'Oh. Right.' She was furious with herself for feeling so let-down. Just what had she been expecting? A cosy lunch for two?

During the hour's journey to Bristol, Max, predictably, was silent, putting a Beethoven tape on the superb stereo and playing it very loudly—and its thunderous strains matched Shauna's mood very well.

The accountant's office was situated in a quiet back-street of the city. On the wall outside 'T. W. Entwhistle' was engraved on a discreet bronze plaque.

Max pushed the bell. 'It'll be useful for you to hear the financial side of things. Try and pick up on the main points and remember them.'

The fairly humble exterior of the building was deceptive. Inside it was luxuriously well-appointed, with subdued wall-lights and several small glass bowls of cut flowers. A smart brunette at the desk stood up as soon as Max walked in.

'Hi, Max! I was sent out for pastries and told to make lots of strong black coffee,' she smiled.

Shauna found herself wondering if this kind of treatment was given to *every* client. Somehow she doubted it.

'It smells good,' murmured Max appreciatively. 'Thanks, Katrina.'

'And I'm to show you straight in.'

'Good. This is Shauna Wilde, my secretary.'

The two women nodded at one another, and Shauna followed them along a narrow corridor where Katrina lightly tapped the door and held it open.

'Mr Ryder,' she announced.

Shauna was partially hidden by Max and was grateful for this when she saw the woman behind the desk get up and walk towards him, her hands out-stretched to grasp his.

'Max,' she smiled.

'Hello, Trudy.'

It was impossible to read anything in his voice and Shauna wondered why she should be so surprised that Max's accountant was a woman. After all, lots of women were accountants these days, though she doubted whether many of them looked like Trudy Entwhistle. She was superb—with sleek hair the col-our of polished mahogany caught into a sophisticated chignon, out of which not a single hair protruded. The slim and obviously well cared for body was clothed in a cotton jersey dress of pristine whiteness which, though neither low-cut nor short, contrived to cling to every slender curve. Sooty-lashed brown eyes regarded her directly. 'Hello,' she said coolly.

Max moved aside. 'This is Shauna Wilde—my new secretary. Shauna—meet Trudy Entwhistle, my accountant.'

'How do you do?' said Shauna politely.

'A secretary?' queried Trudy, looking her up and down. 'Lucky you, Shauna!' Tiny white teeth were bared in a smile. 'It must be wonderful to have a job which carries no responsibilities. What I'd give,' she sighed, 'to be able to knock off at five o'clock every night without a care in the world.'

'Shauna works hard enough,' said Max, amusement in his voice.

Trudy turned to him. 'I'm *sure* she does. Come and sit down, Max. Shauna, could you pour the coffee?—it's on the side.'

Shauna gave an imitation of a smile which turned into a grimace. She was certain that Max saw it, but, frankly, she didn't care. Pour the coffee! Just who the hell did Ms Trudy Entwhistle think she was? She'd like to pour it all over the expensive rug which lay in the centre of the room!

However, she opted for the dignified option, which was to up-end the pot into the tiny china cups and hand them out.

While she sipped, Shauna attempted to do as Max had asked—to listen and to store up information— but this proved harder than expected since Trudy Entwhistle seemed hell-bent on clarifying just how long, and how intimately, she'd known Max.

Shauna thought that she would stand up and *scream* if she heard Trudy's confident voice say again, 'You remember that, Max, surely—that was

the day...' The sentence would then be completed
haltingly, and with a good deal of eye contact and
soft, gurgling laughter. She was so *obvious*, thought
Shauna scornfully—although she had to admit that
once she got down to business she was very good
indeed. Shauna listened as she rattled off a stream of
information, then sat back and smiled at Max.

'I had a phone call from Harvey Tilton's accountant. Did you know that he, Harvey, Harvey's son
and their wives are touring England? And that
they're in the Cotswold area for the next few days?'

Max nodded. 'Yes, I phoned him last night after I
spoke to you. I'd originally planned to entertain him
on the London leg of his trip, but I explained the
circumstances and now we're going to meet up while
they're in Oxford. They're coming to Seekings for
dinner on Saturday.'

Trudy gave a slow smile as one slim leg was
crossed over the other. 'And do I assume,' she said,
looking directly at Max, her eyes widening with
pleasure, 'that you'd like me to take over my usual
role—as your hostess?'

Shauna felt slightly ill as she tried not to imagine
just *what* duties Trudy performed as hostess, when
Max's next words astonished her.

'No, thanks—Shauna's going to do that.'

Which was the first *she'd* heard about it!

'Oh, is she?' said Trudy, looking at Shauna with
cold eyes.

Max glanced at his watch. 'We won't take up any
more of your time, Trudy.'

They all stood up and Trudy turned to Shauna.

'I'm sure you'd like to freshen up,' she said, with a smile which stopped short of the brown eyes. 'I'll show you where.'

In the wash-room, Trudy turned to her, an expression of mock concern on her face. 'My dear, let me give you a tip or two. You don't stand a hope in hell with Max if you wear your heart on your sleeve, the way you're doing.'

Beads of sweat breaking out on her forehead, Shauna put her wrists under the cold tap. 'I don't know what you mean,' she muttered.

A shrug of the elegant shoulders. 'His last secretary fell in love with him and paid the price. When *will* you girls realise that you can't just marry the boss and be carried away on his white charger? Men like Max want their women to be achievers, not hangers on.' There was a parody of a smile on the glossy pink lips. 'And with all due respect—a man like Max isn't going to have much in common with a typist, now is he?'

Shauna turned the tap on full and a jet of water sprayed out, covering both women with little droplets of water.

'Oh, I'm so sorry!' she babbled, grabbing a handful of the green paper towels and dabbing at Trudy's spotted white dress. 'Here, let me.'

'Get *off* me,' said Trudy, between gritted teeth.

Max made no comment when they reappeared, but an eyebrow rose into the dark hair.

Trudy gave him three kisses on alternate cheeks and, amid entreaties that he call her, they left.

He was silent for a while in the car, and so was

Shauna, still thinking about Trudy Entwhistle. Was she really being transparent about the way she felt for Max? Or was Trudy just suspicious of any woman Max associated with? There had been something about the familiarity with which she'd treated Max that had made it very obvious that they'd once been lovers. And were they still? Max turning down Trudy's offer to help him entertain suggested otherwise.

He broke the silence. 'You know Harvey Tilton's an American I've done a lot of business with?' he asked.

She nodded. 'He has an option on twenty-five per cent of the villas in the new complex?'

'Right.' There was a pause. 'Feel up to playing hostess?'

She was still smarting from his accountant's gibes. 'But if Trudy's used to entertaining with you—she might be a better choice?' she hinted recklessly.

He glanced at her. 'Trudy is a brilliant accountant,' he stated, not answering her question at all.

She'd need to be, thought Shauna. She sure as hell wasn't talented at industrial relations! But then Max pushed a cassette tape into the player, which eliminated any further conversation.

Shauna was secretly delighted to play hostess, even more so when Max left the menu to her. So the 'typist' knows *something*, she thought, as she sucked the end of her pencil and tried to imagine what Americans would most like to eat in an English home.

On the evening of the dinner party, Bianca helpfully ate early and disappeared to her room to watch television.

Shauna dressed carefully in a short electric-blue silky dress with a cross-over bodice, and was standing admiring Mrs Robert's beautifully laid table when Max came slowly down the stairs dressed for dinner, and her heart gave an alarming thump. She had never seen him dressed formally before and the black jacket echoed his dark hair. She thought that the trousers had been cut by a genius, or perhaps it was just his physique which set them off—the soft cloth couldn't quite disguise the muscular thighs beneath. Remembering Trudy's comments, she tore her eyes away and started re-folding a napkin.

The Americans arrived promptly and Shauna was introduced to Harvey Tilton and his wife Connie—a fit-looking couple in their forties—together with his son Brett and fiancée Patti.

'Pleased to meet you, Shauna,' grinned Harvey, as he pushed a towering replica of himself towards her. 'Brett's being groomed to take over from his daddy—so he'll probably drive us mad by picking Max's brain all evening and talking about nothing but finance!'

Shauna laughed, finding the American's friendliness infectious. 'I don't mind a bit,' she insisted.

Harvey mimed shock. 'Say! A beautiful woman who likes business—no wonder Max has hidden you away down here!'

'Harv-ee!' said his wife. 'Stop that! You're embarrassing Shauna.'

It was true. Shauna felt herself blushing to the

roots of her hair and was fortunately distracted by Patti asking who had made the floral centrepiece—but not before she had seen the corner of Max's mouth lift very slightly in a sardonic expression which spoke volumes.

The other couple who made up the group were Harvey's accountant 'Buzz' Arnold and his wife. Buzz was in his late twenties, a good-humoured man almost as tall as Max, and Shauna thought that his wife Wendy looked as if she had been reared on orange juice and sunshine—she looked so healthy—with lightly tanned skin, gleaming white teeth, and a fall of sun-streaked hair to her shoulders.

Max moved round the room to pour the champagne. When he reached Shauna, her hand shook very slightly. He steadied her glass. 'I'm waiting to see you blush again,' he murmured.

'Don't hold your breath!' she snapped, furious with him for drawing attention to it.

They ate the delicate canapés which Mrs Roberts had brought in.

Dinner was almost ready when the telephone started ringing. Shauna looked at Max. 'I'd better get that,' she said. 'Mrs Roberts is just about to serve the soup.'

'Take it in here,' he said shortly.

It was Portugal and Max's lawyer there needed a subtle point of clarification to be made on a contract. Shauna knew what Max had intended, and spoke animatedly in her fluent Portuguese. When she had replaced the receiver, she found their guests staring at her.

'Wow!' said Connie. 'That was *brilliant*, honey! Imagine being able to speak Portuguese—why, Harvey and I can barely get our act together to order two Cokes!'

Shauna smiled. 'It's easy for me—I learned to speak it when I was little.'

'And is Portuguese the only other language you speak, Shauna?' asked Wendy.

There was a small silence. Shauna, slightly embarrassed at all the attention, opened her mouth to reply, but someone was there before her.

'Heavens, no,' came a wry voice. 'Shauna speaks four, at the last count—don't you?'

She looked at him quickly, but there was no answering stare which might have told her just what he was thinking. Instead, his mocking smile was for the whole company.

She heard Harvey's aside.

'You've sure got a gem there, Max.'

And the dry reply.

'Haven't I?'

The scallop soup was received with lavish praise.

'Your choice, honey?' Connie asked Shauna.

'Naturally,' replied Max urbanely.

'But Mrs Roberts cooked it,' butted in Shauna. 'She's an excellent cook.'

The good food and the company were making her settle back and really enjoy the evening. If only Max would relax a bit, she thought, instead of keep giving her those curious looks.

Although he chatted charmingly with his guests, she got the feeling that he was apart in some way—

observing things, observing her—and always with that slightly sardonic, mocking smile.

Not that Harvey and his party seemed to have noticed, or perhaps they were used to Max and his cool manner—they certainly bubbled over with more than enough enthusiasm to compensate for any lack of his.

Saddle of lamb was next, with vegetables from the garden.

'This is a truly *British* meal,' enthused Wendy. 'Mrs Roberts should come and cook in our hotel.'

'They have what they call an "international" menu,' explained Connie. 'We keep telling them— we haven't come all the way to England to eat French or Italian food!'

Max had told Mrs Roberts to leave after the main course, and Shauna was in the kitchen getting the lemon meringue pie out of the oven when she heard someone come in the kitchen behind her. She was unable to turn round because of the hot dish in her hand, but she immediately felt the unmistakable presence of Max even before she heard the deep, drawling voice.

'So when's the cabaret?' he enquired, leaning back against the wall, his hands in his pockets, regarding her.

'I *beg* your pardon?' She put the pie carefully on the Aga and turned to face him. As always, the enigmatic face was a mystery to her.

He gave a half-smile. 'Well, this *is* the Shauna Wilde show tonight, isn't it? I'm thinking of laying odds on who'll come out with the next profuse compliment. Brett is currently expressing the opinion that you're wasted as my secretary—the last suggestion was that the United Nations might be suitable recipients of your combined linguistic talents and good looks. I just hope we aren't going to have his fiancée marching out on us!'

'That's not fair!' protested Shauna. 'Brett's just being charming—that's his way—they all are. And I certainly didn't intend for him to be anything other than that.'

The green eyes glinted. 'No, you didn't, did you? You don't go looking for compliments, do you, Shauna? You just get them. And there's the rub— you're completely oblivious to it all.'

His remarks puzzled her. She couldn't decide whether or not he was disapproving, and she was absolutely certain that Brett had eyes only for his beautiful fiancée. Nevertheless, she chatted almost exclusively to Patti during coffee and found her delightful company.

'I've seen the most *beautiful* wedding gowns in a shop in Oxford,' she confided to Shauna. 'I'm half tempted to buy my dress here and have it shipped back home.'

'Oh, no! Not weddings again!' Harvey winked at Shauna. 'That girl's got a one-track mind—all she ever wants to talk about is weddings!'

'Ignore him,' smiled Connie at Patti.

'Well, maybe Shauna wants to talk weddings, too,' interjected Patti, then leaned forward. 'How long have you and Max been living together, Shauna?'

There was a moment of awful silence. Shauna was appalled, feeling her face flame and then blanch, looking to Max for some light-hearted comment which would erase the unintended *faux pas*, but there was none. He continued to sip his brandy with remarkable composure, as though the comment had just washed over him. Which no doubt it had, she thought bitterly. People probably made assumptions like that about Max all the time.

It was left to Harvey to break the silence, but with a suggestion which Shauna could have done without.

'Hey!' he exclaimed. 'It's been a great evening— what say we roll up the rug and end it with a dance or two?'

Everyone enthused over the idea, bar Shauna and her boss, but Harvey took over and put some dance music on with alacrity. The two married couples immediately and unselfconsciously began to dance, and Shauna managed to escape from the room to put some more coffee on.

She returned eventually and was coaxed into dancing in turn with Harvey, Brett and Buzz, and it was impossible not to relax and enjoy herself again with their good-natured chatter. Warm-faced and laughing, she was about to go out again to refill the cream jug, when Harvey caught her by the shoulders.

'We can't have this!' he exclaimed. 'A pretty girl not dancing and, much as I'd like to monopolise you all night—I guess I ought to give the only single guy in the room a chance!'

Shauna caught a glimpse of Max's face. 'Oh, no— really...'

Harvey smiled. 'Don't think he's going to take "no" for an answer, honey.'

And, true enough, Max was moving towards her, his face resigned, perhaps realising, she decided, that it would be impossible for him to refuse to bow to the collective pressure of everyone urging him to dance.

He certainly didn't look as if he were looking forward to it, she thought, feeling ridiculously flustered. It was easy to snap confident rejoinders at Max when he wasn't standing a warm, brandy-scented breath away, waiting to take her in his arms, which was, presumably, why her response made her sound about the same age as Bianca. 'I don't—I mean—you don't have to,' she stumbled.

He laughed then. 'I know that,' he said, and put his arms lightly around her waist.

She could scarcely breathe and he'd hardly touched her. She fought for an excuse which would save her from discovery. Any minute now and she was going to blurt it out—how much she cared for him, cherished him, and wanted him. Any minute... 'I'd better go and see to the coffee,' she said desperately.

'Shut up and dance,' he smiled, and pulled her into his arms properly.

Her body moulded itself into his as though it had been designed for only that purpose. She had her hands on each of the broad shoulders, her head bent, the curls hiding her face—but she could feel his breath, and his heartbeat.

She let him lead her, her reservations vanishing as she experienced the sheer joy of being held by him. The sweet throb of desire had her in its thrall, so that when he tightened his hold even more, making some soft muffled noise at the back of his throat, she could no longer resist—even if she had wanted to. She knew that he was slowly dancing her out of the room—away from their guests and the music—but the music was unnecessary for the particular dance they were creating. She should go back to the others, she thought fleetingly, but she was powerless to move away from him.

They found themselves in the study where only the silvery moon—suspended like a giant football outside the window—illuminated the pale oval of her face.

They stopped and she continued to let her head hang down, until he pushed her chin up with the tip of his forefinger, so that their eyes met at last.

'Are you going to look at me now?' he said softly, and the finger moved to trail slowly along the outline of her mouth, which instantly began to tremble. And then, as she had somehow known he would all along, he bent his head to kiss her.

It was nothing like that first kiss. Nothing. That had been short, almost brutal, hard, and somehow desperate. This was an explicitly sensual kiss, slow and deliberate, and every second of it—from the start when his tongue traced tiny circles on her bottom lip, to when it moved with exciting intrusion inside her mouth—told her in no uncertain terms that he wanted her.

She was in his arms, being kissed to death, and he was moving with her until he had her pushed up against his desk. He leaned over her, so very dark and muscular, dominating her utterly, and, as one taut thigh thrust forward, her legs parted automatically to accommodate it.

She felt his hand slip inside the silky material of her dress to move it aside and she trembled as he found her breast, touching and massaging it through the lace of her bra. She could feel the tip, painfully alive with pleasure, straining against the thin material, and the lace irritating her, constraining her.

She had her hands coiled in his hair, but she inadvertently dug her nails into his scalp as she felt his other hand brush lightly over her stomach, and down further, to enticingly circle the soft flesh of her thigh. And when one finger moved to brush lightly over the line of her panties she found herself wantonly pushing against his hand, a tiny cry wrenched from her lips.

She began to stroke her hand over the fine lawn of his dress shirt—spreading her palms luxuriously and possessively over his chest, hearing the small sigh of pleasure which escaped his lips as she did so. And then he found the front clasp of her bra, unclipping it easily, so that her breasts spilled out, and he bent his head to take one swollen tip into his mouth, his tongue erotically teasing it so that it throbbed with a spasm of pleasure so intense that she felt she might buckle and faint, and her hand went out automatically to support herself, colliding instead with the telephone—and there was a loud crash as it hit the parquet floor.

Max terminated the kiss immediately, and, as she

heard him swear, she turned her face up to him, seeing anger in the green eyes as he released her.

He stood looking hard at her, shaking his head, and she could hear the disbelief in his voice. 'What are you doing to me?' he exclaimed. 'You're my *secretary*, for God's sake! Do you realise that we've got guests—*guests* in the next room?' he said savagely, and then his voice dropped. 'I must be out of my head.'

She was still too shaken, too aroused to speak, and he must have seen it, for he looked down at her, taking in her flushed cheeks, mussed hair and her disarrayed dress.

With a small sigh, he quickly refastened her bra and pulled the bodice of her dress straight again. 'You're in no state to go back in there,' he said. 'It wouldn't take much for them to figure out what we've been doing.' He shook his head again. 'Unbelievable,' he said, as if to himself, before picking the phone up and placing it back on the desk.

'You'd better go to your room,' he muttered. 'I'll make your apologies for you.' And with one movement, his hand pushed through his hair to leave it as unruffled as if he'd done nothing more than walk out into the lightest breeze. And without another word, or further look, he walked coolly from the room.

CHAPTER EIGHT

IT TOOK several minutes for Shauna's limbs to stop shaking sufficiently for her to make her way silently upstairs to her bedroom, her thoughts in turmoil as the reality of what had just happened hit her. She and Max had been petting like teenagers while important clients were dancing only yards away. Just imagine if Harvey or his wife or any of the party had come after them.

She groaned as she turned on the taps to run a bath—*now* what would happen? She scrubbed at her body in the bath as if by washing every inch of her she could wash away the memories which would not leave her.

But when she came to soap her breasts, she felt that restless yearning begin to invade her once more, as she recalled his hand, stroking and caressing her, extracting little ripples of pleasure from her responsive body. Her flesh burned where he had touched her, just as if he had taken an iron and branded her with fire.

She buried her face in her hands despairingly as the suspicions of the past few days resolved themselves into one truth so blindingly clear that she must have been a fool not to have realised it before. She was in love with him. This overwhelming sensation which had thrown the rest of her life into grey insignificance—this was love. In spite of all the warnings from people like Trudy—and disregarding his own wishes—she had committed the sin of her predecessor and fallen in love with Max. But it was up to her to make sure that he didn't realise—or even guess at it—because he had made it quite clear from the very beginning that he didn't want her—not in that way, anyway—and if she were to ever coexist with him again she must be prepared to forget it had ever happened. The question was whether she would be able to do that.

And how was Max going to react when he saw her? Would he simply be able to shrug it off as he had done tonight—as a minor aberration on his part, but nothing to get excited about? Or would he find such intimacy intolerable for their future working relationship? She remembered the way he had said 'What are you doing to me?' It had sounded like an accusation. But surely he couldn't blame her? Hadn't they both momentarily lost control?

The next morning was Sunday and she stayed in bed late, knowing as she did so that she was delaying the moment of reckoning—her confrontation with Max.

She dressed in jeans and a cherry-coloured sweater, brushing the newly washed hair and then catching two long strands at the side with red slides. The red contrasted vividly with her hair, making her look strangely exotic, and, as she went slowly down the stairs, she wondered what the scenario for today would be.

For the last few Sundays, the three of them had

breakfasted together. Max and Bianca had gone riding, while Shauna read the papers, and after lunch they had all gone striding through the woods, ending up in the library, playing Scrabble and doing justice to one of Mrs Roberts's enormous teas. Somehow, she couldn't see that happening today.

She was right. As soon as she walked into the breakfast-room, she saw that Max was not wearing the faded jeans and rather shabby sweater he normally wore for riding, but an elegantly cut suit, with a pale blue shirt which lay silkily flat against the broad chest. Bianca sat opposite him, a belligerent expression on her face.

'Good morning,' said Max formally. 'What would you like for breakfast?'

The sight of the kidneys and bacon, the dish of scrambled eggs and the rack of toast suddenly filled her with nausea. This was not, she realised, going to be as simple as she had imagined. 'I'll just have coffee, thanks.'

He poured her out a large cup of the strong, fragrant brew and handed it to her.

'Thanks. Not riding this morning, Bianca?' The child hadn't looked this miserable for ages, she thought.

'No,' said the girl sullenly. 'Dad's going out.'

She met his gaze with a question. 'Out?'

She thought he looked uncomfortable as he pushed his half-empty plate away from him. 'I have to go to Cheltenham for the day. As it's Sunday, I wondered if I could prevail on you to look after Bianca for me?

You can have a day off in the week to make up for it, of course.'

She tried not to flinch. He couldn't have reinforced her position as an employee more surely if he had written it on the walls in letters ten feet high. 'Of course I don't mind,' she said stiffly. 'Looking after Bianca is a pleasure, not a chore.'

The green eyes narrowed. 'Thank you.'

She met his gaze mutinously. 'You're welcome.'

'Of course, Dad only goes to Cheltenham for one thing,' Bianca sniped. 'He's going to see Marta.' She turned to glower at her father. 'Aren't you?'

A chord of memory struck. A low, husky voice on the telephone—ages ago, at the London flat. That had been Marta, Shauna recalled.

'I will probably be seeing Marta, yes. Not that it's any of your business, young lady. You'll have a fantastic day with Shauna, you know you will.' He pushed his chair back and stood up.

She watched as he bent to kiss his daughter and was offered a very cold cheek in return. She took a huge mouthful of coffee and scalded the inside of her mouth as she strove to act unconcerned. Unconcerned, her left foot! Who the hell *was* Marta?

Shauna stood outside the breakfast-room as Bianca leaned on the front door jamb, waving goodbye as he roared away in his Mercedes. She saw dejection written into the set of the girl's shoulders, and impetuously she ruffled the thick blonde bob.

'What would you like to do today?' she asked.

Bianca shrugged. 'I don't really care.'

Shauna put an arm round the narrow shoulders and

squeezed them. 'Oh, come on—your every wish is my command.'

This produced a grin. 'You can't ride, can you?'

Shauna shuddered. 'Horses—yeuk! They terrify the life out of me!'

'Just what *can* you do?'

'Walk?'

Bianca laughed. 'I guess we'll walk, then!'

Wrapping themselves up in boots and thick coats and hats and scarves, they took sketch-pads and pencils and a big bag of stale bread to feed the ducks, and drove to a local beauty spot.

The morning was brightly clear, the grass crisp with frost which looked like icing sugar. They had been walking for about a quarter of an hour when Shauna did exactly what she had spent the last fifteen minutes vowing she would not do.

'Who's Marta?' she asked casually.

Bianca kicked at a stray pebble with some gusto. 'She's Daddy's number one mistress.'

Shauna frowned. 'You mustn't use that word,' she reprimanded automatically. It had been precisely the answer she had been expecting but it still made her heart sink like a stone.

Bianca turned candid green eyes to her. 'Well, she is. A mistress goes out with a man for all the things she can get out of him, like money and jewels, doesn't she?'

Shauna felt she was skating on very thin ice here. 'Er—yes.'

'Well, there you are, then!' crowed Bianca triumphantly. 'They're only interested in Daddy's money—they wouldn't go near him if he wasn't rolling in it.'

Shauna had been about to say that Max Ryder had far more to recommend him than mere wealth, but she stopped herself just in time. 'Your father is entitled to choose who he likes as friends, and he has a right to expect you to be polite to them,' she pointed out gently, wishing that she'd never started this conversation.

'Sorry,' Bianca sighed. 'Marta is Daddy's girlfriend.'

Shauna walked straight into a muddy puddle without noticing. 'Oh,' she said, in a small, empty voice.

'Well, that's what she likes to call herself. Daddy calls her his "friend". Whenever there's a party or a "do" he nearly always takes her, if she's not away working. She's often abroad. She's a model,' she confided.

'Oh,' said Shauna faintly, wishing that she hadn't asked, wishing that her stomach would stop sinking like a runaway lift.

Bianca kicked at another stone. 'I hate her. When Daddy's around she's all sweetness and light, but as soon as he goes out of the room it's "Bianca, *do* stop slouching", or "Isn't it time you went to bed, Bianca?"'

'I'm sure she's very nice, really,' said Shauna lamely, wondering how much of Bianca's rebellion lay in the fact that she obviously didn't hit it off with her father's partner.

'And I don't know why Daddy describes her as his "friend", when I know they sleep together.'

'Bianca!' Shauna was suddenly glad that she'd eaten no breakfast because there would have been no guarantee that it would have remained in her stomach, and she was angry with herself for the turn the conversation had taken. 'You mustn't say that—you don't even know if it's true.'

'Oh, yes, I do—because she told me.'

Shauna stood stock-still, aghast. 'She actually told you?'

Bianca nodded. 'Daddy wasn't there. He'd have been furious. She was yawning, and she said, "That's your father's fault—he kept me awake nearly all night", and then she giggled. Yeuk! I think she only said it to make me jealous.'

'But Bianca,' interposed Shauna gently, 'why should she want to do a thing like that?'

'Because she thinks that Daddy won't marry her because I wouldn't accept her as a stepmother.'

'And is that true?'

Bianca grinned. 'Too right! I'd hate her to be my stepmother—I wish he'd marry you!'

Shauna took hold of Bianca's shoulders and crouched down so that their eyes were on a level. 'You may wish it, Bianca—but it isn't going to happen. Wishing doesn't make something come true. I'm just his secretary, that's all.'

They spent the whole morning tramping around the countryside, Shauna striding out with fierce determination, as if by keeping herself occupied she could prevent herself from thinking about what Bianca had told her...

She dreaded going back to the house, at having to

face him. Knowing... Knowing what? That he'd spent the day in another woman's arms? Perhaps allowing him the freedom to caress her as he pleased last night had whetted his appetite for fulfilment. Her cheeks burned with shame in the darkness.

As they approached the house, there was indeed a car parked at the front, but it was not Max's Mercedes. Shauna jammed the brakes on. Oh, please don't let him have brought her here, she prayed. Not that.

'Recognise the car?' she asked Bianca.

Bianca shook her head. 'No idea. Oh, goody—we hardly ever get visitors.'

Shauna realised that she was playing for time as she helped Bianca out, convinced that the car must belong to Marta, and that she and Max would be sitting cosily by the fire in the sitting-room, or, worse still—in his bedroom.

She started to get the key out of her handbag, but Mrs Roberts must have heard them, for she had opened the door and was standing there, an odd expression on her face.

Bianca ran in. 'Whose car is it?' she demanded.

Mrs Roberts stood looking at her. 'You've got a visitor,' she said unnecessarily. 'It's Mr Hamilton.'

'Rupert!' yelled Bianca excitedly.

Rupert. Shauna blinked. Now where had she heard that name before?

'Uncle Roo!' Bianca squealed. 'Oh, yummy! Where is he?'

'I'm right here,' said an amused voice. 'What a

wonderful reception from my favourite god-daughter.'

'Your only god-daughter,' protested Bianca, and then she ran and hurled herself into his arms with all the speed of a young gazelle. He scooped her up into his arms, and then, over the top of her head, he saw Shauna—still standing in the shadows—for the first time.

He put Bianca down and looked at her. 'Well, well, well,' he said slowly.

Shauna looked back at him. He was just a little taller than herself, and very slim. His face wore the deep tan of the ardent skier and this made his blue eyes seem even bluer. He was dressed in a beautifully cut jacket underneath which she could see a soft cashmere sweater which matched his eyes perfectly. His hair was blond—very blond—and tumbled in a fashionably cut style around his neck.

He had the kind of confidence and magnetism which were natural by-products of money and breeding.

The blue eyes flashed with interest. He extended an elegant hand. 'Rupert Hamilton,' he smiled. 'Who's *enchanted* to meet you.'

CHAPTER NINE

'WELL, well, well,' Rupert said again. 'Who have we here? A mysterious black-haired beauty who doesn't speak.'

Shauna, who had so psyched herself up for a confrontation with Marta, smiled at him. 'Hello,' she said.

'This is Shauna,' announced Bianca. 'She's Daddy's new secretary—and she's great.'

Aristocratic-looking eyebrows were raised. 'A secretary, you say? And one who seems to have won the affection of the dreadful young Bianca. My, my!'

Shauna, deciding that she ought to start asserting herself as an intelligent adult, and not as some dumbo, held out her hand to him. 'I'm Shauna Wilde,' she said. 'And I'm very pleased to meet you.'

He took her hand and lifted it very slowly and deliberately to his lips, holding it there while he held her gaze with heavily lashed eyes, in such an overly theatrical gesture that it would have been laughable had it not been so effective.

'Enchanted,' he murmured. 'Max always did have the most impeccable taste, but you, my dear, are quite a refreshing change from the rather *outrée* type he usually favours.'

Shauna reflected, as she tugged her hand away,

that everyone she met seemed to take great delight in telling her how unlike the beautiful women Max usually associated with she was. She turned to Bianca.

'Why didn't you tell me that your godfather was coming over?' Or, more importantly—why hadn't Max?

Bianca frowned. 'Because he never tells me. And anyway, he hardly ever comes to visit.'

Shauna raised her eyebrows but said nothing. Now why, she wondered, was that?

'Now, now.' Rupert ruffled Bianca's hair playfully, and shrugged expressively at Shauna. 'It's because I'm such a busy man.'

'Busy going out to parties,' giggled Bianca. 'Did I tell you we saw you in a magazine at school, Uncle Roo?'

'Good picture, wasn't it?' he smiled.

'I'm afraid that Max isn't here,' Shauna began, remembering with a pang just where he was. 'We're not expecting him back until late.'

Bianca tugged at his arm. 'What are you doing here, Uncle Roo?'

He twitched his nose. 'I'm visiting my dear old mama for Christmas.'

'So that means we'll be able to see *lots* of you! Oh, good-oh!' exclaimed Bianca delightedly.

'Does Max know you're coming?' asked Shauna.

The blue eyes had suddenly grown very cold. 'Hardly. There isn't much love lost between Max and myself. I expect you've found how perfectly impossible he can be?'

Well, she had. But she wasn't about to start telling this man about it, and being disloyal to Max. Not, she thought, that he deserved her loyalty. She pushed the thought, and the mental pictures of him cavorting with some stunning model, away, and turned her attention back to the present.

'Will you be staying for a while? For tea…?' She found herself in the odd position of hostess.

Rupert smiled and walked over to Mrs Roberts, who had remained listening to the entire conversation. 'I'd love some of Mrs Roberts's famous fruit-cake.' He put his arm around the shoulder of the plump housekeeper. 'Even though she didn't offer me any herself.'

Mrs Roberts, looking unusually disgruntled, shook the elegant arm off as if had been a fly. 'Oh, go away with you, Mr Hamilton—that's enough of that. I'll get you your tea, though it's more than my job's worth…' She marched off in the direction of the kitchen.

'Bianca, why don't you take your godfather into the sitting-room, while I go and help Mrs Roberts?' Bianca, at any rate, seemed genuinely fond of Rupert, thought Shauna, even if he didn't rate too highly with Max or Mrs Roberts!

Rupert was eyeing her speculatively. 'Oh, Mrs Roberts can manage,' he said airily. 'Why don't you come into the sitting-room with us, Shauna, and let me run my fingers through those delicious black curls?'

There was something so outrageously over-the-top about him, that Shauna laughed aloud. She shook her head. 'Better not—I can hear Mrs Roberts muttering from here—I'd better go and help her.'

She ran lightly into the kitchen, where Mrs Roberts was banging cups and saucers on to the silver tray. Shauna took them from her. 'Here, let me,' she said. 'You'll smash them like that.'

The older woman unwrapped the rich fruit-cake from its covering of greaseproof paper. 'He isn't going to like it,' she declared darkly.

'Who isn't?'

'Mr Max. Likely as not, he'll hit the roof when he comes back to find *him* here.'

Shauna privately thought that the housekeeper was making Max sound like some Victorian despot! Surely he couldn't dislike his daughter's godfather that much? Anyway, it was absolutely nothing to do with her, and she wasn't about to start taking sides. And personally, *she* thought that the blond, beautifully spoken man seemed perfectly charming.

And wasn't it actually rather pleasant, she thought, to have someone new around the house? Someone, moreover, who was giving Bianca a great deal of pleasure.

They had tea, and during it Rupert regaled them with stories and scandals about the aristocratic world he inhabited. At nine o'clock, Bianca was packed off to bed with the promise that she could see Rupert the following day. Shauna came downstairs from saying goodnight to find him warming his hands in front of the fire. He had removed his jacket and had lit one of the smaller table lamps. Without the jacket, he looked less imposing and, therefore, less threatening, and there was, thought Shauna, something not unflattering about having a rather attractive man heap compliments on you. Particularly when your ego had taken such a battering recently.

He turned round as she entered, running his left hand through the thick blond curls in an unconscious gesture of preening. 'I suppose I'd better be going,' he said. 'Unless you're allowed to offer a poor traveller a drink? Or wouldn't Uncle Max like it?'

She hesitated. Well, why not? she thought defiantly. Why not have a drink with a perfectly nice man who had spent the whole afternoon making them laugh. She could just imagine how *Max* had spent the afternoon.

'What would you like?'

'A whisky and soda. Shall I do the honours? I think I can still remember where the drinks cabinet is. Can I get you one?'

She usually drank wine, but she couldn't really ask him to open a bottle just for her, so she nodded. 'Just a small one, please.'

She decided that his idea of a small one and hers must have been two entirely different concepts because when she took a mouthful she nearly spat it out, it tasted so bitter, but she didn't want to seem gauche by asking him to weaken it—particularly as he had just started to tell her about the time he'd met Elizabeth Taylor. So she quietly drank the Scotch, and listened.

By ten, she felt just a little bit merry, and he had persuaded her to put some music on the compact-disc player.

'It's too late,' she giggled. 'I don't want to wake Bianca.'

'We won't—we'll turn the volume right down low. Come on—you must! There'll be balls galore this Christmas and I haven't danced in ages—and as I've got two left feet you've to help me practise.'

Put like that, it sounded like fun, although she thought that he must have been exaggerating his lack of prowess because it was obvious he was a very accomplished dancer, even though he held her far closer than she would have liked. Trying to keep the atmosphere light, Shauna wriggled a little to try to relinquish Rupert's hold on her.

'Goodness—you're a sexy little dancer under that air of innocence, aren't you?' he laughed.

'Yes, she is, isn't she?' The voice cut through the music like a knife slashing through silk, and she looked up in horror to see Max standing in the doorway, surveying the scene before him with open contempt on his face. He took in the whisky-filled glasses and the ruffled cushions on the sofa, and Shauna realised how it must look through his eyes, remembering in horror how her dance with Max had ended with her half-naked in his arms. She was about to move Rupert's vice-like grip, but Max's words beat her to it.

'If you get any closer, you'll be in danger of asphyxiating her,' he drawled, a cold ring to his voice. 'Perhaps you'd like to put her down now?' It was a question which brooked no answer other than the affirmative.

Rupert stepped back dramatically, his hands raised

in mock supplication. 'It's swords at dawn, I suppose?' he exclaimed, looking to Shauna for support, but she dropped her eyes to the carpet, embarrassed.

For answer Max advanced slowly across the room, a kind of black fury on his face. Shauna saw Rupert blanch beneath the golden tan, and he began backing away, until eventually Max almost had him pinned up against the wall, his face just a few inches away.

'You know, Max—you could teach the SAS a thing or two...' Rupert's voice tailed off as he met the icy green eyes.

'What the hell are you doing in my house?' Max hissed, in a soft voice which only seemed to emphasise the cutting edge of his tongue.

'I'm here to see my god-daughter—it *is* allowed, you know.'

Max looked around the room in mock search. 'Then where is she? I can't see her.'

'She—she went up to bed a little while ago,' interposed Shauna, with a slightly desperate ring to her voice.

He didn't even acknowledge that she had spoken, merely carried on talking in that dangerously flat voice. 'So while the cat's away...? Tell me, Rupert—while my daughter slept, did you think that you'd make it doubly worthwhile and seduce my secretary while you were about it?'

'But it wasn't like that!' cried Shauna.

He met her gaze for the first time, the narrowed eyes slowly flicking over every inch of her body, and she had to suppress a shiver as she met his critical gaze. 'No?' he queried softly.

She realised that one of the combs which had kept a mass of the dark curls off her face must have somehow become lost, and that her eyes were bright and glittering, her cheeks all flushed—due to the unaccustomed whisky, no doubt. She looked like a woman who had been interrupted in the early stages of lovemaking—while nothing could have been further from the truth.

Rupert was looking from one to the other with interest. 'Why, Max,' he said slyly, 'I do believe you're jealous.'

He was rewarded with a look which could have frozen at ten paces. 'Don't tempt me, Rupert. I'm about two seconds away from planting my fist in that pretty face of yours.'

The blond man gave a nervous laugh. 'But you can't stop me from seeing Bianca, can you? I *am* her godfather, and you did agree to it, or have you conveniently forgotten that?'

Max suddenly sounded unutterably weary, Shauna thought, as he moved away. 'No, I haven't forgotten, and I have no intention of stopping you from seeing her. Just make sure that you telephone first, in future. I do not want you in my house when I'm not here.' A furrow appeared between the dark brows which framed his eyes. 'What is this, anyway? A lightning visit amid your social whirl? Passing through?'

Shauna couldn't miss the look of pleasure which appeared on Rupert's face.

'Sorry to disappoint you, dear boy—but I'm visiting my mother for Christmas. So we'll be neighbours again for a little while, at least.'

A muscle was working overtime in Max's cheek. 'How delightful,' he said sarcastically. 'And now, if you don't mind—I've had a very long day. You can see yourself out. You know the way.'

Rupert needed no second bidding. He picked up his jacket and slung it over his shoulder in record time, then turned and gave Shauna a smile which showed off every one of his dazzling white teeth. 'Nice to have met you. Pity to have broken up the party, but no doubt I'll be seeing you. Goodbye, Max—perhaps you could try suing the charm school!' He sauntered out of the room, and Shauna saw Max clenching his fists by his side.

They stood in silence until they heard the front door slam, heard the engine of his car revving up, scattering gravel as it roared away up the drive.

And suddenly all the fight seemed to go out of him. Shauna saw his hands relax; saw the tight muscular tension in his face replaced by a bleak, empty look which in its way was somehow more frightening than his anger.

She searched his face for a friendly sign, a sign that he was on her side, but there was none. He barely looked at her as he poured himself a large whisky, without offering her anything.

She curled a long strand of hair around her index finger in an unconsciously nervous movement. 'You don't seem to like him very much,' she said, stating the obvious and knowing how trite it sounded even as she said it.

He looked at her then, giving a short laugh before

swallowing another mouthful of whisky. 'He's not my favourite person.'

She knew that she should feel irritated at his evasiveness, but she wasn't; instead she found herself in the invidious position of feeling guilty—and she didn't have a clue why. 'Why do you dislike him so much?' she asked. 'He seemed OK to me. A bit of a smoothie, perhaps, but harmless enough.'

She wished she hadn't asked, since she was rewarded with a chilly look. 'What goes on between Rupert and myself is of no concern to you, Shauna.'

Like a child wrongly accused of stealing, she found herself with the need to account for herself. 'He's been invited to a lot of balls this Christmas, and he needed someone to practise the waltz with, that's all...' Her words tailed off into an embarrassed silence, and she couldn't miss the faint curl of his lip.

'Really?' he mocked her. 'I had no idea that the waltz involved both partners grinding their pelvises together—but perhaps it's a new variation?'

She almost gasped aloud. The insult hit her like a pail of cold water. 'But it wasn't like that,' she protested, stung, and then she registered that his expression of disgust had intensified, and anger, a slow, insistent anger, began to build up inside her at the unjust criticism.

What God-given right did he have to talk to her in this way? Talk about double standards—*he* had just been off on what was obviously a sexual assignation with Marta, so what right did he have to come storming in here, just because he'd caught her dancing with a man?

'And what about *you*?' she taunted. 'Have you had a nice afternoon, Max?' She put on a sweetly sarcastic voice. 'How's dear Marta?'

Green eyes narrowed to shards of glass as he surveyed her. 'You don't know what you're talking about.' The voice was quiet, and controlled, but there was an underlying menace which warned off further questions.

She chose to ignore it. 'Oh, don't I? Well, I'm not *stupid*. Everyone knows what your relationship with Marta is, and, bearing that in mind—I doubt if you spent the day playing Scrabble with *her*, did you? I expect you had far more grown-up pursuits to follow!' She knew that her voice had a wild, high quality which bordered on hysteria, but she just couldn't stop the accusing words.

She saw anger darken his face, and his hands instinctively tighten into those tense fists again. And she saw by his face that she had gone much, much too far. She waited for the curt dismissal, the instruction to be gone in the morning, but he said nothing, simply stood regarding her with cold eyes.

Perhaps he was waiting for her to offer to go of her own volition—the self-imposed exile. She would have to suffer none of the ignominious treatment of being put out on the streets, jobless and homeless. That might rest a little too sharply on Max's conscience.

So she waited, and so did he. And she had proof then of just how much she did love him. For though

he obviously wished her gone and regarded her, un-
justly, as having the morals of an alley cat, she could
stare back at him and still feel an implosion of desire
which dominated every fibre of her being.

If, even with that expression of distaste, he had
walked over to her then, and started to kiss her and
touch her, and set her on fire with need—she would
have let him. Let him take her to wherever he
wanted, and make love to her.

And maybe that was what love was—desire, with
the absence of all pride.

CHAPTER TEN

'I'VE dictated enough work to keep you occupied all day,' said Max coldly. 'I'll sign it when I get back. I'm taking Bianca out for the day.'

Shauna silently watched as he left the study. She had been dreading facing him after last night's awful confrontation with Rupert. She supposed she just ought to be grateful that he hadn't mentioned her outburst about Marta, she thought as she began typing. Or any of the rather sordid accusations they had each hurled at the other.

She found dinner that evening a difficult meal to endure, with only Bianca's chatter covering up both adults' lack of communication.

The days which followed were awful—with Max seeming to physically distance himself from her as much as possible. The work he left for her to do was demanding, and at any other time she would have welcomed the responsibility, but as it was—all she could think about was how much she missed his company.

Shauna was alone in the house one day when the telephone rang.

'Hello,' came a horribly familiar low voice.

'Hello?' replied Shauna, striving for a professionalism she was far from feeling.

'Is Max there?'

'No, I'm afraid he isn't. He's out with Bianca.'

'Oh.'

'Shall I...can I take a message?'

'Please. Just tell him that Marta rang, will you?'

'Yes, I'll tell him.' Shauna replaced the receiver slowly and sat staring at it for a long time.

'You've had a phone call,' she told him when he came in.

The green eyes surveyed her without emotion. 'Yes?'

'Marta rang.'

He nodded. 'Thanks.'

She felt a primitive urge to do him violence—to fling herself at him and pummel his chest with her fists, or something. Instead, she continued to type, like an automaton.

At dinner that night, Bianca turned to her. 'You will be here for Christmas, won't you, Shauna?'

Christmas was a subject she had deliberately pushed to the back of her mind. It always created something of a problem for her, with no family, but there were always friends to go to. But this year...

'I hadn't really thought about it,' she hedged.

'Oh, but you *must*, mustn't she, Dad?'

Max looked up. 'Shauna knows she's very welcome,' he said. 'It's entirely up to her. She may have friends she wishes to visit.'

Damn him, and his indifference, thought Shauna; why couldn't he just say stay, or go—give her some idea of whether or not he *did* want her there, instead of that chilly social mask he presented?

'Well, then,' smiled Bianca triumphantly. 'That's settled.'

And she was right of course, Shauna knew that. For where else would she have gone? And, more importantly, where else would she have wanted to go? Because however foolish she convinced herself it was—she *wanted* to spend Christmas with Max. And his indifference towards her didn't seem to alter that fact at all.

Two days before Christmas, they stopped work completely. At least, she thought thankfully, there was so much going on at Christmas that Bianca didn't seem to have picked up on the strained atmosphere between the two of them. She hoped.

Rupert visited to see his god-daughter, and Shauna was just returning from a brisk walk across the crisp, frozen grass of the December fields when she saw him getting into his car.

His handsome face lit up when he saw her, and he leaned against the car, one hand resting on his hip.

'So tell me, you rosy-cheeked beauty,' he said, without preamble. 'Are you coming to my party?'

It was impossible not to smile at his irrepressible flirting, she thought, glad that he hadn't brought up the scene of the other night. 'What party?'

He sighed. '*The* party, my dear. The party of the decade. People will kill to come to it—and the lady says to me "what party?" Chez Hamilton, on the twenty-sixth.'

She hastily did a mental calculation. Bianca was flying up to her grandparents in Scotland on Boxing

Day, and she and Max had planned to drive back to London.

She shook her head ruefully. 'I'll have gone by then. But thanks anyway.'

He affected a wounded expression. 'The gods most certainly do not love me! But if you change your mind…it starts at eight at Roakes House.'

She smiled. 'If I'm around—I wouldn't miss it for the world!'

He blew her a kiss and climbed into his car. He seemed in a hurry to get away, and she couldn't blame him. She stood for a moment watching the car drive away, lost in deep thought, and when she moved towards the door she started to find Max standing there, solid and dark, his stance both enticing and menacing as he watched her, faded denims stretching almost indecently across the firm muscular length of his legs, his dark features giving little away, and yet she couldn't mistake the flash of anger in his eyes as he watched Rupert's small sports car drive away.

She met his eyes defiantly. Perhaps he would like to have had written into her contract that she shouldn't converse with people of whom he didn't approve! He might have intimidated her into babbled explanations the other night, but he certainly wasn't going to get a repeat performance. 'Is anything the matter, Max?' she asked.

'What did he want?'

'Do you mean Rupert?' she asked, her voice all sweetness.

'You know I do,' he rasped.

She lifted her head high, so that the hood covering it slipped back to reveal the abundant cascade of jet-black curls, and she saw him step back a little, an unfathomable expression on the stern features. 'He was inviting me to a party he's having at his house.'

He scowled, looking astonishingly like his daughter. 'And are you going?'

Clear grey eyes met narrow green ones. Just what did he think he was playing at? *He* didn't want her, but he seemed far too concerned that somebody else might. Rupert didn't hold a candle to her boss as far as she was concerned, but she certainly wasn't going to give him the satisfaction of knowing that.

'I can't go,' she told him. 'Because it's on the twenty-sixth, and we're going back to town.' She saw him relax. 'Otherwise, I'd love to have gone,' she finished, and saw him glower again.

'Bianca's up in the attic, getting the tree decorations. She wanted...she wondered if you would help us decorate it?'

It had obviously cost him a huge effort to ask it, and it was patently not something that he particularly relished, and neither did she. There was something almost ridiculously intimate about dressing a Christmas tree, especially if it was with a man you'd fallen hopelessly in love with. She opened her mouth to decline the offer, but Bianca put paid to that, whirling out of the door like a dervish, yards of tinsel strewn around her neck like a dozen glittering scarves. She looked anxiously at Shauna, then back to her father.

'Did you ask her, Dad? Will you help us, Shauna? Oh, *please*?'

She looked down into the shining green eyes, so heart-catchingly like his, and smiled. 'Of course I'll help you. Where's the tree?'

'We'll have to go and choose it from the farm,' trilled Bianca excitedly. 'Won't we, Dad?'

Max looked as though someone had suggested a trip to the dentist, thought Shauna as she put her hood back up.

The three of them piled into the Range Rover, and Shauna surveyed the wintry landscape where the bare branches of the hedgerows which lined the lanes were so frosty that their tips looked as if they had been dipped in white paint.

They chose the biggest Christmas tree they could find and spent the afternoon decorating it.

Shauna was perched on the top of the ladder, when it wobbled precariously, and, as Max reached out to steady it, his hand brushed against her denim-clad thigh, and it was as though an electric shock had swept through her.

'That bolt needs tightening,' he muttered.

'Thanks.' Her voice was shaking, and it had nothing to do with an accident averted.

Her Christmas Day was actually much better than she'd anticipated, probably because they seemed to spend the entire day eating! She smilingly listened to Bianca's chatter as she unwrapped presents, and, if her laugh was brittle at times, she was sure that no one noticed it.

Bianca had bought her a whole array of matching

combs, of every conceivable colour, and Max handed her a very large and very expensive bottle of perfume and, as she stammered her thanks, she found herself wondering what he had given to Marta. What a strange partnership they had. If she was his girl-friend, then why wasn't she here over Christmas?

By late afternoon, she was standing in front of the mirror in the dining-room. She had just finished pinning a strand of hair up with one of the combs Bianca had given her. It was black, and matched the clinging jersey dress. With most of her hair shimmering down her back, only the pale oval of her face showed against the blackness. She heard the softest of sounds and turned round to find Max silhouetted in the doorway, and she wondered how long he had been standing there.

The green eyes gave absolutely nothing away; at that moment he seemed nothing more than a polite stranger. 'Bianca's upstairs packing,' he said, sounding as if he'd chosen his words with care. 'Her flight's very early. I thought it would be best to start back to town as soon as possible after I get back.'

'Sure,' she nodded.

There was a long pause. Again she got the sensation of a rehearsed speech. The panacea for her disappointment that he hadn't made love to her.

'It hasn't been easy, this time here,' he said at last. 'I know that. But I want you also to know that I'm very grateful for everything you've done, especially for Bianca.' His mouth relaxed just a little. 'She's very fond of you, you know. Very fond.'

'I like her, too.'

'Yes, I know.' He cleared his throat. 'Can you be ready to leave as soon as I get back tomorrow morning, at around eleven?' There was another pause. 'I'm going off for a few days until the New Year. To the Cotswolds. I meet up with friends there every year. I'll drop you off in London first. It'll give us a break from one another—you can have the flat to yourself.'

But I don't need a break from you! she wanted to tell him, even while the cold stone of despair settled in the pit of her stomach as she tried to block out the picture of Marta—beautiful Marta—joining him. Because Cheltenham was in the Cotswolds, wasn't it? But none of these chaotic thoughts showed in her serene, frozen features. She was getting to be an accomplished actress, she reflected sadly.

'And when I get back—well, everything will be back to normal.'

'I hope so.' Whatever 'normal' was. Would anything ever be normal around this man?

The following day she waved farewell to a tearful, yet excited Bianca, amid promises to write. She felt a pang as the Range Rover tore off down the drive, with Max at the wheel. The reason for their close confinement was now gone and they would find it easier to avoid one another in town, but she would miss the elegant beauty of Seekings, the slow pace of rural community life. Even in these few short weeks Mrs Roberts had made her feel as though she belonged there. And let's face it, she thought, that was an all-time first.

Refusing to allow herself to become maudlin, she

packed her cases and sat down with a coffee to wait
for Max. She sat in her customary window-seat, enjoying her last few moments of the beautiful landscape outside, when a tableau began to develop before her as tiny flakes of snow started to fall—small
scurries of them to begin with, then becoming great
white blobs the size of coins, looking for all the
world like a child's painting.

Within the hour the scene was transformed. Grass
was now barely visible beneath the bright mantle.
The leaden grey sky spilled the snow out relentlessly,
and by twelve the whole landscape was covered by
a thick, silent blanket.

By twelve. She started as she glanced again at her
watch. Where on earth was Max? She strained her
ears to listen for the deadened sound of the four-
wheel drive as it bumped down the drive, but there
was nothing.

She switched on the radio to hear the usual dire
predictions by the weathermen, with warnings for no
one to leave the house unless their journey was 'absolutely necessary'. Oh, Max, she thought. Just come
home.

By three he still hadn't appeared or phoned and
the light had started to fade. She was now seriously
worried, imagining him stuck in drifts along some
impassable country land, and was contemplating
whether or not to ring the police to ask for advice
when she heard his car draw up outside.

The door flew open and wind and snow blew in
round him like a cloud, and she ran forward without
thinking.

'Oh, Max,' she cried. 'Thank God you're back—I've been so worried.'

He took a step back, as if frightened she might hurl herself into his arms. 'I tried to call from the airport, but I think the lines are down. I would have tried again, but I didn't want to risk stopping.'

'Is Bianca all right?'

He nodded. 'The flight was delayed while they cleared the runway. I waited at the airport until news came in that they'd arrived in Scotland. By the time I started back the roads were already quite bad. I was lucky to get here at all. If I'd been in an ordinary car, I reckon I'd have been stuck there for the night.' There was a pause. 'This means, of course, that we shan't be able to get back to London, certainly not tonight.'

She bit her lip. 'Of course.' The big house seemed suddenly very silent. Bianca had gone away, and Mrs Roberts had long since left. They were cut off, isolated, marooned in a vast house which felt smaller by the second, and, by the look on his face, it was the last thing in the world he would have wished for.

'I'll go and shower. We'll eat in an hour.'

And in that instant she decided that what she was *not* going to do was to be told in that presumptuous way how she was going to spend the evening. She still had her pride, at least, and she was not going to scrabble around gratefully for the small crumbs of his company which he deigned to throw at her.

'Actually, I'm afraid you'll have to eat on your own,' she said coolly. 'I've been invited to a party.'

'Rupert's party?' he asked slowly.

'The very same.'

'You're not going to that.'

She didn't know whether he had intended it to come out as a flat command, but that was how it sounded and the way in which he said it filled her with anger. 'I *am* going,' she corrected.

'You'll never get down to the village in this weather—it's like Antarctica out there.'

'But that's not why you don't want me to go, is it, Max? This all has to do with Rupert, doesn't it?'

His voice was cold. 'He isn't your type.'

Her temper snapped. 'Oh, here we go again. You're full of advice, aren't you? What I want. What I don't want. How do you know what my "type" is? And I've made my mind up in any case—I'm going to the party whether you like it or not.'

'Then I'll drive you.'

'Oh, no, you won't,' she answered with icy dignity, but he had stepped forward and grabbed her by the upper arms, as if he were about to shake her.

'Oh, yes, I will,' he hissed. 'You can go to your damned party for all I care, but I'm not having you risking death to do so. What time do you want to leave?'

'At eight o'clock,' she blurted out, and ran upstairs to her room as fast as her feet could carry her, collapsing on the bed as soon as she'd slammed the door shut behind her, beating a helpless fist into the feather pillow, as if it were Max's chest she was hitting.

The harsh words had shaken her. She didn't understand him. Why *shouldn't* she go?

She spent hours getting ready since there was nothing else to do. Her hair took ages to dry properly, but it was worth it afterwards, for it shone like coils of ebony satin.

She had only one dress in her wardrobe which was suitable for a party such as Rupert's and that was one she had bought in Paris, en route to Portugal. It had been in a sale, naturally—a fantastic bargain, but she'd never had cause to wear it before.

Natural reticence made her hesitate a little before trying it on, but she gave a satisfied smile as she surveyed herself in the mirror. Daring, yes—but perfect.

In scarlet lace, it was outwardly demure with its high neck and long sleeves, but the buttoned bodice was fitted, emphasising the tiny waist, and the skirt lay snugly across her bottom, ending just above her knees and showing her long, black-stockinged legs. She would wear her wellingtons there, she decided, thinking about the snow—and change into the high-heeled black shoes when she arrived at Rupert's.

Like a complicated piece of fretwork, she began to pile the dark curls on to the top of her head, securing the whole lot in place with one linchpin of gold.

She darkened her eyelashes and applied scarlet lipstick to the wide lips more out of an act of defiance than anything else, though she wondered why she did it since the only man she was seeking to defy wouldn't even be at the party.

At just before eight, she was ready. Her wellies were down in the hall, she remembered, so she picked up her warm overcoat and, wrapping it around herself, she stepped out into the corridor.

Putting her shoes in her handbag, she tiptoed downstairs in her stockinged feet. She reached the bottom and saw that a fire had been lit in the study and standing, his back to her, was Max.

He must have heard her, for he turned slowly, his face forbidding, a glass of whisky in his hand. Without a word he slowly drank the contents of his glass then put the glass down on the mantelpiece and continued to stare at her, his hands resting on lean hips, an indecipherable expression on his face.

'I'm going out now,' she told him.

His eyes were skimming from the top of the elaborate hairstyle, down the all-concealing coat, to the slim ankles in their sheer stockings. 'So I see,' he grated.

She began to wish that she had insisted on walking, however great a folly that might have been. Well, she certainly wasn't going to *beg* him to take her. She gazed at him questioningly.

'And is the current fashion to go shoeless?' he enquired sarcastically.

'I'm going in my wellingtons—it *is* snowing,' she tried to smile.

It was as though something inside him had snapped. 'Damn you, Shauna!' he exploded. 'I don't want you to go!'

How dared he talk to her like that? 'So you told me!' She tossed her head in an age-old gesture of pique, causing the sensible coat to fall free of her grasp so that it flew open, and he was confronted with the sight of her in the clinging red dress.

He was staring at her, transfixed. 'I don't want you to go,' he repeated, and there was a low, husky quality to his voice.

'I'll bet you don't!' she retorted. 'And what alternative are you offering, perhaps you'd like to tell me that? A gloomy evening while you do your best to avoid me? You don't want me, do you, Max? And yet you can't bear the thought that someone else might!'

She heard a long sigh, like the hissing of steam, escape from the hard line of his mouth.

The air was tight with tension as he stared at her incredulously. 'Not want you?' He closed the gap between them with one purposeful step. 'Not want you,' he repeated. 'Oh, really, Shauna?' The green eyes glittered. 'Come here,' he whispered. 'Come here and feel how much I don't want you.' And in a swift, decisive movement, his hand snaked round her waist, pulling her hard towards him, so that she was moulded against the full length of his body, but, as if that weren't enough, he pushed his hips into hers so that they fitted together, like two parts of a puzzle. 'You see?' he bent and murmured softly in her ear. 'How much?'

It was the most deliberately wanton and explicit thing that had ever happened to her. Every nerve-ending was tingling with awareness. They had been close before, but never this close. The hardness of him jutting against her soft curves. Yes, she could feel his desire for her. Oh, God. She closed her eyes.

It was glaringly apparent—even through the thick denim of his jeans.

His mouth came down on hers, hard, but it met no resistance. He tipped her head back as his tongue probed intimately and she closed her eyes in delirious pleasure as his hand began to move slowly across her back, against the crisp lace of the dress which suddenly seemed an encumbrance.

The blood was singing and rushing through her veins, her heart beating out loudly and insistently like a primitive drum, when the voice of reason began clamouring to be heard.

Every one of her senses began screaming its protest as she pulled her lips away from him, as she tried ineffectually to push at the hard muscle of his chest, her fist balled against the frantic hammering of his own heart.

The green eyes looked almost opaque with desire, their pupils huge, dark shutters. 'What are you doing?' he groaned, pulling her back into his arms, but she kept her head averted, and pulled away. 'Shauna, what is it?'

She forced her ragged breathing to acquire some semblance of normality as she surveyed him. 'I thought this was what you most emphatically didn't want? Wasn't it you who told me "no more"?'

He shook his head. 'I just can't fight it any more. I want you, Shauna.'

Her eyebrows shot up at the arrogant ease of reply. 'Just like that?' Her voice rang out. 'You've changed your mind? You can pick me up or put me down whenever the fancy takes you? Well, I'm sorry,

Max—it won't work. Not with me. I'm not prepared to be your substitute. No one likes to be made love to knowing that they're just filling in for someone else.'

'What the hell are you talking about?'

The pain of being separated from him when her body was crying out for fulfilment made the timbre of her voice unusually brittle. 'You know damn well what I'm talking about! Shall I put it into plain English for you? You need a woman! And you're using me because I happen to be around—because Marta isn't here!'

CHAPTER ELEVEN

Max's voice was ominously quiet. 'What did you say?'

'You heard exactly what I said.'

His face was all dark planes and shadows. 'You don't know what you're talking about.'

The bitterness of the last few days came spilling out. 'Oh, don't I? You aren't denying, are you, Max, that Marta is your mistress?'

'We had,' he said softly, 'an understanding.'

Shauna recoiled. So he didn't even try to deny it. She shut her eyes as if by doing that she could shut out the thoughts which tortured her. When she opened them again, she stared at him—fury darkening the grey eyes. 'Why aren't you with *her*, then? Why don't you go to her, make love to her, and stop using me as a substitute?'

'Stop talking like that!' he yelled.

'Why? Does the truth hurt?' she yelled back. 'Tell me, is Marta busy tonight? Or is it because of the weather? I suppose that if you weren't actually snowed in here with me then you wouldn't have to resort to sex with me!'

'Stop it,' he grated. 'You don't usually talk this way.'

'Well, these aren't exactly usual circumstances, are they?' she asked, sweetly sarcastic. 'And you're not denying, are you, Max, that our—entanglement the other night left you feeling more than a little frustrated? So at the first opportunity you rush off to Marta—who can give you what you didn't seem to want from me?'

He pulled her back into his arms then, and the jarring shock of the renewed close proximity sent her senses reeling, so that she found resistance impossible. 'I'll tell you what happened, shall I, Shauna, if you really want to know? Yes, I had planned to go to Marta that night. Because, yes, I thought that there was only one sure-fire way to get you out of my system...' His eyes had become hooded, cautious.

'Marta and I have known one another for a long time. We're both adults. No ties. No questions. The only kind of relationship which suits me. An easy understanding which suited us *both*. Until now. Yes, you stirred me up that night. I won't deny that I wanted you in a way that I haven't wanted a woman for a long time. But you work with me. You share a flat with me. An affair would complicate that—and I'm not looking for a partner. And so I intended to go to Marta.' His eyes gave nothing away. 'But it was...no good.'

'I don't understand,' she said coldly. If he had taken a blunt, heavy instrument and smashed her over the head with it, he could not have hurt her more.

'Do you want me to spell it out in words of one syllable?' he said bitterly. 'I didn't even get there— I just drove around for hours and hours, my head in a spin. I couldn't have gone to bed with Marta that night, nor anyone else for that matter. Because some dark-haired witchy woman had got underneath my skin, had got into my blood, and I didn't want any-one but her.'

She stared at him stupidly. 'What are you saying?'

'That I want you, Shauna. *You*. Very much.'

But he was saying it as though he was still fighting it, she thought desperately, even while his eyes were devouring her. There was a muscle working overtime in his cheek; she could see a pulse hammering under the smooth brown skin of his temple.

And suddenly she knew that she wanted no turning back, not any more. She loved him. She wanted him too much. If she let this moment go, she might never have another like it, with the promise of everything she knew that he would give her. She didn't care whether it was right or wrong. She wanted this man, but it went deeper than that. Desire, yes—but there was need, too. Real need. There was an empty space in her mind and body and soul. A space that only he could fill. A flickering flame just waiting to grow into a glowing blaze, a flame which he had ignited and only he could extinguish. She wanted him—and to hell with the consequences. She would never be able to work for him again after tonight, in any case.

His eyes were riveted to the heaving movement of her breasts. He stood as if carved from stone—silent and unmoving. Now, she thought. Now.

Very deliberately, she raised her hand to remove the glittering golden pin and it fell to the ground with a little clatter as the mass of dark curls tumbled down around her shoulders like a mantilla. She let her heavy coat slither to the floor, and as she did so she saw him start.

'Shauna...' he said unsteadily.

She had not finished. Slowly, she started to undo each of the tiny, covered buttons of the bodice.

He was watching her, mesmerised.

She took her time. She could hear his ragged, uncontrollable breathing puncturing the silence as her fingers slowly released button after button. The final one free, she smiled, her eyes widening with pleasure at the look on his face as she peeled the bodice right down, revealing the lush honey-coloured breasts, with their rose-dark nipples.

And it was as though someone had breathed sudden life into him. His eyes darkened. He beckoned very slowly. 'Now come here,' he whispered.

She went, willingly, her arms automatically going around his neck, while he grasped the slender nakedness of her waist.

He groaned as he buried his face in her hair, his hands moving to cup and caress each breast, his mouth starting out on a moist, sensual path from neck to mouth, so that when he finally crushed her mouth with his lips she returned the kiss with a feverish intensity which equalled his.

With one fluid movement he slipped the dress down over her hips and then effortlessly lifted her high in the air, so that she was free of it and left wearing nothing but her lace panties and black stockings.

Still kissing her, he pushed her down on to the softness of the Persian rug, and leaned over her, his hand lightly circling each breast in turn, so that she made a tiny cry at the back of her throat.

He heard it and bent his head to her ear. 'You,' he whispered, 'are very beautiful. And I am feeling slightly over-dressed.'

'Oh, Max.' Her voice sounded thick and slurred. Her nipples felt bruised and hard as they brushed against his shirt. She tightened her arms around his neck, but felt him removing them and she opened her eyes, terrified that he was going to stop.

He must have read the question in her eyes. 'Oh, no,' he murmured. 'I'm not going anywhere.' And he stood up, his eyes never leaving her face as he slowly began to unbutton his shirt. He pulled the shirt off and threw it aside, revealing the magnificent torso she'd seen that first night in the flat, the smooth brown skin sheathing the rippling muscle beneath.

She lay, arms above her head, watching his every move. His eyes travelled over every inch of her, lingering on her breasts until she felt them tingle and throb, their tips jutting towards him in tight twin erections, as if he were touching them instead of just looking at them. His gaze moved down to the tiny flimsy wisp of her panties, the little lacy suspender belt, and the black stockings which clung to her long legs.

His hand lingered on the button of his jeans. 'How far do you want me to go?' he grinned.

'Everything.' Her husky reply was barely audible. She started to tremble as he slid the zip down with a tantalising lack of speed. The jeans came off slowly, inch by inch, until he stood in front of her, gloriously proud in his nakedness.

Her pupils dilated as she saw how aroused he was, and without realising it she licked her bruised lips and he saw it, and the game suddenly stopped and he was lying on top of her, his eyes dark with passion, and she felt his need pushing insistently against her stomach.

He traced a lazy line from stomach to thigh, a finger moving to find the moist scrap of her panties, and she gave a stifled moan.

'Now these,' he whispered, as he slid them down past her knees, 'I think we'll dispense with. But these...' his hand rested on a silk-stockinged thigh, 'I think we'll leave on, shall we?'

She was past caring, or answering—he had her in such a feverish state of wanting that she felt she would explode soon. She moved ecstatically as his fingers explored the soft, satiny centre of her that cried out for his possession. And it seemed that he knew she could wait no longer, for he thrust into her powerfully, without warning, filling her totally with himself. She astonished herself with her own frantic movements, wrapping her silk-clad thighs around his back, capturing him—when, as if answering an unspoken need, he drove into her harder until, with a sharp cry that was torn from her lips, she fell over the top, spinning out of control, aware then of spasm after glorious spasm pulsating around his hardness. And when he cried out too, she enfolded him fiercely against her breasts, their bodies joined, the waves

ebbing and dying in unison—bringing utter content-
ment, and peace.

She awoke to find him watching her and he made
slow love to her all over again, and, later in the night,
when the fire had died, he carried her up to his room
and laid her on the bed.

He knelt over her, his eyes skimming her from
head to foot, as if he had a need to memorise every
inch of her. He ran both his hands down over the
contours of her body, moulding them briefly to her
breasts, and down, over her stomach, over her thighs,
resting at last on her ankles, still in their black stockings.

'I think these can come off now,' he murmured.
'Mmm?'

'Anything you like,' she said throatily, and he
laughed delightedly.

'Oh, sweetheart—you don't know what you've
just let yourself in for,' he teased.

'I do...' Her drowsy words faded as the insistent
pleasure began to build up again.

His hand moved slowly up her leg, so slowly that
it was sweet torture, and she waited breathlessly, letting out a tortured little cry as he halted at her stock-
ing top, a forefinger moving within the lacy rim, before unclipping it and slowly sliding it off.

When he had each leg bare, he began to kiss her
toes, then her ankles, her knees and the inside of her
thighs. And then his mouth found the velvety core,
moving so intimately against her that she felt a brief
moment of stunned shock before the slow heat took
over and she could scarcely believe when it happened

again, her delirious cry sounding loud in the stillness of the night. She was still shuddering uncontrollably when her hands reached down for him blindly until she had located the broad bank of his shoulders and he moved to lie above her, laughing a little as he bent his head to kiss her.

'Shauna...' he groaned. 'Oh, God. Feel. Feel what you're doing to me.' And he pulled her even closer.

She felt the hardness of him, the throbbing power of his arousal which filled her with a sense of wonder that he wanted her again so badly, and so soon.

She awoke slowly the next morning, naked and glowing beneath the rumpled sheets, and it took a few seconds for her to register that he was no longer beside her.

She stretched luxuriously, her long arms moving uninhibitedly above her head, frozen in an indolent pose. Part of the sheet slipped to reveal a naked brown thigh, and she buried her face in his pillow as she re-lived the memories of the previous night, moment by glorious moment.

It had been indescribable, and Max, as a lover, quite perfect. There had been only one other man in her life, and that had been Harry. He had been serious. She had *thought* she was serious. After the kind of deliberations which had never even entered her head with Max, she had gone to bed with him, and the sex had served to diminish, rather than enhance the relationship. They had agreed to part as friends shortly after.

But with Max—it had been something else. He

had made love to her almost all night long—she hadn't thought that possible. He had done things to her which should have made her blush, and yet she was filled with impatient longing to have him do them to her all over again. He had slept briefly with her held tightly in his arms, and she had drifted in and out of a dazed slumber, filled with happiness every time she opened her eyes to find her gorgeous, naked Max beside her. And now, without him, she felt as though she'd lost a part of herself. Where was he?

She sat up, taking in the surroundings which last night had gone ignored. It was an overwhelmingly masculine room with dark crimson walls and framed sporting prints predominating. Through the open door of his wardrobe she could see piles of expensive-looking sweaters stacked.

This was a room where a woman would only have one place, and she was in it. All of a sudden, she felt like an intruder, and she pushed the sheets aside and padded over to the door to where a towelling robe of Max's hung. She put it on and pulled the belt tightly around her waist, ran her fingers through her curls to untangle them a little, and went off in search of him.

In the mirror in the hallway, she caught sight of a sparkling-eyed girl with pink cheeks flushed with happiness. That's me! she thought in delight.

She could hear noises coming from the kitchen, and she moved lightly towards it.

As she was barefooted, he hadn't heard her. He had his back to her and was filling the percolator.

She looked at him adoringly, at the broad shoulders and the long, clean line of his limbs. At the way the dark hair curled on to his neck.

He was wearing jeans and a sweater, and a feeling of regret filled her. She would have much preferred to forgo the coffee and have him wake up naked next to her.

'Hello, you,' she whispered softly, and he turned round, his face carefully composed, not looking like Max at all.

'Good morning,' he said. 'Would you like some coffee?'

'Love some,' she lied, her heart thudding with fear. She didn't want coffee, she wanted him to come over to her and kiss her, and tell her she was beautiful, and rid her of the insecurity which had suddenly threatened to overwhelm her. Instead of which, he was looking at her as if she were a stranger, with that horrible polite little smile on his face.

He handed her the cup, but her hand was shaking so much that it danced wildly in the saucer, shattering the silence with its clinking clamour. She put it down on the work surface quickly.

All at once she felt totally unsure of herself, remembering that she had been the seducer last night. It had been her act—her flagrant and provocative strip-tease—which had pushed him over the edge—beyond reason and into her arms. If today he was regretting what had happened, she had only herself to blame.

Suddenly, she could bear it no longer. 'Max,

you're regretting last night, aren't you? Wishing that
it had never happened?'

There was a long pause. When he looked up, his
eyes were guarded. 'I don't think that now is a very
good time to talk,' he said abruptly. 'Drink your coffee—and then you'd better get dressed. I have to
drop you back in London, before I leave for the
Cotswolds.'

She stared at him as if he had just uttered the most
foul obscenity. 'Cotswolds?' she echoed foolishly.

'Yes. It's a long-standing arrangement. You knew
that.'

Yes, she had known. But she had thought—what?
That last night had changed things? And why should
it have done? What had he said to indicate that it
might be otherwise? Nothing. Absolutely nothing. He
had taken her to bed, and she had *known* that part of
him was unwilling to. But what kind of man could
resist that kind of temptation? It must have been the
most unsubtle come-on since time began.

She felt her cheeks grow hot, and, afraid that she
might suddenly start to cry, she turned away rapidly,
blinking back the tears.

'I'll go and get dressed,' she said in a calm voice
that seemed to come from a long way away.

'I'll wait here.'

He obviously wanted to be nowhere near her.

All the while she was getting ready, she had to
fight to suppress the mental images which were
crowding her mind with sickening clarity. Of Max—
doing all those things to Marta that he had done to
her, last night.

True, he had said that he couldn't have gone to bed with Marta or 'anyone else for that matter', because his thoughts had been full of Shauna. But that was before he'd taken her to bed, and, presumably, he had now got her out of his system, leaving him free to return to Marta once more. He had certainly acted as though he had got her out of his system. Why, he had scarcely been able to be civil to her this morning. He hadn't spoken more than a few words to her.

She sank on to the bed, her head in her hands, shoulders shaking convulsively. What did she expect, when she'd behaved like a cheap little tramp?

The journey back was worse than atrocious. The roads were still fairly treacherous, and Max needed every bit of his wits to keep the Range Rover on the road, and out of the drifts on either side.

But even taking into account the conditions, there could be no denying that an awkward silence had invaded the car when their journey started, and it was multiplying by the moment.

The silence grew so lengthy and so brittle that it became impossible to break. For what would they have said? What could they have said, given the circumstances?

For how pitiful it would have been to have heard their dramatically opposing views, from Shauna's 'I love you, Max', to his 'thanks, but no thanks'.

She was glad when they hit London, even though she knew that the sooner they arrived, the sooner he would be gone.

In the flat she heard him moving around in his

room. She stood, feeling totally alone as she stared sightlessly out at the panoramic view.

She heard his footfall behind, but she stayed unmoving.

'Shauna?'

Feeling empowered to face him, she turned, but any hope of a change of heart died instantly on seeing his face. It was as coolly indifferent as it had been all morning.

'I have to go now.'

'Yes.' She was astonished how normal her response sounded.

'I'll see you when I get back. We'll talk then.'

'Yes, Max.' It was an automatic reply. She scarcely registered what he was saying.

'Goodbye.' He hesitated as if to say something more, but evidently changed his mind, for then he turned on his heel and left, without uttering another word.

CHAPTER TWELVE

ONCE Max had gone, Shauna allowed herself the luxury of tears. She lay on her bed like an emotional teenager, and howled. By the time she'd finished she had a blotchy face, shiny nose, and was sniffing like someone with severe adenoidal problems. And still didn't feel any better.

She took a shower—there hadn't been time at Seekings. Max still clung to her skin; the masculine scent of him seemed to surround her, and she was strangely reluctant to wash it away.

And even when she was clean, she still ached, and was tender—there were several small bruises where he'd delectably bitten and sucked at her skin. It was as though she would never be able to rid herself of him.

With hair dripping like seaweed, she made some coffee and sat down to think.

Wouldn't it just be best if she left while he was away? Threw herself on the mercy of Harry and Nick, and stayed with them until she found somewhere of her own?

But wouldn't that be the cowardly way out? Running away had never solved anything. If there was to be nothing between them, then surely it would be better if she faced up to it. Max had said that they would talk when he returned. About what? About what a wonderful time he'd had in the Cotswolds with Marta?

She clenched her fist very tight and pressed it to her lips. What had she expected? Wedding bells? Max had been quite straightforward about the relationship he had with Marta—'the only type of relationship which suits me'. And yes, he had desired Shauna enough to stop him from visiting Marta that night, but now his desire had been satiated, and, in going to bed with him, surely Shauna had lost her elusiveness, and her desirability. For a man like Max would be so used to getting just what he wanted from any woman that surely to remain immune to his charm would be the only way of guaranteeing any degree of respect from him.

She had thrown herself at him. He had been fighting the attraction, but she had stood in front of him and stripped to the waist in an attempt to seduce him.

And the next day, what had happened? He had leapt out of bed and distanced himself from her as much as was humanly possible. He had driven her back to town, as hastily as possible, and had left her for a pre-planned holiday with the woman he had shared his life with for goodness only knew how long.

Perhaps in the sophisticated world these people inhabited this kind of liaison was par for the course. Perhaps Marta understood and forgave Max his little 'indiscretions'. The fist pressed tighter against her mouth, as she fought to control the tears.

Yet, still, she hoped. She didn't contact either Harry or Nick. Instead she hung around the flat, hoping against hope that Max might ring her. But he didn't. Not the first night, or the second either.

By the third, she was feeling like a caged lioness with the sentence of death hanging over her head, when there was a loud ring at the door. She jumped to her feet, and spoke into it breathlessly.

'Hello?'

It was Charlie, the commissionaire. 'There's a gentleman down here to see you, Miss Wilde,' he said.

Even though logic told her that Max certainly wouldn't have announced his presence through Charlie, still she hoped. 'Who is it, Charlie?'

'It's a Mr Hamilton.'

Rupert! If she hadn't been preparing to go to Rupert's party the other night, then the whole bed bit with Max might never have happened. And yet she found herself wanting to see him, hoping that his flippant sense of humour might rock her out of the doom-laden mood which was enveloping her. She cleared her throat. 'That's all right, Charlie,' she told him. 'You can send him up.'

Rupert rapped on the door seconds later. 'Hello, beauty,' he said without preamble, then looked at her more closely, and his eyes widened. 'Or should I say—the beast? What have you been doing to yourself? You look dreadful!'

There was no way she was going to tell him, telling would only make her think about it, and she was sick to death of thinking about and analysing the whole sorry affair. 'Lack of sleep, combined with a heavy cold,' she muttered, which was half true. 'What are you doing here?'

He grinned. 'I pursued you! There's nothing I find quite so attractive as a woman who plays hard to get. I thought you'd come to my party—I really did. So when you didn't I decided to come calling.'

'Oh,' she said listlessly. Flirting was right at the bottom of her list of priorities today.

He frowned a little, and sat down on one of the sofas, spreading his legs before him elegantly, and threading his fingers together before his chest in an almost prayer-like attitude. 'Where's Max?'

A hammer pounded at her chest. 'In the Cotswolds.'

'Ah, yes—his yearly ritual. I hear that the luscious Marta is moving into the big-time. Apparently she's landed *Vogue*, and *Elle*.'

The hammer became heavier. Rupert had made the connection that Marta would be there, too. She found herself looking helplessly at him.

'So you're free tonight?' he smiled. 'No evil boss standing over you as your fingers whizz over the word processor?'

She managed a wan smile. 'No.'

'Good!' He grinned. 'Want to come to a party with me?'

Did she? She hesitated. Why not? she thought defiantly. Why mope around, waiting for a phone-call which patently wasn't going to come, while Max wined and dined Marta in the Cotswolds? Why *should* she stay at home? In truth, she could have done with a long bath, a glass of wine, and a full night's sleep. But sleep was at a premium lately, and she'd probably spend the night tossing and turning.

There was a sense of retaliation in her reply. 'Thank you, Rupert—I'd love to come out with you.' Anything Max could do, she could do better.

Rupert looked her up and down. 'You're going to need a bit of time to cover up those bags underneath your eyes—so get cracking!'

An hour later, Shauna emerged from her bedroom wearing the scarlet lace dress. As she'd slowly buttoned it up, she had had to close her mind firmly to the vivid memories of Max pushing the gown to the floor, Max pulling her naked into his arms... Those thoughts were nothing but self-destructive.

She'd left her hair loose, and it snaked down her back in a froth of jet curls. As she appeared, Rupert gave an appreciative whistle. '*Unbelievable*,' he murmured.

The party was in Chelsea, and was rowdy, noisy and reeking of far too much money. There were a lot of people called Sophie and Henrietta and once Rupert called 'James' across the room, and at least eight people turned round.

There were bottles of warm champagne everywhere, and Shauna found herself sipping some out of a silver christening mug, listening while Rupert and another man argued fiercely over whether the property market would ever recover.

At eleven, they all convened to 'Lulu's' nightclub, where the party continued.

From time to time, Rupert would give Shauna a comforting squeeze on the shoulder. 'Enjoying yourself?' he queried.

'Mmm!' Another sip of the tepid fizz. Was she

enjoying herself? Not really. But it was a damn sight better than being back at the flat, feeling sorry for herself.

The music changed down to slow and smoochy, and Rupert took Shauna into his arms. The wine she had drunk had made her feel just nicely mellow, and properly relaxed for the first time since Max had driven her back. He bent his head to whisper, 'Having fun?'

And strangely enough, considering the circumstances, she was—simple, uncomplicated fun, with a simple, uncomplicated man. 'Yes,' she nodded. 'I am.'

He immediately tightened his hold and began to rub his hand down the back of her neck, but Shauna stiffened and he must have felt it, for he stepped back a little, and looked at her questioningly. 'No?'

She shook her head ruefully. 'No. But no offence?'

He shrugged easily. 'None taken.'

What a wonderfully uncomplex man, she thought sadly. Why couldn't she fall for someone like Rupert?

At two o'clock, they began to gather up their belongings, smiling as they made their way through the crush. Rupert had his arm tightly around Shauna's waist to guide her through the crowd, and, when they pushed their way out into the night, there was a shout, and a blinding flash, which startled Shauna, causing her to fall back against him.

She blinked in confusion as Rupert bundled her into a cab. 'What was that?'

'The bloody Press,' he told her. 'They prowl around like vultures.'

But Shauna thought he didn't look displeased.

Perhaps due to the wine and the dancing, she slept deeply, not waking up, amazingly, until almost ten-thirty, then lay there until eleven, knowing that, pride or no pride, she would wait for however long it took for Max to come back, to hear what it was he wanted to say to her.

She dressed in jeans and an old sweater and was just stifling a yawn when she heard a key in the door and in walked Max. Marta went straight out of her head and her first instinct was to hurl herself eagerly into his arms, but something in his face stopped her.

'Max...?' she said diffidently.

'Feeling tired, are we?' he asked, thinly veiled contempt in his voice.

Her eager expression became wooden as she stared into his cold, indifferent face. She had hoped against hope that he would still want her, but she had been wrong. There could be only one reason for this harsh, frightening Max. He wanted her out of his life. She struggled to say something which would not have her pride in tattered shreds in front of him.

'Did—did you have a good time?' she stammered, her voice dangerously close to tears.

At the gauche question, something inside him seemed to snap and he grabbed her shoulders with a force which made her wince with pain.

'How could you?' he spat out. 'Couldn't you even wait for a few meagre days?'

She shrank away from the blazing venom in his

eyes. His grip on her was like a vice. 'You—you're hurting me,' she said weakly.

He didn't relinquish his hold on her at all. 'Hurting you? Believe me, Shauna, I'm using every bit of restraint in my body at this moment. I'd like to kill you,' he hissed. 'Or perhaps I know a better way to get to you. Shall I turn you on? And then leave you? Leave you wanting me? Hmm? Shall I do that? Would you like that, Shauna?' he whispered. 'Would you like me to...?' The words he used were not loving words. He pulled her into his arms and pressed her close to him, and, even while she recoiled from the violence in his tone, her body reacted involuntarily to the movement. He must have felt it, too, for she saw her self-disgust mirrored in his eyes, and he dropped his hands immediately, as if she were a piece of old garbage he could not bear to touch.

Sanity fought to make itself heard. Even if he had decided that he no longer wanted anything to do with her, that did not account for this—this seeming hatred of her.

'What is it, Max?' she croaked, from terror-dried lips. 'What is it?'

'What is it?' he mimicked tauntingly. 'As if you didn't know. And who did you have lined up for tonight? Rupert again? Or someone else?' He stared at her consideringly. 'I must say, you had even *me* fooled with your enthusiastic once-in-a-lifetime response—quite the little actress, aren't you?'

She prayed that none of this was happening to her, that she was in the midst of some diabolical nightmare. 'I don't know what you're talking about,' she muttered wearily.

'Then maybe this will help,' he said, with icy disdain. He pulled out a newspaper from the inside pocket of his jacket. It was one of the popular tabloids. It fell open at the gossip column, and there, coming out of the nightclub, was a picture of Shauna and Rupert.

It had never occurred to her that they might use it—true, Rupert was a minor aristocrat, but she, Shauna, was of no consequence.

She looked more closely at the photograph. As a piece of evidence it was about as damning as you could get. They said the camera didn't lie, but in this case they'd got it wrong, for it looked like a photograph of a couple who couldn't keep their hands off each other. Like lovers.

It was all there to see. Rupert's hand clasped tightly and protectively around her waist. Her flushed and shining face frozen in a smile as the long tendrils of her hair splayed all over his white shirt-front where she leaned against him.

She looked up to find the green eyes surveying her coldly. She made one last, desperate bid. 'It wasn't like that!' she cried, knowing the futility of the words even as she uttered them.

'Oh, sure,' he ground out harshly. 'And there's gold at the end of the rainbow.'

He wasn't even giving her a chance, she realised, and stared at him then, recognising an irrefutable truth. That in a way he had wanted this. He wasn't looking for a partner, he had told her that, and now here she was, handing to him on a plate the perfect excuse to reject her.

Her words of denial died on her lips. What was the point of begging him, pleading with him to believe her? Why humiliate herself further? He seemed to have one rule for himself, and another for her. *He* could go tripping off with Marta, and yet he had blown a fuse at a stupid little photograph in a down-market rag, without even bothering to validate it.

He didn't want to believe her. He wanted to find her guilty, and, in so doing, that allowed him to reinforce all his prejudices against women. Only he could destroy those prejudices, and he simply didn't want to.

Even if she could convince him that in this case the picture told the wrong story, would he ever truly believe her, or trust her? There was no trust left in Max's heart—that was a truth she had hit on weeks ago—and to live without trust would not be living at all.

'I want you out of here,' he said in a flatly controlled voice, before he turned away and walked towards the door.

'Oh, don't worry, Max—I'm out of here. Nothing in the world would make me stay!' she called at his retreating back, wanting him to hear that her own voice was controlled too, in a last wild attempt to hang on to an appearance of dignity.

But she wasn't even sure that he could hear her, and the last thing she saw was the line of his broad shoulders, now hopelessly distorted as she viewed them through a veil of tears.

CHAPTER THIRTEEN

LIFE in the flat was cramped. Very cramped. Naturally, Shauna was glad to have a roof over her head, and grateful to Harry and Nick for taking her in so suddenly, and without question. And questions must have been swarming around in their minds that morning, when she had turned up with her suitcase, not crying, but clearly in a terrible state.

And she decided fairly quickly that two and a half years on down the line she had changed the way she liked to live. She had tolerated the mess at twenty-one, but now she preferred a calmer, more ordered life.

Each morning, when she opened her eyes to the unwashed dishes, the overflowing ashtrays, shoes kicked hither and thither, she heaved a great sigh and tried to put all comparisons with Seekings out of her mind.

She couldn't really close her eyes to the mess, either, since she was sleeping in the sitting-room. There were only two bedrooms—Harry had the smaller one, and Nick shared his with Heather, his girlfriend. Consequently, Shauna had to wait up until everyone else was ready to go to bed, or 'crash', as they insisted on putting it, the smell of wine and smoke making her feel nauseated. Harry, in the meantime, kept making jocular suggestions that she share his room, and, although he was light-hearted about it, she knew that he would have been delighted if she *had* taken him up on his offer. Because of this, Shauna no longer felt as relaxed in Harry's company as she used to, afraid that any great show of friendship might be misinterpreted.

She quickly found herself a temping job. It was about as menial as you could get—invoice typing in an airless office with two other girls—but at least it didn't require any brainwork—her mind felt totally numb, and she wasn't sure that she could have coped with anything more demanding. And at least it paid her contribution towards the rent.

In her spare time, she went flat-hunting, gloomily looking over dingy and over-priced lodgings which all seemed to share two distinct characteristics—they all smelt, and the bathrooms should have carried a public health warning.

On the subject of Max, she did not dwell at all. Thoughts of Max were taboo, they led nowhere, and, besides, other thoughts had now blocked out *all* thoughts of Max because the last couple of mornings had brought about a very real fear indeed...

One Wednesday evening, almost three weeks after she'd left Max's flat, there was a loud rat-ta-tat on the door. She stirred a little in the armchair. Keeping very still seemed to make the sickness retreat a little. But Harry and Nick and Heather were all out, so she'd have to answer it. Not that it was likely to be for her—no one knew where she was living. Apart from Max—and *he* wouldn't come.

It was Rupert. He frowned when he saw her. 'You

look even worse than last time I saw you!' he exclaimed.

'Thanks a bunch.' But she couldn't be cross with him for long. His voice held no malice, only concern. 'How did you know where I was living?'

'Max.'

Her heart raced. 'What did he say?'

Rupert shook his head. 'I didn't actually speak to him. His new secretary gave me your address.'

His new secretary. 'He's replaced me, then,' she said in a small, resigned voice. In his office, and in his bed.

Rupert was looking at her closely. 'Are you OK, Shauna? Can I come in?'

She nodded. 'Sure.' She saw his nose wrinkle a little as he stepped inside. She'd cleaned the sitting-room, but Buckingham Palace it wasn't. Well, it was too bad.

To her surprise, his face held an unusually gentle look. 'Shauna, what in hell's name are you doing here?'

Grey eyes were turned moodily in his direction. 'What does it look like? I'm living here.'

'But why? It's dreadfully small.'

It was proving impossible to stop her voice from trembling. 'Because I had nowhere else to go, that's why!'

'But you were happy at Max's, weren't you?'

She turned on him; she knew that it wasn't his fault, but she couldn't help herself. 'Yes, I was very happy at Max's, but he thinks...thinks...' Her voice faded away into a whisper.

'Thinks what?'

Her grey eyes glittered with unshed tears. 'He thinks that I'm having an affair with you.'

He shook his head in disbelief. 'No, he can't. Why should he think that?'

'Because of the photo, of course!' she cried.

'The photo?'

'In the paper! In the wretched gossip column!'

Rupert stood up abruptly, and stared at her. 'He thought that?' he said slowly, then nodded his head, as if in confirmation of his own question. 'Yes, he would,' he said, almost as an afterthought. The bright blue eyes were questioning. 'And tell me something, Shauna. How do you feel about Max?'

She shook her head. 'It doesn't matter any more. It's too late.'

'No!' All at once, his voice sounded very adult and serious as he read the answer in her eyes. 'It's not too late. It's never too late, Shauna. Only death makes things too late…'

Shauna frowned as she saw pain shutter the usually carefree face, and, moments later, it was as if he had been galvanised into action, for he moved quickly towards the door.

'Aren't you going to stay—for tea, or something?' she asked, thinking as she did so how tired her voice sounded.

'Things to do,' he said briskly, and shut the door behind him.

Harry and Nick still hadn't returned, and Shauna had been sick twice, when the door went again. She sighed as she got up to open it, then almost crumpled when she saw who it was who stood there, dripping wet, as though he had been standing in the rain for a long time.

She stared at him, white-faced. 'What are you doing here, Max?'

'May I come in?'

She hesitated. What good could come from seeing him?

The green eyes narrowed. 'Please?'

She nodded, afraid to speak, and opened the door for him.

He bent his head a little as he stepped inside. The flat, which was small anyway, immediately shrank to doll's-house-like proportions. He seemed almost larger than life—she'd forgotten the glowing vibrancy which he gave off as an aura.

She had expected to feel a mass of confused emotions. What she had not expected was to find that she felt exactly the same about him. There was still that warm rush of longing, still the desire to be encircled in those strong, protective arms. Her body still knew a sharpening reaction to his proximity. He had broken her heart and she was fickle enough to love him still.

They faced one another across the shabby hearth-rug. She thought that even in a few weeks he looked different. Thinner, with skin stretched tight over a face which was rigid with tension. And she knew that she looked different, too. Pale-faced and hollow-eyed.

'You've lost weight,' he said eventually.

'Yes.' She wanted to scream, to cry, to run into his arms, but she still didn't know why he was here. Her eyes widened questioningly. 'Why are you here, Max?'

'Rupert came to see me,' he said.

She shook her head in vehement denial. 'Well, he shouldn't have done. He had no right.'

'No.' The word was a flat contradiction. 'I had no right. No right at all to accuse you of something of which you were innocent.'

She felt that her knees were going to buckle under her, and perhaps he saw the slight sway, for he put his hand out as if to steady her, then withdrew it.

'Will you sit down, Shauna? I have something that I want to tell you.'

She complied automatically, her body sinking gratefully into the bursting leather armchair. Grey eyes clashed with green. She felt herself instinctively softening under his gaze, and her lashes quickly dropped to conceal her eyes. She didn't want him to know how vulnerable she was around him. Not now it was all over.

'I never told you very much about my wife,' he began, in the tone of someone who wanted to get the story over with. 'But you guessed that it was not a happy marriage, didn't you?'

She nodded. There had been a cool distance in his voice whenever he had spoken of Blanche, like a man describing a stranger—not a much-loved spouse. She found herself imprisoned in the bright green gaze of his eyes.

'When I met Blanche, we were both very young.

She was a very beautiful woman—and I was knocked for six by her.' He ran his hand through already ruffled dark hair. 'I guess we mistook lust for love,' he said at last.

There was a short, intense silence. Shauna could scarcely breathe. Where on earth was all this leading? But she said nothing, just sat and waited.

'She became pregnant.' The voice was harsh. 'And, for the sake of the baby—we married. It was a mistake.' He met her eyes then, staring at her with a candour which triggered off a feeling of hope.

'I'm not saying that we didn't try—because we did. But we were both so very young, and basically incompatible and—it was a difficult time. I was working all hours to get the business started, and, consequently, I was hardly ever there. We had a beautiful house, but not much cash.' He hesitated. 'And then Rupert came back.'

'Rupert?' she echoed, confused.

He nodded. 'We'd grown up together, gone to the same school—we were the best of mates. He wanted to see the world, and when he arrived in Australia he liked it so much that he decided to stay. He didn't come back until Bianca was a few weeks old, when he met Blanche for the first time.' The lines around his mouth were carved as if in stone. 'Rupert had plenty of money to throw around—he was a pretty attractive prospect, and,' he shrugged, 'he and Blanche—fell in love. I didn't know a thing about it—didn't even guess—I was too busy starting up the business.' There was a pause. 'The night she died she was leaving me to go to him.'

Suddenly, she understood. Everything. His furious reaction to the newspaper photo. It must have seemed like a particularly warped instance of history repeating itself. 'Oh, Max,' she cried. 'For God's sake— why didn't you tell me about Rupert?' she demanded.

'When? When I was so busy procrastinating about my own feelings about you? Trying to stay away from you, to fight the way I felt about you? What right did I have to tell you who you should or shouldn't see? I had intended to tell you when I got back from the Cotswolds, but then...'

'But then there was supposed evidence linking me to Rupert,' she said slowly. 'Oh, Max—you didn't even give me a chance to explain. I thought that you were glad of a reason to end it.'

'Glad?' His voice was bleak. 'I wasn't thinking straight at all. I was struck by a jealousy so blinding that I just lashed out. I'd never felt that violently about a woman before, not ever. Afterwards, when I'd had time to think about it, I realised that everything I knew about you—everything in your soft and gentle and funny nature—belied what I believed. Only I thought it was too late, by then. I thought that you'd despise me for my lack of faith. Rupert came to see me today. He told me that it was time we buried the past, for Bianca's sake. That we should each stop blaming the other for Blanche, that she was dead now, and nothing could bring her back. He also told me that there was nothing between you, that, yes—he'd tried it on. But that he was sorry he had because when he saw you, how miserable you were and—'

'Yes,' she said, bitterly. 'Poor little Shauna, moping and pining inside on her own.'

'How miserable I was,' he finished quietly.

She looked up, her grey eyes disbelieving. 'And why should you be miserable, Max?'

'Because I love you.'

Bizarrely, the sound of a car hooting outside the flat intruded on her consciousness. She blinked as if she had imagined it.

'I love you,' he said again, very steadily.

This time she was blinking back salt tears which slid down the back of her throat. She had some questions of her own. 'And what about Marta?' she whispered. 'She was staying in the Cotswolds, too, wasn't she? Were you having a final fling with her?' she finished bitterly.

'What?' he breathed incredulously.

'Marta was there, wasn't she? Why else did you run off the following morning, as if you couldn't wait to be away from me, as if you couldn't wait to get back to her?'

'Yes, Marta was there,' he said quietly. 'I had to get away that morning because I realised that I'd fallen in love with you, and that terrified the hell out of me.' He smiled at her. 'You once asked me what had made me so cynical about women—well, I'll tell you. After Blanche had died there was never a shortage of women, but the fact that all my money was tied up in the business with none left to throw around meant that I was never considered husband material.'

He gave a dry laugh. 'How all that changed once I started making it. Those same women suddenly found an overwhelming urge to settle down and discovered that all they had ever really wanted was to bake bread and be waiting by the fireside every night.

'But you,' his gaze softened, 'were different. I knew that you didn't give a damn for the money. I knew that you genuinely cared—and not just for me, but for Bianca, too. That night I spent with you I finally admitted to myself what I think I'd known all along—that I didn't want the kind of ''no ties, no questions'' relationship that I was used to. Not with you. That with you it was serious business.' The voice lowered. 'All or nothing. The real McCoy. But I also owed it to Marta to tell her that I'd finally fallen in love.'

The impulse to throw herself into his arms was as strong as she'd ever known it. But not yet. 'And what about Trudy?' she persisted.

He laughed. 'I went out with Trudy *years* ago. I kept her on as my accountant because, as I told you—she's superb at her job.' He saw her face. 'However,' he amended hastily, 'I have been thinking of moving to a larger firm of accountants for some time. Listen, sweetheart—there's no one but you. Not since the first day you walked into my office, looking so fresh, and young and vibrant—so different from the other women. You have managed to become a part of my every waking moment. My daughter loves you, Mrs Roberts loves you—every damn person you meet loves you. I was being spectacularly dense not to realise that I was among them.'

He smiled. 'I wasn't looking for love, Shauna, or expecting it. It just crept up on me. The night I spent with you was the most perfect of my life, but I just needed a bit of space—to think things through. The question is,' and here he held his hand out to her, 'whether you think you could consider sharing your life with a man to whom trust doesn't come very easily?'

There was no contest. No contest at all. The bottom line was that they loved one another, and wasn't love the finest foundation for trust which existed? She caught the hand and smiled into his eyes. 'I would consider it,' she said, very softly. 'Because I love you very much, and you're going to learn that you can trust me whatever happens.'

He cupped her face in his hands to look at her for a long, precious moment before lowering his mouth on to hers to kiss her with a sweetness which took her breath away, so much that, trembling, she broke the kiss to lean weakly against him, her mouth against the strong column of his neck, her warm breath fanning the smooth skin there.

'And let's face it,' he mused, 'if I hadn't been in love with you, I'd have sacked you weeks ago!'

'Why, you—' But the playful punch was deflected, caught and kissed.

'Can we go home soon?' he whispered. 'Because if those flatmates of yours walk in, they may get something of a shock!'

'Why?' she enquired with teasing innocence as he began to kiss her, but then she gave a small whimper of delight mingled with shock as he moved her hand down to touch him and she realised just how badly he wanted her.

'Let's go home to bed,' he growled. 'Before I do something which could ruin my reputation forever.'

She took a deep breath; she still wasn't sure how he was going to take this. 'Before we do, there's something I ought to tell you.'

Shauna rolled over, reaching out automatically for her watch on the bedside table.

Max gave a muffled moan of protest and his hand moved sensuously round her waist and up, to stroke expertly at her breast. She gave a little sigh of pleasure, but, remembering the time, moved her warm body fractionally away from his.

'Come back here,' he murmured, pulling her back firmly into his arms, to rub the hard evidence of his arousal slowly against the high firmness of her bottom.

'Max,' she protested unconvincingly. 'You really ought to be getting up.'

'That's exactly what I had in mind,' he said wickedly, as he began to kiss the sensitive area behind her ear.

'Max!' The hand had moved from her breast and was now tracing light circles over her flat stomach. 'Stop that! I ought to think about giving David his breakfast.'

'Bianca will do that,' he said easily. 'She's off to university tomorrow, and she'll miss her little brother.'

Shauna snuggled luxuriously into his arms.

'We've hardly seen him since she's been home for the holidays.'

'That's because she loves her brother, and she likes to give her parents a break,' he smiled.

'You must be very proud of her, darling,' she whispered, running a forefinger lightly over the broad chest.

He propped himself up on one elbow and looked down at her lovingly. 'I am,' he agreed. 'And I still find it hard to believe that our tearaway schoolgirl should have turned her hand to law—and won a place at Oxford, to boot. But most of it's down to you, sweetheart—you brought such love and stability into this house when you married me. Bianca couldn't help but flourish, and neither could I.'

He smiled at her tenderly and she was reminded of his face a long time ago, in a small flat on a cold winter's day.

Laughter lit her eyes. 'Do you remember the day I told you I was pregnant?'

'Do I? You sent me reeling!'

She grew warm with pleasure under the approbation in his eyes. 'I was scared you'd mind.' It was not the first time she'd said it.

'Mind? *Mind*?' he chuckled. A lazy hand brushed lightly over her breasts. 'Do you think it's time we started making some more?'

'Oh, yes, please,' she said softly.

'Well, then,' he teased her. 'You shouldn't try and stop your husband from doing what comes very naturally. Now,' he drawled, 'just where was I?'

He moved his hand back to her stomach, and in a

leisurely way began to trail it slowly downwards until he had reached the tangle of silky hair, and beyond. She gave a sharp gasp of pleasure. His fingers stayed right where they were, but unmoving, and his eyes were twinkling.

'Want me to stop?'

'No—oh,' she shuddered.

'Sure?'

'Yes!'

'Then tell me you love me.'

'Oh, Max,' she breathed. 'I love you very much.'

'That's good,' he said contentedly, and he bent down and began to kiss her.

INSTANT FIRE

by
Liz Fielding

For my mother,
who opened so many doors.

CHAPTER ONE

THERE was an urgency about the ring and Joanna groaned. It was the first Saturday she hadn't worked in weeks and she had planned a lazy morning. She pulled on her dressing-gown. 'I'm coming,' she called, as there was a second peremptory burst on the bell.

The postman grinned as she opened the door. 'Sorry. Miss Grant, but this one needs signing for.' Jo took the recorded delivery letter and signed where the postman indicated. 'Thanks. You can go back to bed now.' She glared at his back, then turned the letter over. The envelope was thick. Nothing cheap about whoever sent the letter inside, she thought. She opened it and unfolded the single sheet. She read it quickly through and frowned. It was from a firm of solicitors offering to purchase, at a very good price indeed, a block of shares she had inherited from her father.

She read it through a second time. The purchaser was not named. 'A gentleman has instructed us...' that was all. Jo shrugged and threw the letter on to her desk to answer later. It didn't matter who the 'gentleman' was. Her shares in Redmond Construction were not for sale.

'You, lad!'

Jo flung a contemptuous glance over the scaffolding. Another short-sighted idiot who assumed that because she was on a construction site she must be male. Nevertheless she inspected the figure standing in the yard with interest. He was leaning against a gunmetal-grey Aston Martin and despite the foreshortened angle she could see that he was well above average height. In fact, she thought, dressed in a beautifully cut lightweight tweed suit, he was an altogether impressive figure, and gave the disturbing impression that he wasn't short of anything.

'What do you want?' she called down.

He raised a hand to shade his eyes against a sudden shaft of sunlight breaking through the clouds.

'I'm looking for Joe Grant. Is he up there?' he called.

'I'll come down,' she shouted, swinging herself on to the first of a series of ladders to descend the fifty-odd feet to the ground and then turning to face the stranger. She had been right about his height. Despite owning to five feet ten inches in stockings she was forced to look up into the lean, weather-beaten face of a man whose very presence commanded attention. And into remarkable blue eyes which contrasted vividly with a pelt of black curly hair that no amount of the most expert cutting would ever quite keep under control. Blue eyes that were regarding her with puzzlement, as if he knew something wasn't right, but couldn't quite put his finger on what was bothering him.

The sudden rise in her pulse-rate at the sight of this tanned stranger, the heat that seared her cheekbones and parted her lips, an immediate recognition of some deep primeval need that he had stirred, shook her easy assurance.

She clamped her lips together. 'Well?' she demanded and her voice was shockingly sharp in her ears.

A slight frown creased his forehead. 'My name is Thackeray,' he said, his soft voice seeming to vibrate into her very bones. 'I'm looking for Joe Grant. A girl at the office told me he was working here.'

Jo stuck her hands deep in her pockets in an unconsciously boyish gesture and walked quickly away from him. 'You'd better come over to the site office, Mr Thackeray,' she looked back over her shoulder and called to him.

'I've been to the office already. He's not there.' He seemed reluctant to follow her.

'He will be.' Jo opened the door and waited. The man shrugged and moved after her and she went inside, removing her hard hat, enjoying the small triumph of satisfaction at the exclamation from behind her as a thick mop of dark blonde hair swung free to frame her face. She shrugged out of the ancient Barbour, several sizes too large, and turned to face him. 'I'm Jo Grant, Mr Thackeray. Now, what exactly can I do for you?'

A smile charged his eyes with warmth as he acknowledged his mistake. 'I can think of any number of things. Accept my most humble apologies, perhaps?'

'Perhaps,' she conceded, cloaking her heart's racketing response to his smile in cool politeness. This man had never been humble.

'Does it happen often?'

'Often enough. There's no reason for you to feel stupid.'

'Oh, I don't,' he said, easily. 'Dressed in an outsized

jacket, wellingtons and a hard hat, even the most glamorous woman might be mistaken for a boy.'

His amusement was galling. And she hadn't missed
the implication that since she wasn't glamorous it was
perfectly reasonable for him to make such a mistake.

'Perhaps you would get to the point, Mr Thackeray?'

'The point, Miss Grant?'

'You were looking for me. You've found me.'

'Oh, the point!' The smile died on his lips and his
expression became quite still. 'The point is this, Jo
Grant. I came to ask the bearer of that name out to
lunch. So? What do you say?'

Jo drew her brows together in genuine surprise.
'Lunch? Why on earth would you want to take me out
to lunch.'

He looked at her more intently. 'You would find
such an invitation surprising?' he asked. There was a
certain practised charm about him and she realised,
with a slight shock, that he was flirting with her.

'Of course I'm surprised. You don't know me.'

'True,' he conceded. 'And I have to own up to the
fact that the Joe Grant I'm looking for weighs around
fifteen stone, has a beard and is in his fifties. But I am
very happy to accept you as his substitute.'

Jo sat down rather suddenly. 'No substitute at all,
I'm afraid. But I'm the nearest you're going to get. My
father is dead.'

'Joe's dead?' There was no disguising the shock in
his voice. 'But he was no age.' He seemed genuinely
upset and for a moment stared through the window.
Then he looked down at her as if seeing her for the
first time. 'You're Joe's daughter? The one in the pic-

ture on his desk?' He frowned. 'But you were all spectacles and braces.'

Jo remembered the dreadful picture in an old frame that had been almost buried among the clutter on her father's desk. 'Yes, I'm afraid I was. Poor Dad. I usually managed to avoid having my photograph taken, but that was a school job. There was no escape. Mum felt obliged to buy it but out of deference to my feelings she wouldn't put it next to my sister's.'

'Really? Why was that?'

'Heather has curls, straight teeth and twenty-twenty vision.' She shrugged. 'Dad took pity on me.'

Measuring blue eyes regarded her with provoking self-assurance. 'I'm certain you'd give your sister a run for her money these days, Miss Grant.'

She smiled slightly. 'I'm afraid not, Mr Thackeray. Heather is still the family beauty. I had to make do with the brains.'

'Poor you.'

Jo stiffened. 'I don't require sympathy, Mr Thackeray,' she blurted out, then coloured furiously at her stupid outburst as she saw the laughter lighting the depths of his eyes. This man was getting under her skin, breaking through the barriers she had erected as part of the price for her acceptance in a man's world.

'Your self-esteem still seems in need of a little propping up, if you don't mind my saying so. But I have to agree that you have no need of sympathy from me, or anyone else.' Before she could reply he had changed the subject. 'Joe said you planned to follow in his footsteps. I thought he was joking.'

'So did he, Mr Thackeray. By the time he realised his mistake it was too late to do anything about it.'

'Did he try?'

She remembered the pride on his face at her graduation, her mother's delight. 'Not very hard,' she assured him.

His look was thoughtful. 'I see.'

She had assumed he would take his leave once he had discovered that his errand was fruitless. Instead he folded himself into the chair at the side of her desk.

'I'm very sorry to hear about Joe's death, Miss Grant. What happened?' There was a genuine concern in his face which brought the old familiar ache to her throat. She stared hard at the schedules on the desk in front of her until the dangerous prickling behind her eyelids was under control.

'He was in his car. Apparently he had a heart attack.' Jo dragged her mind back to the present and looked up. 'It was three years ago.'

'I'm sorry. I didn't know. I've been overseas, working in Canada. I've been renewing some old acquaintances and when I phoned Redmonds' office to ask for your father they said—'

'It's all right. A simple mistake. It happens all the time; I should have learned to be less prickly by now.' She offered him her hand and a slightly rueful smile. 'Joanna Grant.'

His grasp was warm, the strong hand of a man you would want on your side. 'Clayton Thackeray.'

'Well, I'm sorry you had a wasted journey, Mr Thackeray.'

'Hardly wasted.' His eyes were intensely, disturbingly blue, and she looked hurriedly away.

'I'm not much of a substitute for Dad.'

'I liked and admired your father, Joanna. But it occurs to me that lunch with you will be every bit as enjoyable. And you're a great deal easier on the eye. Now that you've dispensed with the braces.'

'Don't be silly,' she protested. 'You don't have to take me...' He waited, his face betraying nothing. 'I shouldn't...'

'Why not?' he asked.

'Because...' There was no reason, apart from the fact that she wanted to go far too much for her own peace of mind.

He smiled as if he could see the battle taking place inside her head. 'Force yourself, Joanna.'

'I...' He still had her hand firmly clasped in his much larger one. 'Thank you.' She found herself agreeing, without quite understanding why. Except that she didn't think he was the kind of man who ever took no for an answer.

'My pleasure. I booked a table at the George on my way through the village. I'd planned to take your father there.'

'Did you? Then I'd better change my boots.' She put her head to one side and decided it was her turn to tease a little. 'But you don't have to impress me, Mr Thackeray. I'm just a site engineer. I usually have a sandwich down the pub.'

Laughter produced deep creases around his eyes and down his cheeks. 'I'm not looking for a job, Joanna.

And my friends call me Clay. Do what you have to.
I'll wait in the car.'

She kicked off her boots, slipped her feet into narrow
low-heeled shoes and ran a clothes brush over her grey
woollen trousers, wishing for once that she had a skirt
to change into. Her soft cream shirt had been chosen
more for comfort than style, but at least her sweater
was a pretty, if impractical, mixture of pink and white.
A gift from her Heather, her older sister, who ran a
stylish boutique and never ceased in her attempts to
add a little femininity to Jo's wardrobe which tended
to run to hardwearing clothes suitable for the site. She
took down the calendar that hid the mirror, her one
concession to vanity in this male world, and regarded
her reflection with disfavour.

Then she shrugged. 'Don't kid yourself, Jo,' she told
herself sternly. 'He's taking you out to lunch because
he knew your father. Don't get any silly ideas.' She
pulled a face at herself, but nevertheless Heather would
have been pleased to see how long her little sister spent
on her hair and make-up.

Clay Thackeray ushered her into the car, opening the
door and settling her comfortably before sliding into
the driving seat. She was aware of interested eyes
watching from every part of the site and knew that she
would be teased mercilessly for the next few days by
men opening doors with exaggerated politeness, offering her their arm on the scaffolding. They wouldn't
miss a trick.

'It would be just the same if you were a man being
picked up by a girl, you know. Probably worse.' He
reversed the car and turned into the lane.

She laughed. 'Do you read minds for a living?'

'No, but I was a site engineer myself once.'

'Were you?' Jo gave him a sideways glance from under long, dark lashes. He'd come a long way from that lowly position. 'And I have no doubt that a great many girls picked you up.'

He turned and smiled. 'A few,' he admitted. 'And your father certainly knew how to tease.'

'Yes, he did.' She had worked on sites with him during the long summer holidays from university and she had seen him at work. Had been the butt of his jokes, too. The slightest mistake was ruthlessly exploited. She had hated it, but it had toughened her up. The Aston purred as he drove gently down the lane. 'This is a lovely car.'

'Yes, it was my father's. He hasn't driven it much in recent years but he wouldn't let me buy it from him until he considered I was old enough to be trusted with it.'

'And are you?'

'Thirty-three?' he offered. 'What do you think? The old man wanted to wait another year. He didn't have his first Aston until he was nearly thirty-five. But I forced his hand. I threatened to buy a BMW.' He turned into the George's car park.

'What a dreadful thing to do!' But the laughter in her voice softened the words.

'Wasn't it?' Their hands touched as he reached to unclip her seatbelt and they looked up at the same moment. For a long second Jo thought the world must have stopped spinning. 'I want to kiss you, Jo Grant.' His voice grated over a million tiny nerve-endings and she swallowed. Her pulse was hammering in her ears and she could hardly breathe. Girls weren't supposed to kiss men they had just met. They certainly weren't supposed to admit they wanted to.

Jo fought the inclination to meet him halfway and lifted one brow. 'And do you always get what you want, Clayton Thackeray?'

'Always,' he assured her.

Flustered by the unwavering certainty in his eyes, she made an effort at a laugh. 'Really, Mr Thackeray, I thought the form was that you wine and dine a girl before you make a pass,' she said, attempting to hide her bewildering, unexpected hunger for this man, bury it under a flippancy she was far from feeling.

Clay Thackeray stared at her for a moment, then he released the seatbelt, making her jump, breaking the spell. 'You're right, of course. And this is only lunch. I'll have to give some thought to the question of dinner.'

Before she could gather her wits he was opening the car door for her. His hand under her arm seemed to burn through the sleeve of her jacket and neither of them spoke as he led her inside the restaurant. Clay caught the eye of the waiter and they were shown straight to their table in the corner, overlooking the river.

Jo kept her eyes firmly on the view from the window, anything but face the man opposite. She spent her working life with men and they rarely managed to find her at a loss for a word. But right now she couldn't think of a thing to say. At least nothing that made any sense.

No such problem tormented Clay. 'Let me see if I can read your thoughts again,' he suggested. Jo's grey eyes widened. The disturbing thoughts racing unbidden through her mind were not the kind she wanted him to read. 'Duck?' he said softly, a suspicion of laughter in his voice.

'Is that an instruction or an observation?' she asked, making a supreme effort to keep the atmosphere light.

'An observation,' he replied, drily, pointing to the birds on the riverbank. 'You seem to be fascinated by them; I thought perhaps you were deciding which one you wanted for lunch.' He offered her the menu. 'Or perhaps you'd rather run an eye over this?'

Jo buried her face in the menu and by the time the waiter returned to take their order had regained something of her natural composure.

'Something to drink?'

'A pineapple juice topped up with soda, please.'

Clay relayed this request to the waiter and added a mineral water for himself.

'You said you have just come back from Canada?' Jo asked, leading the conversation into neutral territory. 'What were you doing there?'

'Working. My mother was a French Canadian. When she died I realised how little I knew about her or where she came from. I wanted to find out.'

'And now you're having a holiday?'

He hesitated for a moment before he said, 'Not exactly. But I'm looking up old friends. When the receptionist at Redmonds said Joe was working here it was close enough to home to take a chance on finding him at the site.'

'Home?' She tried to ignore the treacherous rise in her pulse-rate at the thought of him living near by.

'I bought a cottage on the river at Camley when I was over at Christmas.'

He was staying, and she was ridiculously, stupidly pleased. 'I love Camley. It's so unspoilt.' She was babbling, but he seemed not to notice.

'Yes. It's the reason I bought the place.' He pulled a face. 'Stupid, really. My offices are in London; a service flat would be a lot less bother. But I couldn't resist the cottage. It's old and it needs a lot of work, but I suppose that was part of its charm. The builder has finished putting the structure to rights and it's habitable, but I'm just camping there at the moment.'

'So you're not going back to Canada?'

'Not permanently. At least for the foreseeable future.' He regarded her with steady amusement. 'Are you pleased?' he asked.

The arrival of the waiter saved her from the embarrassment of a reply and she regarded the poached salmon he placed before her with a sudden loathing for its pinkness…the same colour that she was only too aware was staining her cheeks.

'Hollandaise?' Forced to look up, she discovered that he wasn't laughing at her as she had suspected. His smile was unexpectedly warm. 'I am,' he said. 'Very pleased.'

She swallowed and took the dish he offered. 'Did you work with Dad for long?' she asked, the catch in her voice barely noticeable.

'He was my first project manager. I came to

Redmonds from university and was put to work under him. I was very fortunate. You must miss him.'

'Yes, I miss him. I wanted him to...' Her voice trailed away. That was too private a need to be shared. Not something to be spoken aloud.

Sensitive to the fact that he had strayed into dangerous territory, he changed the subject, describing his life in Canada, the country. On safer ground, Jo at last began to relax.

When coffee arrived he sat back in his chair and regarded her seriously. 'So what are your career plans, Joanna? Surely you don't intend to stay on site?'

'I was the first woman that Redmonds employed as a site engineer,' she said, with a certain pride. 'I plan to be the first woman they appoint as a project manager.'

If he was surprised he hid it well enough, but his next question suggested that he had some understanding of the problems involved. 'Does that leave you any room for a personal life?'

'Not much,' she admitted.

'But what about marriage? Raising a family?'

'Men manage to have both.' She was no stranger to this argument. Her sister had tried so many times to persuade her to take up a more conventional career that she had once offered to make a tape recording and play it at least once a day to save her the bother. But Heather had long since stopped trying to change her and confined her efforts these days to improving her wardrobe.

'True, and probably not very fair. But men don't get pregnant. Climbing up and down ladders might get to be a bit of a problem, don't you think?'

Since Jo had no intention of getting pregnant in the foreseeable future, she ignored the question and glanced at her watch. 'It's late. I should get back.'

Clay regarded her thoughtfully for a moment, but didn't pursue the subject. Instead he summoned the waiter and asked for the bill. 'Now, about dinner. Where shall I pick you up?'

Surprise that he should want to see her again made her laugh a little uncertainly. 'There's no need, Clay, really. It was very kind of you to take me out to lunch, but—'

'I didn't bring you here to be kind.' He leaned forward. 'I still want to kiss you, Jo Grant. You were the one who stipulated being wined and dined first. Of course, perhaps you've changed your mind.' His eyes glinted wickedly. 'In which case I'll be happy to oblige right now.'

'I didn't…' Joanna bit back the denial and stood up. It was a ridiculous conversation and she had no intention of prolonging it. Clay rose and she smiled, graciously, she hoped. 'Please don't let me rush you.' She offered Clay her hand and he shook it solemnly. 'Thank you for lunch. I won't trouble you for a lift. I can get a taxi back to work.' She moved swiftly across the dining-room, making for the pay-phone in Reception, where she searched furiously in her bag.

'Can I offer you some change?' He was leaning against the wall, watching her.

'No, thank you,' Jo said coldly. Then, as she realised that she had none, she changed her mind. 'Yes,' she snapped.

'It'll be at least ten minutes before one comes,' Clay

said, gently, offering her a handful of silver coins. 'Why don't you want me to take you?'

She refused to meet his eye. Selecting a ten-pence coin, Jo fiercely punched in the number of the local taxi service listed by the phone.

'Don't you want me to kiss you?' he asked, seriously. 'I rather thought you did.'

The phone was ringing in her ear. 'Keble Taxis, how can I help you?'

'I should like a taxi to collect me from the George as quickly as possible, please,' Jo said, studiously ignoring the man at her side.

'We're rather busy at the moment,' the girl told her. 'It'll be twenty minutes.'

'Twenty minutes!'

Clay took the phone from her hand and spoke into the receiver. 'We'll leave it, thank you.' He hung up. 'I can't have you late for work, can I? Not a dedicated career-woman like you. You'll be quite safe, I promise.'

Before she could protest further he had opened the door and swept her towards the car. Settled against the worn leather, Jo was aware of a certain breathlessness. On site, except for visits from the project manager, she was in control. But she had somehow lost that control when Clay Thackeray had walked into her office. The word safe was completely inappropriate. He was a dangerously disturbing man.

They didn't speak as they sped along the country lanes and it was with a certain relief that Jo saw the site earthworks appear above the hedge. Clay pulled into the yard and stopped. She tried to escape but he

was faster, catching her hand as she moved to release
the seatbelt, holding it against his chest so that she
could feel the steady thudding of his heart.

'Now you have to decide, Jo Grant.'

Jo glared at him. 'You promised!'

'Did I?' He challenged her softly. 'I remember saying that you would be safe. I didn't specify what I
would keep you safe from.'

How could such open, honest eyes hide such a de-
vious nature? she fumed. 'In that case I'll get it over
with now, if it's all the same to you.' Ignoring the fact
that they had the rapt attention of the site staff, she
closed her eyes and waited. A soft chuckle made her
open them again. Clay was shaking his head.

'Round one to you, ma'am. On points.' He leaned
across and pushed open the door for her. For a moment
she sat, completely nonplussed. 'Well? Are you going
to sit there all afternoon? I thought you were in a
hurry.'

'Yes.' She made an effort to pull herself together.
'Thank you again for lunch,' she said, auto-matically.

She climbed from the car and walked quickly across
to her office, firmly refusing to give in to the impulse
to look back.

It was Thursday before he phoned. A whole week.

'Joanna?' Her heart skipped a beat as the low voice
spoke her name.

'Clay?' she echoed the query in his voice, but ruefully acknowledged that the man knew how to play the
game. She had been on tenterhooks all week, expecting
him to turn up at the site every moment. The mere

glimpse of a grey car was enough to send her heart on a roller-coaster. But he hadn't come and she had called herself every kind of fool for refusing his invitation to dinner. And then called herself every kind of fool for wanting to get involved with him. He was completely out of her reach. She hadn't the experience to cope with such a man. She hadn't the experience, full stop.

'How are you, Joanna?' She could almost see the cool amusement in those eyes.

'Fine, thank you. And you? Are you enjoying your holiday?'

'Not much. I've been in the Midlands all week on business. But you could change all that. Have dinner with me tonight.'

'Have all your old girlfriends got married while you've been away?' she parried, a little breathlessly, not wishing to seem too eager.

He chuckled. 'Most of them. It has been nearly seven years. Will you come?'

'I...' For a moment there was war between desire and common sense. Desire had no competition. 'I'd love to.'

CHAPTER TWO

It was late when Jo finally parked the car behind the old house in the nearby market town of Woodhurst. She let herself into the first-floor flat that she had rented for the duration of the job and dumped her shopping on the kitchen table.

She wasted very little time in the shower and quickly dried her hair, a thick, dark blonde mop, streaked with pale highlights from so much time spent out of doors. There had been a time when she had wondered what it would be like to have curls like her sister, but had long since accepted the fact that they weren't for her. Her nose was a little too bold and her mouth overlarge. Curls, a kindly hairdresser had told the fourteen-year-old Joanna as he'd cut away the disastrous results of Heather's attempt to provide the missing locks with a home perm, were for those girls whose face lacked character. She hadn't believed him, even then, but these days she was content with a style that needed little more than a cut once every three weeks to keep it looking good.

Satisfied with her hair, she spent a great deal longer than usual on her make-up and painted her nails pale pink. Tonight she was determined to be Joanna Grant. Jo the site engineer could, for once, take a back seat.

She had few evening clothes and she hadn't needed to deliberate on what she would wear. She stepped into a floating circle of a skirt in pale grey georgette and topped it with a long-sleeved jacket in toning greys and pinks with a touch of silver thread in the design. She fastened large pale pink circles of agate twisted around with silver to her ears and regarded the result with a certain satisfaction. It was quite possible, she thought, with some amusement, that, in the unlikely event they should bump into any of her colleagues tonight, they would be hard pressed to recognise her.

Slipping her feet into low-heeled grey pumps, Jo spun in front of her mirror, coming to a sudden halt at the sound of her doorbell. She stood for a moment, as if rooted to the spot, vulnerable, uncertain of herself. Then the fear that he might not wait lent wings to her heels as she flew to the door.

Clay, his tall figure a study in elegance in the stark blackness of a dinner-jacket, was leaning against the stairpost regarding the toe of his shoe, and he glanced up as she flung open the door. He started to smile and then stopped, cloaking the expression in his eyes as he straightened and stared at the girl framed in the doorway.

'Are those for me?' Jo asked finally, to break the silence.

He glanced down at a spray of pink roses as if he couldn't think where they had come from, then back at her.

'I rather think they must be.'

'Come in. I'll put them in some water. Would you like a drink?' she asked, trying to remember what she had done with a bottle of sherry left over from Christmas.

'No, thanks.' He followed her into the cramped kitchen and watched as she clipped the stems and stood them in deep water to drink.

She turned to him. 'These are lovely, Clay. Thank you.'

'So are you, Joanna. No one would ever mistake you for a boy tonight.' He took a step towards her then turned away, raking long fingers through his hair. 'I think we had better go.' For the briefest moment it had seemed as if he was going to kiss her, and the thought quickened her blood, sending it crazily through her veins. Instead he opened the door and she followed him down the stairs to the waiting taxi.

'Where are we going?' she asked.

'A little place I know by the river.' This deprecating description hardly did justice to the elegant restaurant overlooking the Thames and she told him so.

'I thought you would like to come here.' He seemed oddly distracted.

'It's beautiful.'

He turned and looked down at her. 'Yes. It is.' He lifted his hand to her cheek, his fingertips lingering against the smooth perfection of her skin. 'Quite beautiful.'

'May I show you to your table, sir?'

Clay dragged himself back from wherever his thoughts had taken him and he tucked his arm under Joanna's. They made a striking couple as they walked across the restaurant and several heads turned to follow their progress. Joanna was usually forced to disguise her height when walking with a man, never wearing high heels and, if not exactly slumping, at least keeping

what her father had laughingly described as a very relaxed posture. Now, beside the strong figure of Clay
Thackeray, the top of her head just reaching his ear,
she stretched to her full height, human enough to enjoy
the knowledge that she was envied by at least half the
women present. Probably more.

Afterwards she couldn't have described anything
they had eaten or much of what they had talked about,
although she thought he had told her something about
a consultancy that he had begun in Canada and his
plans for expansion into Britain. All she could remember was Clay's face in the candlelight, his hand reaching for hers across the table, the words, 'Let's go
home.'

In the back of the car she curled against him as if
she had known him for years. His arm drew her close
and it seemed the most natural thing in the world to
rest her head on his shoulder. She didn't think about
where they were going. She didn't care, as long as he
held her.

The car eventually stopped and she lifted her head.
'Where are we?' she asked.

'You are home, fair lady. Where did you expect to
be?'

Glad of the darkness to hide her blushes, she allowed
him to help her from the car.

'I'll see you to your door.'

She turned to him at the top of the stairs. 'Would
you like a coffee?'

'I think I'm going to have enough trouble sleeping,
Jo.' His arm was around her waist and she didn't ever
want him to let go of her. As if reading her mind, he

pulled her closer. 'But, before I go, I believe you promised me a kiss.'

She lowered her eyes, suddenly shy. 'Now?' she asked.

'Now,' he affirmed, and his lips touched hers for the briefest moment, the time it took her heart to beat. He drew back the space of an inch, no more. 'Joanna?' His voice was a question and an answer. Then his mouth descended upon hers and her willing response answered any question he cared to ask.

When at last he released her she could hardly support herself, and he held her in the circle of his arms and stood for a moment with her head upon his shoulder.

'I must go.'

'Must you?'

'Don't make it any harder.' He kissed the top of her head and she looked up, but he seemed to be far away, no longer with her. She fumbled in her bag for her key and he took it from her and opened the door.

'Can I see you tomorrow?'

She hesitated for a moment, but then he smiled and on a catch of breath she nodded. 'Yes.'

He raised his hand briefly. 'I'll pick you up at seven.' Then he was gone without a backward glance and for the first time in her life she felt the pain of being torn in two. Her other half had walked down the stairs in the palm of Clay Thackeray's hand.

Joanna wondered briefly, as she stood under a reviving shower, exactly what she had thought about before the appearance of Clay Thackeray. Since his appearance a week earlier he had filled her waking hours completely, and a good few of her sleeping ones.

A ring at the door put a stop to these thoughts and she grabbed a towelling wrap and went to answer it.

'Clay!'

'I'm a little early,' he apologised.

'Just a little,' she agreed, laughter dancing in her eyes. 'I thought we were meeting at seven p.m., not seven a.m.'

'I had this sudden yearning to know what you looked like first thing in the morning.' His eyes drifted down the deep V of her wrap and she grabbed self-consciously at it and tightened the belt, feeling at something of a disadvantage alongside the immaculate dark blue pin-striped suit and stark white shirt.

'Well?'

'Exactly as I imagined. No make-up, bare feet, hair damp from the shower...' she lifted her hand self-consciously, but he anticipated the move and caught her fingers '...and quite beautiful.' He stepped through the door and closed it firmly behind him.

She laughed a little nervously and stepped back in the face of such assured advances. 'Compliments so early in the morning deserve some reward. Would you like some breakfast?'

One stride brought him to her side. He slid an arm around her waist and drew her close. 'That, sweet Joanna, rather depends upon the menu.'

Jo's breathing was a little ragged. 'Eggs?' she heard herself say. He made no response. 'I might have some bacon.' His eyes never left hers. 'Toast?' she offered, desperately. 'I haven't much time. I have to get to...'

He leaned forward and brushed his lips against hers and she no longer cared about the time.

'You, Jo. Don't you know that I want you for breakfast?'

He pulled the knot of her wrap and she made no move to stop him. Last night she knew that with very little persuasion she would have fallen into bed with him. He had known that too. It had been far too easy to fall in love with him. In the long, wakeful hours of the night she had determined that this evening she would put on some emotional armour along with her make-up. But, almost as if he had anticipated this, he had outmanoeuvred her, taking her by surprise with this early-morning raid. No make-up. No armour. No clothes. The harsh ring of the doorbell made her jump and he straightened, a crooked smile twisting his mouth.

'Saved by the bell, Jo.' For a moment he held the edges of her robe, then he pulled it close around her and retied the knot before standing aside for her to open the door.

'Sorry, Miss Grant. Another of those recorded delivery letters for you to sign. You'd better pay up!' She smiled automatically at the postman's bantering humour and signed the form. This time she didn't bother to open the letter, but threw it on the hall table.

'Aren't you going to open it?' Clay asked. 'It looks urgent.'

'I know what it says. It's from someone who wants to buy some shares I own. I've already told them I won't sell.'

'Oh? Maybe they've increased their offer.'

She frowned. 'Do you think so? I wonder why they want them?' Her eyes lingered for a moment on the envelope. 'Perhaps I ought to find out—'

'Forget them! They're not important.' She lifted her eyes to his and all thoughts of shares were driven from her head as he kissed her once more. But the moment of madness had passed and when he finally raised his head she took an unsteady step back.

'I really must get ready for work, Clay.'

'Must you?' He frowned, then shrugged. 'Of course you must. And I'm delaying you.' He turned for the door.

'Clay, why did you come here this morning?'

He paused for a moment, his knuckles white as he gripped the door-handle, as if debating with himself. When he looked back it was with a deadly and earnest force. 'I thought we might have dinner at the cottage tonight,' he said. His eyes were unreadable.

She didn't stop to think. It was already far too late for thinking. 'I'd love to,' she said, the words barely escaping her throat.

She stood in the hall for a long moment after he had left, then, gathering her wits, she turned to get ready for work. Her eyes fell on the letter and impatiently she tore it open. Clay had been right, the offer had indeed been increased. His apparent omniscience gave her a ridiculous burst of pleasure.

Clay arrived on the stroke of seven and Jo picked up the soft leather bag that held everything she might need. She locked the door behind them and opened her bag to drop in the key, then turned to see him watching her.

'Got everything?' he asked.

'Yes, thank you.' Her cheeks were warm as she turned to follow him down the stairs to the waiting car.

The cottage was beautiful and very old, built of narrow autumn-coloured bricks, with a drunken pantile roof where a pair of fantail doves, golden in the evening light, were flirting. The garden had been neglected, but already work had begun to restore the stone pathways and a dilapidated dovecote. He helped her out of the car and for a moment she just stood and took it all in.

'It's lovely.'

'I'm glad you like it. Come and see what I've been doing inside.' Her heart was hammering as he led her up the path and opened the door, standing back to let her step across the threshold and into the hall.

The floor had been newly stripped and repolished and a jewel-rich Persian rug lay before them. She dropped her bag at the bottom of the stairs.

'Hungry?' he asked.

She shook her head. 'Not very. Will you show me round?'

'The grand tour?' He laughed. 'It won't take very long.'

The colour in her cheeks deepened slightly. She just needed a little time to gain her bearings. It would have been so much easier if they had gone out somewhere first. Good food, wine, eased the way.

'This is the study.' His voice made her jump. He opened a door on the left and led the way into a square room littered with wallpaper off-cuts. 'I've been trying to decide which paper to use.'

Glad of something positive to think about, Jo picked up various samples and held them against the wall. 'I like this one,' she said, finally.

'That's settled, then.'

She spun around. 'But...it's your choice.'

'Yes. I know.' He held the door to let her through. 'That's the cloakroom. Storage cupboard,' he said carelessly, as they passed closed doors. 'And this is the morning-room.'

'This is a cottage on a rather grand scale,' she said, admiring the use of yellow and white that would reflect the morning sun. She walked across to a pair of casement windows and opened them, stepping out into the garden. 'You're on the river!' she exclaimed. 'I hadn't realised.' She walked quickly down to the small mooring with its tiny dock.

'There's a boathouse behind those shrubs, but the roof has collapsed.'

'Will you rebuild it?'

'Maybe. Is it warm enough to eat out here, do you think?'

'Oh, yes! I've a sweater in my bag.' Once again the betraying heat stained her cheeks at this reminder.

'Go and get it while I organise the food.'

'You haven't finished the guided tour,' she said quickly. Then wished she hadn't.

'We've the whole evening. Don't be so impatient, Joanna. You'll see everything, I promise.'

She stood for long moments in the hall, making an effort to bring her breathing back under control. It was idiotic to be so jumpy. She was grown up. Twenty-four years old. She found the cloakroom and splashed cold water on to her face. Her eyes seemed twice their normal size in the mirror, the grey abnormally dark. 'Come on, Jo,' she told her reflection. 'You want this man so much it hurts.' If only he would make love to her, all her nerves would be swept away. But it was almost as if he was going out of his way not to touch her.

He had spread a cloth under a willow tree, its curtain providing a cloak of privacy from the passing boats, and was uncorking a bottle.

'Mrs Johnson has done us proud,' he said, as she settled on the rug beside him.

'Mrs Johnson?'

'She cooks, cleans, looks after me like a mother hen.'

'Oh.' Jo wasn't sure she liked the idea of an unknown woman cooking a seduction feast, wondering how many times she had done it before.

He handed her a glass of wine and touched the rim with his own. 'To Love.'

'Love—?'

'"'You must sit down,' says Love, 'and taste my meat.' So I did sit and eat.'"' He solemnly offered her a crab bouchée.

She quickly took one, but it seemed to fill her mouth and stick there. He topped up her glass and she drank nervously. For a moment he watched her, then he toyed with his food.

'How's Charles Redmond these days?'

'Charles?' She frowned. 'Of course, you must know him. He's made a good recovery by all accounts.'

'Will he retire, do you think?'

'I doubt it. The company is his life.' She was so glad of something ordinary to talk about, she didn't stop to consider that her boss was a very odd topic of conversation in the circumstances. She even began to enjoy the food. At last, though, the late May sun had dipped behind the trees and the temperature dropped sharply.

'Come on, you're shivering. I've kept you out here far too long.' He caught her around the waist and hurried her indoors. 'This way.' Clay led the way through a door to the right and turned on a lamp which softly illuminated the drawing-room. The floor was richly carpeted in Wedgwood-blue and a large, comfortable sofa was set square before the fireplace. Behind it stood an eighteenth-century sofa table. A well-rubbed leather wing-chair flanked the hearth. The only modern touch was the hi-fi equipment tucked away in an alcove. He bent and put a match to the fire. 'Warm yourself. I won't be a moment.'

Jo stood in front of the large open brick fireplace, watching the flames lick around the logs, wondering, with a sudden attack of nerves, if she was being an absolute fool. She had prided herself on her detachment, her ability to hold herself aloof from the idiotic disenchantment and pain she had seen her friends put themselves through. She had her job, her career to keep her content. Now here she was, in danger of falling into the same dangerous trap.

'Joanna?' His voice pulled her back to him and she understood then, as they stood side by side in the flickering firelight, just why people made such fools of themselves. Clay solemnly handed two glasses to her and, not once taking his eyes from hers, opened a bottle of champagne and allowed the golden bubbles to foam into them.

He raised his glass in silent homage to her. Jo sipped the champagne, hardly conscious of the bubbles prickling her tongue; only the heightened sensation of expectancy seemed real. The tiny nerve-endings in her skin were all at attention, tingling with nervous excitement, and quite suddenly she was shaking. Clay rescued her glass and stood it on the great wooden beam that formed the mantel.

He drew her into his arms, moulding her against his body, his eyes hooded with desire. 'I want you, Joanna Grant,' he said, and his voice stroked her softly. She leaned her head back slightly and smiled up at him, her self-possession a paper-thin veneer masking the ridiculous racketing of her heart, and as his lips touched hers she closed her eyes.

She thought she knew what it was like to be kissed by Clay Thackeray. Perhaps it was the champagne, or perhaps it was just that she had been anticipating this moment all day. For a few moments his wide, teasing mouth touched hers in a gentle exploration of the possibilities. Then he paused and she opened her eyes, parting her lips in an involuntary sigh as old as time, any lingering doubts having long since evaporated in the heat beating through her veins. He kissed her again, fleetingly, his eyes locked on to hers, then swung her into her arms and carried her to the sofa, sitting with her across his lap, her arms around his neck. For a

moment his gaze focused on her mouth. Gently he outlined her lips with the tip of his finger. She moved
urgently against him and whispered his name.

'Patience, my love. I want to enjoy you. Every bit
of you.'

He peeled away her sweater, but his fingers were
almost unbearably slow as they undid the buttons of
her blouse and pushed the heavy cream silk aside. He
kissed the soft mound of her breast where it swelled
above her bra, then, edging the lace away, his mouth
sought the hard peak of her nipple and she cried out
as he drew it between his teeth and caressed it delicately with his tongue. Her breathing was ragged and
there was a throbbing, desperate ache between her
thighs which was strange and wonderful and which she
was woman enough to know that only he could ease.

Her fingers dug into his shoulders. 'Clay…' Her
voice was pleading.

He raised his head and frowned slightly. 'Have all
your lovers been so hurried?'

'No…' But he wanted no answer; his mouth began
a thorough and systematic plunder of hers, preventing
her attempts to explain, then driving them out of her
head altogether.

After a while he raised his head. 'I think it's time
we went to bed.'

She raised lids heavy with desire and with her fingertips traced the strong line of his jaw and the small
V-shaped scar on his chin. She drew her brows together
in concentration. 'Clay…' He caught her fingers, kissing each one in turn as she struggled to sit up. 'You

should know…that is, I think I'd better tell you that I haven't ever—'

'Haven't what?' His mouth continued to caress her fingers and for a moment there was only silence in the flickering firelight. Then he realised that she had ceased to respond and he raised his head. 'What is it?'

'It was nothing important, Clay.' She tried to keep her voice light, conversational, but to her own ears failed dismally.

'You picked a hell of a moment to play games, sweetheart.' There was a slight edge to his voice. 'If you've got cold feet you only have to say.'

'No.' She threw him a desperate look. 'I just wanted you to know. That's all. I wanted you to know that I'm…' She cleared her throat. 'I haven't…' Why was the word so difficult to say? It was nothing to be ashamed of, after all. It just seemed silly. But surely by now he must understand what she was trying to tell him. Why on earth was he being so *slow*?

He was staring at her, a slight frown creasing the space between his brows. 'Joanna Grant,' he said at last, 'are you trying to tell me that you've never done this before?' She nodded, her face hot with embarrassment. 'That you're twenty-four years old and still a virgin?'

'There's no need to repeat yourself,' Joanna said, fiercely proud. 'I'm well aware how ridiculous I must seem.'

'I…' He seemed for a moment quite unable to speak, then he lifted her on to the sofa and stood up. 'Hardly ridiculous. But unexpected. To say the very least.'

She stood up, then, horribly, embarrassingly conscious of her state of undress, turned her back on him to straighten her clothes. She couldn't understand why it took so long, hardly aware how her fingers were trembling on the buttons. Finally, though, it was done. Pale and empty, she forced herself to face him.

'Could I ring for a taxi?' she asked, with as much dignity as she could muster. 'I think I should go home now.'

'I'm sorry, Joanna.' His regret sounded genuine enough, as well it might, she thought. He looked almost angry. 'I just hadn't anticipated this situation. Most of the women I've known are rather more—'

'You don't have to draw a picture, Clay.'

She should have known. He was used to sophisticated women who knew exactly how to please a man. Why had she ever thought he might be interested in her? Except that he had been, until she had been stupid enough to own up to her virgin state. It wasn't as if she wanted it. There had just been so many other things, important things she had to do.

She fled to the cloakroom. Like the other rooms she had seen, it had been gutted, and there was the smell of fresh plaster. The fittings were starkly new, but the tiles were still in their boxes, stacked against the wall, and the floor was bare board. He'd only just moved in. 'Camping' was the word he'd used. The quality of the fittings gave the word a slightly surrealistic edge. Not that it mattered.

She regarded herself in the mirror. Her cheeks were flushed and her lips red and swollen. She sighed and opened her bag to repair the damage as best she could.

Her sister had once suggested, quite kindly, that virginity beyond the age of twenty was an embarrassment she should try to resolve as quickly as possible. Apparently she had been right, but just now she didn't feel much like telling her so.

Clay was waiting when she emerged. He crossed the hall quickly to take her hand but she avoided his touch. 'Is there a telephone?'

'You don't have to go, Joanna. Can we talk?'

'Talk?' What on earth was there to talk about? she wondered. She hadn't come to talk. Her chin high, she turned away from him before she weakened. 'I'd prefer it if you would call a taxi.'

'Damn your taxi!' He reached for her.

'Now, Clay!' she demanded. If she let him touch her she would lose her hard-won self-control and simply weep.

For a moment the tension held him in suspension, neck muscles knotted into cords, hands clenched. Then, as if he had made a decision, he nodded slightly and relaxed.

'Perhaps you're right. Now is not the time. I'll take you home.'

'There's no need to put yourself to the trouble.'

'There's every need, Joanna. Don't argue.'

She made no further objection, sensing that it would be pointless, but she shook away his steadying hand at her elbow as she stumbled on the uneven path in the gathering darkness.

He insisted on seeing her to the door. She unlocked it and with a supreme effort managed a smile as she turned to face him.

'Goodbye, Clay.' She offered him her hand, sure

now that she was safe. His expression grave, he took it, holding it for a moment as if he would say something. But he didn't speak. Instead he raised her fingers to his lips.

Before she could recover from her surprise he had turned and disappeared down the stairs. She ran to the front window in time to see the car door slam. It remained at the kerb for so long that she began to think he might get out again, but then, very quietly, the car pulled away and disappeared down the street.

No longer needing to keep a rigid control upon her feelings, she let out a long, shuddering sob.

Monday was a bad day at work, but Jo welcomed the problems. It used all her energies, blocked the need to think. She had spent the weekend with her sister, avoiding thinking, for once welcoming the disapproval of the long hours she worked, the unsuitable job. Thinking wouldn't do. She had made an utter fool of herself over Clay Thackeray and she would have to live with the memory of her humiliation for a very long time, but the longer she could put off thinking about it, the better.

'Good morning, Jo.'

Her heart sank. A visit from the project manager was the last thing she needed this morning. She turned to the sleek, tanned figure and forced a smile to her lips.

'Hello, Peter. We didn't expect you back until tomorrow. Had a good holiday?'

'Wonderful, my dear. The Greek islands in May are a perfect joy. You should have come with me.' He didn't exactly leer; he was never quite that obvious.

But he hid his resentment at being landed with a
woman on his site under a surface skim of flirtation
that grated like a nail on a blackboard.

She shrugged and sighed. 'Someone has to stay and
do the work. And I'm sure the company of your wife
was adequate compensation. Do you want me to walk
around with you?'

'No, it's nearly lunchtime. I've just come to take you
all down the pub for a drink. A thank-you for all your
hard work while I've been away. I'll give you a lift.'
He placed his hand on her elbow and steered her towards his car.

Jo bit down hard to prevent herself from screaming.
Not that he ever did anything that could be grounds for
complaint. Just the innuendo and the proprietorial hand
to her back, whenever there was anyone to see, to give
the impression that she belonged to him personally.

Jo made for a table by the fireplace, but he moved
her on to a secluded corner. 'It'll get noisy there when
the place fills up.'

She fumed while he fetched the drinks. It wasn't as
if he was interested in her, and for that at least she
supposed she should be grateful. He was only interested in having the world believe that she was besotted
by him.

'Now, my dear. Tell me everything that's happened
while I've been away. Any problems?'

'Nothing major.' She smiled. 'You should have had
another week in Greece.' The sentiment was heartfelt.

He leaned closer and placed his hand on hers. 'I
couldn't stay away that long.'

She looked up with relief as she heard the door open-

ing in the corner. It would be the men from the site.
But it wasn't them. Clay Thackeray stood framed in
the doorway, very still, taking in the picture the two of
them presented. For a moment their eyes clashed, then
Clay took a step forward, his face taut with anger.

Quite deliberately Jo turned to Peter and smiled into
his startled eyes. 'I'm glad. I've missed you, darling.'
She leaned forward and kissed him lightly on the
mouth.

His reaction should have been comic. It was a moot
point who jumped most visibly—Peter, leaping to his
feet, or Jo, at the crash of the door rattling on its hinges.

It was late when she drove home. The truth of the
matter was that she didn't want to go back to her empty
flat. At least while she was working she had something
else to think about. Finally, however, the figures began
to swim in front of her eyes and she was in danger of
falling asleep over her desk. She parked the silver Mini
in her allotted space and walked slowly up the stairs.

She was near the top when she became aware of an
obstruction, and for a moment she stared uncompre-
hendingly at the long legs barring her way.

'You're very late. It's nearly nine o'clock.' Clay's
voice was accusing.

She glanced at her watch. Anywhere to hide her face,
to hide from him the betraying leap of joy at seeing
him again. 'I've been working late.'

'I saw you working, at lunchtime.' His jaw muscles
tightened. 'Who was he?'

It was too late to regret her stupidity. She had behaved very badly indeed and had the unhappy suspi-

cion that Peter would make her pay for that when he had got over the shock. But it wasn't too late to retrieve a little self-respect.

'What's the matter, Clay? Did you change your mind?'

He stood up. 'This is hardly the place to discuss it.'

'This is the only place you're going to discuss anything. Because I have.' She turned away so that her eyes shouldn't betray the lie.

'Are you really so fickle?' He descended to her level and grasped her face between his hands so that she was forced to look at him. 'Who was he?' For a moment she glared furiously up at him, defying him to make her speak. He leaned closer. 'Who was he, Joanna?' he repeated, the velvet drawl of his voice contradicting the gem-hard challenge in his eyes.

'Peter Lloyd. He's the project manager.' The muscles in his jaw tightened and she closed her eyes. 'He's just come back from holiday.'

'You appeared to be very pleased to see him.'

'Did I? Maybe I was, Clay.'

'Maybe.' He suddenly released her and she rocked back on her feet. 'He didn't hang around for long, though. Or perhaps he came back tonight?'

'You stayed to spy on me?' Her eyes widened in surprise. Then a flash of anger sparked through them. 'You should have stayed longer, then you'd know whether he came back.'

'No!' He stepped back. 'No. I didn't do that. I was too angry to trust myself at the wheel of a car. I sat in the car park for a while, that's all, and I saw him leave, then a while later you all went back to the site.'

She frowned. 'I didn't notice the Aston in the car park.'

He shook his head. 'It needed some work. I borrowed a car from the garage. Look, Jo, this is silly. Can't we go inside and talk?'

She hesitated for a moment then shrugged and unlocked the door. 'Why not? I know I'll be safe in your company.' She threw her bag on the sofa and turned to face him. 'Won't I?'

CHAPTER THREE

'MAYBE.' He seemed to fill her sitting-room. 'Have you eaten?'

'I'm not hungry, Clay. I'm just tired. All I want is a shower and my bed. Just say whatever it is you feel you have to and go.'

'You have to eat.' He turned her in the direction of the bedroom and firmly steered her towards it. 'Have your shower. I'll get you some food.'

She dug her heels in. 'I don't want anything from you, Clay.'

'Yes, you do.' His hands were still on her shoulders and his grip intensified. 'So you'd better go and shower now, before I lose all semblance of self-control and remind you exactly what you want from me.'

She fled. Locking the bathroom door firmly behind her, she stood against it, her whole body trembling with the longing for him to slake the shattering need that the slightest touch of hand awoke in her. A longing that wouldn't go away.

'Damn you, Clay Thackeray,' she whispered to herself. She took deep, calming breaths and gradually began to regain control of herself. Slowly she undressed, and stood under a fierce shower trying to work out what Clay wanted from her. She had already offered him everything a girl could give a man and he had rejected it in very short order. Angrily she flicked the switch to cold.

Shivering, she quickly dressed in cream cord trousers and an oversized fleecy sweatshirt. The blue was faded and the Prince of Wales feathers of Surrey Cricket Club were barely visible, but it had been her father's and it was a comfort in her misery.

As she opened the bedroom door she heard a key in the lock. Clay appeared carrying a plastic bag. 'I borrowed your key. Hope you don't mind.'

'When you said you were getting food, I had assumed you were going to cook,' she protested. 'I could have made an omelette or something.'

'You said you were tired,' he said. 'Have you got any chopsticks?'

'I'm afraid not. I just use knives and forks.' Her lips imitated a smile.

He shook his head and tutted. 'How very conventional.'

'I've recently discovered that stepping outside the bounds of convention isn't that good for my ego,' she replied, sharply.

He smiled. 'I promise I'll do my best to restore it.' With a wry smile he dumped a pile of magazines on the floor. '*New Civil Engineer*. I might as well be at home.'

'I'm sure I can find you a copy of *Vogue* if it will make you feel more comfortable,' she offered, but he ignored this and began to lay out a series of aluminum dishes on the glass-topped coffee-table.

'Plates?' he suggested.

'Has anyone ever told you that you have a very managing disposition, Clay Thackeray?' she remarked, crossly.

'Managing is what I do best, Joanna Grant, so you'd better get used to it.'

'Yes, sir,' Jo snapped, but fetched a couple of plates and some cutlery from the kitchen. Clay piled a plate with food and handed it to her. She stared at it in dismay. 'I can't eat all this!'

He helped himself to food. 'Convince me that you've had a proper meal today and I'll let you off with half,' he offered.

'I don't suppose you'd take a doughnut into consideration?' He paused in the act of spooning rice on to his plate just long enough to hand her a fork. She made no further protest. At least eating precluded conversation.

'More?' he offered, as he watched her finish.

Jo shook her head. 'No. But thank you.' She forced a smile. 'I was hungrier than I thought.' She began to clear the dishes into the kitchen. 'Now, perhaps you'll tell me why you're here?' It seemed easier to ask the question while she was occupied. 'What exactly do you want from me?'

He had followed her, and his voice at her ear made her jump 'Maybe,' he said, very softly, 'I did change my mind. Maybe I can't get the thought of the other night out of my head.' He reached out and caught her wrist. 'Maybe I've been driven to distraction by the thought of you offering yourself to another man…I have the feeling that Peter Lloyd wouldn't be so tactless as to refuse you. Or is that where you've been all weekend?'

Jo stared at his hand, at the strong fingers curled around her wrist, the same fingers that had elicited such a eager response from her. She ignored his question. 'Is that how you see me?' she asked. 'Desperate? Realising how late I've left it and throwing myself at every man who comes my way in the hope that one of them will take pity on me?' She shuddered, resisting to no purpose as he pulled her into his arms, wrapping them around her, holding her close.

'Is that how you see yourself?' She looked up into his eyes but, startled by the intensity of his expression, she buried her face in his sweater. 'Joanna?'

'It wasn't like that. I just never met anyone before…' Her voice was muffled and he caught her shoulders and held her away from him.

'What wasn't it like?'

She concentrated very hard on the stocking-stitch pattern of his sweater. 'You were the first man I've met who just took my breath away. That's all.' The first to make her body sing, her heart do somersaults, her skin tingle. All the ridiculous things that people wrote in love songs.

'It's that simple?' he asked softly.

'Yes, it's that simple,' she lied. Love was never that simple. She raised long dark lashes and met his eyes head-on. 'You were right in a way, when you suggested that it had become a burden. Although I hadn't realised it myself.' She gave a small sigh. 'It must be so much simpler if you fall head over heels in love when you're sixteen and get the sex thing over with.' She half smiled at herself. 'The older you get, Clay, the harder it becomes. You become choosier, it assumes an importance quite out of proportion to its significance. Then along comes a man who meets all the specifications.' She withdrew from his arms. He made a move to hold her but she put up her hand to keep him at bay. 'Someone experienced enough to make it special.' She dropped her hands to her sides and shrugged. 'I'm sorry to have complicated what to you must have seemed something very straightforward.'

'But you must have met dozens of men.' He sounded genuinely astonished.

'Hundreds,' she corrected him and smiled. 'My friends were convinced that I chose an engineering course because of the men. But the truth was that at university I was working far too hard to get that involved. There was too much to prove.'

'And afterwards? Was there still too much to prove?'

'You mustn't flirt on site, Clay. Not if you expect to be taken seriously. And you get moved about. It's not that easy.'

'It seemed very easy…' He stopped as she swung away from him, walking swiftly into the living-room, leaning her cheek against the cool glass and staring sightlessly out of the window. 'I'm sorry, Jo. That came out all wrong. But it was easy, don't you see? It wasn't just you. I wanted to carry you off to bed the moment I set eyes on you.' He chuckled softly. 'It was quite a relief to find out that you were a girl, I can tell you.' He came up behind her and put his arms around her and rubbed his cheeks against her hair. 'The chemistry was right.'

'Chemistry?' she asked a little breathlessly, as she felt his body stir against her and the instant liquid fire course through her veins as he dragged her back against him.

'Lust at first sight.' His voice grated softly at her ear. 'So we'd better do something about it, don't you think?'

Lust? Surely it had been more than that, even for him? 'Desire' was the word that sprang unbidden to her mind. Or was that merely a euphemism for the raw need he had so unexpectedly awoken in her? Burning her from the inside out so that she thought she might explode if he didn't assuage her longing with his lips, his hands... She shuddered. Whatever it was he was offering, she wanted him.

'Now?' she asked.

'Such flattering impatience, my love. But there are one or two details to be sorted out first. Friday's a good day for me. And we'll have known one another for two weeks. That's almost respectable.'

She gasped, turning sharply in the circle of his arms to face him. For the second time she had offered him everything she had to give, and this time he had to consult his diary?

'A whole day, my love?' She echoed his endearment coldly. 'Are you sure you can spare it?'

His voice was cool. 'I think I can spare a whole day for our wedding.'

'Wedding?' She was sure she had misheard him.

'Well? Do you accept my proposal?'

'What proposal?'

'Just this. If you want my body you're going to have to take it on a permanent basis. Marry me, Joanna Grant.'

'That wasn't a proposal, Clay, it was a command.'

His mouth described a curve from her ear, along the line of her jaw, and for a moment she clung to him, the heady sensation of his lips against her skin driving the ability to reason from her mind.

'Do you prefer that?'

'I hardly know you,' she objected, faintly.

'You hardly knew me on Friday,' he pointed out, with perfect accuracy. 'It didn't seem to matter then.'

She blushed furiously. 'That was different.'

'No, it wasn't.' He wrapped his arms about her, regarding her upturned face from under heavy lids. 'Not a bit different.' Before she could extricate herself, his hands were sliding under her sweatshirt and stroking the satin skin of her naked back. His brows shot up. 'No underwear, Miss Grant? How very shocking.' His hands moved to caress her throbbing breasts, his thumbs brushing the hard budding tips. Then his mouth was on hers and his kiss was binding her to him with the fierce promise of untasted pleasures.

When at last he raised his head, she clung to him weakly. 'I don't know what to say.'

'There's nothing to say, my darling. You've already answered me.'

She took a slow, deep breath and shook her head. 'You don't have to marry me, Clay.'

'I believe you made that plain enough.' A tell-tale muscle was working at the corner of his mouth. 'But I'm making it a condition.'

'Why, Clay? People don't marry for *lust*.'

'Really? Why else would they marry?' He held her lightly, felt her betraying body tremble in his arms and, certain now of victory, he smiled. 'I want you, Jo. And when I saw you kiss Lloyd today I knew just how badly I wanted you.'

'That's silly…' she protested.

'Is it?' His voice was silky. 'Convince me.' When he finally lifted his head his breathing was as ragged as hers, his eyes almost black with naked hunger. For a moment he held her so fiercely that she thought he would never release her. Then he drew in a great shuddering breath. 'Friday?' he demanded harshly.

She nodded dumbly, quite unable to speak.

'Witch,' he murmured. 'If you knew more, you would be positively dangerous.' He stroked her cheek with the edge of his thumb. 'I'll pick you up in the morning. We can choose a ring. Nine-thirty. Don't be late.'

It had been an odd week. She had telephoned her office to ask if she could have the rest of the week as part of her leave, but had told no one why she wanted the time off. She had always kept her work completely separate from her private life and saw no reason to change simply because she was getting married.

Her family had been another matter altogether. But Jo had weathered the storm of her mother's disapproval at such a rushed marriage.

'It's madness, Jo!' Her mother had never called her Joanna, she reflected absently. Her father always had, and her sister sometimes, but never her mother. 'What about your career, your ambitions?' she said angrily after Clay had called formally to meet her. 'I guarantee that he'll have you pregnant on your honeymoon and you might as well never have gone to university.'

'Leave her alone, Mum.' Her sister grinned knowingly. 'Not that I disagree in general with your conclusions. Would you like me to help you choose your outfit?' she offered.

Jo accepted with grateful thanks. Heather, ten years her senior and a fashion buyer before the twins had arrived, and she'd begun to run her own boutique, had exquisite taste. She had already turned over the stock at a bridal wear store and picked out three outfits for Jo to try on when she arrived somewhat breathlessly on Wednesday morning.

'Perfect, love,' Heather pronounced, when Jo decided on a simple ivory suit in wild silk. 'Not many women can wear a straight skirt, but you have such a narrow waist and a perfectly beautiful little bottom...' She laughed as Jo blushed. 'He's already told you that.' She gently lifted the wide shawl collar to frame Jo's face. 'This collar is beautiful. It's a good thing you're a standard size; you haven't allowed yourself much time. Although I don't think you could have done better than that in three years, let alone three days.' She laughed. 'And I'm not sure I'm talking about the clothes. Are you going to wear a hat? Try this one.' Obediently Jo tried on the tiny pillbox and immediately took it off again.

'I don't think so. I don't think I've got the right shape head for a hat.'

Heather giggled. 'Not that one, anyway. This might be more you. No, close your eyes.' She fastened the circle of stiffened silk to Jo's head. 'Now look,' she said, with satisfaction.

Jo opened her eyes and for a moment stared at the stranger reflected in the mirror.

'Not bad, eh?' Heather beamed. 'Been hiding your light under Dad's old Barbour for too long. Clay's a clever man to spot you.'

'I took the Barbour off, Heather.'

'I think you'd better stop there, or I might just get jealous. Has he told you where he's taking you for your honeymoon?'

'We only have the weekend. He's in the middle of some business deal.'

'It must be something big to put your honeymoon on hold?'

'Very big.' Jo's smile was automatic. The truth was, she had no idea what the deal was.

'You look utterly charming, my dear.' Clay's father kissed her cheek. 'I'm so glad you didn't make him wait too long.'

'I...he was very insistent,' Jo said and blushed.

'Was he?' The older man regarded his son with affection. 'No point in fighting it, then. He always did get anything he set his mind on. I remember when—'

'I think we can do without nursery tales, if you don't mind.' Clay took Jo's hand and led her firmly away from the small group of family and friends who had come to witness the wedding. 'There hasn't been a moment to tell you how very beautiful you look.' He glanced at their guests and bent his head to her ear. 'Is there any way we could miss lunch, do you think?'

'Such flattering impatience,' she teased him. 'And you're the one who insisted on waiting.'

'Right now I can't think why.'

But eventually lunch was over, the cake had been cut and they had extricated themselves from their well-wishers. Clay drove the Aston through the country roads, turning at last into the lane that led to the river and his cottage. He pulled into the driveway and turned off the engine and silence descended around them.

'Welcome home, Mrs Thackeray.'

'Would you mind very much if I continue to call myself Grant?' she asked, as he took her hand and helped her from the car.

His fingers tightened around hers. 'You want to keep your own name?' His brows drew together as he frowned. 'You have some objection to mine?'

'None whatever, Clay. It's a splendid name. It's just simpler for work.' She lowered her lashes. 'Besides, I married you for your body, not your name.' Then she blushed crimson.

He touched her cheek with his fingers. 'So you did,' he said thoughtfully, then with a shrug he took her arm in his and they walked arm in arm down the path. Clay unlocked the door then turned to her, the slightest smile playing about his lips. 'Shall I carry you over the threshold, *Miss Grant,* or do your unexpectedly feminist views preclude that?'

'Why should they do that?' she asked, a sudden *frisson* of nerves catching in her voice as she noted the dangerous gleam lighting his eyes.

'Because carrying a bride over the threshold harks back to the caveman tactics of slinging the nearest breeding female over your shoulder and carrying her off to mate.'

She laughed a little uncertainly. 'Perhaps we should both step over the threshold together to signify our complete equality—'

'Rubbish!' He didn't wait for her to finish, but picked her up and threw her effortlessly over his shoulder.

'Clay! Let me go!' she protested furiously. He didn't bother to answer, but pushed the front door closed behind him with his foot and carried her kicking and yelling up the stairs, while her hat and shoes flew in all directions.

'Mind the beam,' he cautioned, as he ducked, then he dumped her on the wide bed. She scrambled quickly to the far side as he joined her and jumped to her feet.

'Clay, I won't—' she said, backing away as he advanced towards her.

'Won't what, Miss Grant?' he breathed. And then she was trapped, cornered and he was towering over her. 'Don't you want your wedding present?'

Her mouth dried. She hadn't expected him to be like this. All week he had been so careful not to push the fine strands of self-restraint to breaking-point. Now something seemed to have snapped. She gave a little scream as he caught her wrist and turned it over, raising it to his lips to kiss the delicate blue-veined skin, crossing the palm of her hand with butterfly touches of his lips, teasing the tips of her fingers. He raised his eyes, and she saw then that it was a game and he was laughing.

'Beast!' she said, but softly.

'Not today,' he promised. 'Not yet.'

She discovered that her legs were trembling and as she put out her hands to save herself he caught her and pulled her into his arms.

'And I really do have a present for you.' He took a small box from his pocket and opened it. Inside nestled a small gold Victorian locket. 'It was my mother's.'

'Clay, it's beautiful. Will you put it on for me?' He lifted the locket from the box and she turned and bent her head so that he could fasten it. His fingers brushed teasingly against her neck and she heard a small noise that might have come from somewhere inside her. He caught her hair, raking it away from her neck with his fingers.

'Do you know,' he murmured, 'that in Japan a geisha leaves the nape of her neck unpainted because it is considered to be exquisitely erotic?' He explored the delicate, sensitive skin with his lips, with the tip of his tongue, until she was gasping, breathless as a wave of desire swept over her.

'What else do geishas do?' Jo's voice was husky as he turned her to face him.

His lids drooped lazily, hooding the dazzling blue. 'Why don't you use your imagination?'

'But I don't know—'

'You wanted my body, darling. Take it. It's all yours.'

A tremor contracted her abdomen and her breathing shortened as she reached up to smooth the jacket away from his shoulders. She stretched it carefully across the back of a chair, certain that no self-respecting geisha would drop it on the floor. Then she loosened his tie, taking care not to touch him more than necessary, sliding the silk free of the knot. She folded it and laid it neatly on the chair. Her fingers began to shake as she undid the buttons of his shirt. She glanced up and saw that Clay was holding himself rigid as she slipped each tiny disc from its fastening and she smiled, deep down inside where he couldn't see.

At last it was done. She loosened the shirt, pulling it from his trousers, gently resting her cheek against his chest as she reached behind to free the back. His heart was beating as fast as her own and she brought her hands back to the front, fluttering her fingertips against his skin, over the little whorls of hair, across the small male nipples.

He groaned then and captured her, crushing her against him, his mouth hard on hers. She revelled in the sweet, heady sensation of her victory over his self-control. When, finally, he pulled away for lack of breath, she smiled.

'Shall I go on now?' she asked, but he captured her hands.

'I believe it's my turn.' He undid the three large buttons that fastened her jacket and pushed it back from her shoulders, leaving it to drop to the floor as his hands lingered to trace the long column of her neck. He stroked her gently, the backs of his fingers following her breastbone until they came to rest on her proud cleavage. He bent swiftly and buried his face there and with a cry she caught his head and held him, her fingers twisting in the thick dark curls. There was a sudden welcome freedom from the irksome restraint of lace, then with a fierce shout he lifted her and carried her bodily to the bed.

Joanna turned and woke to find Clay lying on his side watching her.

'If you were a cat, Joanna, you would be purring,' he said, at last.

'If I were a cat, my love, you would be stroking me.' She stretched in invitation and he laughed softly as she turned into his arms. Three nights and two days had only increased the first ecstatic pleasure of their love-making, but now, as she curved against him, he seized her and held her away.

'No, you don't. Honeymoon's over, my sweet. I have to work today, God help me.'

'Work?' She let the word sink in. Then sat up with a shock. 'Clay, it's Monday!'

'Yes,' he said, wryly. 'It's Monday.'

'What time is it?'

'Seven o'clock. But there's no need for you to get up.'

She scrambled from the bed. 'I'll be late.'

'Late?' He sat up, his hands clasped behind his head, watching her scrambling through the drawers. 'Where are you going? Arranged some shopping trip with the delectable Heather?'

'Don't be silly, Clay. I'm going to work.' She found a pair of jeans and held them up. 'Are these mine, or yours?' She turned and suddenly realised that he was very still. 'What's the matter?'

'I just hadn't realised that you intended to rush back

to work. I thought you might spend a few more days totally dedicated to my well-being.'

'Stay at home with me and I'll consider it.' Her generous mouth curved in a smile as she dropped the trousers, and moved towards him.

He caught her wrist before she could wreak havoc on his will. 'I'm sorry, Jo. I did warn you—'

'It must be something very special,' she said, hoping that he might elaborate.

'I'll be back as soon as I can.' He pulled her down and kissed her. 'I promise. Sure you won't stay and keep the bed warm?'

'That's not much of a career move.'

'Isn't it? I thought you might find me a full-time job.'

She straightened. 'Why would you think that, Clay?'

'I can't imagine. Fantasising, no doubt.'

'I'm not the domestic type. Even as a little girl I was always better at mud pies than pastry. What on earth would I do about the house all day?'

He rose in one smooth movement and was at her side. 'I had this vision of you, my darling, in a frilly apron, dusting the bedrooms, baking apple pie—'

Her eyes widened in horror. 'You didn't!'

His face split into a grin. 'No, that wasn't exactly the role I had in mind. Mrs Johnson already does that to perfection.' Jo had met the lady who kept the cottage immaculate and had taken great pains to reassure her that she had no intention of usurping her role. Clay looked suddenly serious. 'But the kitchen garden could do with a good weeding.'

'Sorry. I can't tell a weed from an orchid.'

'It's easy, darling. If you pull it up and it grows again it was a weed. If you pull it up—'

'—and it doesn't grow again, it was the orchid,' she finished.

'Ah, well. It was a nice try. But being married to a career-woman will take a bit of getting used to.' He kissed her shoulder and she turned, dropping the jeans as she reached for him, but he held her at bay. 'It's as well that I have an early meeting, or you, Miss Grant, would be very late for work. Very late indeed.' He kissed her hard then turned her firmly in the direction of the bathroom. 'Don't be long.'

They made an odd pair at breakfast, Clay all tailored elegance in a dark suit and a striped shirt, Joanna in denims and a jumper that had seen better days.

'What time will you be home?'

Joanna added an apple to her lunch-box and considered the question. 'I have to finish clearing the flat. There's not too much left there so I suppose I could do it at lunchtime. But we need some shopping; the fridge is pretty bare.'

'You'll want some money.' He took a wallet out of his inside pocket and offered her some notes. 'Take this for now. I'll organise a housekeeping account for you.'

'I don't need that, Clay. We'll have to sort out some sort of split on expenses.' His expression didn't change and yet she had the feeling she had said something to make him angry. 'The mortgage and so on,' she added, uncertainly, realising as she said the words that she hadn't a clue if there was, in fact, a mortgage on the cottage, or anything very much about Clay Thackeray except that she loved him beyond all reason. But she didn't want him to think that she had married him for a free ride.

A smile creased his eyes and it was all right. 'Thanks for the offer, Jo. But I think I can manage to support us both in reasonable comfort. Besides, you won't always be a working girl, will you? Once the babies begin to arrive you won't be able to contribute to the—er—mortgage.'

'Babies?' She felt a tiny stab of unease.

'You do know where they come from?' he teased. 'Or haven't you been paying attention…?'

'Yes.' Her voice sounded unnaturally loud and she forced her mouth into an answering curve. 'I just hadn't realised it was the gooseberry bushes that needed weeding.'

'I'd better get someone in to do it.' He dropped the notes on the table and stood up. 'I'll be home around seven. Do you want Mrs Johnson to leave something, or will you prefer to cook?'

'I'll cook,' Jo said, without thinking.

'Whatever you like.' He glanced at his watch. 'I've got to go.' He took her in his arms and kissed her with a sweet, fierce urgency that quite took her breath away. 'Take care.'

Jo drove to work but when she arrived couldn't remember any of the ten miles she had negotiated. Once the babies arrived? Her mother had suggested he would want a family immediately, but she had dismissed the idea as ridiculous. Men didn't want families. Babies were things that women yearned for and men put up with as the price for a home, food on the table, a willing partner in bed. She worked with men all day. She heard the things they said, knew what they got up to in the lunch-hours when their wives were worn out with housework and children. Even Heather's husband had briefly strayed when she had been huge with the twins— She cut off the thought. It didn't matter. It wouldn't ever happen to her.

She sighed and reluctantly let the warm memory of Clay's lovemaking go, firmly banishing thoughts of him as far to the back of her mind as he was prepared to stay. She was a career-woman, she reminded herself, but keeping her personal life separate from work had been easier when she hadn't had a personal life.

She spent the morning immersed in the problems that no one else had bothered with during her absence, glad enough, at lunchtime, of a genuine excuse to refuse Peter Lloyd's flirtatious offer of a drink.

'I'm moving the last of my things from the flat,' she said, without thinking.

'You're moving?' he asked, with unexpected interest.

'Yes. Excuse me, I don't have much time.'

'You'll have to let Personnel know your new address. And I'll want your telephone number.' It was a perfectly reasonable request, yet, as always, he managed to endow the simplest request with some hidden meaning.

'My number hasn't changed. I have a portable phone.' She certainly wasn't giving him the cottage number. Cursing herself silently for being so careless, she hurried away before he could ask any more questions. The less he knew about her life, the better.

CHAPTER FOUR

MARRIED life, Jo decided happily, was a lot more fun than living on your own. Waking up to find the man you loved smiling at you was the very best way to start the day. Especially when he then proceeded to kiss her.

'I'm working from home today,' he murmured, throatily, pulling her close. 'Don't rush away.'

The temptation to linger in his arms was almost too much, but today was special and she had to be strong.

'Sorry, my love. You chose the wrong day.' She laughed and tried to wriggle free, but he held her without apparent effort. 'Please, Clay,' she begged as his lips teased her throat. 'I have a meeting at eight o'clock. I want to make a good impression.'

His eyes darkened and for a moment his hands tightened around her waist. Then he released her and rolled on to his back. 'In that case, sweetheart, it would be cruel to detain you,' he said, carelessly. 'Although in my day site engineers weren't invited to meetings.'

'The senior engineer has left, so I'm standing in for him.' It was essential that he understand how important it was to her. 'I'm going to apply for his job. I've as good a chance as anyone. I must make a good impression.' He made no response, and if it hadn't been so silly she could have sworn that he was angry. 'Clay?' She smiled uncertainly. 'I can't be late.'

There was no answering smile. 'If it's so important to you, you'd better get a move on.'

'Don't make me choose, Clay.'

He turned to her, his face unreadable. 'Would it be so very difficult?'

She didn't bother to make breakfast. Instead she slammed the door hard on her way out and drove to work through a film of tears, angry with him for not understanding, even angrier with herself, although she didn't know why.

The meeting seemed endless; Jo's mind kept wandering to Clay, wondering what he was doing. But at last it was over and someone moved that they adjourn to the pub for an early lunch.

'Coming, Jo?' Peter's proprietorial hand was at her back as they stood outside the site office.

She had acquitted herself well at the meeting despite the mental distraction and relief made her generous with her smile. 'You've all held yourselves in check on my account for quite long enough,' she said, excusing herself. She patted Peter's cheek lightly and extricated herself from his grasp. 'You'll enjoy your lunch much more if you don't have to think twice before you tell a joke.' And she could spend the time far more usefully going home to make her peace with Clay. But she didn't have to go home, because as she turned away she saw him.

Clay, clad in close-fitting jeans and a white shirt that billowed loosely, giving him something of the appearance of seventeenth-century pirate, was leaning against the Aston, arms folded, watching them with an ominous intensity. Her heart in her boots, she detached herself from the group and went over to him.

'Hello, Clay,' she said, stiff, in the face of his all too evident displeasure. 'How lovely to see you.'

'Is it?' He opened the car door and held it for her, his eyes daring her to do anything other than get in. She slid into the seat but he didn't speak again until he pulled into a quiet turning and parked under some trees. She turned on him.

'Well? What do you want?'

He stared straight ahead, through the windscreen, his knuckles white where he gripped the wheel. 'I'm not quite sure. I know that I came to apologise for this morning. I wanted you to stay with me. Understandable, but not exactly fair.'

'No. Not exactly fair.' She glanced at him uncertainly. He sounded reasonable enough, but she wasn't convinced. 'If one of the men had been late, you see, no one would have said a word. But I have to be…well, I don't have to spell it out, do I?'

He ignored this. 'But then I came face to face with my wife, my very professional wife, a wife who is so very professional that she prefers people to think she isn't married, and who mustn't be late for meetings on any account, flirting with that pompous ass.'

'Tell me, Clay,' she said, making her voice very quiet, in her determination not to shout, 'what do you object to most? The flirting? Or the fact that I chose to do it with a pompous ass?'

'Both!' He seized her shoulders and glared angrily at her for a moment. 'If I see that man lay so much as a finger on you again, I'll knock that expensive dentistry clean down his throat. And—'

'And what?' she demanded. 'What will you do to me, Clay? Shake me like a naughty schoolgirl, until my teeth rattle?'

For a moment he held her, his fingers biting painfully into her shoulders. Then, with effort, he slowly regained possession of himself.

'There would be little point in that. I'm perfectly aware that you can't be browbeaten by me, or anyone else. But I do have one weapon that we both know you can't resist.'

Rigid with anger at his distrust, she told herself that right now resistance would be easy. But his mouth on hers was warm, gentle, and as his hands slid from her shoulders to her back, drawing her closer, she whimpered, quite unable to help herself.

When, apparently satisfied that he had proved his point, he at last let her go, she blinked back a film of tears, feeling totally humiliated by the casual ease with which he could dominate her body.

'I should have done that this morning,' he said angrily.

'My job is important to me, Clay.'

He grasped her chin and forced her to face him.

'You've made that abundantly clear. If you want to be a career-woman, Jo, you've got it. And you can call yourself Miss Grant until the cows come home if it pleases you. But don't ever forget you're my wife. First, last and everything in between.'

'Why should I want to forget?' she demanded

through angry tears. 'Why on earth do you think I married you?'

The curve of his mouth was pure insolence. 'You married me, Joanna, because your body suddenly realised what it was made for. And because I wanted you to.'

'Did you? Why? Just why *did* you marry me?' she demanded.

For a moment he stared at her. Then he turned abruptly away and he reached for the ignition. 'I'll take you back.'

He dropped her off just as the others came back from the pub and they stood watching the car with open admiration as it disappeared down the road. Peter Lloyd stopped her as she passed him. 'Who was that?'

She didn't want to talk to him, would give anything never to set eyes on him again. 'Clay Thackeray,' she answered as briefly as she could.

'Thackeray,' he repeated thoughtfully. 'Clay Thackeray. The name rings a bell. What does he do?'

'Do?' she asked, coldly.

'It's probably just a coincidence, but I saw him at the office yesterday being given the grand tour. There have been all sorts of rumours flying around about a take-over ever since Charles Redmond's heart attack. The company has a big fat pension fund. Very tempting for a certain type of businessman.'

'What sort?' she asked, curious despite herself.

'The sort that only cares for profit and doesn't give a damn about the little people who make it for him.'

'Clay isn't like that,' she said, shocked. 'He's a civil engineer. He knew my father.'

He gave her a long, hard look. 'Well, you probably know far more about it than me; you've that nice parcel of shares your father left you. But better beware.' He leered suggestively. 'Mr Thackeray might just have more than one motive for romancing you.'

'I'm sorry, I've heard nothing. Will you excuse me, please?' She didn't wait for his reply. But in the privacy of the office she searched in her handbag for the letter she had received from the solicitors with an increased offer for her shares.

He had seemed to know. And his arrival had coincided with her rejection of the first offer. For a long time she stared at it. Then, her heart hammering painfully in her throat, she reached for the telephone. It had been stupid to ignore it. If she knew nothing about an attempted take-over she had no one but herself to blame. She had a responsibility to Redmonds and to herself as a shareholder. The least she could do was find out what was going on. Not that she thought Clay was involved, not for one moment. But, when she had asked him why he had married her, he hadn't given her an answer. And he hadn't mentioned his visit to Redmonds.

The simple truth was that she hardly knew more about his business activities now than on the day they met. On their marriage licence he had stated his occupation as company director. When she had asked him what company he had smiled.

'Half a dozen at the last count, but it's all right, I don't expect you to have heard of any of them.' Then he had kissed her, his warm mouth driving all other thoughts from her mind.

That evening she pulled an old shoe-box out of her wardrobe and found her share certificate. It was worth more than money to her. Her father had helped Charles Redmond when the company hit a bad patch years earlier. He had borrowed on his life assurance and this block of shares had been his reward. Redmond had wanted him to join the board, but her father had declined. He wasn't interested in the wheeling and dealing of company finance. He had been a civil engineer and never wanted to be anything else. And he had left the shares to her because in a man's world she would need an 'edge'. She hadn't expected them to come to her so soon and had felt, guiltily, that her mother should have had them. But her mother had taken her father's view and refused her offer.

'What are you doing?' Startled, Jo looked up from the floor, where she was sitting surrounded by papers. She hadn't heard him come up the stairs.

'I was looking for something. She tried to push the certificate back into its folder, but Clay stopped alongside her and took it from her hands. He examined it thoughtfully then met her watchful eyes.

'This should be in the safe downstairs, Jo,' he said. 'It's a very valuable document.'

'I know.' His eyebrows rose sharply at the abruptness of her reply. 'I thought it should be in the bank,' she hedged. 'That's why I was looking for it.'

'Have you decided to sell them after all?' There was a more than casual interest, she thought, although his expression was carefully shuttered. She tried to remember whether she had mentioned that the offer had been for Redmonds shares. She thought not.

'I have no plans to sell them at the moment. I just thought the certificate should be kept more securely.'

'You're right. Would you like me to do it for you? It could just as easily be kept in my safety deposit box.' She wondered, uneasily, if simply possessing the certificate so that she would be unable to sell to anyone else would be enough, the 'edge' that he might need if he was trying to gain control of Redmonds.

'I... The arrangements have already been made. I'm going up to town tomorrow.'

'I see.' He surrendered it to her, unwillingly, she thought. 'In that case I'll leave it for you to deal with. Look after it.'

She placed it back in its folder and attempted to gather the rest of the papers together, but his brooding presence made her clumsy. Finally he swept them up and shuffled them up into some order before handing them back to her. They had hardly spoken beyond the need for politeness since she had come home. Now he touched her cheek very gently.

'It's a lovely evening, Jo. Why don't we take a walk along the towpath?'

She made an effort at a smile. 'A walk?'

'Just as far as the Ferry? For a drink?'

'Yes, if you like. I'll be right with you.'

The river was busy. A fine July had brought out the pleasure boats, and the holiday cruisers were already thick on the water. For a while they walked without speaking. Jo couldn't think what to say that wouldn't bring them back to the reason for the strained atmosphere. Then Clay spotted a family of ducks and caught her hand as he pointed to them.

'There's a nest just by our mooring,' Jo said, her voice shaking with the helpless longing to forget everything that had happened since she got up this morning and go back to yesterday. 'They haven't hatched yet…' Her voice trailed away.

They walked on. 'I've been meaning to talk to you about the mooring. Have you any strong feelings about boats?'

'In what way?'

'Any way.'

'No,' she said. 'I don't think so. But then I've never been in anything bigger than a dinghy with an outboard motor.'

'I can do a little better than that. I had someone over this morning to look at the boathouse. I've decided to have it restored.'

'Restored?' She considered the possibility of restoring the collapsed heap that glorified in the name of boathouse. 'There's precious little left to restore. Surely a more appropriate word would be ''rebuilt''?'

'Perhaps.' He almost smiled. 'But rebuilt to the original plan. I should have saved myself the fee and consulted you.'

'I should have thought you could have worked that out for yourself.'

'I could do it all myself, Jo, from the foundations up. But it wouldn't be a cost-effective use of my time.'

'Wouldn't it?' She tried not to dwell on exactly what he considered an appropriate use of his time.

'Well, I'd need a labourer. How would you feel about taking the job on?'

'It might be fun,' she said, her mind smiling at the

thought of the two of them working together. Reluctantly she switched the picture off. 'But I take your point. Who is going to do the work?'

'Redmonds. They do a lot of work on the river so they were the obvious choice.'

'Redmonds! Oh, that's wonderful.' The words were expelled on a sudden breath of relief at such a simple explanation for his presence in the office. She had been screwing herself up to ask him about it. Now suddenly it was all right.

'I'm glad you're so pleased,' he said drily. 'I thought I'd better keep it in the family.' He had stopped and was looking at her oddly. 'What is it?'

'Absolutely nothing.' She threw her arms around his neck. She knew she was grinning idiotically, but couldn't help herself. 'Except I'm incredibly hungry.'

'Are you?' His arms were around her waist, drawing her against him. 'Well, you had no lunch and you didn't eat much dinner.'

'Neither did you. Perhaps I should leave the cooking to Mrs Johnson.'

'There's nothing wrong with your cooking. I just didn't feel like…' He stopped. 'Jo, let's go home.'

Later, lying in the darkness, Jo went through the day again in her mind, trying to work out why it had gone so dreadfully wrong. It all came down to trust, she decided. Clay had no reason to be jealous of Peter, stupidly over-reacting to what he imagined he had seen. And she had been no better. The slightest hint that Clay might be working against the best interests of Redmonds and its staff had raised her suspicions. Because, she decided, sleepily, outside of bed she and Clay were still relative strangers. But that was something time would mend. She smiled as he drew her into the circle of his arms.

'Go to sleep,' he murmured.

'Make me.'

'If you're coming up to town today,' Clay said, over breakfast, 'why don't you come to the office?' Jo jumped guiltily. How on earth had Clay found out that she was going to the solicitors today? 'You did say you were taking your share certificate to the bank.' His expression was appraising and she knew her cheeks had gone a betraying shade of pink. 'Unless of course you have some other plans?'

'Oh, no.' And even as she said the words she knew she should have told him. But it was too late. She made an effort to pull herself together. 'That is, I'd love to see your office. I'll be finished by twelve, I should think.'

'In that case I'll have my secretary write in "Miss Grant" for lunch.' He stood up and dropped a kiss on the top of her head. 'Don't be late.'

'No, sir! See you later.'

At eleven o'clock she was in the city office of a firm of solicitors that appeared to have been in business since Victoria came to the throne. It was possible, she thought, that one or two of the staff were the original employees.

But Mr Henry Doubleday was not one of them. Smooth, well groomed, he put himself out to charm her. Yet when she rose half an hour later she was hardly any wiser. She had an offer for her shares from a gentleman who preferred to remain anonymous. An offer that Mr Doubleday took great pains to point out was well above the market value.

She asked if anyone else had been approached, but he 'wasn't at liberty to say'. She asked why the gentleman was prepared to pay so much. That, again, was confidential. She asked how they knew she had the shares and he told her that it was a matter of public record. She hadn't realised that.

It quickly became clear that she would learn nothing from this man. Not that it mattered any more. She excused herself, promising to give the offer further thought. She had intended to give some truth to her lie and go to the bank to leave the share certificate, but, glancing at her watch, she realised she would have to leave it until after lunch. She hailed a cab and gave the driver the address of Clay's office, which turned out to be an impressive city block.

The lift took her to the twenty-first floor and she stepped into an impressive, thickly carpeted foyer presided over by a beautiful red-headed receptionist. The girl ran an expert assessing eye over Jo's clothes and clearly found her suit wanting.

'Mr Thackeray is expecting me,' Jo said, interrupting the examination. 'Joanna Grant.'

'Miss Joanna Grant?' she asked, consulting her list. A second appraisal apparently confirmed her first opinion that this woman had no business bothering the likes of Clay Thackeray. Jo nodded and the girl waved at a chair with a sigh. 'Take a seat. I'll see if he's free.' The girl's offhand manner might have been amusing if Jo had felt less vulnerable, and for the first time she felt a pang of regret at retaining her own name. Then she dismissed the feeling as ridiculous. When she made it to the top of her profession everyone must know she was Joe Grant's daughter.

The girl telephoned and seconds later Clay was there, extending his hand in formal welcome. 'Miss Grant, how kind of you to come.' His expression was deadpan and she took the proffered hand and shook it gravely.

'Mr Thackeray? I've heard so much about you.'

'Should I be worried?' he asked, earnestly.

'Very!' she whispered. Then, louder, as she looked about her, 'I'm looking forward to seeing your offices.'

'I'm afraid there's no time now.' He placed a hand at her elbow and moved her firmly towards the lift, pausing briefly at the receptionist's desk. 'I should be back by two-thirty, but if Henry arrives before I do give him some coffee and tell him I won't keep him long.' His smile was warm.

'Yes, Clay.' The girl's eyes devoured him and Jo subdued with difficulty a wild stab of jealousy. The lift doors slid open. They stepped inside and she turned on him.

'Does that girl know you're married?'

'I'm not in the habit of discussing my private life with my staff. An attitude you should find some sympathy with.' His expression was unreadable. 'Does she bother you?'

'Should she?' She thought she was smiling. She hoped she was.

'Apparently she does.' He raised one shoulder in the slightest shrug, then smiled. 'I'll make you a promise,

Jo. The day you agree to use the name Thackeray, I'll put an announcement in every national newspaper to tell the world that you're my wife.'

'I'll let you know,' she said, with a carelessness she was far from feeling.

'Any time.' The doorman hailed a cab and Clay told the man to take them to Greek Street and they were disgorged a while later at the restaurant door.

They were directed upstairs and shown to a table in the far corner. 'We'll be able to see everyone from here,' Clay said. Jo looked around her with interest at the signed photographs of actors and actresses that covered the pale green walls. Her eye halted on a familiar face at a nearby table.

'Isn't that—?'

Clay didn't take his eyes off her. 'I expect so. It usually is whoever you think it is.'

They both ordered monkfish in a shellfish sauce and sat back to enjoy the comings and goings of the famous, and Jo forgot about shares and concrete and beautiful redheads as Clay set out to amuse her.

'Do you come here much?' she asked after the waiter had brought them a dish of strawberries. 'Everyone seems to know you.'

'Now and then. When I want to entertain special people.'

'Who, for instance?'

His eyes flickered over her and he smiled. 'Just business, Jo.'

She fiddled with her spoon. 'I don't think you ever told me exactly what your business is.'

'No.' He sat back, regarding her thoughtfully. 'There

always seems to be so many more interesting things to do when I'm with you.'

She blushed faintly. 'You could tell me now.'

His dark brows drew together. 'Is it important?'

'I'm interested in everything about you,' she said, and sipped her wine as her mouth dried.

He shrugged. 'I told you, I'm a consultant. I identify problems in the management structure of companies and put them right.'

'But you're a civil engineer,' she said, confused by this slightly ominous reply.

'Initially, yes. But, unlike your father, Joanna, I never found concrete to be an all-absorbing interest.'

'You would have taken the seat on the board,' she murmured, more to herself than him, but he immediately picked her up.

'Seat on the board?'

She found herself telling him about the time her father had helped Charles Redmond save the company and his refusal to join the board.

'I hadn't realised that Joe had been offered a directorship. He should have taken it.' He regarded her thoughtfully. 'Maybe you should demand it now.'

Startled, she looked down to hide the sudden reawakening of all her fears from his all-seeing eyes.

'Don't be silly. I know nothing about business.'

'Nothing?' She held her breath momentarily, convinced that the time had come and he was going to ask her for her shares. Instead he laughed. 'If keeping your share certificates in a shoe-box is anything to go by, I would have to agree.'

She let out a long sigh of relief. 'It was Dad's box.'

'Do you know something? I'm not a bit surprised. If your father had hopped to work on one leg you would probably do the same.'

The fierceness in his voice shook her. 'I'm not...' Her voice trailed away under his scornful look.

'Aren't you?'

She took a deep breath. 'I always wanted to be just like him, Clay. He was so funny. So clever. And when he took me to see the huge things that he had made I wanted to do it too.' More than that she would not say.

He took her hand. 'Joe Grant was one of the best men I've ever met, my love, but I never wanted to marry him, even at one remove. And he had his faults like everyone else. Perhaps it's time you tried being Joanna. She has a right to a life of her own.'

His perception was frightening. She turned quickly away and, spotting a new celebrity, diverted his attention and the moment passed.

It was only when she was on the train and the ticket collector asked to see her ticket that she realised she still had the share certificate in her bag.

It had been an inconclusive day, she thought, unhappily. She had found out nothing that was any real help. If Charles Redmond had been available she would have gone to see him. But he was recuperating in the south of France from a mild heart attack and wouldn't be back for another couple of weeks.

It occurred to her that he might not even know what was going on, and she pondered on the wisdom of writing to him. She didn't want to give him another heart attack. But there was no reason why she couldn't write to ask how he was, just mentioning the offer casually, asking his advice. And, the decision made, she felt instantly better. She didn't know why she hadn't thought of that sooner. Instead of going back to the site, she called at the office to get his address from his secretary.

She was sitting at her dressing-table sealing the envelope when she heard Clay calling.

'Jo? Where are you? I've got something to tell you.' His feet pounded up the stairs and she jumped guiltily as the door swung open. As she turned her bag crashed to the floor, its contents sliding and rolling across the polished boards.

Clay surveyed the wreckage with amusement. 'Come on, I'll give you a hand.'

Jo's eyes fastened on the envelope containing the share certificate, convinced that Clay would be able to see straight through the thick manila.

'Leave it. I'll clear it up in a minute. What's your news?' She tried to distract him. But he had already bent down and his fingers had fastened over a small black plastic case. He straightened and extended it to her, in the flat palm of his hand.

'What's this?' he asked.

Jo, almost heady with relief, looked from the small inoffensive rectangle and up into the face of her husband. It was stiff, set with an ominous expression that sent a swift shiver of apprehension down her spine.

'You know what it is,' she said, quietly.

He shook the package slightly, and the pills rattled in their little plastic bubbles. 'Oh, yes, I know what it is. But I should like to know what it is doing in your handbag.'

'Does that need an explanation, Clay? I have a ca-

reer. In fact I applied for the senior engineer's job today and I'm sure I'll get it. You can just imagine the
response if two months later I leave to have a baby.
Redmonds would never employ another woman on site.
And who could blame them?'

'I am completely indifferent to Redmonds' policy on
the employment of women. I *do* care about this.'

She avoided his eye. 'I'm not ready to give up everything I've worked so hard to achieve to have a family.'

'You don't think,' he said, with a painful, icy calm,
'that it would have been…polite…to impart that particular piece of information to me?'

'This is ridiculous, Clay. We're grown up, for
heaven's sake. Surely you didn't expect me to produce
a son and heir nine months to the day of our wedding.'

'A daughter would be equally acceptable.'

'I don't believe this. You never said anything about
children when you asked me to marry you. Demanded
that I marry you.'

'Forgive me for being somewhat slow-witted, but I
thought that marriage was a total commitment. Or don't
you love me quite enough to want to bear my children?'

'Love?' The tears were biting at her eyelids now,
but she refused to let them fall. When had he ever
spoken of love? 'Surely we married for lust, Clay. Isn't
that what you said?'

His hands closed tightly on the small package. 'I
hadn't realised that you had taken me quite so literally.'
His eyes were gem-hard in the evening light and she
stepped back, suddenly afraid.

'Going somewhere?' he asked, and he moved swiftly to block her exit.

'I have to get dinner,' she babbled.

'Later.' He let the small packet fall from his hand and caught her wrist, jerking her close. Then with his other hand he began, very slowly, to undress her. 'Right now, I'll settle for lust.'

She fought him, beating at his shoulders in silent fury but he ignored her onslaught, not hurting her, simply holding her in an iron grip until at last she stood panting, her naked breast heaving against a shirt-front from which the buttons had been ripped in her struggles.

'Clay, please!'

'Please what, Jo?' His mouth began a series of lightning raids across her shoulder, while the tip of his thumb grazed a betraying nipple already fiercely to attention. She moaned, an urgent fire kindling deep within her as he touched her, caressed her, played her body with the skill of a virtuoso, until she was tearing feverishly at his clothes.

There was a savage magnificence about their coupling that had nothing to do with love. And when, at long last, it was over, there was no tender rest to be found in Clay's arms. Instead he held her fiercely at arm's length, raking her with eyes numbing in their cold intensity, his teeth bared in a predatory grin.

'Whoever would have guessed, Miss Grant, that beneath that cool exterior there lurked a sleeping tiger?'

She wrenched herself free and fled to the shower, turning it to a biting cold, desperate to cool the hot shame of her own wanton response to him, desperate to hide from those knowing eyes, but his laughter, real or imagined she hardly knew, followed her there, echoing in her head.

After a long time she wrapped herself in a towelling robe and emerged. He was lying back on the pillows, turning the pill case between his fingers.

'Do you still want these?' he asked, without expression.

She was unable to answer. She didn't know what she wanted any more beyond the gentle comfort of his arms. But that was denied her. He rose in one smooth movement from the bed and she dragged her eyes away from the magnificence of his body, wincing as he pressed the package into her palm and wrapped her fingers firmly around it.

'Here, then. But don't take them on my account, sweetheart. I'm going to Canada tomorrow.'

'Canada?'

'That was my news. I thought you would have liked to come with me for a belated honeymoon. But clearly your career has to come first.' He pushed her fringe back from her eyes. 'You are your father's daughter, Jo. Right down to the cement dust in your hair.' She reached for him, wanting to hold him, convince him of her love, but he turned to open the wardrobe and began to throw clothes into a holdall.

Fear stabbed through her. 'You said tomorrow.'

'I'll stay at the airport hotel tonight. What's left of tonight.'

'Clay, please!'

He raised his eyes to hers. 'Sorry, darling. I've had more than enough for one night.' Her breath came in a sharp, cold gasp against her teeth and, apparently satisfied, he zipped the bag closed. 'We'll talk about our marriage when I get back, Jo. In the meantime, perhaps it's time you gave some thought to your priorities.' With that, he walked into the bathroom and closed the door firmly behind him.

CHAPTER FIVE

JOANNA was dressed and waiting when he came down into the hall and he glanced at his watch.

'Not going to bed? It's a little early for work, even by your standards.'

'Not at all. The site is working round the clock,' she said, calmly, determined not to be drawn into a game of sniping.

'Well, you'll be able to keep really busy while I'm away,' he said, cruelly, 'without anything as tiresome as a husband to distract you.'

She shook her head. 'I wasn't included in the night-shift rota. Clay—'

'And you stood for that?' His mouth twisted in a mockery of a smile. 'You're slipping. Isn't that some sort of discrimination?'

'I was glad,' she said urgently, seeking to convince him. 'I wanted to be home with you.' He merely raised a disbelieving brow and for a moment she froze. Then she reached for her bag, fumbling for her keys so she wouldn't have to see the cold, hard expression in his eyes. 'I—I dressed because you'll need a lift to the airport.'

'I've already called a taxi. It will be here any moment.' As if to confirm his words a car horn sounded at the gate.

'When will you be home?' she asked, trying desperately not to let him see how much the effort of making polite conversation was costing her.

'I'll let you know.'

Her fragile mask began to slip. 'Can I have your address? A telephone number?' She was reduced to begging and didn't care.

'If there's anything urgent my office can find me.' He opened the door and paused against the dark rectangle of the sky. Then he disappeared into the dark. She wanted to run down the path, chase the headlights' bumpy passage down the lane. Tell him how much she loved him, make him listen to her, promise him anything. But she clung to the doorpost, sinking to the floor, resting her cheek against the cool ancient wood, until the birds roused her with their dawn clamour.

She rose stiff with cold and climbed the stairs. The contents of her bag were still scattered across the floor and she picked them up, stuffing them in anyhow. All except the pills. Those she threw, one by one, into the toilet and flushed them away. She dropped the empty packet into the bin. When Clay came home they would talk, she decided. Thrash it all out. Everything. Then, perhaps, they could pick up the pieces and start again.

The days passed. She missed him so much that it was like a pain. She longed simply to hear the sound of his voice, but he didn't telephone or write and she tried to tell herself that he was right. She needed time to make decisions about her future. But when the phone did ring she ran to answer it, breathless with hope, only to be disappointed.

Her mother invited her over for the weekend and she thought it would help to fill the numbing loneliness.

But two days of putting a brave face on for her mother made her wish she had stayed at home where her pallor could remain unremarked upon and she wouldn't have to field carefully couched questions regarding the likelihood of her starting a family.

On Sunday afternoon an urgent summons from Peter was a welcome opportunity to escape.

'Sorry to call you out, Jo,' Peter said, as she arrived. 'But Mike's been rushed to hospital with suspected appendicitis and I've got a family do.'

'It's no problem.'

'Not for you, maybe. But it is for me. You're not supposed to be working the night-shift.'

'That's silly.'

'Yes, I know. I told them at the office that you'd have a fit. I was amazed, frankly, that you took it so calmly.'

Jo shrugged. 'Well, don't worry. I shan't mention it if you don't.'

But it was a long night and it was with infinite relief that she saw Peter's car turn into the yard. She finished signing the last of the worksheets and almost fell into her car.

'I don't think you should drive, Jo. Come on. I'll give you a lift.'

Peter's face swam above her and she didn't bother to argue. She felt giddy, sick with tiredness, and had almost to be helped to his car.

She woke as the car stopped outside the cottage. 'What?' For a moment she was totally confused. 'Oh, I'm home.'

'Safe and sound.' He leaned across and opened the

car door, halting, his face far too close to hers, something uncomfortably close to a leer curving his lips. 'Don't I deserve a reward?' Before she could move he had touched her lips with his own. She pushed him away and began to climb quickly from the car but his voice followed her.

'Well, now I know why you didn't make a fuss about the night-shift.'

'I'm sorry?' Her voice was forbidding.

'That's not a car I'm likely to forget.'

Jo focused on the Aston standing on the gravel driveway, suddenly wide awake at the implications of what she could see. 'It's not what you think, Peter,' she said quickly and opened the gate.

His laughter followed her. 'That rather depends upon what I'm thinking.'

But she hardly heard him as she ran down the path to the cottage. It had all become too silly. She was married, for heaven's sake. She had clung to her father's name for long enough. She wasn't Jo Grant any more. Clay was home and her joy at that fact was an end to all the uncertainties. Nothing was more important than her love for him.

The door opened as she raised her key to the latch and he stood back to let her inside.

'Clay!' she exclaimed and threw her arms around him. 'I'm so glad you're back.' He made no move to hold her; instead he reached over her head and pushed the door. It shut with a crash behind her and she jumped and stepped back, feeling foolish. 'I'm sorry I wasn't here when you arrived. You must have wondered...'

'Must I? Well, you didn't keep me in suspense for very long,' he said evenly. He turned abruptly and left her standing in the hall.

She followed him into the living-room, realising that something was very wrong. 'If I had known you were coming I would have left a message.' He didn't answer, didn't even bother to turn around. 'You said you would let me know when you were coming home.'

He turned then, his eyes wintry. 'How inconvenient that I chose to surprise you.'

'Inconvenient?' she echoed, blankly.

'I did ring your mother when I got home, assuming that you would be there. My father told me you were going there for the weekend when I telephoned him a couple of days ago.'

'You were able to use a telephone, then?' she said, suddenly furious for all the heartache she had endured. 'I thought perhaps you must have lost the use of your dialling finger.'

He ignored this outburst. 'He said you were with your mother,' he repeated. 'So I called her.'

'I was there.'

'Undeniably. Except you left there just after tea on Sunday. Called away to work, she said. She was very convincing, but then, I expect she believed it.'

'I was,' she repeated, helplessly.

'All night, Jo? When I distinctly remember you telling me that you had been excluded from the night-shift.'

Cold apprehension clutched at her insides as she realised what he was implying. 'For heaven's sake, Clay, ask Peter; he'll tell you—'

'Of that I have no doubt. I'm sure he has his own reasons for covering his tracks. A wife, for one. Maybe I'm wrong, but he has the look of a married man. But perhaps she's more forgiving than I am.'

'I have been working for the last twelve hours, Clay. I'm too tired to argue with you.'

'In an expensive silk blouse and a skirt? Pushing credibility just a bit too far, wouldn't you say?'

'I borrowed a pair of overalls from…' She stopped. She had done nothing to be ashamed of. Nothing to excuse herself for. 'This is ridiculous. I'm going to have a shower and go to bed. We can talk when you're feeling a little more rational.' She walked quickly away from him and hurried to the stairs, but he followed her.

'If you plan to sleep in my bed, be sure to change the sheets before you leave.' The slashing edge of his voice was like a knife, cutting so deep that nothing could ever stop the pain, bringing her to an abrupt halt on the first rise of the stairs. She turned, her hand clutching at the rail to prevent herself from falling.

'You want me to leave?'

'Oh, yes, Jo. I want you to leave. Before I get home this evening. I'm afraid there's nothing generous in my nature where you are concerned. I won't share.'

The hard, uncompromising planes of his face swam before her. She blinked the tears back. She had been ready to give up everything she had ever wanted to be with Clay Thackeray, but he had told her to go. Leave. And none of it was true. She reached for him, determined to get through to him somehow.

'Don't touch me.' His voice was low. He had not raised it above a polite conversational tone throughout, yet it vibrated with menace. She pulled back her fingers as if she had been burned.

'Clay,' she appealed desperately, making a last attempt to get through. But his face was shuttered, closed to her. He was convinced she had spent the night with Peter Lloyd and nothing she said was going to change his mind. And she would not grovel. If he had so little trust in her, perhaps it was better to end it quickly. A sharp stab of guilt caught in her throat. There had been precious little trust on either side.

Pride was all that remained. Marry in haste, the old adage went, repent at leisure. Well, she had her promotion; that was a start. She would just have to ensure that she had no leisure to waste on regret.

She said nothing—she was no longer capable of speech—and he nodded, as if satisfied that he had made his point, before turning for the door. He stood for a moment in the opening and took a deep breath and, when he turned back, just for a moment her heart flickered back into life.

'I'm sorry, Jo. I should have remembered that when you wake a sleeping tiger you have to stick around to keep it under control.' Then he was gone. She heard the throaty roar of the Aston as it disappeared down the lane. Then there was silence.

She sank to the stairs, her legs unable to hold her, and sat there for a while, quite numb with shock.

The ringing of the telephone brought her to her feet. It might be him, she thought wildly. He might have changed his mind. She reached for the receiver, but the answerphone cut in and she remained motionless, her hand ready to snatch it up at the first sound of his voice. The message ended, the tone sounded.

'Hello, Clay? This is Henry Doubleday. Redmond's found out what you're doing and it's all going to pieces. I think we'd better meet as soon as possible.'

The man hung up. Henry Doubleday. She frowned, trying to clear her clouded brain, to think where she had heard the name before. Then she remembered.

In a sudden panic she flew up the stairs. She packed her clothes, flinging them into suitcases without care. She had to get away, get everything out of the cottage before he returned, because she was never coming back.

She stripped the bed and pushed the linen into the washing machine, then set the programme. He would have to remake it himself, or maybe Mrs Johnson would. It was no longer her concern.

At last it was done and she summoned a taxi. The driver surveyed the quantity of her luggage, the boxes of her possessions and, about to complain, saw Jo's face. He carried them unprotesting to the car. 'Where to, miss?' he asked, finally.

For a moment she couldn't think. Where on earth could she go? To her mother, or her sister? 'To a hotel,' she said, eventually. 'Somewhere reasonable in Woodhurst.' Somewhere to crawl away and lick her wounds in private.

'The Red Lion?'

She nodded. The Red Lion would do as well as anywhere. It no longer mattered where she went.

*   *   *

Joanna pulled sharply at the fingers of the thin leather gloves she used for driving, using them as an escape valve for her anger.

'Late, Peter?' He didn't improve, she thought. He had put on weight, and the smooth tanned lines of his face were beginning to sag. At least out on site he had had some exercise to keep him in trim. She had never been able to understand why Charles Redmond had taken him on to the board. She stood in the open doorway of the boardroom. How like him to have their meeting in the grandeur of the oak-panelled room, where he could demonstrate his new power.

'We were expecting you two hours ago. I suppose you had car trouble?' The sneer in his voice was the final straw. He was convinced that she used her friendship with Charles Redmond to keep her position, to rise steadily up the ladder, despite everything. But now Charles was dead and he thought she was fair game. Well, she wouldn't go down without a fight.

'If you ever bothered to listen to the weather forecast north of Bristol, Peter, you would know that my site is under four inches of snow. The road across the Beacons was closed at Storey Arms and I had to wait for a police convoy.' She paused to draw breath. 'I finally got to the Severn Bridge just as it closed because of high winds and had to drive up to Gloucester in a two-mile queue of lorries. Now, perhaps you would like to tell me exactly what was so important that I had to be here this afternoon, when I would much rather have been building a snowman!'

'Mr Lloyd sent for you at my request, Miss Grant. I thought it was important that you should meet your new chairman.'

Joanna spun in the direction of the soft, well-modulated voice that even now had the power to make the blood leap in her veins, bringing a flush to her skin and making her heart beat unbelievably fast. She took a step into the room and closed the door. It was him. Sitting at the far end of the long polished table, the window behind him so that his face was in shadow.

'Please come and sit down. I'm sure Mr Lloyd will be happy to fetch a cup of coffee for an old…friend.' His eyes gleamed coldly.

'I…' She looked at Peter and then back to her husband. She nodded, helplessly.

She wanted to shout at him, ask him what he thought he was doing to come crashing back into her world when she had finally reached a state where peace seemed a possibility. But if the past two years had given her nothing else, it had given her self-control. She jerked a nervous glance to the secretary's office next door. No. More than self-control. Much more.

He indicated the chair beside him and she walked slowly down the room, her feet sinking soundlessly into the soft carpet. She lowered herself, very carefully, into the chair beside him and stared unseeing at the cup Peter placed in front of her. 'I'm sorry to hear that you have had such a bad journey.'

'You could have rung in,' Peter interjected. 'You have a telephone in your car.'

'It…it isn't working.'

Clay made a note on the pad in front of him. 'I see that you've been running the site at Brynglas ever since the project manager went on sick leave.' She nodded silently, a hard knot in the pit of her stomach. 'You're several weeks behind.' He sounded reasonable enough and yet she was sure that something bad was going to happen.

'Yes.'

'Six weeks.' Peter's voice rang with satisfaction.

Clay shot him a silencing glance. 'You are being relieved of that position as from today.'

Her head jerked up then and she faced him. Was the destruction of her career to be his final revenge? 'For what reason?'

'Company restructuring.'

'Are you dissatisfied with my work?' she asked, coldly. 'I will have to ask you to justify any complaints.' She glanced across at Peter. She had been so sure when the summons came that he wanted to tell her in person that he was the new chairman and her days were numbered. She could have fought Peter, but Clay? When had she ever been able to fight him?

There was a tap at the door and the secretary put her head around it. 'I'm sorry to interrupt, gentlemen. Jo, have you got a bag for Alys? Bit of an emergency.'

She caught her breath and glanced quickly at Clay. His face, half-shadowed, was expressionless. She rose. 'I'm sorry, I left it in the car.'

'Give me a key. I'll see to it.'

Clay's voice was shatteringly loud in the silence that followed the woman's departure. 'You've brought your child into the office?'

'What can you expect if you allow women the sort of freedom she's had?' Peter was unable to hide his triumph.

She turned on him. Anywhere but at the stark blue

eyes of her husband. 'What did you expect? Should I have left her on a Welsh hilltop in the care of the site foreman?'

'You should be at home looking after her. The office is not an appropriate place for a baby.' Peter knew that she had had a relationship with Clay and she realised with disgust that he was thoroughly enjoying the situation.

'I'm well aware that you vetoed a crèche facility in the office, Peter. But I'm not your only employee with a baby. You have at least one father who is bringing up a child on his own.'

'Enough!' Clay's voice cut through their bitter exchange. 'I have no interest in your domestic arrangements, but my secretary has better things to do than play nursemaid.' His glance fell on Peter Lloyd. 'I won't keep you.' His voice was dismissive.

He turned to Jo, his eyes holding her as surely as shackles. She wished he would not look at her. It was too painful. The memories, she found, even after all this time, were still too raw.

He finally broke the silence. 'How are you, Joanna?'

'As you see me, Clay.'

'Tired and alone. The lovers soon fell out, it would seem.' His eyes flickered to the doorway through which Peter Lloyd had departed.

She turned angrily. 'I'm tired because I've had a tiring day. And no, Clay, I'm not alone.'

'The situation has a certain irony, wouldn't you say? It must cramp your style considerably. But you've managed to see that your career has not suffered. You still give that your first concern.'

'Not my first, Clay. But I haven't neglected it for
the simple reason that I need a job. I don't work for
myself any more, Clay. I work for my daughter.'

'But the child's father...' His voice trailed away as
if he couldn't bear to say the word.

She caught and held the cry of anguish in her throat.
'I have never asked him for anything.'

A black scowl darkened his face. 'He should still
provide for her. Good God! He knows. He said, just
now, that you should be at home with her.'

She wondered if he would believe her if she told
him the truth. What he would do. She shuddered involuntarily.

'I think perhaps I had better clear up one thing. Clay.
Peter is many things, most of them unspeakable, but
he is not the father of my child.'

He stood up so suddenly that she jumped. Then he
turned his back to her and walked to the window, staring down into the car park below. When he turned back
to face her his mouth was twisted into the semblance
of a smile.

'That's the thing with late starters. They are so enthusiastic.'

She had asked for that, but it still hurt and she had
taken more than enough punishment for one day. She
stood up, carefully gathering her gloves and bag, self-
respect requiring that she withdraw in good order before she broke down completely.

'I haven't congratulated you on your appointment as
chairman. I rather thought Peter would get the job.'

'I'm sorry to disappoint you.'

She hesitated, wanting to get away, needing to find

a dark hole into which she could crawl and lick her wounds. But she had to know why he had come back. 'What are you going to do with Redmonds? Will you break the company up?'

'Break it up?'

'That's what "restructuring" means, isn't it? Sell off the valuable assets and junk the rest. I helped to stop it the last time you tried, but with Charles gone I don't suppose anybody cares very much. Except the people who will be out of work as a result.'

He was beside her before she could move, his face just inches from her own. 'Just what exactly did you think you were helping to stop?'

She could see the small scar on his chin where an irate workman had once hit him with a shovel and she felt a certain sympathy with the man. It was so close that if she just moved her weight to her toes she could touch it with her lips. And she longed to. Even after all he had done to her, he still evoked an almost animal response from her.

'Mummy!' she turned to see her daughter racing up the length of the boardroom towards her.

Jo scooped up her daughter and held her tightly. A fair mop-haired creature, a tiny miniature of herself in every respect, except that her bright blue corduroy dungarees echoed eyes that every day were a wrenching reminder of Clay. She turned to him and the child stretched out chubby starfish hands to him.

He stared at her with a look of such hunger that Jo's heart missed a beat and for a moment she thought he would touch the tiny fingers. Then he jerked abruptly away.

'We'll continue this in the morning.' His voice was harsh. 'Please be in my office at nine o'clock.'

'I'll fight you, Clay,' she said fiercely.

He smiled slightly. 'I look forward to that battle.' When she made no answer he walked to the door and opened it. 'It will be interesting to see what weapons you can muster. After all, you sold your shares to Charles two years ago.'

She had hoped to bluff him. Hoped he didn't know that. But it seemed he knew everything, except that she loved him and that Alys was his daughter. 'Nine o'clock. Don't be late.'

'If you're going to fire me, Clay, I'd rather you did it now. There's no need to dramatise it any further.'

'Your preferences are no concern of mine and your...daughter is nearly asleep.'

She looked at the fair head nestling on her shoulder. 'It's been a long day.'

'How do you manage?' Surprised at the edge of concern in his voice, she raised her eyes to his.

'The same way that thousands of other women manage, Clay. Childminders. Family. Taking her to work when, like today, everything else fails.'

Then he said, brutally, as if regretting his sudden lapse into humanity, 'I thought that you were far too careful to fall into that trap.'

'We all make mistakes, Clay.' She stroked the child's head and added almost to herself, 'At least I managed to do one thing right.' His sharp intake of breath brought her back to reality. 'I must go.'

'Yes. And please make alternative arrangements for tomorrow. This isn't a nursery.'

*　　*　　*

Her mother fussed over them both, asking no questions. It wasn't until Alys was asleep and Jo was curled up in her dressing-gown in front of the fire that she broke the news.

'Clay's back.' Jo sipped her cocoa. 'He's the new chairman of Redmonds.' Her mother's unexpected in-precation sent her eyebrows rocketing.

'You'll resign, of course.'

'I may not have to.'

'Oh, darling, he'd never have the nerve to sack you!'

'They call it restructuring these days.'

'If I get hold of him, he'll be the one...'

'No, Mum. Please. It's all over and forgotten. For the moment he's my boss. I'm seeing him first thing in the morning. When I know what he's got in mind, then I can make decisions about the future.'

'You won't listen to my advice?'

'No need, I think I can guess it. Run away?'

'Hard and fast. He hurt you, Jo. I don't know how because you never saw fit to confide in me, but I saw what it did to you. You can't go through that again, and besides, you've Alys to think of.' She stiffened. 'Would he try and get custody of her?'

'No.' Her mother deserved some sort of explanation. She had never asked what had gone wrong, never criticised. She had been proved right and that had apparently been enough. She didn't need to say 'I told you so' and for that Jo had been grateful. 'Clay is under the impression that Alys is the result of...of...a fling.' She watched with a kind of awful fascination as a tear fell into her cup.

'A what?'

'When he went to Canada.'

'The man's a fool. And so are you if you want to keep him ignorant. He's only got to look at the child—'

'Apparently not. He saw her today.'

'But her eyes, Jo!'

'I wouldn't have taken her to the office if I'd known he would be there. But it didn't matter. He never noticed. And there's no reason for him to see her again.' She looked up. 'Will you look after her tomorrow?'

'If you moved back home you would never have to worry about babysitters again. You could just get on with your career. You've done so well.'

'Have I?'

'It's not the time for doubts. Your marriage was just a blip. An aberration. But it's out of your system now and you're moving on.' She frowned. 'You will be careful, won't you? He's a dangerous man. Strong, wilful.'

'Yes, Mum. I'll be careful.'

'Don't fuss, Jo. I can look after Alys. I'm far more worried about you. That man...' She regarded her daughter with concern. 'Why don't you just take leave in lieu of notice?'

'I can't do that.'

Her mother shrugged philosophically. 'No, I suppose not. You never did do things the easy way.' She looked admiringly at her daughter's clothes. 'At least you're going down with all flags flying.'

Jo checked her reflection in the mirror. The suit, with its plain, old gold, collarless jacket and soft skirt in a bold abstract print of white and black and the same old gold, had come from her sister's boutique. She wound a scarf of the same material around her neck and nodded.

'Yes, Mum. All flags.' Today was definitely not a day for jeans.

'Miss Grant?' She paused in Reception an hour later and looked at the man who had spoken to her.

'Yes.'

'I'm from Pentagon Motors. I've come for your car. Could I have your keys, please?'

She looked at the keys, still in her hand, and the Pentagon key fob. The leasing company for all the company cars. She had heard of such things happening: being sacked and having to get a bus home. The modern equivalent of having your sword broken and the epaulettes ripped from your uniform.

'It's...I haven't...I need to clear it out.'

He shrugged. 'If you insist. Can you do it straight away? I haven't much time.'

She stiffened. 'Of course.'

She led the way to the car park and unlocked the car. There wasn't much. Some maps. Driving shoes. She bent to pick them up and discovered a feeding cup that Alys had dropped.

'What about the boot?'

'No. It's empty.' The man was looking expectantly at her. 'Here.' She handed him the keys and he climbed in, driving away with the sort of fierce bravado that some men seemed to feel was necessary in the presence of a woman. Or maybe he was just as embarrassed as she was. She walked back into the office and up to the first floor.

His secretary waved her to the door. 'Go straight in. He saw you arrive and he's waiting for you.'

So, he had watched the little performance in the car park. She straightened her back and opened the door. He looked up briefly from his writing block and motioned her to a seat.

'Sit down, Joanna. I won't be a minute.' He carried on writing in his bold, incisive hand, giving her a moment to notice the fine sprinkle of grey hair at his temple. Then he threw down his pen and sat back. 'Would you like some coffee?'

'No, thank you. I can do without the niceties. I'm not prepared to sit and let you gloat, Clay. You've humiliated me enough for one day. Say what you have to and then let me go.'

'Humiliated?' He frowned. 'In what way?'

She stood up. 'Do you want me to make it easy for you and resign?'

'For heaven's sake sit down. You never used to indulge in hysterics.'

'I've never been sacked before.'

He fixed her with a glare that riveted her to her seat. 'I haven't asked you to come all this way to sack you, as you so inelegantly put it.'

'Then why have you taken my car?'

'Taken your car?' He looked at her blankly.

'Did you enjoy the performance? I understand from Mrs Gregg that you watched from your window.'

'What the hell are you talking about?'

'I was mugged in Reception by a driver from the leasing company. You might at least have waited until afterwards...'

Light at last dawned. 'You complained last night of a faulty car phone. Pentagon were asked to fit a replacement as soon as possible. I had no idea they were coming today.'

'Car phone?' She stared at him. 'Then why on earth didn't the man say?'

'I imagine he thought you knew. And now we've cleared up one misunderstanding we'd better move on to the next. I have brought you in from the site, Jo, because I want you working here. In the office.'

'No!'

She might never have spoken. 'You've proved yourself in every possible way to be competent, hardworking and reliable. Even in the most trying circumstances. Reading between the lines of your weekly reports, the last few months at Brynglas cannot have been easy. And, despite Lloyd's attempts to blacken you, I am well aware that, when you took over, the job was ten weeks adrift.' He sat back in his chair and regarded her from beneath hooded lids. 'He's very anxious to get rid of you, did you know?'

'I'm not surprised.'

He waited for some sort of explanation but she said nothing more. He had no doubt already made up his own mind about why Peter would want to be rid of her and nothing she said would change it.

'No, I don't suppose you are. But he is going to be disappointed. However, if you're going to progress further in your career you need some management experience.'

Progress? What on earth did that mean? 'And if I prefer to stay out on site?'

'At the moment you have no choice in the matter.'

'I could leave Redmonds.'

'Not so easy at the moment. You did say you needed a job?' He regarded her thoughtfully. 'I wonder what sort of reference Lloyd would dream up for you?'

'He wouldn't dare!'

'You're prepared to take the risk?' He was provoking her deliberately, but she was determined not to rise to the bait. Apparently satisfied with her silence, he continued. 'You've proved you can do the job out there at the sharp end. Now it's time to demonstrate that there's more to Miss Joanna Grant than reinforced concrete. Or are you afraid to try?'

CHAPTER SIX

CLAY was challenging her head-on, forcing her to make a decision that would affect the rest of her life. In daring her to stay and face him he was instituting a war of nerves, and Joanna wasn't about to turn tail and run. She met the mocking question in his eyes and forced her lips into an answering smile.

'What exactly are you offering, Clay?'

A glint of satisfaction lit those seemingly bottomless blue depths and her smile faltered. It was hard enough to sit opposite the man she loved so much that each day it was a physical pain which could only be defeated by working herself until she dropped. His father had said, the day they were married, that Clay always got exactly what he wanted. Now she wondered with a qualm of unease just exactly what he wanted from her.

'I have a job for you in the planning department.'

'Planning!' At her arrogant gesture of dismissal his face darkened.

'You can have your say when I've finished. Be quiet and listen to what I'm offering before you dismiss my proposition out of hand.' His voice rattled against her and, stunned into silence by his blazing arrogance, she found herself doing exactly what she was told. When at last he had finished he leaned back in his chair. 'Now, you may speak.'

'I…hardly know what to say.'

'Well, I have achieved something.' His mouth finally twisted in the semblance of a smile. 'Does that mean you're tempted by my proposition?'

Of course she was tempted. He knew her too well, knew exactly what would hold her, and he had held out the sweetest plum. But first there would be six months in the planning office, every day spent under his eye, at his beck and call, subject to his whim. Her mother's advice to run as hard and fast as she could rang loudly in her ears. She needed time to think and so she countered his question with one of her own.

'This is a long-term proposition, Clay. What happened to the restructuring?'

'The restructuring?' For a moment his dark brows drew together in a frown, then he leaned towards her and instinctively she edged back. 'The restructuring is on hold, Jo.' Even across the vastness of his desk the threat was clear. 'Until I have your answer.'

For a long time she didn't say anything. Somewhere a telephone was ringing. There was a burst of laughter in the corridor. Outside these four walls, she thought, people were going about their business quite unaware of this quiet drama taking place in Clay's office that could affect all their lives.

'How long do I have to think about it?' she said, at last.'

'Not long. Henry Doubleday will be here at eleven. You've met, I believe?' he said. 'I shall have to know by then.' His eyes gave her no clue to his thoughts. And when he spoke his voice held none of the warmth that for a few weeks, a painfully few, had had the power to bring her total happiness. 'Last time I made a bid for this company, Jo, you thwarted me. Now I'm going to make you pay for that.'

She felt her blood run to ice. The ruthless man sitting opposite her was her husband. The father of her child. The man she had loved. A catch in her throat caught her by surprise; still loved, although he had broken her heart beyond mending. And he was going to punish her for something she had never done. She held herself very still. It was vital that she didn't show any emotion, then at least she would prevent a total defeat. She raised her clear grey eyes to meet his. 'You were going to destroy Redmonds,' she said, with only the faintest betraying tremor in her voice. 'You told me yourself you have no interest in mere "concrete" any more.'

'It has its uses. I'm always happy to gather another profitable company under my wing.'

'Even if you had to marry me to make certain?' No wonder it had been so easy for him to walk away. Perhaps he had never intended to stay.

'My mistake. But now I'm giving you a chance to redeem yourself. Once again the fate of Redmonds is in your hands, Joanna.' He glanced at his watch. 'And time is running out. What shall I do? Save it or throw it away?'

'You're the consultant, Clay. What would you advise?'

'I'm in the happy position of being unable to lose.' He shrugged and leaned back in his chair. 'The choice is all yours.'

'There doesn't seem to be much choice involved. I cannot just sit back and allow you to throw Redmonds to the wolves. I accept your offer.'

His smile was chilling. 'I thought I could rely upon you for blind loyalty to your company. You should try it on people occasionally.'

She blenched. 'Not totally blind,' she said, desperately. 'There are two conditions, Clay.'

'What makes you believe you're in a position to make conditions?' His cynical demand brought a flush to her cheeks but she refused to back down.

'I'm making these.' He raised a condescending brow and nodded for her to continue. 'If we're to work in the same building, Clay, the past must be forgotten.'

A vein beat fiercely at his temple. 'Have you forgotten it? Have there been so many other men in your life that you can blot out memories of what it was like to lie in my arms?'

She hadn't forgotten. Not for a moment. Even as he spoke she felt the fiery colour rush to her cheeks as her body responded to the pictures his words evoked. Apparently satisfied with the effect of his words, he made a dismissive gesture. 'You said two conditions.'

'I want to buy back my shares.'

A faint smile curved his lips. 'Can you afford them?'

'I still have the money from the original sale.' Money that she would need to buy a home for Alys. It had been a rash demand, a symptom of her need to patch up an ego battered by his insolent demands. Clay Thackeray was altogether too much in command and she wanted to see him stopped in his tracks. But he was unmoved.

'You once told me that you knew nothing about business, Jo. I think perhaps the shares are safer in my hands for the moment.'

'And my other condition?' she persisted desperately.

For a moment their eyes locked. Then he stood up. 'I'll think about it.'

She rose to her feet. 'Make sure you do.'

He nodded. 'If you insist. But it might be safer to let sleeping dogs lie. Now, I'll take you down to Planning and get you settled in.' He reached for her arm and she jerked nervously at his touch, afraid of the power he still had to raise her pulse-rate, but he tightened his grip, ignoring her reaction. It was just chemistry, she told herself. Nothing else. But it made no difference to the way her pulse raced.

'I know my way,' she said quickly.

'I don't doubt it.' And she knew there was no further point in protesting. With Clay there never was. 'You'll be wanting your things from Brynglas. I imagine you've quite a lot of stuff there?' he said, conversationally, as she allowed him to lead her down the stairs.

'Quite a lot,' she agreed dully. Most of it belonged to Alys.

'Shall I have someone collect it for you? Or would you like to borrow a transit van and fetch it yourself?'

'I have to go back. I can't just abandon Mrs Rhys without a word of thanks after all she's done for me and Alys.'

'You'll need to take two days, I imagine?' His voice remained light, only the tightening of his jaw muscles suggesting any emotion.

'Yes.'

He stopped, forcing her to do the same. 'Will your mother take care of...Alys?'

'Yes. She'll be happy to.'

He seemed surprised, and it was a relief to reach the planning department, although when he had gone and she was able to think clearly again she realised that he hadn't in fact agreed to either of her conditions.

'Well?' Her mother had waited until Alys was in bed before she began her interrogation.

'I've a new job. In Planning. I'll be working at the office for a while.'

'The clothes must have made the hoped-for impression, then.'

'What? Oh, I suppose so.'

'Although it doesn't sound quite your cup of tea. Are you really going to take it?'

'It won't be like working in the office when I was expecting Alys.' Jo pulled a face at the memory of the weeks stuck behind a drawing-board. 'I'll be working on a major new project and then Clay's promised me the job of agent for the temporary works.'

'Good lord!' She saw the brief gleam of triumph in her mother's eyes, but it was quickly extinguished. 'And just what does he want in return?' she asked.

'Nothing!' Even to her own ears she sounded a little fierce, as if she was trying to convince herself. 'It's a fantastic opportunity, that's all,' she added, less emphatically.

'So you'll be staying on?'

'You could sound a little more enthusiastic. I thought you'd be pleased. Can you put up with us for a few weeks until I can find somewhere to live?'

'As long as you like, you know that.' Her mother's

look was measuring. 'But I'm still not sure that it's wise. Can you cope?'

'Cope?'

'Come on, Jo. You toughed it out, never let the mask drop, but I saw what it did to you when you split up with Clay. Can you really manage to forget that?' There was no answer. 'Can he?' she added, as an afterthought.

'Clay and I are history.'

'So are Antony and Cleopatra.' She shrugged. 'Oh, well, it's another step on the ladder. Just remember that I warned you. Stay clear of him.'

'I'll remember. Oh, I'm borrowing a transit van to go to Brynglas and collect all our stuff. Will you look after Alys, or shall I take her with me?'

'Leave her with me. I can spoil her rotten for a couple of days without you scowling at me.'

Jo wrapped up in warm black dungarees and a bright red ski jacket against the long journey. A horn sounded in the road and she grabbed her bag, kissed Alys and hugged her mother.

'There's the driver. I'll get back tonight if I can. It depends on the weather.'

Jo hurried down to the gate and opened the van door. 'Clay!' She took an involuntary step back, then managed to pull herself together sufficiently to offer a smile. 'How kind of you to bring the van yourself.'

'It was no trouble. Your mother is waving, Jo. Do you think she's seen me? Shall I wave back?' She looked around and saw her mother at the window.

'No!' If her mother saw Clay she would be sure to

think the worst. She waved herself and he pulled his mouth down in a provoking little smile.

'Very touching. Now get in. I'm in a hurry.'

She swung herself up and fastened her seatbelt. 'So why are you here?' she asked, as they headed for the main road. 'Surely we're not that short of drivers.' Then she frowned as he took the slip-road to the motorway. 'This isn't the way back to the office.'

'How perceptive. I was going up to Brynglas anyway. It seemed an unnecessary waste of fuel for us to travel separately. And as your belongings won't fit in the Aston—'

'You're going…?' She turned on him. 'You planned this deliberately! How could you?'

'Easily. You didn't think I brought you into the office out of the kindness of my heart, did you? You'll have your promotion at the end of it, but in the meantime don't expect to enjoy yourself. Particularly not with your male colleagues.'

'You haven't got a heart!' she gasped.

'No?' His mouth clamped down hard for a moment. Then he managed a smile. 'No. Not any more. But I do remember what it was like to have one.'

'Take me home right now!' she demanded.

He ignored her and she glanced helplessly around. They were hurling relentlessly down the motorway. It was miles to the next services and she doubted that he would stop even if she begged him.

'Why have you done this?' she demanded. Then colour washed her face. She couldn't, wouldn't put into words the disquieting thoughts spinning around her head. 'What do you want from me?'

'Why should I want anything? I've already had everything on offer.' His brows rose at her involuntary imprecation.

'I—I don't want to go to Brynglas with you.'

'That's no surprise. I'm sure you have plenty of loose ends to tie up that I'll get in the way of. But it's too far for you to drive both ways in a day and I have no intention of allowing you the luxury of an overnight stop. With two of us to drive we can come back tonight.'

'There's precious little luxury at Brynglas,' she snapped.

'We'll see.'

For a while they drove in silence as they negotiated the busy stretch of the M4, but as the traffic thinned he began to ask her about the job. He was so matter-of-fact and businesslike in his questioning that soon she was responding quite naturally.

'It must have been difficult for you,' he said finally. 'Since the project manager took to drinking whisky for breakfast, in preference to tea.'

She stared at him. He was very well informed. She had never said anything. Never even hinted at the problem. 'I never shared breakfast with him, so I couldn't say.'

'No?' She refused to dignify the suggestion with an answer and he shrugged. They were approaching the bridge and he took the slip-road. 'But speaking of breakfast reminds me that it was a very long time ago.'

She glanced at her watch. 'It's rather early for lunch.'

'Not too late for a second breakfast, though.' He

pulled up in the services car park and turned to her. 'It's a long time since we shared breakfast, Joanna. But I'm willing to take the risk if you are.'

'Risk?' she asked, defiantly. 'What risk?'

He jumped down and came around to her door and opened it. 'Who can say?'

'Clay!' she warned and suddenly felt very alone with him.

'Well?' he laughed softly. 'Are you going to join me? Or are you just going to sit there and wish you had?'

'I'm going to join you, of course.'

He lifted her down and for a moment stood with his hands around her waist. It would have been so easy to put her arms around his neck and kiss him. Despite everything she still wanted to. There was still that instant attraction between them, like iron filings to a magnet. Instead she pulled back, lifted her chin and tightened her coat around her to keep out the biting wind. And anything else that was trying to get in. 'In fact, I'm very hungry,' she said, with a bravado she was far from feeling.

They piled their plates with food and went to sit at a window overlooking the Severn. The huge towers of the bridge stood clear of a low mist that enveloped the estuary, giving a magical air to the view.

'I've always loved this bridge. It's quite beautiful when you can't see the lorries and the toll booths.'

'Beautiful?' Clay regarded the bridge without enthusiasm. 'It's functional, up to a point. But not quite my idea of beauty.' He turned to face her. 'Not that I should be surprised. We manage to differ about most things.'

'Managed, Clay. Past tense.' She bent her attention very firmly to her food but he hadn't finished.

'I'm having some difficulty with our agreement, Joanna.'

'You're not trying hard enough.' But suddenly her appetite had gone.

He reached out and captured her hand, holding it when she would have pulled free to escape the instant fire of his touch. He rubbed idly at the plain gold band he had slipped on to her finger the day they were married. When he looked up, his eyes were wintry. 'You seem to have managed well enough.'

'It takes practice,' she told him with all the chill she could muster and jerked her hand free.

They arrived at Brynglas shortly before twelve and Mrs Rhys hurried from the farmhouse to meet her as she stepped stiffly from the van.

'Come in, *cariad*. Out of the cold.'

Clay stayed in the van. 'I'll be back later. If you can have everything ready to load we'll start straight back.' He frowned. 'I thought you said it was under a pile of snow up here?'

'That was last week,' Mrs Rhys told him. 'It's rained since then. But the snow will be back soon enough.'

'Do you want me to come with you?' Jo asked. 'You don't know the way.'

'I'll find it. You've enough to do here.' He drove away.

She spent several hours packing, then dismantled the cot and began to carry everything down the narrow

stairs. It took longer than she expected and when Mrs
Rhys suggested something to eat she was more than
happy to accept.

Afterwards she settled her rent and gave her the present she had brought, a huge printed Liberty scarf and
a pair of black leather gloves. Then they sat by the fire
to wait for Clay.

'She's like him, your little one,' Mrs Rhys said finally. 'About the eyes.'

Jo frowned. Mrs Rhys knew nothing about her past
relationship with Clay, yet she had seen in an instant
the likeness between them. 'We're not...together, Mrs.
Rhys. Clay has taken over the company I work for,
that's all.'

'Well, there's a pity.'

'I'd rather you didn't mention anything.'

She glanced up. 'No. I see. It's dark. I'd better draw
the curtains.

Jo glanced anxiously at the clock from time to time.
It was nearly six o'clock when the crunching sound of
tyres on gravel sent her rushing to the window.

Mrs Rhys let him in and ushered him to the fire. 'Sit
there and warm yourself. I'll get you some soup.'

'Is it always this cold here?' he demanded, as he
rubbed his hands vigorously before the flames.

Jo grinned. 'Stick around. It's only November; the
best is yet to come.' She left him to his soup and started
loading the van, hurrying to get out of the icy wind.
'It's all done. I think we'd better get going, Clay. It's
started to rain.'

'I've made you a flask, Jo,' said Mrs Rhys before
they left. 'You might be glad of something hot.'

'Bless you.' She hugged the woman. 'I'll bring Alys back in the summer to see you.'

'Come up for the shearing, *cariad*. She'll love it.' She smiled at Clay. 'You'll all be welcome.'

Jo held her breath, but Clay apparently read no special meaning into the words and merely thanked the woman for her hospitality.

'I'll drive,' Jo volunteered.

'No. I'll take this stretch. You can have it when we get to the motorway.' For a moment she considered arguing; she knew the roads up in the hills far better than he did. But he had claimed the driving seat and fastened his seatbelt. 'Come on,' he said, impatiently. She felt an odd reluctance to surrender herself to his mercy once more. She glanced back at Mrs Rhys, standing in the square of light in the doorway that somehow represented safety. Then she raised her hand and climbed in.

He fired the engine and, avoiding as many pot-holes as possible, left the farmyard. Once he had negotiated the narrow lane they might have been the only people left on earth.

They had been travelling for twenty minutes or so, Clay taking it rather more slowly in the dark, when the rain turned quite suddenly to snow. It wasn't settling much on the roads, but the hillsides rapidly began to whiten and the huge flakes flinging themselves out of the darkness and swirling in the headlights made it difficult to tell where the road ended and the rocky hillside began.

'Should we turn back?' Jo asked, anxiously.

He glanced at her. 'We should be all right...' She

shouted a warning as a sheep loomed suddenly out of
the darkness and halted, panic-stricken, in the headlights. Clay swerved to avoid hitting it and there was
the ominous sound of tearing metal from underneath
the van. With a muffled curse he turned off the engine
and jumped down to see what the damage was.

'Well?' she demanded.

He got up and brushed the snow from his knees. 'I
can't tell without a torch, but I don't think it's good. I
can hear something dripping.' He sounded remarkably
sanguine, she thought irritably, and looked around.
There was not a light to be seen and they hadn't passed
another vehicle since they left the farm. She saw him
grin in the light from the headlamps. 'Thank goodness
for Mrs Rhys and her flask. I have a feeling that we
may need it before morning.'

'Morning?' The prospect of a night alone in his company was daunting. 'Surely we can try and get to a
garage?'

'I don't think we'll be going anywhere. Get back in.
There's no point in getting any colder until I've found
the torch.' She complied without demur. The snow had
wet her cheeks and the wind was cutting viciously. She
rubbed them, already shivering. 'What's the chance of
some other vehicle coming along before morning?' he
asked.

'Not very high,' she was forced to admit. 'This is a
forestry road. Another few weeks and you won't be
able to move for rally drivers, but right now it's a bit
off the beaten track.' She glanced out at the swirling
blizzard. 'And let's be honest, if you didn't have to go

somewhere, would you venture out on a night like this?'

'Frankly, no. In fact I can't think what I am doing out on a night like this when I could be sitting in front of Mrs Rhys's fire.'

'I'm sorry.' She began to shake.

'Oh, come on, Jo.' He put his arms around her. 'It's not that bad.' His arms were strong and his voice convincing and she felt safe pressed up against the warmth of his chest.

'Isn't it?' She looked up and for one giddy moment thought that perhaps it wasn't.

He grinned. 'I'm sure I can think of something to do that will keep us warm.' With a shock she recollected where she was. And just who had his arms around her. There was no safety there. He laughed softly as she jerked back, but he made no effort to restrain her. 'No? In that case I'd better summon assistance.' He produced a portable telephone from his jacket and punched in a number.

'How long?' she asked, when he had finished.

'They said twenty minutes.'

'They always say twenty minutes,' she said dismissively. 'How long really?'

'I would say a more realistic estimate is likely to be nearer three or four hours.'

Her heart sank as she recognised the truth in what he said. 'Maybe we could do something ourselves,' she suggested.

'What exactly?'

'Unless we look we won't know,' she said, crossly,

and opened the glove compartment. 'There's a torch in here.' She flicked it on and handed it to him.

'Oh, no. If you're that keen you can come and hold the wretched thing for me.' She didn't wait for a second invitation. She opened the door and quickly clambered down. The road was ankle deep in slushy, semi-liquid snow. Clay swore as he skidded on the surface and called a warning back to her. But it was too late. One foot went from under her and before she could save herself she was over the edge and rolling down the snow-covered hill.

'Jo!' She lay for a moment in the dark, breathless and too winded to reply. 'Jo, for heaven's sake answer me!' His anxious voice drifted down to her, but all she could do was lie quite still while she struggled to regain her breath. It was the sound of his feet crashing and slithering down the hillside that jerked her into movement.

'I'm all right,' she managed to croak. 'For goodness' sake stay there.' But he didn't, coming to a halt beside her, showering her with more wet snow, most of which seemed to find its way inside her jacket and down the back of her neck. She was still clinging desperately to the torch and now he eased it away from her numb fingers and flashed it quickly over her.

'Have you broken anything?' He felt urgently at her legs and arms.

She shook her head. 'No, just a few bruises. You should have stayed up there. Now we both have to get back up.' She shivered convulsively.

'Let me worry about that.' He put his arms around

her waist and lifted her to her feet. For a moment everything spun giddily and she clung helplessly to him.

'Put your arms around my neck,' he commanded. Slowly, almost mesmerised by the force emanating from his powerful body, she obeyed, linking her fingers behind his head, the warmth of his skin giving her strength. Then he swung her up into his arms and carried her back up the hillside. Once he stumbled on a snow-covered rock and swore viciously.

She lifted her head from his shoulder. 'I can manage, Clay. Put me down.' But he took no notice, holding her closer if anything. And she was glad. Ridiculously, stupidly glad.

It was warmer inside the van, out of the wind, but already the temperature was dropping as the engine quickly cooled. He held her for a moment, cradling her on his lap until the trembling began to lessen.

'I'm sorry, Clay. I feel so stupid!' she muttered into the wet cloth of his jacket.

'With good reason,' he said, softly.

Something in his voice made her look up and she saw with a shock that his hair was sticking wetly to his forehead. 'You're soaking. Oh, lord!' she moaned. 'What a mess. I'll get a towel.'

The need to do something for him put strength back into her limbs and she scrambled into the back of the van and tore at the tape on the boxes with her numb fingers until she found one containing her linen. She pulled out her quilt and sheets and found her towels at the bottom. She handed one to him, quite suddenly unable to meet his eyes. He held it for a moment then he made an exasperated sound.

'You've cut your hand. Here, let me.' He took her hand and wrapped one of the towels around a cut that was beginning to ooze blood.

'I c-can't feel a thing,' she said, then gasped through her shivers as he pulled her against him and began to rub hard at her hair with a towel.

'Now get out of these wet things,' he said. Before she could object he had peeled off her coat and begun to unfasten the clips of her dungarees.

'No!' she protested, but they were sticking wetly against her legs and the snow melting inside her collar was beginning to run down her back.

'You never used to be so shy, Joanna. If you don't get them off you'll freeze.' She made no further protest as he undressed her, lifting each foot obediently at his command, trying not to think about his hands as they brushed against her, his fingers on her skin as he peeled off her sweater. But when he began to rub her vigorously with the towel it was more than the cold that was making her shake.

'Stop. Please stop,' she begged.

'Sure?' His voice was harsh as he wrapped her in the quilt, holding it firmly around her for a moment until she had the wit to grab at it. Then he began to dry his own hair. For a moment she watched him, helplessly mesmerised as she remembered the days, pitifully few of them, when she could have done that for him. 'Pour yourself some coffee.' His voice, sharp, intimidating in the confines of the van, made her start, bringing her sufficiently to her senses to turn away as he pulled off soaking trousers.

It's just chemistry, she reminded herself. Nothing

else. The way that dynamite was just chemistry. Jo sipped at the steaming coffee, but, no matter how hard she tried to control them, her teeth wouldn't stop rattling. She watched as he flattened one of the boxes and covered it with her sheets to made a bed of sorts.

'You should be warmer here. Lie down.' She was beyond argument and he lay down beside her, covering them both with the quilt, immediately disappearing under its folds to rub some life back into her legs, peeling off her damp socks to work on her feet. 'Stop, p-please!' she begged, as his touch kindled more than heat. But it seemed forever before he surfaced and every inch of her was glowing with a painful fire.

'Warmer?' She nodded. He rolled on to his back and closed his eyes. 'Your turn.' She swallowed. The thought of deliberately reaching out to touch him was so disturbing that for a moment she didn't think she would be able to do it. But she had to because it was her fault. If she hadn't insisted on looking at the van they would both still be dry. Tentatively at first, and then with more urgency as she felt how cold he was, she chafed at his legs and feet.

'That's enough!' His voice was ragged and before she could object he had put his arm around her and pulled her close. She lay rigid in his arms, knowing the slightest movement would be enough to send them both out of control. So she stayed very still, her ear pressed against the hard wall of his chest, listening to the steady, even thumping of his heart competing with the rising noise of the wind as a thousand memories, brought to vivid life by his closeness, fought for space in her brain. Then a sudden fierce gust shook the transit and she let out a cry of alarm.

Clay crooned softly as she clung to him, holding her tightly while he murmured soft comfort-words into her hair.

'Clay, I'm frightened. Will we freeze to death?'

He lifted his head and in the eerie light reflecting from the snow she could see his eyes. 'No. We won't freeze.' Then he closed them and she saw nothing at all as his mouth descended, blocking out the faint light, the cold, the emptiness.

She caught the warm familiar scent of his skin, and as his fingertips stroked very gently across her neck her lips parted in an involuntary gasp of longing. For a moment the world hung in the balance.

CHAPTER SEVEN

FOR a moment only. Very slowly Joanna drew back from the abyss, gently disengaging herself from the temptations of Clay's arms. His grip tightened and she froze.

'I—can't, Clay,' she whispered.

'No?' His lips teased her throat and she swallowed hard, fighting the desire that blazed like a match struck in the darkness, holding herself rigid against the sweet need to draw close and find comfort in his arms. He raised his head and stared at her for a moment that seemed to last forever.

'I can't,' she repeated, helplessly.

He released her abruptly and sat up. She longed to call him back to her, longed for him to hold her again. But it was time for her to be strong. She had to be strong for Alys.

He turned his back on her. 'If you've any clothes in those suitcases behind you, this would be a good moment to put them on.'

For just a moment she considered trying to explain. Alys had been denied the joy of a complete family. She had no father and there would be no brothers and sisters. What she did have, what Jo gave her gladly, was the right to expect her mother to think of her first, always before herself.

His back, however, did not invite conversation.

Shivering, she left the warmth of the quilt and in the dim light from the cab found a tracksuit and some socks. Dressed, she felt less vulnerable, and she hunted until she found an old pair of men's socks that she wore in her wellingtons and a sweatshirt of her father's.

'Will these fit you?' she asked doubtfully. He took the sweater without a word and pulled it on, straining it severely across the shoulders. The socks were better and she had a sudden uncomfortable feeling that they might once have been his. But he said nothing. Instead he pulled the cover over him and turned on his side. For a moment she sat hugging her knees, wondering what on earth to do.

'Try and get some sleep, Jo. It'll be a long night.'

Sleep. She would have laughed if she hadn't felt quite so much like crying. She wouldn't, couldn't lie beside him. Then, with a sudden jolt, she realised it wasn't necessary.

'Clay!'

He turned over and stared up at her. 'What is it, Jo? Changed your mind?' he asked, roughly.

Grateful for the darkness that hid her burning cheeks, she ignored his crude gibe. 'We can use your telephone to call Mrs Rhys. She'll come and fetch us in the Land Rover. At least we won't freeze to death.'

'We won't freeze to death here,' he said, heavily.

'Please!' At her soft plea he sighed, but sat up and retrieved the phone from his jacket.

'What's her number?' he asked, and punched it in as she repeated it. 'It's unobtainable,' he said, after a moment. 'Could the wind have brought down the line?'

Jo bit her lip. 'It could have. Try again; maybe you

misdialled.' She repeated the number again and he shook his head and held out the receiver for her to listen.

'Nice try, Jo. But you're stuck with me. Now, try and get some sleep.'

She lay down then, trying not to touch him, although in the confined space that was difficult. Then he turned over and put his arm around her and she stiffened. But there was nothing threatening about the gesture; he was offering simple human contact and she found herself relaxing into the welcome warmth of his body.

'Jo?' The sound of his voice and the sudden coldness at her back woke her and she struggled stiffly to sit up.

'What is it?'

'The breakdown truck.' A light swung vivid flashes of yellow across his face in the darkness and he grimaced as he hauled on damp trousers. 'Better get your things together,' he advised, before jumping down to explain the situation to their rescuer.

The driver of the rescue vehicle was horribly cheerful. 'Good morning, Mrs Thackeray.' She jerked involuntarily at the unfamiliar sound of the name and glanced at Clay but his face was unreadable, all yellow and black shadows. With any luck hers would be the same. 'Sorry we've been so long. I was telling your husband that it's been a bad night all over. It seems to be clearing up now, though.' The moon made a brief appearance from behind the clouds and for a moment everything sparkled. 'Why don't you go and get in the cab? It's warm in there and we'll soon have this loaded up.'

Eventually the van was loaded on to the trailer and Clay climbed into the front with the driver.

'Would you like a sandwich, Mrs Thackeray?' he said, leaning back and offering her a plastic box full of thickly cut cheese sandwiches.

Clay threw a hard look at her, daring her, it seemed, to contradict the name. 'No, thank you.' She remembered to smile. At least she hoped what she was doing was smiling.

'Mr Thackeray?' he offered. Clay shook his head.

The driver took them to a garage where Clay arranged for the van to be repaired and hired another one to get them home. They transferred her boxes and bags in total silence and finally set off with Clay at the wheel.

They drove through the snowy darkness for miles and the silence stretched endlessly between them. Jo couldn't think of a way to break it, and anyway Clay seemed lost in thought, hardly aware of her existence.

At the bridge he headed for the services, cutting off her protest that they should push on. 'I need some coffee to keep me awake.'

'Oh!' She felt stupid and in an effort to make amends she suggested breakfast. 'You must be hungry.'

'Yes. I'm hungry.' He stared at her for a moment. 'But it'll keep.' He opened her door and she tried to move but her limbs had stiffened from her fall and he lifted her down, holding her against his chest as her legs buckled. 'Safer to leave it at coffee. Breakfast could so easily become habit-forming.'

'It won't,' she said, with a fierceness she hoped sounded convincing. She had come as close to that danger tonight as she was ever likely to. Despite the desperate yearning for him, as potent now as when his lips had first claimed hers, from somewhere she had found the strength to reject him. Not because she wanted to, but because she had to. They had wasted their chance at love and she wouldn't take whatever second-best he had in mind.

It was light when Clay finally turned the van into Mrs Grant's drive. She was at the door as they climbed down and hurried out as she saw them.

'Jo! I've been worried sick.' Her eyes fell on Clay and her worst fears were apparently confirmed.

'We broke down, Mum. We're all right. If I had thought you would be worrying I would have phoned. But I didn't think you would welcome a call in the middle of the night.'

'It was when I heard the forecast on the television. I telephoned Mrs Rhys and she told me you'd left hours before.'

'We…' Her mother's words sank in. 'Telephoned Mrs Rhys? But her phone was…' She turned on Clay, who regarded her without a flicker of expression, except, she thought, for something in his eyes that might have been amusement at how easy she had been to fool. Disconcerted, she looked away.

'Come along in, both of you. You look frozen.'

'I'll unload the van and get away, Mrs Grant,' he said, stiffly.

One look at his gaunt white face, shadowed where he needed to shave, and she softened despite herself. 'No. Come in by the fire. This will wait. Have you had breakfast?'

He glanced at Jo. 'I thought we'd better get back. I guessed you would worry.' Jo stifled the words that leapt to her lips and he raised one brow in mocking salute to her self-control. It would keep, she thought, following her mother into the house, but vowed that he would have a full account of her feelings on the matter when she felt stronger.

'Sit there, Clay.' Mrs Grant left him in an armchair by the fire and turned on Jo. 'You'd better get into a hot bath, right now.'

'Mum—'

'Later. She pushed Jo towards the stairs and she dragged herself up and stood for a while under a hot shower, afraid that she would fall asleep in a bath. She dressed in soft grey cord trousers and a yellow sweat-shirt and went to look in on her daughter. Alys wasn't in her room and in a sudden panic she ran down the stairs.

'Where's—?'

'Shh.' Her mother placed a finger to her lips and indicated Clay, slumped fast asleep in the armchair. 'I just rescued his cup in time. Come into the kitchen and have something to eat.'

Alys was already there, munching happily on a toast soldier that she offered to her mother. 'Mummy!'

'Hello, my sweet. Have you been a good girl?' It was easier to chatter to the child than meet her mother's knowing eye, but eventually she would have to be faced and the sooner the better.

'I'm sorry you were worried, Mum. The van broke down up in the mountains and we had to wait hours for a tow-truck.'

'That's close enough to Clay's explanation,' her mother said. 'The only thing neither of you has explained, Jo, was how you came to be together in the first place.'

'He had to go to Brynglas to see the site.'

'And you invited him along with you?'

'No!'

Her mother raised an eyebrow. 'But he came anyway. Well, I did warn you.'

'Yes, Mum, you warned me. But you really don't have to worry.' She gazed at Alys. 'My emotions are quite under control.'

Her mother's eyes shifted to the doorway and she spun around. Clay was standing there, a dishevelled figure in the bright kitchen.

'I'd better go.' He turned to Jo. 'Can we unload now?'

'Jo and I can do that later,' Mrs Grant interjected. 'Jo will drive you home now. You look as if you might fall asleep at the wheel. She can bring the van back to the office tomorrow.'

He looked as if he would refuse and Jo, realising the truth in what her mother said, quickly intervened. 'Mother's right, Clay.'

For a moment he stared at her, then he shrugged. 'Who's arguing?'

She turned to give Alys to her mother, but Mrs Grant shook her head. 'I'm afraid you'll have to take her with you, Jo. I've an appointment with the hairdresser in twenty minutes.'

Jo stared at her mother. 'But—'

'If you'll excuse me.' She nodded. 'Goodbye, Clay.'

He offered a half-smile. 'Mrs Grant.'

Jo shrugged. 'Come on, Alys. Let's get your coat on.' She was conscious of Clay standing behind her as she pulled the bright jacket over the child's dungarees.

'She's very like you.'

'Yes,' Jo quickly agreed. 'Everyone says that.' Before she could react he had bent and picked Alys up, holding her at arm's length, staring at her closely. Alys closed her eyes and giggled delightedly, kicking her little legs.

'Is there nothing of her father in her?'

'A—a little.'

His mouth tightened. 'How little?' he demanded.

'If you knew—him, you would see.' She took Alys from him and hurried outside to her car and fastened her firmly into her car seat.

Clay climbed into the passenger seat and closed his eyes. He didn't open them again until she pulled up outside the cottage. She left the engine running and waited for him to get out. He didn't move.

'You're home, Clay.'

He turned and looked towards the cottage. 'Yes. So I am. Come on.' He opened the door.

'No.' His face was implacable and she looked quickly away. 'I don't think that's a good idea.'

'That wasn't a request, Jo.' He grimaced as he straightened. 'God, I'm stiff. Bring Alys, then you'll be quite safe. That was your mother's intention, I take it?'

Jo glanced back at her daughter and frowned slightly. 'Maybe.' She certainly hadn't been going to the hairdresser. Clay opened her door and she climbed out, every bruised muscle shrieking from maltreatment.

As she followed him up the path a movement on the roof caught her eye. The doves were tumbling in their crazy, free-fall flight, just as they had been the very first time she had come here.

'Look, Alys!' she said. Clay stopped for a moment and watched them both and when Jo looked up she saw his forehead crease slightly, as if trying to remember something. It brought her back to earth with a sudden shock. 'What do you want, Clay?'

He dragged himself back from wherever his thoughts had taken him. 'Want?' he asked. Then, as if something had struck him as particularly amusing, he smiled. 'It's time for that breakfast you keep promising me. I'm starving.' He didn't wait for her answer, but turned and opened the door and disappeared inside.

She stood rigid with shock. How dared he? Well, he could whistle for his breakfast. 'Come on, Alys.' But as she turned the little girl slipped her hand and dived through the doorway. 'Alys!' She could hear the soft burble of laughter disappearing towards the drawing-room, and a sudden vision of a fine nineteenth-century porcelain figure of Napoleon on horseback that adorned the sofa-table sent Jo racing after the child.

She came to an abrupt halt in the doorway. The furniture was covered in dustsheets and there were no ornaments to be broken. She took her daughter's hand and walked slowly around the ground floor. The desk in the study was uncovered and had obviously been used recently, but the morning-room was sheeted and the curtains drawn against the light. The kitchen was clean, tidy enough, but didn't gleam the way it had under Mrs Johnson's lavish care.

The fridge revealed little more than a few basic necessities and Jo took out a box of eggs. She had the oddest feeling as she opened the cupboards, knowing exactly where everything would be, that nothing had been touched since she left.

Upstairs she could hear the shower running and she quickly began the task of making scrambled eggs and toast. She put some coffee in the cafetière and set the kettle to boil. Alys had found a cupboard to her liking and had begun to empty it on the kitchen floor, heaping baking tins in an unsteady pile, but Jo had no time to stop her. She was desperate to have everything ready so that she could beat a hasty retreat the minute Clay appeared.

She wasn't sure when she realised the water had stopped running, but something made her turn, and he was standing in the doorway watching her. He was wearing only a short towelling robe and his hair was still wet. She watched in desperate fascination as a droplet of water ran the curve of a tight curl and hung shimmering before splashing on to his neck and running down into the folds of his robe. She quickly put the plate on the table and pressed down the cafetière.

'Won't you join me?'

'I—no.' She turned away and began to pick up the dishes that Alys was playing with, pushing them back into the cupboard.

'Leave it,' he commanded. 'Mrs Johnson will be in later. I expect she'll want to start from scratch.'

'It's been a long time since she was here.' She had to say something.

'It's been a long time since anyone was here. I haven't quite made up my mind whether to move back in or sell the place.'

The thought of anyone else living in their home tugged at her heart-strings, but she had to face reality.

'It's a shame to leave it empty. Where have you been living?'

'I took a service flat in town after you left.'

'I didn't leave. You threw me out.'

'You would have stayed?' His mouth curved in distaste. 'Should I be flattered?'

She didn't reply. There seemed nothing to say. 'We'll be going, then.'

'Sit down, Jo.'

'I don't think—'

'How fortunate for you. Get another cup and sit down. I want to ask you something.' She sank on to the seat opposite him and watched him eat the breakfast she had prepared.

'Well?'

'Can your mother cope with...?' He indicated Alys. 'She seems to be a handful.'

'It's not ideal. But while I'm staying there I think she would be hurt if I found a childminder. Once I've moved out, then it will be different.'

'Moved out?' He looked up. 'You're looking for a place of your own?' A vein began to throb at his temple. 'Or perhaps you're not on your own?'

She felt the colour leave her face. 'I'm a big girl, Clay. It's a long time since I lived at home.'

'Living with your mother must be rather cramping.' She was too shaken to make any response and he shrugged and poured himself another cup of coffee. 'You made a valid point the other day about the need for a crèche. I've had Personnel run a check on numbers and I believe we should go ahead.'

'Why would you do that?' she asked, suspiciously. 'It was vetoed before.'

'You're a single parent,' he said, with careless insolence. 'Surely I don't need to spell out the benefits to you?'

'There's no such thing as a single parent, Clay,' she replied with chilling intensity. 'It takes two people to make a baby.'

'A fact I'm well aware of. But which two?' His voice was cutting. 'You were careful enough to see she wasn't mine.'

Alys looked up from the floor and Jo glared at Clay. 'This conversation is at an end,' she said, with quiet force.

'Not quite.' His eyes were glittering hard. 'I have to know if you loved him.'

'With all my heart, Clay. Until the day I die.' To be able to say the words was a kind of relief. He didn't know, would never know that she meant him. But she knew and rejoiced as she said it. Then she saw the ice in his eyes and the joy froze into a hard, painful knot where her heart was beating far too fast.

'So where is he now?' he demanded. She moved back under the naked savagery in his face, until the chair back stopped her. It seemed forever that they were locked into that look. He straightened abruptly

and turned from her. 'What a waste,' he said, con-
temptuously. 'Will you use the crèche if I go ahead?'

She blinked, momentarily thrown by the sudden shift
in subject. 'Of course. But I don't understand what you
will get out of it.'

'A loyal workforce.' He leaned across and caught
her hand. He frowned and looked down, for a moment
focusing on her wedding-ring. Then, his mouth a hard,
thin line, he went on, 'Good engineers are hard to find.
And we have an agreement. I wouldn't want you to
have any excuse to say that you must stay at home to
look after Alys.'

She jerked her hand away. 'I can't afford to stop
work on a whim to look after my daughter.'

'No? Not even with the money from your shares?'
he demanded and his cold eyes froze her to the chair.

'I need that to buy somewhere...' She stopped. She
was saying far too much.

'Somewhere to live?' he finished thoughtfully. 'Your
demand to buy them back was nothing but a bluff and
I let you off the hook. How careless of me. It won't
happen again.' He smiled quite suddenly. 'So you think
the nursery is a good idea?'

'Long overdue,' she agreed, somewhat raggedly.

'Then consider it a fact. And just think how grateful
all the other mothers who work for me will be to you.'

'And fathers. On behalf of all your employees I
thank you for your generosity.' From somewhere she
found the strength to stand. 'Come along, Alys. Time
to go home.'

For once the child responded immediately and Jo
swept down the path and tucked her into her car seat.

As she turned the key in the ignition she glanced back at the cottage, saw Clay drawing back the curtains to let in the light and wondered if he had made up his mind to stay or to sell.

She spent the rest of the day recovering from what her mother infuriatingly referred to as her 'night on a bare mountain' and by the following morning was almost able to ignore the colourful crop of bruises decorating various bits of her, thankfully on the less exposed parts of her anatomy.

Next day she arrived at the office to find herself a heroine. 'However did you persuade him?'

Jo shifted uncomfortably. 'Persuade who?' she asked, but she had a feeling that she already knew the answer to that question.

'Mr Thackeray, of course. He's going ahead with a crèche.' The receptionist, who had two small children, was desperately grateful. 'I heard him, Jo! He was standing right where you are now and he told Peter that you had convinced him that it was the right move to make.'

'Peter Lloyd?'

'Yes. He was absolutely livid!'

'I'll bet. He thinks all mothers should be at home puréeing carrots for their offspring,' she said, flippantly. But she wasn't feeling flippant. If Clay had stood and discussed the plans in Reception, it was because he wanted everybody to know what was going on. Jo shivered and wondered if she was catching a cold.

The day continued with a series of interruptions as she received calls of congratulation from members of staff. By early afternoon it was clear that everyone in the building knew that a nursery was proposed and she was the person who had persuaded the new chairman to make this concession. At three o'clock she was summoned to Reception for a delivery and, curious, she hurried down.

The basket of red roses was ostentatious. More, she thought angrily, it was positively vulgar. More appropriate for a film-star's dressing-room. Jo turned over the card. Nothing discreet in an envelope. Just a scrawled message for anyone to read, and undoubtedly the receptionist already had done so.

'A night to remember,' it read. It was unsigned, but the bold, slashing handwriting was unmistakable. Jo flushed deeply to the roots of her hair. Well, now everyone would know how she had managed to 'persuade' Mr Thackeray that the company needed a crèche. Or they would think they did, which came to the same thing.

She plucked the card from the basket and tore it in two and dropped it in the waste basket. Then she turned to walk away. 'Aren't you going to take the flowers, Jo?'

She stopped and tried on a smile for size. Surprisingly, her face didn't break. 'Why don't you keep them here to decorate the hall? I really don't have room for them upstairs.' After all, they were for public consumption. He might as well get his money's worth. And her reputation was a small enough price to pay. But there were no more interruptions, only curious glances.

At five, lost in concentration, hardly aware that

everyone had suddenly found something important to do elsewhere, she looked up to find herself alone except for Clay, leaning nonchalantly in the doorway. She glanced around and offered him a rueful smile. 'You certainly know how to clear a room.'

'It takes years of practice.' He perched himself on the edge of her desk. 'You came to the office in the van. May I offer you a lift home?'

'I'd love one.'

He had clearly expected a swift rebuff and his eyes narrowed. 'Would you?'

'Of course. I've no particular affection for public transport, and besides, I'd hate to spoil your fun. You'd better be waiting in the front entrance just after five-thirty. I'd be sorry if anyone missed us leaving together.' He bowed slightly and rose to leave. 'But there is a price.'

He paused, apparently amused. 'You're in no position to make demands, my dear.'

She ignored this. 'I can't quite decide. I was wondering whether I might begin to use my married name,' she murmured, and waited, but there was only the slightest tightening of his jaw to show that he had heard. 'It would reinstate my reputation very nicely, don't you think? Put a stop to a lot of vulgar gossip.' She didn't wait for a reply. 'Or—'

'Or?' he demanded.

'Or perhaps the crèche should be...' She hesitated, wondering just how far she could go.

'Get on with it!'

'Free?'

'Don't be ridiculous, Jo.' He turned to leave. 'I'll see you in reception at five-thirty.'

She picked up a telephone and punched in a number as he walked away. 'Personnel? This is Jo Grant. I have an amendment for your records—' His hand cut off the call and she replaced the receiver and waited.

'You're bluffing, Jo.'

'Am I?'

'You wouldn't use my name when we lived together. You won't do it now.'

She swallowed. 'We all have to make sacrifices.'

His face darkened. 'I had planned to charge fifty per cent of cost. That's very reasonable.'

The phone rang and she placed her hand on the receiver. 'Ten per cent?' she offered.

'Forty?'

The phone rang again and she picked it up, holding her hand over the mouthpiece. 'Twenty?' she countered and answered her caller. 'Hello. Yes, we appear to have been cut off. As I was saying, I have a change for your records.'

'Twenty-five!'

She smiled faintly. 'I'll call you back,' she told the girl in Personnel, and glanced at her watch. 'Twenty-five per cent will do very nicely. I'll meet you downstairs in half an hour.' As he turned to leave she stopped him. 'Clay!'

'Yes?'

'Thanks for the flowers.'

He nodded. 'I'm glad you liked them. They were—' he hesitated, as if searching for an appropriate word '—rather expensive.'

'Worth every penny,' she assured him, although as every head turned to watch her progress through Reception at the end of the day she wasn't so sure.

Clay took his time about settling her in the Aston and she bore it with good grace; he had paid dearly for his fun. But when he pulled into the pub on the ring-road she protested.

'No. After-work drinks are strictly for the boys. I have to get home.'

'I had no intention of taking you for a drink. I just didn't want to sit outside your mother's house with her twitching at the curtains. Will you have dinner with me tonight?'

'I think you've had your way quite sufficiently for one day. Besides, I may not be able to get a babysitter.'

'I'm sure your mother would be happy to oblige. There's something I want to discuss with you. Or per-haps this time I shall be forced to call your bluff.'

She frowned slightly. 'My bluff?'

The headlights of a car illuminated his face. 'There's no way you'd start calling yourself Thackeray, my dear. Is there?' he demanded when she made no reply.

She pulled a face. 'After that horrible basket of roses it would serve you right. And if I did, I'd hold you to your promise to put an announcement in every national newspaper.'

'My promise—?'

'Had you forgotten? Pick me up at about eight. Or would you prefer to meet me somewhere and avoid my mother altogether?'

He smiled a little grimly and reached for the ignition. 'I'll pick you up.'

CHAPTER EIGHT

MRS GRANT was not amused. She had been willing enough to babysit, but when Jo explained why she set her mouth in a grim little line.

'You're mad to go,' she said. 'He'll have you eating out of his hand again.'

Jo shook her head. 'No, I don't think so. He said he wants to talk about something.' She began to pick up Alys's toys. 'I think something I said today...' She clung to a teddy. 'I think he's going to suggest a divorce.'

'Oh.' Her mother took the toys from her. 'That would be a relief. But you'd better go and get ready. In the circumstances you'll want to look your best.'

Did she? She flipped idly through her clothes, wondering just what she could wear that would cover such a situation. She would never have sought a divorce because she would never love anyone else but Clay. But perhaps her mother was right. It would be for the best to cut the invisible ties that held them in thrall, no matter how painful the final severance would be. And there was no doubt that it would be painful. Despite everything, when he was in the room it was as if the lights had been switched on. Harsh light it might be, illuminating all too clearly every crack in their relationship. But for the first time since he had walked out of her life Jo felt alive. And that was dangerous.

She pulled out the dress she had bought for Redmonds' last Christmas dinner. She hadn't gone in the end because Alys had been unwell and there had been no reason since to wear it. Plain black. It seemed somehow appropriate.

She put Alys to bed and they played for a little while, then, when she couldn't put it off any longer, she went to get ready and in the process discovered that her mother was right. It was important that she look her very best.

She took extra care with her make-up, sprayed herself with an exotic scent her sister had bought for her birthday and fluffed her normally sleek hair into something altogether wilder. The dress, a slender tube of black crêpe, slipped smoothly over her hips, stopping just short of her feet, the hem dividing at the side in a graceful curve to display her ankle as she moved.

She fastened long plain gold drops to her ears, but wore nothing around her neck. The drama of the dress, black against the whiteness of her skin as it curved over one shoulder, leaving the other bare, needed no embellishment. Jo turned to examine her rear view in the mirror and wondered, briefly, how her bare arm and shoulder had so miraculously escaped bruising, when the other was a kaleidoscope of colour.

A brisk ring on the doorbell put an abrupt stop to her musings. She hadn't heard the Aston's throaty warning of his arrival. She threw a brief backward glance at her reflection, then hurried downstairs before her mother could say anything that everyone might regret. She caught her breath as she paused in the entrance to the drawing-room. Clay stood, his head bent slightly as he listened to something her mother was saying, his broad black-clad figure graceful, relaxed, certain of his power to charm. He turned and straightened as she moved towards them and as his eyes widened she was glad that she had taken so much trouble over her appearance.

'Joanna...' He reached for her hands and she allowed her fingers to rest in his for the briefest moment. Longer would be too hard.

'Good evening, Clay,' she said, with a coolness that belied the way the blood was racing around her body. 'Has Mum offered you a drink?'

'She did, but I have explained that our table is booked for eight-thirty. We should go now.'

She acquiesced with a graceful nod. 'Where are we going?'

'I've planned a small surprise.'

She smiled slightly. 'Then I'll wait in the hall while you tell my mother where she can reach us in case she needs to get in touch.' A frown creased his forehead. 'Because of Alys,' she explained, and turned quickly away, wrapping herself in a cashmere shawl to disguise the fact that she was shaking with the effort of maintaining a cool poise, of keeping all her feelings firmly under lock and key.

He joined her moments later and his hand at her elbow led her firmly to a waiting taxi. 'The last time I felt like that I was seventeen years old.'

'Really?' she said. 'In what way?'

'Having to report where I was taking you to your mother!'

She stifled a giggle. 'Did she remind you to have me home before midnight?'

He glanced across at her. 'Not in so many words, Cinderella. I think she remembered, just in time, that I'm your husband.' Any desire to laugh deserted her. Apparently satisfied, he went on. 'I never could understand why parents believe that their daughter's virtue is safe until midnight. A triumph of hope over memory, perhaps?' he suggested.

'I'll bear that in mind when boys come calling for Alys.'

He stared at her. 'It's the boys who come calling for you that concern me.'

'If this is the kind of discussion you had in mind it is already at an end. You can take me home right now.'

'Too late.' The taxi pulled up. 'We've arrived.'

Jo looked out of the window and caught a glimpse of lights on the river. And with a sickening lurch of her heart she saw where he had brought her—to the same beautiful restaurant where they had come on that first night. She would never have believed that he could be so cruel.

He held out his hand and she dismissed the idea of refusing to get out of the taxi, demanding that he take her home. There was a challenge in his eyes, a dare. She lifted her chin, placed her hand in his and allowed him to lead her inside.

It hadn't changed. The low ceiling, the soft lighting and candles on the table invited lovers. The last time they had crossed this restaurant floor, happiness had lifted her; she had floated at his side and people had turned to watch them. Now pride kept her back ramrod-straight, kept the smile pinned to her mouth, and still people raised their heads and followed them with their eyes.

At last they were settled in a quiet corner, vast menus before them, and Jo sipped at a glass of champagne to moisten her dry mouth.

'Have you decided?'

'What?' She glanced down. 'Oh, no.' She stared at the jumble of words, unable to make them out. 'I'm not very hungry.'

'Shall I choose something for you?'

She nodded miserably. 'If we must eat.'

'I rather think it's expected.' His look brought the instant attention of the waiter and he ordered for them both, then refilled her glass.

They sat for a moment in silence. 'How is your father?' Jo asked, politely.

'His health isn't so wonderful, but he tries to keep active.'

'He sent me a card. At Christmas,' she explained. 'And a present, for Alys.'

'Rather more than he sent me. But then he believes I've robbed him of his grandchild.'

'I'm sure you've done your best to correct that impression.'

'I'm afraid not.' His eyes locked on hers. 'I preferred to cling to the remnants of my pride.'

Her hand shook and she put the glass down quickly. 'So that's why he wanted to see her? He believes she's yours...'

'It would make him very happy. He's not been too well. Could you bear it?'

'I tried to telephone him, but by the time his card had been sent on to Wales he had gone abroad.'

'He's back now.'

Jo didn't know what to say. Clay appeared to be inviting her to perpetuate what he believed to be a lie. It seemed oddly unlike him.

She was glad of the interruption of the waiter bringing them food. She stared at it for a moment and then picked up her fork and began to push the curls of smoked salmon about her plate.

'You really aren't hungry?' he asked.

She shook her head. Her stomach was tied in knots. 'You brought me here to discuss...something.'

'We've all evening.'

'I'd rather get it over with, if you don't mind.'

'I thought we might...' He stopped. 'This was clearly a mistake, but we can hardly walk out in the middle of a meal.'

'For goodness' sake, Clay. I'm not stupid. I know what you want!'

He put the glass down on the table and looked at her. 'Do you?' He picked up her left hand. 'I rather doubt it. Tell me, why do you still wear your wedding-ring, Joanna? You left your diamond behind, but surely this was the important one?'

'The diamond had an intrinsic worth. This only has a value to me.' She made herself look up. 'Do you want it back?' she demanded.

A flush darkened his cheekbones. 'No, I do not!' His mouth tightened. 'And if it lends you a certain respectability I don't begrudge—'

She erupted from her chair. 'If I had wanted that

kind of respectability, Clayton Thackeray,' she said, not caring who turned to stare at her, 'I could have used my married name any time I wanted.' She wrenched at the ring but it wouldn't come off. 'Damn! It always was too tight. I'll send it to you. By registered post!' She snatched up her bag and ran from the restaurant, pushing past people arriving, too much in distress to care.

A taxi was dropping someone and she leapt in and gave her address. The driver picked up his radio to inform his office.

'Please hurry,' she urged him. But she was too late. The door opened and Clay slid in beside her. The driver turned and eyed them both. 'Same address, madam?'

'Yes, please.'

'But take the scenic route.'

The driver regarded Clay evenly. 'It's the lady's cab, sir.'

Suddenly ashamed of her loss of control, she raised her hand hopelessly. 'It's all right.' They had to talk, and the sooner it was over the better. She shivered.

'You're cold. Here.' He slipped his jacket around her and somehow his arm stayed there, wrapping her in his strength. Just now she needed all the strength in the world.

'I shouldn't have made a scene,' she apologised stiffly. 'I didn't mean to.'

'I found the crack in the self-control…illuminating.'

'I'm glad it served some purpose. But it was the last time. You can have your divorce.'

He swung to face her, a deep frown creasing his forehead. 'Is that what you want?'

'It's for the best.' She looked away, disconcerted by the intensity of his gaze. 'But I think that in the circumstances I really would like to look for another job. Will you let me go? Please, Clay?'

There was a muscle working at the corner of his mouth. 'I can't hold you beyond the three months' notice you're obliged to give.'

The chill flooded back as he removed the comfort of his arm. Three months! Her insides caved in at the thought. It was less than three weeks and already she was at the edge of her endurance. 'Surely you wouldn't force me to continue working for you in the circumstances?'

'I'm letting you off lightly. Three months. I'll expect to hear from your solicitors.' He tapped on the glass. 'Stop here.' The driver pulled up and Clay passed him some notes and climbed out. 'Please take my wife wherever she wants to go.'

'Clay! You can't get out here!' The mist was swirling along the river. 'At least take your jacket!' She held it out of the window but he didn't turn back. 'Idiot!' She opened the door and began to run after him. 'Clay!' He'd disappeared from the road and she swung about her, trying to see where he had gone. Then she realised where she was. After a moment's hesitation she plunged down the towpath, cursing furiously as she stepped in a puddle, slithering on the damp mud in her high heels. 'Clay!' she screamed after him. Something rustled in the bushes beside her and she spun around. There was something there; she couldn't see what. Then it moved again and she took off in panic, desperate to get away from the heavy breathing close at her heels. 'Clay!' she shouted hoarsely, and was brought to an abrupt halt as something grabbed her. She tried to scream, but the terror closed her throat and turned her tongue to wood.

'What the hell do you think you're doing?'

It was him. She saw him as he spun her round and in her relief she threw herself at him, clinging to him while she tried to catch her breath. 'There... was...something...' Braver in his arms, she turned to confront her pursuer. A large black and white dog was sitting on the path, head expectantly on one side. 'Oh!' she gasped, feeling suddenly very foolish. She slumped against him as relief washed over her. 'It was a dog.'

'What did you think it was?' His voice was chilly, shocking sense back into her. She managed to let go and step back.

'You...' she held up his jacket '...left this.' He didn't take it and she let her hand fall. 'I thought you'd be cold.' She shivered, and with a muffled exclamation he took the jacket and draped it around her shoulders.

'Whatever am I going to do with you now?' he demanded.

'Do with me?' She stiffened. 'Do with me?' She stifled a sob. 'Please don't trouble yourself on my account!' She turned and began to walk quickly back the way she had come.

'Trouble?' he yelled after her. She faltered, but stumbled on. 'You've been nothing but trouble since the day I set eyes on you.' She forced herself to keep walking but he caught her arm and swung her round to face him. 'Stop, damn you!'

'Why?' she demanded. 'If I'm so much trouble you should be glad to see the back of me.'

'I know that. I thought I would be. But it didn't work, so I took my chance when Charles died and took control of Redmonds. I wanted to make you watch as I took it to bits. Then I could clear you out of my mind along with the debris. It was the only way I could think of to hurt you the way you hurt me.'

'But...you're expanding, opening a nursery. Oh, God!' With sudden clarity she saw it all. 'It's just a cruel hoax, and when they find out they'll crucify me. I'll never get another job— '

'That was the general idea—'

'And the breakdown?' she demanded bitterly. 'Was that all part of the plan?'

'No. The accident was genuine enough.' He paused, then added, 'But another mile and we would have run out of petrol.'

'So why didn't you see it through?' she demanded, furiously. 'Surely it was a little squeamish to stop at rape?'

'You wouldn't understand,' he said fiercely. 'Not in a million years.' He turned and began to walk away from her.

She followed, suddenly desperate. 'You can't do it, Clay. I'm not asking for myself. I don't matter. Please...I'll do anything you want.'

'Anything?' He paused and his look was cynical. 'You haven't changed, then. I thought...' He threw back his head and groaned. 'God help me, I thought—'

She snapped. 'Thought?' she demanded wildly. 'When did you ever stop to think?' She felt all control slipping away as she flung an angry fist at his shoulder, rocking him back on his feet.

He turned four-square to her, offering himself as a target. 'Yes! Come on, Jo, let it out. You're so bottled up that it's a wonder you don't explode with all that suppressed emotion. I've goaded you, taunted you, embarrassed you beyond endurance and you just take it. What will it take to make you let go? What are you so afraid of?'

'I'm not afraid!' she yelled.

'No? Prove it. Come on. Why have you chased down the towpath after me? Can't you admit the truth to yourself?'

'Truth? What truth?'

'This. The only truth there ever can be between a man and a woman.' He jerked her roughly against him.

'No! Clay!' As she realised his intention she began to struggle.

'Too late, my darling. You said anything. I'm taking you at your word.' His mouth claimed hers with absolute conviction and after the first momentary shockwave, when she could neither move nor think, she found herself clinging to him, responding with a burning urgency that met him head-on.

When, finally, the need to catch breath drove them apart, they stood, their breasts heaving, staring at one another in astonishment. Then she reached for him, lost beyond any sense of danger.

'Not here,' he said hoarsely and grabbed her hand. They ran wildly along the path, carelessly splashing through the muddy puddles, heedless of the curls of mist drifting along the water or a distant church clock proclaiming the hour.

He looped his arm around her waist as he searched for the key to the cottage door, and they almost fell inside as it suddenly gave way under their combined weight.

Once inside, he gathered her once more in his arms, kissing her like a man starved, and Jo wasn't listening to the warning voice of common sense screaming in her ears. She was suffering from a kind of madness, a long-suppressed hunger for him, and she was no longer capable of stopping what was now inevitable even if she had wanted to.

With a fierce, hungering cry he seized her in his arms and carried her up the stairs and over the threshold into what once, aeons ago, had been their bedroom.

She lay back against his chest, revelling in the sight of his body outlined by the damp cloth of his shirt as it clung to his shoulders, and of his thick dark mat of curls decorated with a film of mist.

She wrapped her arms around his neck and slid to her feet, moulding herself against him. Then she began to undo his shirt-studs, frowning in concentration.

'Joanna...' Her name was wrung from him.

She raised her wide grey eyes to his. 'I'm reacting, Clay. Letting go. It's been a long time and I'm not sure I remember how. Help me.'

His hands seized her zip and tugged it and with a soft sigh she shrugged out of her dress, leaving it to ripple to the floor.

He dragged her to him. 'God help me, I can't resist you.' He tilted her face to his and kissed her, a long,

possessive kiss that set her aflame. Then they were
shedding their clothes and she gasped as he reached for
her once more and held her hard against him. 'Is that
what you want, Joanna?' he asked, roughly.

Her legs were too weak to hold her and she clung
to him. 'Yes,' she whispered.

'You're sure it's me you want?' he grated.

'There's never been anyone else…' She moved urgently against him and with a primitive roar he bore
her to the bed, smothering her with wild kisses that
covered her eyes, her chin, her throat until every last
vestige of her hard-won control was shattered and she
was shouting, screaming at him, demanding that he
take her.

He raised his head and for a moment held her,
pinned by his body to the bed, taking in her dark, pas-
sion-soaked eyes and her heaving breast. Then, with a
smile of triumph, he rolled away on to his back.

'Make me,' he invited.

There was a wildness in her that blotted out everything but the two of them. With a delighted laugh she
accepted his invitation, reaching for him, trailing her
fingers through the tight curls of his chest until a fin-
gertip brushed the tiny bud of his nipple and she heard
the sharp intake of his breath. She moved over him,
caressing him with her breasts, outlining his lips with
her tongue, tasting the salt of his skin.

He moved then, to take her, but she stopped him,
holding him in suspense for one long moment until,
very slowly, she lowered herself on to him.

For the space of a heartbeat nothing happened. Then
he seized her and rolled over, until she in turn was the

one who was dominated and she was plummeting in crazy, giddy waves of sensation that swept her to a wild culmination before he surrendered to his own convulsive release. They clung together until the shock-waves passed and at last they were still, entwined in each other's arms.

She must have slept briefly, because when she opened her eyes Clay was standing over her, dressed in a dark tracksuit.

'I've dried your clothes as best I can.'

She clutched the covers around her. 'What time is it?'

'It's after one.'

'So late!'

He nodded. 'I'll bring the car round to the front.'

Thankful for the privacy, she quickly dressed and straightened her hair as best she could, but her reflection in the mirror was brutally honest. To anyone with half an eye to see, it was obvious what she had been doing. She stopped the thought. There would be time enough to worry about that later.

He drove swiftly through the quiet streets, concentrating wholly on the mechanics of driving, leaving her to her thoughts. He stopped the car in the road outside her mother's home, opened the door for her and walked her up the drive.

'Clay—'

'Tomorrow, Joanna. Now is not the time to talk.' He took her key and slid it silently into the lock and pushed the door open. 'I'll come round about eleven.'

'Tonight was just a madness, Clay. I want you to forget that it ever happened. Promise me.'

'Tomorrow,' he said abruptly. 'We'll talk tomorrow. Please, go in.'

'Jo?' Her mother's voice floated down the stairs. 'Is that you?'

'Send her my apologies,' Clay murmured. 'Tell her the pumpkin broke down.' He dropped a kiss on her cheek. 'Goodnight.'

She watched him until he ducked into the car. He raised a hand in salute and then slid silently away from the kerb.

'Jo?' Her mother appeared at the bottom of the stairs clad in a woollen dressing-gown.

'It's me, Mum. Sorry I'm so late.'

'No problem. Alys never murmured.' Her mother regarded her thoughtfully for a moment. 'Well? Were you right? Did he ask you for a divorce?'

'I believe we've settled all the outstanding issues,' she said with a gallows smile. 'He's coming round in the morning to discuss the details.'

'Didn't you have enough time tonight?' her mother asked innocently. She didn't wait for an answer but wandered into the kitchen and put on the kettle. 'Tea?' she offered.

'I'll go straight to bed if you don't mind. It's been quite a week, one way and another.' Not that she would sleep. What remained of the night would have to be spent putting her shattered self-control back together. She just hoped she could find all the pieces.

Alys woke her mother with joyful quacking. 'Ducks! Feed the ducks!' she shouted, and started to quack again.

Joanna lay still for a moment, her limbs oddly leaden, and tried to recall when she had last felt those familiar aches. She hauled herself up and looked at the clock. It was ten-thirty. She frowned for a moment, knowing that there was something important she should remember. Then it all came flooding back. She leapt out of bed and, shutting the door so that Alys couldn't escape, dived under the shower.

The steaming water breathed some life back into her and she dressed simply in a pair of jeans and a soft shirt.

'Mum!' She picked Alys up and carried her down the stairs. 'Mum?'

'In here, dear.'

She followed her mother's voice into the living-room and found her sitting before the fire, talking to Clay, who rose at her entrance.

'Hello, Joanna.'

She paled and had to swallow before the words would come. 'Hello, Clay.'

She knew she was blushing like a fifteen-year-old. Her mother looked from Joanna to Clay, and back again. 'Clay brought you some roses, Jo. They're in the kitchen.'

'Roses?' She made herself smile. 'Not red ones, I hope?'

'Pink seemed safer,' he said evenly.

Alys wriggled free of her mother's grasp and ran to her grandmother. 'Feed ducks,' she said.

'I'm sorry, sweetheart, not today.' The older woman looked up. 'I promised her a trip down to the river this morning. I hate to disappoint her, but I've a slight headache.' She touched her brow delicately.

'I'll take her later,' Jo promised.

'Why wait?' Clay stood up. 'We'll go now.'

'Well, how kind. She's all ready and there's a bag of bread in the kitchen.'

Jo looked from her mother to Alys, who was dressed in her bright blue dungarees that so perfectly echoed her eyes. She wasn't sure what game her mother was playing but she wasn't about to become one of the pawns.

'No, Mum. Not if you're not well.'

'I'm sure your mother would prefer us to take Alys out of her way, Joanna. Get your coat on.'

'But I haven't had any breakfast!'

'It's far too late for breakfast. I'll buy you a cup of tea at the hut in the park,' he offered.

'However could I refuse an offer like that?' she said, furious at the way she was being manipulated. But she went off to dress Alys in her outdoor clothes and then fastened her into her pushchair.

Clay lifted her out of the door and before she could take over had set off down the road. She called good-bye to her mother and raced after him.

'I'll push,' she said.

'I think I can manage. It's not that difficult.' He looked down at her. 'If you were to link your arm through mine we would look like any ordinary married couple.'

'But we're not.'

'Humour me.' He offered her his elbow. She hesitated, knowing only too well how her body reacted to his touch. Aware of her reluctance, he paused. 'I'm not likely to eat you in the street,' he said. With the utmost reluctance she slid her arm through the crook of his arm and he clamped it firmly to his side, giving her no opportunity to change her mind.

He halted at a crossing and waited for the cars to stop. Alys looked up at him.

'Ducks?' she asked, hopefully.

'Soon, sweetheart.' He laughed and turned to Jo. 'She has a recognisable single-mindedness.'

'Yes, I'm afraid so. Clay—'

'We can cross now.'

They walked beside the river in silence, Clay concentrating intently on negotiating the pushchair through the people brought out by the winter sunshine, Jo trying very hard to remind herself that this interlude had nothing to do with the reality of their lives.

They crossed the stone bridge over the entrance to the lock and on to the island where the ducks were greedily waiting for early visitors. She watched helplessly as Clay released Alys and lifted her from the chair, carrying her close enough to feed them.

It all had such a heartbreaking normality. She had rejected all this because she had been hell-bent on a career. Hell-bent on proving to her father—proving to herself—that she was as good as the son he had been denied by her own birth. Now, standing watching Clay and Alys, she realised the sum of what she had lost.

He turned to her and held out the bag of bread. 'Come on.' She joined the two of them in their game reluctantly, not because she didn't want to be part of the charmed circle, but because afterwards, when it was over, the pain would be total.

For a while they watched the little girl toddling about among the birds, chasing them and being chased, Clay guarding her path to the water, taking care that the ducks didn't get too close to her little fingers. Finally, the bread all gone, he picked her up and swung her on to his shoulders. 'Right, young lady. It's time your mother had her tea.'

He gave her no opportunity to object, but strode purposefully back the way they had come, leaving Jo to follow with the buggy. By the time she caught them up they were already inside the cosy park hut, choosing from a display of home-made cakes.

'Can she have one of those?' Clay asked, as Alys pointed to an éclair.

Jo shook her head. 'No. She can have some toast.'

'Spoilsport. What about you?'

'I'll have a slice, too.'

They sat at the table, Alys perched on Clay's knee. He loosened her jacket, fielding her neatly as she made a dive for the salt-pot. 'Oh, no, you don't, miss.' Alys smiled winningly, then turned her attention to the zip on his pocket.

'Jo—' He stopped as the woman brought tea and toast for them all. 'Thank you.' He began again. 'Jo, last night—'

'Last night was an aberration, Clay. It was the tension, the fight. You've no need to feel guilty.'

'I don't.' He frowned. 'I'm sorry that you feel it necessary to pull on a hair shirt.'

'I shouldn't have let it happen.'

'But it did. It was inevitable from the moment you followed me. You must have known that.'

'No!' She saw the woman behind the counter peer in her direction and shook her head, lowering her voice. 'No. It was just madness—'

'Jo,' he interrupted, 'I want you to come back to me.'

CHAPTER NINE

JOANNA felt the blood drain from her face. 'Come back to you?' She shook her head in an effort to clear the hammering from her ears.

He reached across the table and grasped her hand. 'I know you asked me for a divorce, Jo, but think about it.' His eyes blazed at her. 'Think about last night.'

She refused to let her mind draw out the pictures of that fierce passion. He had married her for that, had made no secret of it. It hadn't been enough then. How could it be enough now, with all that had happened a thorny barrier between them? She snatched her hand from his warm grasp. Even the touch of his fingers was enough to weaken her resolve.

'No,' she said, quickly, before the temptation overwhelmed her. 'It's not possible.'

The blue eyes suddenly chilled. 'There's someone else?' She shook her head vehemently. 'What other reason could there be?' he persisted.

'I should have thought that was obvious,' she said, her eyes automatically straying to her daughter.

He glanced down at Alys, perched on his knee, contently chewing on a piece of toast. 'She's beautiful, Jo. Like her mother. If she had been...different—'

'Like her father?' she offered, glad of the sudden chill that drove the weakness from her heart.

He looked up. 'I'd treat her as if she were my own.'

She sat back, suddenly exhausted by the emotional drain of it all. As if she were his own. The words mocked her. Even with the child in front of him, he couldn't see it. She is yours... She rehearsed the simple phrase in her head, but never spoke the words. He would never believe it, no matter how much she protested.

'Please, Clay. Don't go on with this.'

But he persisted. 'What happened was an aberration; I was stupid to have left you on your own.' Once more he fielded her hand as if he knew instinctively that his touch had the power to persuade her. 'I won't, ever again.' There was a fierce implacability about his mouth that gave her the strength to deny him.

'Surely, Clay, that's the point? You'd never trust me out of your sight. I'm sure the cage would be comfortable,' she tried to make him see, 'but it would still be a cage, with you constantly on your guard every time another man came too close, in case I felt like breaking out.'

'No,' he swore. And yet the whiteness around his mouth told her it was the truth.

For a moment she considered trying to convince him that she had never looked at another man since he'd come into her life. Had never wanted to. But he wouldn't believe her. Perhaps he couldn't. And it would destroy her utterly to see the disbelief in his eyes.

'A relationship needs trust, Clay. Neither of us quite succeeded in establishing that. We didn't know each other well enough to marry. It was my fault. I allowed you to overwhelm me because, heaven knows, I wanted to be overwhelmed. But it was too soon. You should have been content with an affair. Although I suspect you had your own reasons for preferring the commitment of marriage.'

'That's not true!'

'You expect me to believe you when you refused to listen to me?'

He was silent for a moment, then his mouth twisted into a self-mocking little smile. 'An impasse.' He lifted Alys down. 'I think we'd better go.'

For a moment she didn't move. An almost unbearable sadness weighed so heavily at her limbs that the effort of standing seemed too much. Clay's hand at her elbow galvanised her into movement and she bent to take Alys by the hand, automatically returning the smiles of two elderly ladies who stood aside in the doorway to let them out.

'What a lovely child,' the first one said, and turned back to her friend. 'Isn't she lovely, Molly? And so like her mother.'

Alys, always delighted with attention, smiled expectantly at Molly.

The old lady reached out and touched the mop of fair hair and looked up at the tall figures of Joanna and Clay.

'Charming. And as you say, dear, she is like her mother.' Then she smiled at Clay. 'But she has your eyes. Quite unmistakable.'

Slowly—almost, Jo thought, in slow motion—he bent and swung Alys up, holding her out in front of him, looking at her as if he had never seen her before. Alys stared solemnly back at her father, then raised her chubby hands to his face. With a sigh he drew her close and folded her tenderly in his arms. Then, without a word, he walked from the hut, striding purposefully away, leaving Jo to hurry after him.

'Clay, wait,' she said, but he took no notice and, hampered by the pushchair, she was forced into a ridiculous half-run in an effort to keep pace with him.

He forged ahead and her heart gave an enormous sigh of relief when he turned into the driveway instead of bundling the child into the Aston and spiriting her away. But her relief was short-lived as he turned to her, hand outstretched.

'Your car keys,' he demanded. Faced with a white-faced man holding her child, she handed them over without hesitation. He unlocked the door. 'Get in.'

'Alys—'

'Leave Alys to me.' She watched as he fastened her securely into the car seat. 'Get in, Jo,' he repeated, quite unnecessarily. She wasn't going to let Alys out of her sight. She slid quickly into the passenger seat and fastened her seatbelt.

He climbed in beside her and carefully backed out of the drive. Then, as if driving on eggs, his concentration total, he drove three silent miles to Redmonds' office. Without speaking, he unfastened Alys and carried her inside.

'What are you doing, Clay?' Jo demanded. 'Why have you come here?'

He glanced at her coldly, not bothering to answer, before turning in the direction of the basement. She was pulled after him by his possession of her daughter, following him down the stairs to the room where the records for all the jobs that Redmonds had ever undertaken were stored. He flicked the bank of switches, flooding the huge area with light, then set off purposefully along the racks of plans and box files, his eyes narrowed, searching.

'What do you want?' she asked, in a sort of desperation. 'Perhaps I can help you find it?'

'Really?' His voice was chilling.

After that she said nothing, merely following him. Alys had fallen asleep across his shoulder, perfectly content, but Jo never let them out of her sight for a moment.

Finally, with a exclamation of satisfaction, he pulled a file from the shelf. He laid it gently on the table, so as not to disturb the sleeping child, and began to turn the pages.

Jo frowned. They were pink time-sheets for the bridge job she had been working on when she met Clay. He leafed through them quickly until he found the day he was looking for and she saw him blench as he flicked through each one, signed by her.

'You worked that night.'

So that was what he was looking for. Proof.

'I told you I did.'

He turned then to face her. 'Could I have been that wrong? Lloyd…'

'Peter brought me home because he thought I was too tired to drive and if I had had an accident he would have had to explain why I was working while he was off at a family party. No other reason. He wouldn't give me the time of day unless I paid him for it.'

He frowned. 'But you...he kissed you. And before. I saw you kissing him before.'

'Yes, Clay. You saw me kissing him.' She shuddered at the thought. 'After you had rejected me. I'd offered you myself without any strings because I had fallen hopelessly, totally in love. At least I thought it was love.' She forced a careless shrug. 'At least you corrected that childish fantasy.'

'Then why—?' He grabbed at her shoulder and Alys stirred. With a smothered oath he released Jo and, as if he had been doing it all his life, gently settled Alys back to sleep. 'Why did you kiss him?' he demanded, his voice quiet but the soft tone as dangerous as ever.

'Because you were there, standing in the doorway of the pub, completely misunderstanding what you were seeing; I was angry. Very angry.' She refused to meet his eye. 'I did it without thinking, to make you jealous. I knew I'd have to pay for it. I just hadn't realised how much.' She made a dismissive gesture. 'Peter Lloyd isn't a very pleasant man. I was half-asleep when he kissed me that time he brought me home, or he would never have got so close.'

Clay uttered a soft groan of pain. 'There never was anyone else.' It wasn't a question, but she answered him anyway.

'No, Clay, there was never anyone else.'

He touched the sleeping child's head. 'She's mine? She's really mine?'

Jo nodded. 'After you left for Canada I did some thinking. I realised how wrong I'd been. I hadn't considered your feelings at all. I'd excluded you. I...I had my own reasons for not wanting a family so soon.'

'Your career.' He bit the words off as if they were something dirty.

She nodded unhappily. 'If you like.' She looked up at him desperately. 'But I threw the rest of the pills away. I thought that when you came home from Canada we could sit down and talk it through. Make some decisions together.' She pulled a face. 'Apparently I did the worst possible thing.' Then she touched the sleeping child. 'Except that it was the right thing. The best thing I ever did.'

'Now you must come back.'

She took a deep breath. 'Because you have your proof? I don't think so, Clay. It's too late for us. You've found your daughter; be content.'

He looked for a moment as if he would argue. Instead he nodded as if he understood how she felt. 'Will you let me see her?'

'Of course.'

He kissed the sleeping head. 'Come on, I'll take you both home.'

'Where is he taking her?' Her mother's lips were thin with disapproval.

Jo shrugged in an attempt to hide her nervousness. 'He said they might go to the zoo. Isn't that the classic Sunday haunt for all separated fathers?'

'That's too far!' she protested. 'He won't know what to do with her.'

'I pointed that out myself but he said he'd think of something. He's very resourceful. He'll cope.'

The sharp ring at the door plucked at her already shredded nerves, and the trembling about her midriff belied her casual acceptance of the possibility that he might have a woman in tow. To her relief he was alone.

'She's all ready.' Alys giggled with delight as Clay picked her up.

'Daddy!' she cried.

Jo had been coaching the little girl with this new word all week, but her timely use of it was totally unexpected. Clay's face whitened. When he had recovered he looked at Jo.

'Thank you.'

She managed a casual shrug. 'It's a new word. I warn you, she'll use it endlessly.'

'I shan't complain.' He picked up the child's bag. 'Where's your coat?'

'Coat?'

'Yes, my dear, your coat.' He looked down at the bag he was holding. 'The contents of this are a complete mystery to me. I shall need walking through the details.'

'But you said you would manage,' she protested.

'So I will.' His smile was inviting. 'If you'll help?'

'And if I won't come?' she asked, suddenly certain that he had intended this from the first.

He looked into the drawing-room. 'I suppose I'd have to stay here all day. If your mother would put up with me,' he added, doubtfully.

'I'll get my coat.'

Alys was already tucked into her car seat when she emerged. Clay had asked to borrow her car for that very reason, offering to loan her the Aston in return. Now she wondered if it had simply been a ruse to ensure that she couldn't be out when he arrived.

They had been driving for a few minutes when Jo realised that he wasn't taking the road to London. 'I thought we were going to the zoo,' she said.

'It's too cold.'

'Alys is well wrapped up.'

'I know. But...' he glanced across at her '...it's my father's birthday. I promised him a special present. Is it a dreadful imposition?'

'You should have told me where you intended taking her,' she said, stiffly. 'I have a right to know. Suppose something happened?'

'But you're with us, so you do know.'

Jo went cold as she realised how easily he could have taken Alys and disappeared without trace and she might never have seen her daughter again. She had heard of such things happening.

'Don't play games with me, Clay. I bore Alys alone and raised her when you chose to think I was nothing but a—a—wanton.' She almost choked on the word. 'Suddenly I'm acceptable again because I have what you most want.'

With a low curse he pulled into the side of the road. 'It wasn't like that. I wanted you to come.' He reached out for her but she flinched away, refusing the easy comfort of his arms. He sat back, staring sightlessly out through the windscreen. 'I would have told you, but I didn't think you'd agree.'

'You thought right,' she said.

'Do you want me to take you home?'

For a moment she sat, her hands in tight fists, forcing herself to remember the pain of his rejection, his unwillingness to believe what she told him. But the face of Clay's father intruded, a gentle man who had been unfailingly kind to her. It wasn't his fault that his son's behaviour had deprived him of his granddaughter's company. She breathed out very slowly and shook her head.

'No. We'll go on. But don't ever try something like this again.' She forced herself to look at him, to ignore the disconcerting hunger in his eyes. 'And, in the future, please make alternative arrangements for the care of Alys, because I shall not be available as a nanny.'

His mouth clamped together in a hard line. 'In that case I shall have to forgo the pleasure of my daughter's company.'

'No, that's silly. You could always find someone—'

'To take your place?' he offered. 'Do you think I would have come back if there had been the remotest possibility that I could ever love anyone else?'

'Love?' The word escaped her lips as, startled by the vehemence in his voice, she turned to him.

His lips curved in a self-mocking little smile. 'Silly, isn't it?' He slid the car into gear and, checking the road was clear, pulled out. Only Alys's occasional muttering broke the silence, mostly unintelligible. But once her high, clear voice called 'Daddy!' and they both visibly jumped.

The visit was not as awful as she'd feared. Mr Thackeray was overjoyed with his granddaughter and the initial coolness between the two men soon thawed in their competition to amuse her. As they were leaving, Clay's father extracted a promise Jo gladly gave: to visit him often.

'Don't feel you must wait for Clay to bring you,' he told her when they were alone.

'I won't,' she promised.

'And if you need anything...' He looked at her fiercely and she realised that he too had those blue eyes. Faded a little, but just as powerful. 'Anything at all,' he reiterated, 'come to me.' He raised his head to stare out of the window to where his son was packing the car. 'You don't have to go to Clay.'

'I never have.'

'No. Well, you're both strong characters. Differences were bound to arise, but I thought...' He shrugged. 'His mother and I married within days of our first meeting, you know. I suppose I'm just a silly old man, but I thought you two had that same "till death us do part" kind of love.'

'Sometimes that's not enough, Mr Thackeray.'

Clay carried in the bag and buggy when they got home and found her reading a note from her mother saying that she had gone to babysit for Heather.

'In that case,' Clay said, with satisfaction, 'I don't feel an urgent need to leave. Can I help you to bath Alys and put her to bed?'

'No.' The word came out too sharply and Jo was sorry for that as he almost flinched at her fierceness, but she was already stretched to breaking-point emotionally. 'It's been a tiring day. Alys has had quite enough excitement.'

'In that case I'll wait until you've finished. There's something I have to say to you, and unless you would rather I make an appointment at the office...?'

'That won't be necessary. Help yourself to a drink; I won't be long.'

Wearily Jo climbed the stairs, Alys a dead weight in her arms. She accomplished her daughter's bath with indecent haste, dressed her in a one-piece pyjama-suit and lifted her into her cot.

'Goodnight, Alys.' She kissed the child and tucked in her teddy-bear.

'Daddy?' she asked.

'Bedtime, Alys,' Jo warned.

Alys stuck out her lower lip. 'Daddy!' she said, raising her voice.

'Did someone call?'

She turned as Alys raised her hands. 'G'night, Daddy!'

He bent over the cot and stroked the fair hair. 'Goodnight, princess.'

Jo stumbled from the room and after a while Clay joined her in the living-room and poured himself another drink.

'You must come back, Jo.' His back was a wall between them.

'Because of Alys?'

'That's one reason. But only one.' He turned then. 'I was a fool. There. I've said it and I hope it gives you some satisfaction. I was jealous because I loved you beyond any reason and you refused to let me into your life.'

'Love?' That word again, and she wouldn't, mustn't allow it to influence her. 'Why do you persist in saying you loved me when we both know why you married me?'

'Do we?' He drained the glass. 'I'm beginning to wonder. If I had wanted your damned shares I could have had them for the asking.' His eyes challenged her. 'That's the truth, Joanna. Be honest with yourself.'

She flushed. It was the truth. He could have taken them from her and she would have begged him to do it.

'Yes,' she whispered. 'It's true.' She raised her lashes. 'So why didn't you?'

'Don't you know? Even now?' He was beside her in a stride. 'Because I loved you. I still love you.' He put his arms around her and held her gently. 'I didn't want to ask you to do anything that might spoil that.' Her sigh was a long, painful wrench from the heart. 'I wanted control of Redmonds—I admit it. More than that: I'll admit I was prepared to seduce them out of you.'

He refused to let her leave the circle of his arms. 'Be still and listen to me. It's time you heard it all.' She stood very still as he continued. 'I came looking for your father to enlist his aid. My solicitors had written to him, offering a good price for his shares, but he had turned it down. Except it wasn't your father I found. It was you. And an odd mixture of innocence and self-assurance you were. I'll confess I didn't know quite what to make of you. But when I trailed the offer of a flirtation you were quick enough to respond.'

She tried to speak then, but he stopped her, holding a finger to her lips. 'Not yet. I haven't finished, my love. I have to tell you that when you lay in my arms and told me you were a virgin I couldn't go ahead with it. Too cynical by half.' He smiled faintly. 'But it was too late, you see; I was bewitched. I was already far too deeply in love.'

She raised her face at last to his. 'But I was certain you married me to gain control of my shares. Not at first, but then there were rumours...'

'The shares had nothing to do with it. Unlike you, my darling Joanna, I was always able to keep my business and personal lives quite separate.' He swept her exclamation aside. 'If you had decided to sell I would have explained. But you were adamant that you had no intention of selling. Henry gained the same impression, and so long as you held your shares I could win.'

'I never meant to sell them. But Charles convinced me it was the right thing to do.'

'I believe you. He was lucky that I ended up with enough stock to fend off anyone else with similar ideas. Redmonds was a company begging to be taken over. An unwieldy management system that was totally out of control and an autocrat at the helm who wouldn't let go even when he was too sick to work.'

'And a big fat pension fund. Ripe for the plucking.'

'Exactly. Just what I didn't want to happen. Redmonds is too good a company to be destroyed that way.'

'You could have explained. All I heard were rumours. Then I discovered you knew Henry Doubleday and it was all too clear.'

'Why didn't you come to me?' he demanded.

She shook her head. 'When I first heard the rumours, first thought you might be involved, I didn't want to believe them. I didn't want to believe what that would mean. I wanted to trust you, believe you loved me. By the time I had proof it was too late.' She forced herself to look up into his face, search for any hint that he was lying. 'You said you bought the company to hurt me—'

'Maybe I did. God knows I tried to hurt you that night alone on the mountain when I had you completely at my mercy. It would have been so easy. But I couldn't. Love was finally all I had.'

'Oh, Clay. I'm sorry. So very sorry. But I didn't know. You never told me.'

'It was careless of me. I assumed you realised. And I'm telling you now. I'll never allow you to forget if you'll give me a second chance to prove just how much I love you.'

She rested her cheek against his broad chest, feeling the steady comfort of his heartbeat. 'It's not just for Alys?'

He held her away from him, his eyes blazing with a powerful emotion that she couldn't begin to understand. 'If you tell me now that it's over, that there's no chance for us, I'll go away. The hurt I inflicted upon you was unforgivable and if you make that decision I'll honour it. Neither you nor Alys will ever be bothered by me again.' His jaw tightened. 'Alys will always be my daughter and she'll never want for anything. I'll support you both gladly, but I can't go on seeing you, knowing that you can never be mine. If that means losing Alys, well, so be it.'

He was shaking, she realised, and she put her arms around him. 'But I don't think you'll make me go away, my darling. Because I remember what you said when I asked you if you loved Alys's father.'

'With all my heart, until the day I die.' She gazed

at him in a sort of wonder, all the pain dissipated in the love that she was now, at last, able to recognise.

'I won't interfere with what you want to do, Jo. You can work, have your career. I promised you the job of your life to entrap you, keep you close to me for a while. It's still yours if you want it.'

'My career seemed very important once,' she said. 'Come and sit down; I have to explain why.' He stiffened, sensing rejection, but she shook her head. 'It's something you should know.'

He nodded briefly and sat beside her on the sofa. 'What is it?'

'It's a story about a little girl. She had an older sister—ten years older. There had been other babies in between, you understand, but none of them had made it to full term until she arrived and the doctors told her parents that there could be no more babies after that.'

He drew in a sharp breath, but she kept going. It was important that he understand. He had the right to understand.

'The father was sad,' she went on, 'because he could never have the son he wanted so much to follow in his footsteps. So the mother encouraged the little girl in a game. She could take the place of Daddy's son, she told her.'

Clay moved to hold her, but she kept him at bay. 'She didn't mind,' she assured him. 'It was fun. She wore jeans all the time and when she had to wear glasses and braces it didn't matter so much, because boys didn't care about things like that.'

'Jo—'

'Fortunately she was clever, and because she competed with the boys at school she shone at the things boys were good at—maths and science.' She smiled slightly. 'She wanted so much to make up to her father for not being a boy. And it was easy enough. She would do exactly what a son would: follow her father into his profession. Show him that it didn't matter...' She was surprised by a sudden sob.

He held her then. 'My darling, please don't go on. I think I understand.'

'It's all right, Clay.' She smiled brilliantly through a film of tears. 'Because she passed all her exams. Graduated. She made it. Became a civil engineer, just like her father. He thought it rather amusing and I think...I think he was proud. But then he died and I had to try so much harder to make it up to him—' She broke off, no longer able to speak, and he cradled her until the sobs finally subsided and she was at rest in his arms.

'Did he know what you were trying to do?'

She shook her head. 'I don't think it ever crossed his mind. I was just his funny little tomboy. Mum...well, she never discouraged me.'

'Oh, God. And I didn't understand. I just thought you didn't care about me, only about your damned job.'

'I should have told you.'

'Did I ever give you the chance? I just blazed away, my male ego bruised and hurting.' He fetched her a brandy. 'Drink this, slowly.' He watched her as she sipped, gasping at the unexpected heat at the back of her throat. 'Do you want to carry on, my love—working?'

'I don't think I'm much good at anything else.'

'You must do exactly what you want.'

'I don't know what I want. Except...' She turned to face him. 'Except I want to go home, with you. If you still want me.'

CHAPTER TEN

'WANT you?' Clay took her face between his hands and for a long, heart-stopping moment his eyes seemed to devour her. Then, so slowly that Jo had time to re-discover every feature, remind herself of every tiny line and scar on his well-loved, weatherbeaten face, he bent to kiss her.

Gently, tenderly, his mouth touched her eyelids, moved to graze the delicate skin at her temples, before taking a diversion to tease the sensitive whorls of her ears. He took all the time in the world, setting her skin ablaze with an answering desire as his lips continued their intoxicating journey across her throat, playing havoc with her heartbeat until the blood was thundering in her ears and she could no longer bear the agony of waiting.

Her lips parted on a soft moan and finally he took pity on her and accepted the invitation of her tongue, his kiss a sweet, wondrous evocation of their love.

It was a long time before he released her, holding her away from him so that he could see her face. 'Does that answer your question?'

His voice stroked her and Jo simply nodded, unable to speak for sheer happiness. Clay folded her in his arms, holding her close. 'Then we'd better make some important decisions.'

She raised her eyes. 'Decisions?' she asked, her

pulse quickening nervously as she saw the intensity with which he regarded her. 'What about?'

'The most important, darling, is where in the world you would like me to take you for your honeymoon.'

'There's no need,' she murmured, and smiled happily. 'I know how busy you are. I shall be perfectly happy just to...begin again.'

'And so we will. But I shall never be too busy for you again, Joanna. Never.' He rubbed his cheek against her hair. 'And besides, the decorators won't finish the nursery for at least ten days. You don't expect me to wait that long?'

She sat up. 'Decorators!' She stared at him. 'You never even considered that I would say no! Of all the conceited—'

He caught her waist and pulled her hard against him. '"With all my heart, until the day I die"...' he softly quoted her, before kissing her again. 'Do you want to change your mind?' he offered at last.

She shook her head. 'No,' she said softly. 'I don't want to change my mind.'

He smiled. 'Well, now that's settled, where would you like to go?'

'I don't know.' She thought for a moment. 'It's too late for beaches and too early for winter sports. Maybe we should wait for a while. Until the summer, perhaps?'

'You're not listening to me, Jo,' he said. 'We're going away for a couple of weeks at least. If nothing else, it will give everyone time to get used to the idea. And when I asked ''where in the world'', I did mean just that. There's the Far East. South America. Australia.'

Her eyes flew open. 'That far?'

'Anywhere in the world you would like to go. Just say the word.'

'Anywhere?' Her lips curved into a dreamy smile.

'Anywhere,' he repeated.

'In that case, my love, I think I should like to spend my honeymoon on a desert island.'

His smile was wolfish. 'A real desert island? Or one with a few home comforts?'

She considered for a moment. 'I think I'd like a few home comforts.'

'Perhaps that's just as well, because I give you due warning—I have no intention of wasting any time spearing fish.'

The Maldives were everything that Jo had asked for and more. For two weeks they swam and sailed and made love as if they were the last two people on earth.

'It's back to reality tomorrow. Will you mind?' Clay asked as they took a last stroll along the beach.

'No. It's been wonderful. But the truth is that it would have been wonderful anywhere with you.'

'Flatterer.' He kissed her ear. 'And you're missing Alys.' She started guiltily, but he was reassuring. 'It's all right, Jo. I miss her too. I can hardly wait to get back and start to be part of a real family.'

'I'll remind you of that when she wakes up in the middle of the night wanting a drink,' she said, with feeling. She glanced at him sideways from under long dark lashes, hesitating to mention what was on her mind.

'Yes?'

He seemed to have the power to read her mind. 'I'm not looking forward to going back to the office. I shall feel like an exhibit at a waxworks. Everyone will stare when we both come back on the same day with these wonderful matching tans.'

'I briefed my directors before I left. They had a right to know the truth before any silly rumours started to fly about when we disappeared at the same time. Especially since I rather gave the game away with that damned basket of roses. I had Lloyd's resignation on my desk within the hour.' He glanced at her. 'I told him there was no need but I think he'll go anyway.' He stopped and pulled her to him. 'You may rest assured that everyone knows that you're a respectable married lady, and always have been. Now, I think we've walked quite far enough. And talked quite enough. This is our last night in paradise and I don't intend to waste a second of it.'

'What shall I put on this branch?'

Jo handed Clay a little wooden doll. 'This should look about right. And I think that's enough. If you hang any more ornaments on that tree it will sink through the floor.' She handed him the angel. 'There's just this for the top.'

He placed the angel on the top and turned on the lights. They stepped back in order to judge the effect.

'It's wonderful, Clay. I can't wait for Alys to see it tomorrow. She was too young last Christmas to understand.'

He looped his arm around her waist. 'I only wish—'

'No!' She swivelled in his arms and placed her hand

over his mouth. 'Don't say it. Don't waste one second on regret. We have the rest of our lives together and that's what matters.'

'You're right, Mrs Thackeray. And I have an early Christmas present for you.'

He bent and lifted a long package from among the piles of gaily wrapped presents waiting for the morning. 'Happy Christmas.'

She took it from him, turning it in her hands. 'What is it?'

'Why don't you open it, my darling, and find out?'

Slowly she slipped the ribbons and opened up the wrapping. 'A newspaper?' She looked at him. 'Is this a joke?'

'It's today's edition of *The Times*. Try the personal column and judge for yourself.'

And suddenly she knew. 'Clay! You didn't!'

'I made you a promise.'

She laughed. 'Oh, Clay!' She quickly opened the paper at the page and then she stopped laughing. He had taken an entire page. Filled it with the words.

I love you, Joanna Thackeray. With all my heart, until the day I die. Clay.

A damp spot appeared on the page, then another. She looked up at him through glistening lashes. 'I've never cried for happiness before,' she said, her voice hardly reaching a whisper.

'I recommend that everyone should do it at least once,' he said, gravely.

'Thank you. I believe it's the best present I've ever

had.' She wiped at the tears with her fingers. 'And I have something for you. I was going to wait until tomorrow to give it to you, but I think you should have it now. It seems the right moment, somehow.'

She untied an envelope from the tree and gave it to him. For a moment he held it between his fingers, then pulled the bright red ribbon that fastened it and drew out a sheet of notepaper.

His eyes narrowed. 'What is this?' he asked.

'You'd better read it and see.'

He flicked the paper open and studied it for a moment, his face darkening as he read the words. 'Why are you doing this?' he demanded.

Shaken by his reaction, her voice trembled. 'I thought you would be pleased.'

'And I thought I made it clear that I don't want you doing anything, anything at all, just to please me. You have a great career ahead of you. You'll be regretting this gesture in a month and blame me.' He dropped her letter of resignation to the floor and moved to the table to pour himself a drink. He turned to her. 'Can I get you something?'

She shook her head, unable to for the moment speak.

'I'll open some wine if you'd prefer?'

'No, I won't have anything. I've given it up for a while.'

He poured himself a Scotch. 'Given it up? Why? Then he swung round and stared at her. 'You're not ill?' His eyes fell on her letter and he went white. 'Is that the reason—?'

'No, my love. I'm not ill. But you did once say that

climbing up and down ladders when you're pregnant is one of the drawbacks of the job.'

'Pregnant!' He was by her side in a stride and seized her by the arms. 'You're pregnant?'

'Are you angry?'

'Angry? Why the hell would I be angry?'

'It's just that you're shouting,' she said, quietly. 'And you're rather hurting me.'

He looked down in surprise and abruptly released her. Then he grabbed her again, pulling her into his arms. 'Oh, dear God, I'm sorry, Jo. It's all my fault.'

She tilted her head back until she could see his face. 'Certainly it's your fault,' she told him severely. Then a smile lit her beautiful grey eyes. 'Who else's fault could it possibly be? But don't be sorry, Clay Thackeray. Don't ever be sorry. Because I'm not. I couldn't be happier.'

'You're sure?' He shook his head in an effort to think more clearly. 'We could have a nanny. You could still have your—'

'My career? No, my darling. Please understand. I've already missed too much time with Alys. That couldn't be helped; I was lucky to be able to work as I did. But there is nothing of the noble gesture about my resignation. I've simply decided that it's time for a new career.' She slid her hands around his neck. 'Wife and mother will do me just fine from now on.'

'Is that a fact?' His eyes gleamed darkly. 'In that case, Mrs Thackeray, I think you'd better start practising. After all, you've a considerable amount of ''wifing'' to catch up on.'

'I'll need a little help with that part of my career plan,' she said.

He swept her up into his arms. 'That, Mrs Thackeray, is no problem. You'll get all the help you'll ever need from me. And I believe we should start right now.'

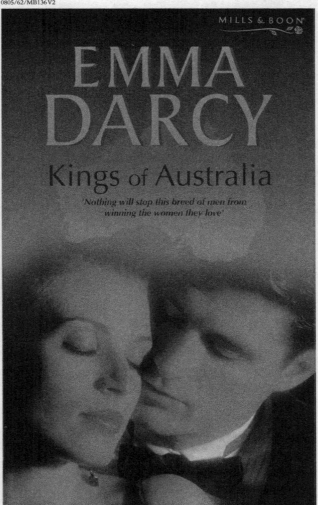

MILLS & BOON

EMMA DARCY

Kings of Australia

'Nothing will stop this breed of men from winning the women they love'

On sale 5th August 2005

Available at most branches of WHSmith, Tesco, ASDA, Martins, Borders, Eason, Sainsbury's and all good paperback bookshops.

0805/024/MB135 V2

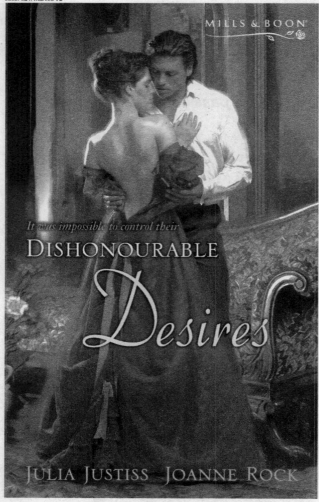

MILLS & BOON®

It was impossible to control their

DISHONOURABLE

Desires

JULIA JUSTISS   JOANNE ROCK

On sale 3rd August 2005

*Available at most branches of WHSmith, Tesco, ASDA, Martins,
Borders, Eason, Sainsbury's and all good paperback bookshops.*

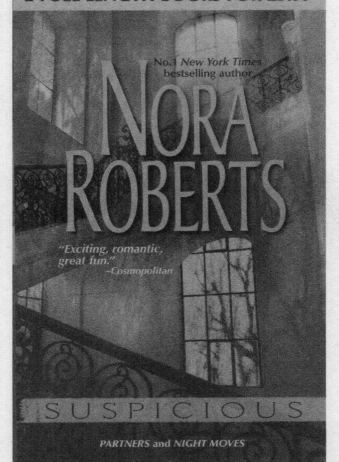

0905/055/SH104 V2

Desert Heat

Susan Mallery
Alexandra Sellers

On sale 19th August 2005

*Available at most branches of WHSmith, Tesco, ASDA, Martins,
Borders, Eason, Sainsbury's and all good paperback bookshops.*

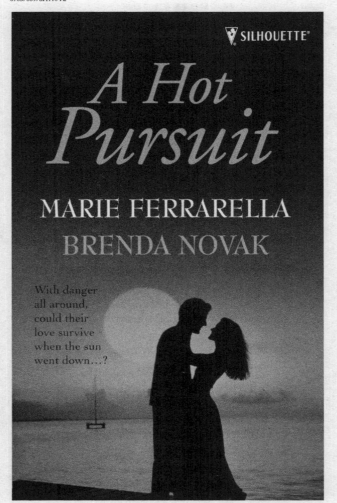

SILHOUETTE®

A Hot Pursuit

MARIE FERRARELLA

BRENDA NOVAK

With danger all around, could their love survive when the sun went down…?

On sale 17th June 2005

Available at most branches of WHSmith, Tesco, ASDA, Martins, Borders, Eason, Sainsbury's and all good paperback bookshops.

Narrated with the simplicity and unabashed honesty of a child's perspective, *Me & Emma* is a vivid portrayal of the heartbreaking loss of innocence, an indomitable spirit and incredible courage.

ISBN 0-7783-0084-6

In many ways, Carrie Parker is like any other eight-year-old—playing make-believe, dreading school, dreaming of faraway places. But even her naively hopeful mind can't shut out the terrible realities of home or help her to protect her younger sister, Emma. Carrie is determined to keep Emma safe from a life of neglect and abuse at the hands of their drunken stepfather, Richard—abuse their momma can't seem to see, let alone stop.

On sale 15th July 2005